LATIN JAZZ

VIRGIL SUAREZ

A FIRESIDE BOOK
PUBLISHED BY SIMON & SCHUSTER INC.
NEW YORK   LONDON   TORONTO
SYDNEY   TOKYO   SINGAPORE

FIRESIDE
Simon & Schuster Building
Rockefeller Center
1230 Avenue of the Americas
New York, New York 10020

First Fireside Edition 1990
Published by arrangement with William Morrow & Company, Inc.

Designed by Patrice Fodero
Manufactured in the United States of America

1   3   5   7   9   10   8   6   4   2

Library of Congress Cataloging in Publication Data

Suarez, Virgil
Latin jazz/Virgil Suarez.—1st Fireside ed.
p.   cm.
I. Title.
[PS3569.U18L38   1990]
813'.54—dc20   89-78136
CIP

ISBN 0-671-70535-0

If this book were a sculpture,
then it stands as a monument for

Luis Navarro Rubio

Acknowledgments

The author wishes to thank the following people who helped in the preparation of this manuscript: James Mosher, Raymond Cothern, Patricia Geary, Robert Houston, Delia M. Poey, Joanna Cole, Elaine Markson, and Harvey S. Ginsberg.

And also Vance Bourjaily and Elliot Fried, for their support and understanding.

There is an old saying in Havana that goes:
"If we lose each other, honey, then meet me in Miami."

PART I

Book of Voices

HUGO / The new epidemic spreads like spilt quicksilver from tip to tip of the island, from the sierras to the bays. On the radio I hear the voice belonging to the enraged Leader blame the C.I.A. for introducing the African fever virus to the pigs, the voice, that fizz-crackle, fizz-crackle voice, that demanding, loud, monotonous voice accuses the Yanquis.

"Y la pregunta es: ¿Que haremos en 1980?" (And the question is: What can *we* do in 1980?) He spits these words into the microphone, and who can avoid imagining them echoing beyond the multitudes gathered to listen and offer support at Plaza de la Revolución in Havana? *"¡Patria o muerte, venceremos!"*

But here in the fields, within the boundaries of Cochiquero, a work camp/prison for political prisoners, the voice comes from an old Marconi radio in the mess hall. It is the same voice which never changes. Yes, it's the Yanquis' fault for the meat shortage, for it becoming so scarce that . . . A soldier, who's been listening while eating his lentil soup, stands up, approaches the radio, and turns up the volume.

The static becomes unbearable. Thus the ten-minute lunch-break is over. Back to the bulldozer waiting outside.

I go from the mess hall tent, under which the soup caldrons sit on red coals, to the field, to the fire, to where the scavengers perch on the branches of the mango trees, the ceibas and guayabas. Not even the crows or buzzards try to escape, suffocating, they wait. They are the jury, the only witnesses to the slaughter. In the distance they blur like thumb smudges on plaster walls.

No map leads to this charred territory.

All the animals afflicted by the epidemic are burned. They are brought in trucks from out-of-the-way villages and towns and cities, clubbed, and pushed down a ramp into the fire. The pigs' leg muscles tense as they crowd in the rear of the trucks. Falter. Hooves slip in resistance, but there are no crevices, gaps, nooks, nor crannies to hold on to. The workers, their tattered clothes and bodies splattered with blood, club the pigs and kick them out of the trucks.

One, two, three little piggies slide down the ramp to a fire which makes their skin bloat, shrivel, and blacken. The fire grows tall, in orange waves. Only the sound of the fire melting eyes, skin, and entrails is heard. A roar.

Wood is thrown in to keep the fire strong. Blazing.

The smell of burned flesh and the heat extend like a mantilla over the fields, from the pit to the barracks, across the marsh to the rice and cane fields.

And the truckloads keep coming from all the provinces of the island, from cities where rumor has it people are destroying their homes by raising animals in their own living rooms. Something that, according to the Leader, goes against reform and most importantly the revolution.

The we've-come-here-to-die-no-one-can-fool-us look hides between each and every wrinkle on the workers' sunburned faces. Sullen, they watch me go by. In turn, I see them moving behind the flames on the other side of the pit, their tired bodies slouching.

Under the shade of a fruitless mango tree, I climb on the hard round seat of the bulldozer and wait for the signal from one of the young soldiers working this shift to push more wood over the side into the pit. That's what I've become, a wood pusher. The pigs, I'm willing to bet, are bludgeoned to save bullets; the ammunition's needed for the war in Africa.

Yes, here I wait, bone weary, sick to my stomach, groggy, while the sun and the fire take their toll upon the raw skin on my hairless scalp. Hairless because we had a lice epidemic break out in the barracks recently. I can feel the pus-filled callouses under gray stubble where the sun has burned the skin.

Two weeks ago I was still at La Cabaña, the prison, but when the virus epidemic started, I volunteered to come out here and work, just to get out. Before that I was in the mental wards in

Mazorra. Never a dull moment . . . I'm not crazy; I am dead . . . Dead now, I failed to pass purgatory . . . I'm deep into hell.

I bite the bottom of my lip and draw blood to taste it, to prove that I'm still alive. The twisted hairs of my mustache the camp barber didn't get with his dull blade under my nose hang over my lips and poke at the cracked tender skin.

Something's happened. Something big. This morning while I washed my face and before the radio was ordered unplugged because the news might cause turmoil, I heard about the Peruvian Embassy break-in in Miramar, Havana. This is what little I managed to hear: The sentries guarding the entrance to the embassy were removed after a bus commandeered by several people crashed through the gates and entered the embassy grounds. After the radio was removed from the barracks, gossip started in the mess hall, outside the latrines and showers. Distorted facts. Some of the other men who heard the news too said that the sentries were removed because it is a government plot to start trouble. Why the Peruvian Embassy? Why not. Maybe it is the only embassy known for providing political asylum. Later, the rumor among the other bulldozer drivers spread, crowds of people started running in to . . . to seek asylum.

Two other drivers on my shift gossip while the nauseating stench of burned flesh drives a desperate it's-now-or-never feeling home. Since I can't hear what they're saying, I imagine it. Will there be another revolution? They ask.

Then thoughts of my Lucinda. Señorita Ochoa. The guerrillera girl I met in Sierra Maestra after I dropped out of medical school at the University of Santiago to go fight. Oh, Lucinda, where the hell are you?

Out of the splendor in the wavering heat of the fire Lucinda evolves. Her lips puckered around my cock. Up/down-up/down. This vision haunts me: She comes to me in the white silk dress she wore for Sunday visits at Mazorra, where she was transferred from prison because of epilepsy. Lucinda, the woman with whom I was reunited after so many years. One Sunday we managed to meet in the laundry room and while we were making love, she went into her second grand mal (the first happened at Sierra Maestra during the revolution). After that incident, the nurse in charge of

Lucinda's ward made sure I was kept away. I found out the hard way I couldn't see her, from a fat orderly who thought he could push me around. The day came when I couldn't put up with not seeing Lucinda, the bastard orderly, the nurses and doctors, and the goddamned institution. So I asked to be transferred back to La Cabaña; I had been brought to Mazorra only temporarily because I had had too many fist fights and injured a couple of guards for which I received several beatings and twenty days in what is called a *gaveta*, meaning a prison cell too narrow and short to be comfortable. I almost drowned in my own shit and piss. "Mental instability," the prison doctor had said.

Oh how I wanted Lucinda one last time! Her breasts and that patch of black fine quiltwork between her legs. Oh, the bittersweet taste of her loins. I sit with the bulldozer levers between my knees while I think of Lucinda on all fours, her buttocks tilted upward. These past few days I have labored around the fire pit from sunrise to sundown and haven't been able to forget her.

Around me now the workers and the soldiers appear like lifesize paper-mâché cutouts propped up against the stillness of the mangroves. No breeze to blow the ashes away. A word comes to mind. Escape. Yes, *fuga*. These thoughts leave me with an overpowering feeling of anxiety and helplessness. But how? I can pay one of the truck drivers to take me to the embassy. Pay him the one hundred pesos I stole yesterday from the spot where I'd seen a man squat and bury it—I thought he was covering his shit with dirt, but then I saw him take the money out of his pocket and drop it in the hole.

E-s-c-a-p-e, there's no better time than now. If I were to get to the embassy, I could leave this place; of course, I couldn't be recognized. Who can recognize this nondescript face, so hard to recall? Besides, by the time they realize I'm missing—one less tired shriveled-up body taking up bunk space—I'll be on my way. Jesus, others have done it in the past and so could I, except those fools were captured and brought back, but now with the break-in. . . .

Drawn flesh—that's my face—drawn flesh, pale, wrinkled, taut over cheekbones and jaw. My dark eyes, which Mama Concha, my mother (God rest her soul) used to compare to my father's, look more alert than usual, but they haven't stopped itching, burning because the ash particles in the air irritate them.

The bulldozers begin to move back and forth on either side of the pit. When the signal comes to push more wood over the sizzling flesh, I press the button that starts the machine, push the levers forward, and move from under the shade. Once again the sun begins to burn my scalp, a pickax on my head. The putrid smell of offal gags me, makes the saliva at the back of my throat knot; webs close my air passage.

Think man, think! How to get from here to old Havana?

The train tracks lie fifty miles north behind the coffee plantations.

The bulldozer crawls closer to the edge of the pit. Are you with me Lucinda? I enter the fire area. Intense heat on my skin. The sparks fly out the mouth of the pit like red-hot bolts.

My eyes hurt so that I have to shut them. Tears run down my charcoal-smeared cheeks. I get closer to the pit's edge.

Here, so close to the fire, all that can be heard are the flames burning the flesh. I feel as though my own flesh is being scraped off with a dull scalpel. I lose my grip on the lever.

I am falling.

Opening the slits over my eyes a little wider, I see him, the soldier signaling to roll back. That I've come too close to the edge.

I am letting go.

The soldier walks over. "Carranza!" he calls out, loud enough for me to hear him over the crackling of the fire and the bulldozer. "What's the matter? What's the problem?"

"My eyes," I start to say, covering my eyes with a rag I keep to dry the sweat off my face.

"You're too close. Way too close. Get back."

I push the levers and return to the shade.

The soldier comes over and asks, "What's wrong with you?"

Wondering if this is the same one who turned up the volume on the radio inside the mess hall half an hour ago, I kill the motor.

"You just had a break," he says.

"I want out!" I say, for a moment forgetting that there is a holstered gun hanging like a bull's cock from his belt, and with the slightest provocation. . . .

"You want out? Sure. I'll let you out. See those trucks over

7

there?" He points to the unloading ramps down which more pigs slide. "Go there and help out. I'll get somebody else to replace you here. Go."

"And to think that I fought in the sierras to end up here, doing this," I say.

"What are you mumbling?"

"Put a bullet in my gullet. Finish me off, will you?"

"What I want to know is," the soldier says, "who sent you here. Your crazy ass belongs in Mazorra."

I start to walk away toward the trucks, but then I stop and turn. I tell him, "Don't you think I know what's going on here? While your mother was busy changing your diapers I was up in the goddamed hills fighting. A fucking worthy cause turned sour. But, never mind. That's gratitude for you." Stop to swallow. "There's no virus, no Yanqui infiltrators causing the epidemic. The Party created this mess and—"

"Come on, stop the nonsense before—" the soldier says, then touches the holster containing his Soviet officer's automatic pistol.

I go to the trucks and when I get there I'm out of breath. The clubs hitting flesh go: thump! thump! Pigs squeal.

Planning how I'm going to escape, as the night claws its hands over the hills on the other side of the camp, is exciting. Do I have the *cojones,* the balls? In twenty-four hours I could be in Havana near the Peruvian Embassy or in Mazorra with Lucinda. With the money I have I can bribe one of these bastard truck drivers to take me there.

But what is really happening at the embassy? What's going on in the rest of the world? The men who told me about the break-in mentioned the bus rushing in. They revealed no more.

I climb onto the ramp and up to the back of a truck. The man clubbing does so inefficiently. Not on first strike. Blood covers his hands and hairy forearms. I start to kick the pigs, some of which are still alive, down the ramp.

"About time I got help," the man says without looking at me.

He is a short, dirty-faced, fat man, who, when he smiles, shows rotted teeth. He keeps wiping his hands on his thighs after each blow. "You should see," he says. "They keep them in their bathtubs, for Chrissakes. In their fucking tubs!"

"Did you actually witness this?" I ask, wondering where he'd keep such an animal.

"Who—who do you think goes inside the houses and brings these fuckers out?"

"Hunger," I reply. "The epidemic's all a lie. One of the many inventions by the Department of Sanitation."

The man ignores me.

"What a fucking waste!"

For a moment Esteban, my father, who lives in California, like a phantom of the fire, appears as clearly as the last time I saw him when he came with Mama Concha to La Cabaña. And what does my father, this certain Esteban, say? "See son," he says. "Is this what you fought so hard for? What you gave up a career in pharmacy for?"

The man clubs another pig. It squeals.

"Don't do a shitty job," I say to the man. "Will you? Kill them, don't—"

"You want to do this?" the man says.

"I didn't say I wanted to, did I?"

"Shut up then. Get them out of here."

"What have you heard about the Peruvian Embassy?" I ask.

The man looks behind him out of the sides of the truck. "This isn't the time to talk."

I smile; the man smiles back, and for a moment I sense that he can read each and every one of my crooked thoughts. He is the type I got along with in prison; all brute strength and no brains. I ask him to get me out of Cochiquero.

"How much money do you have?"

"One hundred."

"That's not enough. I'll do it for—"

A soldier walks by and looks inside the truck, then moves on. The man swings the club as if to hit another pig and gets a trail of blood on the back of the soldier's olive-green shirt.

The soldier turns around and eyes us. We continue working, then the soldier moves on. The man grins up at me and laughs.

"One fifty," he says. "Or no go."

"Hundred's all I have."

He says no go.

9

"Cabrón," I say.

The man regrips the club and swings. I duck just in time, for he barely misses me, hitting the side of the truck.

"I wouldn't risk my chances over scum like you," he says.

I jump out of the back. "Hey, I call out to him. "All right, one fifty."

"¡Metete el dedo!" the bastard says, meaning to go stick a finger up my ass.

I contemplate using the club to bash his head in, but instead I go down the line to the last truck, which is already empty. I climb into the back and sit in one of the corners. Blood and excrement stain the floorboards. I try to catch my breath. Somehow, I think, I'll do it, get the hell out . . . no matter how . . . no matter what.

ANGEL / Los Angeles, city of skyscrapers under ashen skies where so many windows give the impression of individual wasp hives that reflect smoggy skies and more across-the-way hives. Too many cars, buses, trucks. City of speed and races.

For Angel Falcón, Los Angeles brings back memories of when the family had first arrived from Cuba in 1962. They lived on Pico in a three-story apartment building not too far from where they are now passing. He and his wife, Lilián, drive through the downtown panic of pedestrians trying to cross streets, even when the street signals flash: DON'T WALK!

Strewn newspapers and crushed cans clutter the streets and sidewalks, gather by the curb and gutters. Spoiled fruit rots in broken crates. And always the stink of piss and vomit in the air.

People witness two bums fighting over a wine bottle under a fire escape in an alley. Three times a week Angel and his wife come downtown to buy merchandise wholesale to sell in the ice cream truck. Nothing has changed. The poorly dressed Mexican children with hungry looks on their faces remind him of the harshness and struggle of the first days in California, the constant trips to the immigration department.

When he sells the merchandise through the streets of Bell and South Gate—suburbs of the big city—he can see the despair. What a name for a city so full of sin and evil and chaos. The Angels.

The years have gone by quickly, and Angel sees himself, the family, moving farther and farther away from Los Angeles. They can now afford to, he thinks. Lilián and he do their business in Bell, but they live on Evergreen Street, a residential block in South Gate.

It is a humble, three-bedroom, two-bathroom house—Diego, their son, sleeps in the den. Angel likes the back room best because the breeze keeps it cool during the summer afternoons, for whatever little time he isn't out selling.

Angel and Lilián have never been this much together, but now they share at least nine to ten hours a day riding around, selling ice cream, making a decent living. They bought the ice cream truck with the money they managed to save by working at odd jobs, factory work mostly. Perhaps it's what Diego accuses them of that is true: They avoid the problems at home by hiding within the comfortable numbness, motor-warmth of the truck. When they're through for the day, they go home, shower, eat and go to sleep to rest up for the next day.

Seven years ago they started the ice cream business, six months after Concha, Angel's mother-in-law, died. Concha, who always had stories about the past up her sleeve. She often spoke of the good times . . .

He works seven days a week, including holidays when Lilián may stay home and do the household chores. American holidays are the best-selling days. What more can he ask for, considering that the day they crossed the ninety miles from Varadero to Key West, they had nothing but three ragged suitcases filled with old clothes.

Lilián, like her mother, likes to reminisce about how things used to be for the family, the "good days" as she likes to refer to them, before her brother Hugo left the university to join the rebels in Sierra Maestra. Angel, too, has lived through better, like when he owned the two cafeterias in Santiago, on José Martí Street, but why complain? Why bring back something that died the day he arrived in this country?

Esteban, his father-in-law, lives with them. The old man keeps himself busy by doing little odds and ends around the house, watering the flowers or raking dead leaves, but Esteban has never forgotten the past, for in the past he lost, as he says, his identity, dignity, his respect for humanity. In the past or inside the motherland, he still believes that Hugo's alive and well, though the last time they heard from him he was in Mazorra.

Details are hard to keep track of, Angel knows, especially when they have to do with such a stubborn person as Hugo. The truth of the matter is that Angel and Hugo never got along because of Hugo's ideology. Back then he was an idealist, who believed the way to power and justice was through force. Lilián keeps her brother's letters and journal entries somewhere. Hugo could have come down from the hills when it was time to go, time for him to realize that the revolution was being fought for all the wrong reasons.

Because Hugo had not returned from the sierras, Esteban and Concha didn't want to leave. A chain reaction occurred. Lilián wouldn't leave without her parents, so they waited and waited. Finally, after Hugo was arrested and sentenced to twenty years, the family left.

Angel never talks about past mistakes or whose fault it was they didn't leave Cuba sooner because Esteban doesn't like to be reminded of how much better things could have turned out.

Time flies, Angel thinks, at supersonic speeds. His days begin and end the same: with work.

They buy the merchandise from different places. Candies, toys, soft drinks, ice creams. Today he rushes from the candy and toy warehouse in Los Angeles to the ice cream factory near where he lives. It's a new place owned by compatriots, Bebo and Eloisa, a nice family. Julio Iglesias plays on a radio sitting on a shelf behind the cash register. Lilián usually goes to the back where there is a sofa and two armchairs on which to sit and chats with Bebo's wife about her golden years in Santiago before the revolution when she was part of the Highlife on Vista Alegre.

Eloisa, who wears the same dress every day, is in her late forties. It must be the only dress she cares to use to come to work, Angel thinks. Nevertheless, he likes her body. But doesn't stare too much because he doesn't want the owner to notice, or Lilián, though she has outgrown her jealousy.

A quiet man, Bebo believes in listening to people more than in talking, and when he hears a good story, he laughs wholeheartedly.

He tells Lilián how he had been accused of counter-revolutionary activities and was almost sentenced to a firing squad, but they let him go because a cousin of his was a rebel. Yes, back then survival depended on whom one knew. Connections. The bigger the web of friendship, the better the chances of staying alive.

Sometimes the man tells funny jokes, like those by Alvarez Guedez, the humor virtuoso. The dirtier the better; those, according to Angel, are his funniest.

But when there are no stories or jokes to share, they listen to the radio. Angel likes music. One or two tunes. Usually by the end of the third one, Angel's order has been filled and he leaves. By then Lilián reminds him that it is almost eleven o'clock, time to hit the streets.

On the car radio the news of the Peruvian Embassy break-in is alarming. "People are running scared, mad . . . ," the voice on the radio says. "After the sentries were removed from their posts outside the embassy, thousands of citizens have snuck inside the grounds and are seeking asylum. They demand they be given exit visas. According to the government, the situation is under control. The *gusanos,* as a government official calls the people inside the embassy, are people who have nothing to offer the revolution. . ."

Lilián raises the volume and listens intently. "Government officials," the man on the radio continues, "refuse to release any more information concerning the asylum seekers' situation."

"They've really done it now," Lilián says.

Angel tries to imagine the thousands of people crowding the mission grounds, the upturned bus used to ram in through the front gate. "I doubt they'll let anybody . . . "

The news changes to the weather report: The day promises to be sunny, temperature in the mid-seventies. If the temperature drops lower, there'll be a decline in sales.

Lilián seems lost in thought. Probably about her brother. Hugo, Angel knows, is nowhere near the embassy. Political prisoners never seem to find a way out.

Home's the place Angel likes most. He's proud of it no matter how much heartache exists there. For him the way to deal with heartache is to ignore it, make believe there's nothing wrong. Like this separation his son Diego's going through.

Vanessa has left Diego, this much Lilián has told Angel. He and Diego lead separate lives. His son spends most of his time at the club where he plays with his band; Angel with his ice creams. Sometimes a week goes by in which they don't see each other.

Angel and Lilián work all day in the truck; then when the warmth surrenders to the coolness of the evening and the streets begin to empty, they start heading homeward. Most people around this city like to sit outside, especially the men, and chat or drink something cool like beer. Mariachi music fills these streets with old Mexican tunes. Lilián wishes they were Cuban songs instead, like the ones she used to hear when she was a teenager. Songs by Benny Moré, Pérez Prado, or Celia Cruz.

This place is to the Mexicans what Little Havana is to the Cubans. It's like comparing Olvera Street to Calle Ocho. These same Mexican people have become their best customers. The few American families that remain are in the process of putting up FOR SALE signs or have scurried away to cities like Downey, Lakewood, and Cerritos.

Lilián too has a knack for telling stories and anecdotes, something, Angel imagines, she inherited from her mother. She tells stories of how this land belonged to the Mexicans, to the Indians before them—how they lost it, and how they're slowly gaining it back.

Angel figures that if Mexicans are his best customers, then Cubans are his worst. Cubans are smart in a cheap way. They know that they can buy twice as many popsicles at the supermarket for the same amount of money they spend on his ice cream.

He rarely associates with his own people. Some, not all, are full of envy and contempt for what he has worked so hard for. They gather in social clubs like El Holguinero and La Cofradía to gossip and to play games and to talk about the old days, hoping that a coup d'état will occur and they can return. Angel believes strongly that whatever evil has fallen upon the homeland has been there for more than twenty years and, in all probability, is there to stay.

He'd be a fool if he sat around waiting for something to happen so that he can return.

Angel's the first to admit that he likes this country—his country, for he is a citizen now.

Families have come, have settled here, and those families have divided and spread, and new generations have emerged, generations which don't know the meaning of the word struggle. Oh, how they abuse this freedom. His own son doesn't know; when he was taken out of the country he was too young to remember.

Today Angel and Lilián work without breaks until six o'clock. On the way home Angel notices how the street lamps create a long, unbroken bracelet of lights as the sun sets behind the tenements. Angel wonders where it is dawning.

At home Lilián tells her father about the news she heard on the radio. Though Esteban has been home all day, he hasn't heard. He says he's worried because Diego has gone to Pilar's, his wife's mother's house, to find Vanessa.

"That," Lilián says, "won't do him any good." Lilián has never liked the Prados, Vanessa's parents. Her mother's a *metiche,* meaning Pilar's a meddler.

"Let him do what he wants," Angel says, carrying the change box into the kitchen.

"He cares about her," Esteban says. "I doubt it holds true at the other end." Esteban sits at the dining room table, smoking a cigar and drinking a beer. He helps count and stack all the change they make.

"The news," Esteban says, "will be on soon. I—" He drinks. "I want to hear all the details about the break-in."

Ever since Concha died, they've become a quiet family, not separate but silent. While Concha was alive, she kept reminding them of what her husband had lived through. In fact, she always told stories even Angel forgot at times, though he had as much affection for Concha as he had for his own mother, who passed away when he was a young man.

Angel stands by the kitchen sink and slowly washes his hands for dinner. Suds cover the grimy back of his hands. Years of work have taken their toll on them, he thinks.

Nowadays they sit together at the kitchen table, eat together, and sometimes, while they have dinner, Angel likes to think that they are a happy family.

DIEGO / Pilar, your mother-in-law, is in her corner of the worn divan sipping her cappuccino so as not to burn her tongue. She watches *Río Rebelde,* the eight o'clock soap opera on channel 34.

You sit quietly at the other end, feeling the two hits of coke take effect. A slow burning in the upper reaches of your nostrils. There is also a numbness between your eyebrows and a nagging itch at the tip of your nose. Will Pilar reveal V's whereabouts? V stands for venom.

Wife? You've got no idea where . . . didn't come to battle or argue or defend any masculine point, but in peace, to mend . . . You wish to settle things. . . .

The sound of rusty, static voices coming from the console's side speaker breaks the silence, a silence that extends into endless moments as you sink deeper and deeper into the cushioned softness of the divan, alone with your mother-in-law in the stuffy living room of the old house.

Under whose roof is she hiding? Hiding from what? God knows you didn't mean to . . . She wants you to leave her alone (this is all part of her new yearning for independence), and you wish you could, but to forget V would be like forgetting the past, which haunts you.

It is like shrapnel.

Pilar's house looks messy, unkempt, like a house in the process of being remodeled or moved into. The room smells of soiled rags and fried fish, when it had at one time—when Gustavo still lived here—smelled of Pine Sol or lilac air freshener. A dim lamp sheds light upon the film of dust on the television console, lamp table, picture frames, and coffee table, under which the last issue of the telephone directory yellows.

Steam whirls from the porcelain mug to Pilar's eyes and forehead. She leans back with her shoulders bent forward while her breasts under her blue robe spill over her stomach. Blinking to the changing pictures on the screen, she sips slowly.

The glare hurts your eyes.

You do, you do, you do . . . you did? Still do? Love her.

The face of an old woman appears on the screen. Her voice, when she speaks, carries the metallic sounds of make-believe despair. A soft crackle. She seems like an old woman who at the end of her life struggles; afflicted with sickness and solitude, she has to endure her suffering a little longer.

This stuff you bought from Nestor, the bartender at the Toucan Club, the place where you play the *timbales* with the band, is, as he calls it, "brutal," meaning the best uncut cocaine from somebody's private reserve.

"I'm worried about her," you say, wiping your sweaty hands on the knees of your Oscar de la Renta jeans.

"My daughter can take care of herself," Pilar says, not turning from the screen. She blows into her mug and takes another sip.

My daughter can take care . . . Instead of taking this as an insult, you grip the armrest and squeeze until the humps of your knuckles turn white. V, whom you know better than anyone else, is a poor driver. Drives crazier than you do, that's why you never let her drive the Spitfire. *She can't go far unless . . . Her father's in Miami. Yes, that's it, that's where she went.*

Pilar looks fatter since the last time you saw her, two or three months after your separation from her daughter. Fuller cheeks. The indifferent look on her face now reminds you:

She walked through the sliding door out of El Pueblo Market at the corner of Gage and Zoe into the heat of the street. She spotted you getting out of your car. One of the women you were dating while married to Vanessa was with you. Pilar gave the girl a harsh, cold stare. Embarrassed, you turned and headed straight for the IN door. Minutes later you walked out puzzled—Julie followed you in and out—having completely forgotten what you had come to buy.

Through the steam Pilar glances over as though she knows what you are thinking. She hasn't forgotten the incident.

The cool air from the fan on the coffee table hits your face and makes your eyes water. Action fills the screen.

"Amor," a young man says, entering a room

"I don't want to see you ever again," the girl standing by the window is saying. "Leave me alone. Understand?"

"But, Patty, don't be cruel. Forgive me. I promise it won't happen again."

Forgive him, goddamnit!

"Humm," Pilar says, regripping the handle of the mug absentmindedly.

The girl picks up a vase and throws it at the young man's feet. Glass shatters. "If you don't leave me alone I'll scream," she says, then she falls on top of the canopy bed and hides her face under a pillow. The brat.

A couple kisses in a Colgate toothpaste commercial.

There is a moment of silence in which the soft rattle of the fan turning becomes audible. Your ears feel as if they were on fire; your throat's dry. Gritty. Mouth feels like sandpaper.

"How can you watch that, Pilar?" you say.

Pilar, turning from the screen, says, "It's the only thing I watch."

"Watch the American channels. Animal Kingdom, now there's a program for you." She can watch the mating habits of Australian flying lizards.

"There's nothing wrong with this."

What you want to say, confess, is that Julie meant nothing to you, that she had been a companion to make you forget what had gone wrong with your marriage. V wanted to manipulate you. Now you can only call your breakup a mishap, a misunderstanding, or, as Pilar had labeled the situation, "A lesson for you to learn from."

Haven't learned a thing except that being close to someone is better than being alone. V left the apartment a couple of days ago—that much you know. No note, not even a call to say, Hey, I'm leaving you.

And it seems, from the sad expression on Pilar's face, that her loneliness goes far beyond the hurting stage. Gustavo, your father-in-law, left her for another woman.

"You haven't forgotten, have you?" you say.

She asks what you mean.

You stand and turn off the annoying television. Silence.

"What did you do that for?" Pilar says, placing the mug on the armrest.

"I think it's time we talk." You feel like scratching your nose with a file, that's how bad the itch is.

"Threats don't work on me."

She tries to stand, but you block her way. With her arms akimbo, she says, "Turn it back on! This is *my* house."

"Talk. Get everything that's bothering you out."

"Damn you! You are crazy. I've got nothing to say to you, and if you don't get out of here I'm going to call—"

"What do you want from me?" you say, feeling the adrenaline rush.

"I want nothing. I need nothing."

A vision of a dead frog pickled in formaldehyde forms in the back of your mind.

"Then why do you ignore me?"

She slides to the edge of the divan. "I'm not ignoring you."

"You've never forgotten that day you saw me with Julie at El Pueblo?"

"Look," she says and pauses. Then, "I'm not the one you should be telling this to. I don't care."

"If you tell me where V is I just might do that," you say, then move away from the television. "You didn't care that I was with her?"

"What I care about's that you mistreated my daughter. Why? I don't know. You got tired or disappointed or both. Of her. Now you come looking for her. Well, I'm not going to tell you. If you don't love my daughter, why did you marry her?"

You married her, you wish you could tell her, because V was a great fuck—no, no, that wasn't the real reason.

Pilar stands, pushes you out of her way and turns the set back on.

A special report comes on. The anchorman says that there has been a break-in at the Peruvian Embassy in Havana, and that the number of people there is growing by the thousands.

"See?" she says. "I missed that." She sits again.

"It's not that I don't love her—"

"Why did you leave her? Why do you keep coming back? To torment her? To make her suffer more?"

"Wait a minute," you say enraged, "I didn't leave her, *SHE* left me!"

"Who left whom the first time?"

She'd bring this up sooner or later; being predictable comes with old age.

"V's an impossible person to live with," you say, trying to keep your voice down. "She wants to run my life. Always tried to get me to stop playing at the club. I love playing. I've never asked her to stop cutting hair at the salon, have I?"

The watch on your wrist reads seven-forty, almost time to go to the club. The rest of the guys in the band must be there by now, setting up and tuning.

"Have you ever asked how she feels about you?" Pilar looks away. "I think you left her, got tired of warming another's bed, and decided to return thinking that you could do so just like that." Pilar snaps her fingers. "When she said no, that she didn't want anything to do with you, you . . ."

Her words bounce between the walls of the living room.

This thought invades your mind: a pair of maracas rattling, but there's no one shaking them. You realize that if V were . . . were here, she'd have looked at her mother first and then at you. Familial blood. Mother and daughter still attached. What V fails to understand is that marrying a woman so that you can finally have sex with her is a mistake. V stole the kisses and embraces she gave you from her mother. For Pilar sat chaperoning the two of you in this same living room.

"You're not being fair. I came to find out—"

"Not telling you. Even if I knew, I still wouldn't."

Pilar waves her hand as though to wipe you out of her sight. "Let me watch," she says. "I told you, I don't have anything against you, except when it concerns my daughter and her happiness."

"Fine. I didn't mean to . . . Julie meant nothing to me," you say, leaning against the wall.

"Does Vanessa know about Julie?"

"I thought you had told her," you say.

"I never opened my mouth."

She's lying. She probably called V at the hair salon the moment she got home from the market and said, "Guess who I saw just a few moments ago?"

You feel like going to the bathroom so that you can do something about the itch in your nose and the desert dryness in your throat, but instead, standing by the armrest of the divan and putting your knee on it, you ask, "How's Gustavo? Have you heard from him?" Gustavo, the architect.

Pilar leans forward and covers her knees with her robe. "Who knows?" she says. "I don't want to talk about that bastard."

At your wedding, you had been close enough to smell the Bacardi on Gustavo's breath. During the reception (hand in hand, V and you had already sliced the cake and were getting ready to depart for what you hoped would turn out to be a night of constant fucking), Gustavo approached you and fumbled with his words as though he were deeply moved. He began by saying that Vanessa was his treasure, to take care of her, and to love her . . . "I'm not one for sayings," Gustavo said, holding on to your shoulder to keep steady, "but . . . " he paused to suck the last drops of rum from the ice cubes in the plastic cup. "A woman . . . You want to know the truth, Diegito? I can't stand the sight of my wife in the morning . . . And she probably can't stand me, but she pretends better than I do . . . It's a constant reminder that I'm getting old, that I'm going to die . . . but a woman, a woman's that darkness that prevents a man from finding the light switch. Jesus, what a mystery they are! But, hey, what do I know about women, eh?"

The other time you met Gustavo had been at the bank, during a long wait at the teller window. He revealed his plans to leave for Miami, then mentioned something about buying a house on Key Biscayne.

Pilar glances at you as if she isn't sure whether you are going to stay or leave. You yourself don't know, feeling stuck to the spot by the divan.

The pictures on the wall hang loosely on their wires—all pictures of V's evolution from diapers to ruffles to graduation cap and gown to the white silk dress and veil. *Remember the nervous glances that V cast at you when the priest asked if you'd take her to be your wife?*

"If only I'd known, I'd never have come here," Pilar says, creasing the seam of her robe. "Look what has happened. What am I going to do here all by myself? You know I have nothing against this country, but . . . Nonsense!"

All by herself, you repeat, is that a clue? "Tell me," you say, making up your mind to leave.

She grabs her mug and runs the tip of her finger around its brim.

"Too bad I can't go back," she says. "With so much trouble now . . . who knows?"

"I don't know what happened, okay?" you continue. "I've changed. I was in a bind." Wipe the sweat off your brow. "V got tired of coming to the club to watch me play. I guess I got bored too. We lost respect."

"You thought by leaving her all your problems would be solved?" she says. "You should never take shortcuts. They don't lead anywhere."

"I knew that if I didn't get away things would get worse."

"No woman deserves to be abandoned."

"The affair with Julie, that just happened!" She came to the club one night. Easy.

Pilar, in a mocking tone, *"Just happened."* She swallows the last of her cappuccino. "Now it's Vanessa's turn to get away."

Another clue?

She stands up and goes to the kitchen. She opens the faucet and washes her cup. Water runs. When she returns she says, "He ran away." Then, looking at her slippers, "He ran away to another woman."

Watching Pilar slouch back to the divan makes you feel sorry for her, but this has nothing to do with your situation.

"He'll be back," she says. "You'll see. He'll be back and like a fool I'll let him in."

How tired you are of arguments. Your eyes burn as if a heater has been shoved too close to them.

"You're all the same . . . And you watch, he'll be back to have me—"

"Don't!" you say. "Don't do it! You don't have to take him back."

Looking up at the pictures, she says, "You expect her to, don't you? Otherwise you wouldn't be here."

"I'm not Gustavo." You dig into your pockets for the car keys.

"I'll take him back," she says. "I always do." She runs her fingers through her hair. "But I'll never forgive him,"

"Like you won't forgive me." You reach for the knob and turn it to open the door.

"You're *her* problem."

She stares at you the way she looked at Julie that hot August afternoon, the way a snake sizes up its rat. There's nothing left to be said, to be asked. *Where could she be?* One more look at Pilar and the fact that her eyes are closed says that she's not going to tell you. Once and for all, she's not going to tell you.

Promised to love and to honor . . . Love and honor. You leave the stuffiness of the living room for the coolness of the night. Outside on the porch you can still hear the television droning.

V has quit working at the salon. The other day at the bank you found out she had withdrawn half of the nine thousand dollars in the savings account—her half.

The sight of the Spitfire parked across the street is a relief. The drive to Sunset Boulevard is long. The crisp air lapping at your cheeks feels good as you walk toward the car.

The top's already down. You get inside the car, start the engine, and turn on the radio. Music comes on.

In gear now, the car begins to move. As it speeds away, the house in the rearview mirror diminishes and disappears the way ghosts in movies do.

ESTEBAN / Morning of the next day finds him kneeling on the soft earth with his back to the sun. Pruning carefully the dead leaves afflicted by malathion, he sweats and the drops fall from his chin onto his khakis. Sweating in this weather: warm mornings, heat during the afternoons, and windy at night. Santa Ana winds.

He works on his garden between the driveway and the entrance of the house.

Damn helicopters! he thinks. Every night they fly over the city and spray this gooey pesticide, and for what? All it's good for is to kill most of his roses.

They spray to kill a mediterranean fruit fly which City Hall claims poisons fruit. A lie. In all the years he lived in Santiago and ate fruit—mangoes, guayabas, papayas—nothing happened, not even a bad stomachache. If he doesn't take care of these flowers, who will? Not Angel. His son-in-law's always too busy with his ice creams. The truck, the merchandise, the customers. His daughter Lilián lives a hurried life, from the market to the house to the truck . . . And Diego. God knows that boy's got enough to worry about with Vanessa. Diego must have done something to her (hit her?); otherwise why would she leave him?

In the driveway sits his grandson's car, top up, and covered with white spots. He's going to be angry when he wakes up and sees it.

Esteban has been working on his flowers since sunrise. These were Concha's, his wife's, favorite roses ever since he knew her. The roses grow more buds than ever open, in bunches, and now he cuts some that the pesticide has damaged. From yesterday to today, Poof! Gone. What a shame.

Pinching here and there, he prunes slowly, carefully, as though he's been a gardener all his life and these are not real roses but ones made from fine porcelain. The thin stems he touches gently and cuts as close to the top as possible, while the cut pieces lie strewn around his knees. Steady are his hands; his fingers seem to be tiny tentacles, feelers. Paprika-colored spots the size of pinheads cover his hands and forearms. Armies of them. He wipes his hands thinking for a brief moment that they are only dirt particles sticking, but they aren't. The sun, he then figures, or, rather, being under it for so long has caused this. He can't help but wonder about skin cancer. Now his back and knees begin to ache.

So much to do, he thinks. Weed out, rake, water. This is the time when the avocado tree drops a lot of leaves. Why doesn't Angel cut the son of a bitch down? He has never liked big trees or bushes—big trees steal light from little plants.

What the plants need is water and a little fertilizer to rejuvenate them. Yes, fertilizer, he needs to buy some. The things I do for Concha, he thinks. Been doing them since she died, and not a sign. Every morning for the last eight years he has done this because the pruning takes his mind off things. Off how much he misses his wife. This was the time when they used to get up and stay in bed for a while, then make love. She loved it from the back. This thought excites him so that his prick gives a little tug.

Pain attacks his ankles and toes when he reaches to overturn a rock from under which a mustard-colored, wide-eyed salamander runs.

Esteban sits in the shade the house casts on the grass, then begs Concha to come to him, to form herself ephemerally from the grass dew surrounding him, out of the dirt; and for a moment he believes she does.

She walks toward him from the distance. It is an image of her he has seen before—the same one as in a black-and-white photograph he keeps, torn, dog-eared and faded by age to a coffee-stain yellow—an image he preserves in the last drawer of his dresser under his mended socks. Concha is dressed in one of her ornate lace and silk dresses she wore on hot afternoons when she sat on her rocking chair on the portico of the Spanish house in Santiago de Cuba. These dresses he enjoyed most, not for their intrinsic beauty, though they were beautiful, but for the youth they brought his wife. Her face so smooth and perfect under the slight shade from the porch awning. Ah, those pulpy lips! One day she came to the kitchen (neither Hugo not Lilián was in the house) and sat on his lap. Before he knew it she had unzipped his pants and gotten him in her. He loved these surprises.

"Esteban," a voice calls.

Though he keeps his eyes shut, he recognizes his friend's voice.

He looks pale, so Domingo tells him.

"I'm all right," Esteban says. "Been out here too long today, that's all."

Domingo Sosa. Thin, which makes him look frailer than he actually is, balder, and with long hairs protruding from his nostrils. He looks as if he hasn't slept for days. His face is dark and wrinkled, but his eyes behind his glasses, in the years Esteban has known him, have preserved a mixture of alertness and curiosity.

"Did you hear the news?" Domingo asks.

"The break-in, yes, I stayed up last night."

"So many people. Something's bound to happen this time."

"Doubt it," Esteban says, resting his hands on his hips. I'll have to wait and see, he thinks, otherwise I'll lose my mind thinking about Hugo.

"They used a bus to ram their way in." Domingo tsk-tsks, then puts his hands behind his back.

Esteban bets that the whole incident's just another rumor snowballing from Miami.

"Anyway," Domingo says, "I come to speak to you. Urgent matters."

As he stands, Esteban wonders what these *urgent* matters could be. He senses Domingo's restlessness quickly and asks him if he'd prefer the coolness of the inside. "I'll make coffee," he says.

"Sounds like a good idea." Domingo looks down at the cut plants.

"The spraying's killing all the plants. Look how many leaves I've cut." He shows Domingo a small mountain of snipped buds, petals, and leaves.

"Terrible," Domingo adds, "just terrible. If I were any younger, I'd do something about it."

Younger. Domingo's only two years older than I am, Esteban thinks, sixty-five. But he is right, though; something's got to be done about all this spraying and those helicopters flying amok. Domingo was a lawyer in Santiago. Came to the states with most of the money he had saved in Cuba, bought a lot of property whose value has steadily increased over the years.

"Who knows when the bastards plan to stop. Epidemic, eh? Sure." Esteban puts the pruning scissors in the wallet pocket of his work khakis, and leads the way across the yard and down the driveway.

"Lilián and Angel gone?" Domingo asks.

"Went to buy more merchandise," he says.

"Those two want to get rich."

Soon they'll return with a trunkful of cardboard boxes. Ice cream. A traffic jam's all it takes for it to melt. One day his son-in-law's going to open the trunk and find a creamy pool of melted ice cream.

Domingo asks about Diego.

"Inside sleeping. He's got bucketfuls of problems. Separated. Well, she left him." Haven't I told him all this the last time we played chess? Esteban wonders. "Ran away. He's going crazy looking for her. You know how these young people are."

"Not all are young people ," Domingo murmurs.

"That's what happens when you marry so young." Concha and he got married when . . . Well, times were different then.

"Does he still play at the club?"

"Every night." Esteban has told Diego that Vanessa probably went to live with her father in Miami.

"Good. It probably takes his mind off things."

Esteban holds open the screen door, whose hinges are loose. If Angel doesn't take some time off his ice cream to do repairs around the house, it'll fall apart. Esteban can see it now: one door-slam and Boom! There go the roof and walls.

Inside Esteban waits for his eyes to adjust to the dark before he walks down the hall to the kitchen, where Domingo usually sits on one of the dining-room chairs. This time, though, he remains standing by the back door. Esteban offers him half of a cigar he takes from a cabinet drawer. Domingo refuses.

When he turns the radio on, music comes on. He expects the news soon. After Esteban washes the dirt off his hands, prepares the espresso coffee maker and puts it on the stove, he leans against the refrigerator ready to listen.

"Ruthie," Domingo says, and which he pronounces *Rusi*, "tells me I'm incapable of taking care of myself, Esté." He folds his arms over his belly. His elbows make a W.

He listens intently.

"My own wife wants to dump me in a convalescent home. Something one of her doctor friends suggested. She tells me, 'You're getting too slow to look after yourself, and I can't do everything for you. I'm too busy with work.' Damn her, Esté. She insinuates that I'm losing touch with . . . You know it isn't true."

"She's the one losing her mind," Esteban says, "not you. Why don't you do this: Hire one of these young girls to take care of you, you know, and let Ruth come home one day and find the two of you—"

27

"She's got witnesses. Her nurse friends at the hospital. She wants to take me to court to prove to a judge that I'm not well. I might be old, damn it, there's not much I can do about that, but I'm not senile."

Far from it, friend, Esteban thinks. Listening to all this nonsense makes him angry. He draws closer to Domingo to place his hand on Domingo's bony shoulder. Esteban remembers the day the police came to close his pharmacy in Santiago. It was such a shock that he didn't speak to anyone for days, not even to Concha. Domingo, he knows, lost not only his law practice, but his son, who was killed shortly after the triumph of the revolution for counterrevolutionary activities, whatever they were.

Domingo's eyes water, but no tear dares to jump out of his eyes. Esteban has seen him upset before, but never like this. Señora Sosa's a bitch, he thinks. She's the type of woman who throws things away as easily as she obtains them, Esteban can tell; Domingo has become a thing no longer needed, an obstacle.

"If she gets witnesses," he tells Domingo, "so can you."

"But she's got the doctors—"

"Let the doctors go screw themselves."

A smile appears on his friend's lips.

Coffee drips from the beak of the espresso maker. Esteban quickly turns the stove off and pours two cups. Domingo takes his and blows into it.

"Want something to eat?" Esteban asks, opening the refrigerator. He sees that the carton of milk is almost empty. Diego drinks milk faster than Lilián can buy it. He closes the door.

"I don't know what to do," Domingo says. "I've got nothing here. No wife, no daughter, no home."

"Come on, cool off."

Without Domingo, there would be no more chess games, card games, or dominoes, but they haven't played in a long while. No more conversations about the past.

"If she puts me in a convalescent home," he says, slamming his fist down on top of the counter, "I'll run away."

"Get that out of your mind."

"What about court? She's got notarized papers from this lawyer, from doctors."

"You are just absentminded, your condition's not chronic," Esteban says, and immediately feels sorry for having said *chronic*. It isn't the word he intended to use.

I know what she wants, Esteban thinks. By putting him in a convalescent home, the court grants her the right to dispose of all their property, the land, the apartments, all of the real estate Domingo's worked so hard to obtain.

"I've always envied Concha for having such good qualities," Domingo says. "She was a family woman, Esté. My wife, she's ..."

Ruth can go wipe her mouth clean of all the vileness that comes out of it. Very little, in fact, can be said about Ruth. Her only good quality might be that she understands her daughter, but Julie neither cares nor loves nor understands either of them. Just a young slut. Came by a few times to see Diego. The last he heard she moved to New York and is now living with some mafioso.

Domingo drinks the last of his coffee in one gulp (one day he's going to snap his neck) and sets the cup down on the stack of doilies by the radio. A more relaxed look appears on his face. He wants to know if Esteban has received any news from Hugo.

"The last letter came from Mazorra," Esteban says. "He's still there."

"Better off there than at La Cabaña."

In prison, Esteban has heard reports from political prisoners who have been released, that those bastard guards and wardens and sons of bitches who run prisons like Boniato, La Cabaña, and El Príncipe, do their very best to break your back. Through physical and psychological torture, they wear down your human dignity. Someday, they'll pay. Look at the Jews; every time they get their hands on a Nazi bastard, they hang them, shoot them. They deserve to be buried alive.

Mierda. Both places are shit. He remembers the disgusted feeling that overcame him the day he got to visit Hugo at La Cabaña. The inmates lived like animals. Filthy, vermin-ridden cells, no room to move in. The food was mush, fit for pigs and dogs—if those poor souls *indeed* got any food. Inhumane and barbarous treatment, that's what it was, what it still is.

"I've found Lucinda again, Father," Hugo wrote. "And we're happy together." But no one knows Hugo better than he does, not

29

even Concha knew him as well. Hugo's made out of some hard material I lack, Esteban thinks, but who can say that Esteban Carranza doesn't have guts, *cojones*.

"Maybe," Domingo says, "they'll let him come."

"That would be a miracle."

Domingo slides his hands in his pockets and says, "If something were to happen and suddenly you had to go get Hugo, would you let me come along?"

What does Domingo know that I don't? Are they really going to let these people out of the embassy? But Hugo's a political prisoner, not an asylum seeker. Political prisoners are never freed. Asylum seekers do crazy things like take over embassies. Everybody on that island is looking for the best way out. Only political prisoners have the balls to reject the system and voice their opinion—that's what gets them behind bars.

"Are you hungry?" is what Esteban asks Domingo.

"Something's going to happen. I can feel it, Esté."

"If you stay, I'll fry a couple of chicken filets and some plantains."

"Not hungry," Domingo says. Then, "Count on me, Esté."

"We'll have to wait and see what happens, won't we?"

For all he knows, this is only a hoax set up by Cuba's government to create confusion, or alarm the Cuban community here in the States.

Esteban picks up a rag off the sink and starts to wipe the stove.

"I must go," says his friend.

"Stay a while longer. How about a game of chess?"

"I've got to run," Domingo says. He starts for the door.

"Don't forget to listen to the news," Esteban tells him, checking the batteries in the portable radio.

He takes the radio with him as he accompanies Domingo to the sidewalk. After they say goodbye, he returns to his garden. All these years of struggle and this is all that remains: the sound of the wind dragging dead leaves across the cement. Is silence all that's left, Concha? He turns on the radio, sighs, kneels once again, and with the scissors in hand cuts away all the withered parts of his miniature roses.

* * *

CONCHA */* . . . out of the past. Songs. A medley of voices. Good times. A way of life in another place, another time. When she was a young girl her father took her sailing once. The boat, which he had rented for the summer, was called **La Perla** . . . a long time ago.

Favio Lara, her father, a short, but strong man of thirty-five, with a full and dark beard covering his face. That morning La Perla—her mother stayed at the beach chalet—sailed out of the bay swept by a strong breeze. Her father seemed to be in a jovial mood. A song came from his lips, a tune he sang without knowing a lot of the words to it—he hummed along places where he got lost.

It was a mild, sunny day. Quiet. A tingle of salt hung in the warm air. She was thirteen and the only thing she liked about the sea was its color, the way the coral reefs and sandbanks formed patterns underwater. Schools of silver fish flashed by under the boat. The boat, which sliced the waves, bobbed; and the motion made her dizzy at first, a little faint; but then, with a steady wind, she felt better.

They sailed past keys and islets on whose sands pelicans and gulls nestled or stood preening their feathers. Egrets, on one leg, stood with their necks held in the shape of a question mark.

Away from the bay now, away from the shore, the land became a huge mass, the hump of a monster rising out of the water. This was what Amerigo Vespucci and before Christopher Columbus must have seen from the distance. Trees of the deepest emerald. Indigo water ending at the edge of the whitest sand.

The wind whipped the clouds up from behind the mountain peaks. The grandeur of the panorama took her breath away. Made her giddy. She felt nervous and scared and excited all at the same time.

Her father, who had gone down into the cabin, returned dressed in shorts. Towel in hand, he approached the stern, tufts of premature white hair showing on his bare chest.

"Change into your bathing suit and let's go swimming," he told her.

She watched as he stood on the edge of the deck, stretched his arms, inhaled, and dove in. He went under and stayed down for what seemed like an eternity. When he surfaced, he blew a stream of water in an arch out of his mouth.

"Come on sweets," he called from the water. "Come join me. The water's wonderful."

"I'm afraid," she told him. She was stretched out on the deck with her arms behind her head.

"Of what?"

"Everything. Big fish."

He laughed and started to swim toward the boat. The muscles on his back tensed and flexed as he moved his arms out in front of him.

She knew how to swim, it wasn't that that kept her from jumping in. She wore a red-and-white striped bathing suit and a funny-looking hat her mother had insisted on to keep the sun off her face.

Her father asked her to help him climb aboard. She sat up and gave him her hand, and when he grabbed hold of it he pulled her into the water.

She let out the scream just as she went under. He was laughing when she came up and held on to his wide shoulders. Her father brushed her hair out of her face.

"The hat's ruined," she said.

"I'll buy you another," he said and kissed her on the cheek.

Now she moved away from her father and when she was at a distance she said, "I'll race you to the boat."

"Bet me something first," he said. Droplets of water glistened in his beard.

"Like what?"

"Some information."

"What kind of information?" she asked, slowly kicking her feet.

"Tell me about him."

"Who, Father?"

"The young man."

"Young man. What young man?" she said playfully and swam away.

"Come back, tell me more." Her father laughed.

"It's my secret."

"I want to hear about him." he said, swimming toward her. "Your mother's told me he walks you to school."

She swam around the front of the boat to the other side where she stopped and listened for the sound of her father coming after her. Favio climbed aboard instead and went down to unpack the lunch Rosario had prepared for them.

The young man was her secret, she thought, moving until she reached the ladder and climbed on deck. She sat down to eat the sandwich and drink the juice her mother had made. It was summer and though she was having fun, she couldn't wait to get back to the city. There Esteban was waiting.

May 1958

Mama Concha:

I don't know if these letters will ever reach you. I hope they will, but I'm compelled and determined to write it all down for the great moment that it is. That it will be. There is a lot of time to be made up for since I joined the revolution late.

My motives escape me now that I'm here among the vines and foliage, out of danger for the time being. Maybe I had to leave the city because I figured things this way: A man must stand on his own two feet. If he believes in something, he must not speak about it or kill it with words and speculation. Instead, he must act. Action's the word. I have taken the initial step, and I am proud of myself for doing so.

At this very moment, I am holding a Winchester rifle, dry mud caked on its strap. Yes, it's loaded, and its long barrel looks as black and shiny as a crow's feathers, and as smooth. The weight of it pleases me. This, Mother, is what will make those bastards listen. I am not one for names. Nothing else will do. They are not going to stop their butchery. Words have no meaning when somebody's after you.

Since I am a new recruit (the youngest in the group), they have me doing night-watch guard duty. It gives me a chance to think and put things in perspective. Sometime soon I'm supposed to meet the commander of this unit, a certain Lobo Morales, whom his men seem to admire and look up to, when he returns from a mission. He's the one who came up with this bit of advice: "Keep your gun pointed at the dark."

Tell Father I know how disappointed he must be. He's a stubborn man. I couldn't explain myself away to him any more than I can get up and walk inside the presidential palace and arrest the son of a bitch. Call me an idealist. Fine. I don't want a comfortable life with all its toppings: a family, beautiful wife and children, a house in Vista Alegre, and an income from the pharmacy. I'm not the type. Tell him that no matter what, I love him.

Action is the antidote that cures restlessness, Mother. Consider me gone from your side, but whenever you look up at these hills, think of me.

When I look at the future I see the brightest glare. Tell Father I couldn't picture myself dealing with scales and measures, pills and powders, liquids and lotions and potions . . .

All I ask is that you understand, Mother.

Up in arms,
Hugo.

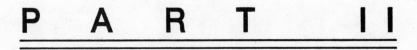

PART II

Book of Places

DIEGO / The Toucan Club's the only club in town that plays merengue, salsa, and latin jazz, good music to dance to. Long ago it used to be the finest Mexican restaurant on Sunset Boulevard until don Carlos Piñeda bought it and turned it into one of the best nightclubs, with the largest dance floor. The other thing that makes this place great is the influx of women. A mine. Men are outnumbered five to one. That's the way don Carlos likes to keep it.

Once in the parking lot you park facing a brick fence. There is a huge billboard at the corner. On it is a Ferrari with working headlights. LET THE WILD INTO YOUR LIFE! it says. Red, V's favorite color. The bitch left without a warning.

Getting out of the car and advancing toward the entrance, no longer do you feel the itch in your nose. This stuff's a killer. Check the tie knot on the side mirror. Didn't get cut shaving, a miracle. In a hurry you went from Pilar's to your parents' and found the house empty. Your grandfather must have gone out somewhere, he usually stays at home to catch the news. Certainly he must be excited about the break-in.

Black marble and mirror cover the facade of the two-story building at the back entrance. Multicolored bright lights hide among the flowers, tropical plants, and miniature palm trees which give the place an air of grandeur. Topaz water cascades from a fountain filled with Japanese carp.

On the glass revolving door you find your face slightly askew, with the corner of your mouth doing a tightrope balancing act. Coke, you think, always numbs the face, especially that area of the forehead between the eyebrows. The tie hangs a little too far to the right, nothing a little twist and tug won't fix. Ahhhhh, Bill Blass!

The bouncer, better known as Pelican because of his big nose, is taking the cover charge and doing the hand-stamping tonight. He greets you with a Hey-you're-late look. From what you've heard and seen, he doesn't like you. Sometimes you get the feeling that not too many of the employees here do. They probably envy you because you have it so easy being the leader of the band.

The interior decor is Caribbean style: dry reeds, bamboo, wicker—lots of wicker furniture, baskets, ceiling fans—and gourds that hang from the walls and columns.

Two girls dressed in low-cut, tight-fitting evening dresses go by and smile.

In his giant birdcagelike booth hanging from the ceiling at the other side of the dance floor, Tictacs, the deejay, notices when you come in and says into his microphone, "Welcome to the Toucan Club, ladies and gentlemen! Hope you have a great time here tonight. This is the last song before the band takes the stage. Enjoy!"

You walk toward the stage through the crowded bar behind which you see Nestor, the bartender who handles your drinks and sends them up to the stage. He's an old friend.

"Nestor," you call out to him, "hear the news about the break-in? Trouble, trouble."

He looks over and does a thumbs-up gesture. Also, he wears an earring on his left ear. Soon he'll send over his specialty: a Kamikaze with blue curaçao and a sprig of mint.

On stage the rest of the band has already tuned up and is anxious to get started. They take their places. You take yours behind the see-through Plexiglas timbales, remove the sticks from the skins, and signal Tictacs to cut his music.

The stage blacks out. *"Damas y caballeros,"* Tictacs introduces the band, *"con sabor latino, para la gente latina, la gran orqueta del Club Toucan!"*

A spotlight shines center stage; then, as the other lights come up and you snap your fingers on the countdown, the band plays the first tune with gusto, an original called, "Negra Criolla," meaning creole black woman.

Immediately the dance floor swells with couples. Women in

fancy silk dresses move their hips to the beat. And what delicious hips they are, swaying to the rhythms of the congas. They dance close to the stage where the sound is loudest.

A fine sense of music tells you that the electric piano's not keeping time. One look behind you and the problem becomes evident: Flaco, the piano/pianola player, isn't there. Instead, Chucho, one of the trumpet players, stands behind the piano.

"Why isn't Flaco here?" you ask Godoy, who sits next to you slapping his tumbas.

Godoy shrugs.

That's going to cost Flaco. Don Carlos is tired of hearing excuses. This is your band, so your neck's on the cutting block. But this is strange that Flaco's absent. He's never been late.

Forget it. Concentrate on keeping the rhythm. Tuc, tuc, trrrr-tuc, tuc . . . A towel with which to dry sweaty hands and sticks hangs from the stand between the drums.

Music begins to soothe, and the following conversation takes place inside your head. A little voice: Hey, bastard! You killer, you . . . That's right, you dumb son of a bitch. Ever hear of cellicide? . . . When million of cells are exterminated by drugs and alcohol? . . . So what . . . So what! So fuuuuuck you!

The stage lights hurt your eyes and so you look in the direction of the bar. There, Maruchi, the new waitress, dressed in a red leotard which has long black plumes attached to the back and black fishnet stockings, waits for her order to be filled. Nestor is talking to her.

She delivers her drinks, then slowly begins to move toward the stage and leaves a drink on the edge. She looks up, smiles. Her V-cut uniform shows a lot of cleavage.

Bend over for a quick sip. The Kamikaze burns on its way down. Boy, a couple more of these and the lights'll spin. But you know how to administer your booze, and drugs. Life, you think, is all a matter of checks and balances—booze slows down the coke.

Almost finished with this first tune, you begin to loosen up a bit. A smile of approval for the way the band's hiding Flaco's absence forms on your lips. Relax, man, relax, you tell yourself, a mighty long night still lies ahead.

* * *

HUGO / Cochiquero lies between ash and smoke, cinders and rubble. Between sugarcane fields and a muddy river which hides among the hills in the distance. This camp holds no boundaries, no barbed wire or electrical fences. No, none of these physical confinements. It's an open camp in the middle of a vast terrain of red earth, surrounded only by sparse trees and shrubs. The limits here are kept imaginary, enforced only by guards, dogs, and where-do-you-think-you're-going? bullets fired in the dead hours of night.

Like a wounded bird, the sun takes its time descending, and my wait for darkness becomes tiresome. I sit on the edge of an empty water trough, digging my heels into the dirt and dust. Like other things now, thoughts have to be portioned; for time cannot be wasted. In a hurry, no time to slow down and ponder over *what ifs* or minute details. This is 1980. Month: April. Day: I heard it mentioned on the radio, the sixth.

Thoughts of the embassy come and go.

From here the trucks on the other side of the fire pit blur as the sun goes down leaving a red glow in the sky.

The night shift begins. Workers come and go from the mess hall to the sleeping barracks, out of which emerges the sound of men undressing and coughing, sometimes retching. A couple of guards leave the mess hall chatting, toothpicks in their mouths. Their talk is loud, as though they haven't realized that day noise has ceased.

Ask him who finds himself bent over the latrine hole vomiting what the night was made for and he'll tell you that it was made for suffering and denial. And, in the end, morning and death.

To escape from a place such as Cochiquero one has to move about as one should always go about in Cuba: carefully. One mistake and . . . As far as I'm concerned, they are like hounds, bred to detect suspicion.

It is dark enough now for the caged dogs behind the barracks to howl to let whoever feeds them know that they are hungry.

I stand and walk away from the trough slowly. Hands in pockets. But I try not to walk too slowly for I might attract attention. Inching toward the other side of the fire pit where the truck driver should be waiting, I check the rolled-up money in my back pocket.

A guard walks by and I say, "Wonderful night, eh?"

"What's so wonderful about it?" he says and walks inside the mess hall and gets a place at the end of the food line. Tonight's dinner, from the greasy smell in the air, is mashed potatoes and fried eggs.

Some of the workers go by and look, hunger-ridden behind their dirt masks. If they only knew what I'm up to, they'd laugh. *What?* they'd say. *You plan to escape? Ha!*

Only two bulldozers remain on the outer edges of the pit. At night the work slows down considerably. That's why some of the truck drivers, if they came to deliver late in the afternoon, spend the night and leave before dawn.

In the dark everything gets lost. I sneak from tree to tree behind the guard post, cut across the empty shower area, and move to the other side of some tall shrubs. Breathing becomes difficult, so I stop to catch my breath. The time for real *cojones* arrives, and a nervous twitch attacks my left shoulder blade.

The chirping of the flames embracing new flesh drowns the noise of my steps as I move out into the open. Finally when I reach the other side I see the silhouette of somebody behind the windshield of a truck whose plate number I remember.

"Hey!" a voice says.

I stop abruptly as if I had come to the edge of a precipice, then turn around.

A soldier stands behind me, close enough to the pit so that with one push . . .

"What are you doing?" he asks, his face hardly visible in the shadows.

"I couldn't sleep," I tell him, "so I figured I'd come out and help unload." There are liars and then there are liars, but none as good.

The young soldier looks me over and says, "This isn't your shift. If you work now doesn't mean you'll get a break in the morning."

"I understand," I say and realize, once he turns and faces the glow of the fire, how young this son of a bitch is.

"Go over to that truck," he says and points to the one in the middle. "They need help there."

"Great," I say, then smile, "I can't sleep with those bastards.

They cough and puke all night long."

The soldier can't help but smile, for he probably knows what it's like to live under such conditions.

"Just give them a hand."

"Are there any more trucks coming?"

"I don't know," he says, then turns around and walks in the opposite direction, toward the other side of the pit.

To make sure he's not going to follow me, I walk to the truck. There, two black men are struggling killing a last pig. Since they haven't seen me and it seems like they don't need my help, I fall to my knees and crawl under the truck.

The ground's damp, and I can't help but wonder if blood has leaked from the cracks between the floorboards. It's blood, all right. It smells rancid and I feel it sticking on my fingertips.

I move out from underneath the truck, stand up, and run to my truck. On the other side I reach for the door handle, pull the door open, and climb inside. "I've got the money," I say to the fat man who's got his muddy work boots up on the dashboard.

The truck driver holds out his hand and says, "All of it."

I reach inside my back pocket and withdraw the bundle of bills.

"Look," I tell him, handing him the folded bills. "I tried to get the other fifty, but I—"

"You don't listen, do you?" the man says and starts to count the money.

We exchange glances.

I grin. "I know somebody in Havana who'll lend me the rest."

He shakes his head. "That's not good enough."

The brightness of the fire across the loading ramp is reflecting off the man's large eyes.

"Fuck!" I say, resting my arms on my thighs. There's a wide crack on the dashboard which looks as though somebody had cut the vinyl with a serrated knife.

"I'll take you if you give me that," the man says and points to my chest.

He wants the gold chain my mother gave me before I started at the university. "Are you crazy?" I say. "This thing's solid gold. This is worth more than—"

"Hey," he says, "I don't have to take you anywhere, understand? I can sit here and sleep."

"Tell you what. This'll be collateral. When we get to the city I'll give you the rest of the money."

The man turns and looks out the dirty windshield as though he is calculating what I've just told him. The stubborn bastard.

"Take it off," he says.

"No, no," I tell him, getting angry enough to call the whole thing off. "Either I wear it or I'll have to hire some other driver."

"Okay," he says. "How about if you take it off and hang it from this sun visor."

"Go fuck yourself," I say and reach for the door handle.

"All right," the man says. "All right, goddamnit!"

Nervously, he puts the money in his shirt pocket, starts the truck, and shifts gears. We move out. On the rearview mirror the night swallows the camp. Forty miles per hour, that's what the speedometer reads. Go faster, I think, or we'll never get there.

"Stay down until I tell you to come up," he says. His hands, dirty and large, seem to be one with the wheel.

I do as he says. The cabin reeks of piss and excrement and blood. How many pigs has this truck brought to slaughter?

Once out on the dirt road, the truck driver fishes a cigarette out of his other shirt pocket.

"Let me have half?" I ask, picking at a scab on my head which hurts when I touch it.

He looks down at me and smiles. "You want a lot of things, don't you?"

"I haven't had a cigarette in days."

"This is my last one," he says.

"Be a good samaritan," I say. "Break it in half."

This makes the man laugh, so he reaches over and hands me the cigarette. I take it, snap it in half and give him the filtered end.

"Uh-uh," he says, "give me the other half."

Smart bastard. He takes his half, puts it to his mouth and lights it. When he lowers the match, I lean forward and light my own and swallow a mouthful of smoke. Smoke rapidly fills the cabin.

My eyes water while I breathe in the smoke.

"What are you going to do once you're in the city?" the driver says as he rolls down his window.

"Don't know," I tell him. "One thing at a time."

"You're crazy."

"Listen, my knees are starting to hurt. When can I come up?"

"When I tell you to." The man takes a last drag off his cigarette then crushes the butt in the ashtray.

"What the hell's going on in Havana anyway?" he asks.

"Something big, I hope."

"That embassy break-in stuff might be a trick, you know."

"No tricks," I say. "Not when sentries get killed."

The driver grows pensive. I can feel every pothole or rock the truck goes over as it moves down the road away from the camp. A cramp on my lower back makes me groan.

"Can I come up?"

"No. Stay there. An army truck's following us."

A sharp pain runs up my spine. Not out of danger yet. I lean against the hard metal door while scattered thoughts of Lucinda come to me. Lucinda standing by the window of her room looking out at the ravine at the end of the patio.

The man notices that I'm dozing off, so he tells me to get some sleep, for, he assures me, it's going to be a long drive to the city. He himself yawns, then starts to drum his hands on the wheel and whistles a tune I haven't heard in years.

DIEGO / Finished with the first set, the band goes on a break. Tictacs starts spinning his records. From Godoy and Negro, who play the flute and tenor sax, you try to find out what happened to Flaco. They don't know.

"He didn't call?" you ask.

"Chucho's fucking up," Negro says. "He can't play that damn piano." Negro acts jittery, more nervous than usual.

"Somebody's got to play it," Godoy says.

"Okay," you tell them. "Here's what we gonna do, all right? On the next set, Godoy, you replace me on the timbales. Negro, play the tumbas."

"Who's going to play piano?" Negro wants to know.

"I will," you say, then suck the blue residue from the bottom of your glass and set it down on the floor.

"Uh-uh," Godoy says.

"Fuck," you say, holding the sticks in one hand and the towel in the other, "we'll have to rework the order of the song list. That way we'll be able to alternate on the instruments."

"Okay," Negro says. His teeth, against his black face, look so bright under the lights. "Sounds good."

You leave Godoy and Negro onstage so they can change everybody's song list for the next set. What a fucking night, you say to yourself as you go to the bar for another drink.

It's hot around the bar, so many people and they are all smoking. A thick cloud of smoke shrouds Nestor behind the counter. Maruchi approaches you from behind and puts her hand around your waist. You feel the smallness of her thin fingers against your back.

She says hi as you turn around to face her. You thank her for the drink.

"Don't thank me, thank Nestor," she says and smiles.

Yes, Nestor, who at this very moment's calling for you to go over to the corner of the counter where he's mixing two tequila sunrises. Maruchi carries away her tray.

"Thanks for the drink, bro," you tell him, pointing to the tip of your nose.

"Hey," Nestor says, "the boss wants to see you."

"Upstairs?"

"Where else?"

You study the faces of the people sitting across the bar. There's this guy with a hat on and his collar turned up talking to this black-haired girl who doesn't look too interested. "Got any family at the embassy?" you ask.

"I don't think so, but if I did, I wouldn't hold my breath."

"Why?" Dating is a game.

"It's a big publicity stunt, might be a trap or something."

"It looks legit to me."

"The place must be a madhouse," Nestor says.

"Imagine," you say and move away from the bar.

At the end of the hall upstairs, the office is between the two bathrooms. You decide to visit the john before confronting the boss. Inside, Jorge, the bathroom attendant, is rearranging his colognes on the sink counter. A man finishes washing his hands and Jorge hands him a towel. The man dries his hands, checks his hair in the mirror, digs in his coat pocket for his wallet, removes a dollar, and drops it on the counter.

What you like most about this bathroom besides its cleanliness is that you can hide from the noise and pandemonium. The smell of the deodorizer pill sitting inside the urinal is strong. Facing the Royal Flush urinal, you say, "Hey, Jorge."

"*¿Qué pasa?*" he says. With paper towels Jorge soaks up the water splashed outside the sink.

"Know how to play the electric piano?" you say to humor him.

"Why you ask?"

"Flaco didn't show up, man. That son of a bitch." Finished pissing, zip, and tuck the shirt in.

"Wish I could help you out, bro," Jorge says, brushing your lapels, "but I'm not as lucky as you Cubes. Born with the beat."

"I thought Chileans were born with the beat, too," you say and laugh.

"Not with that kind of beat, understand?" Jorge swings his hip back and forth.

"Ah, that one we can all dance to."

"On the house," he says and splashes some Yves Saint Laurent cologne in your hands. He knows that your favorite cologne's Calvin Klein, but he says this is real good. Knowing what to recommend and to whom is the sign of a good bathroom attendant, which Jorge is.

Leaving a dollar in Jorge's jar, you exit the bathroom. On the EMPLOYEES ONLY door you knock and wait for an answer. Don Carlos opens the door and tells you to have a seat. He's on the phone.

In disorder, don Carlos's office looks smaller than it actually is, more like a cubicle. Papers and invoices cover his desk, dust and carbon-paper smudges have turned his white calculator gray, and the glass cover on his desk has a huge crack at the corners. You sit down.

Don Carlos is about your father's age—forty-two or -three—

and his face is nothing but a compilation of contortions and nervous tics. Something to do with an accident where he used to work. A heavy piece of metal fell on his back and broke several vertebrae. He was an invalid for a year, then with an operation and physical therapy he was able to walk again. He sued the company and got close to a million in damages. "Pain and suffering," he said once, "are the x factor in a lawsuit. In other words, big money."

From what little you make out of the conversation, he's talking to his wife about the break-in and the possibilities of . . . he's off the phone.

Leaning back on his swivel chair, don Carlos says, "You look surprised."

"A little," you say and sink deeper into the chair.

"Didn't you tell me once you had family back home?"

"An uncle," you say, "but I doubt he's at the embassy."

Don Carlos mentions all the family he's got in Havana. A brother, a sister, and her family.

Don Carlos places his hands behind his head. "I don't know what the hell's wrong, but I've made up my mind. I might have to take a trip to Miami," he says, "but that's only if my family gets out of Cuba. If they do, then I'm going to leave my wife in charge here, and I want you to help her make sure everything keeps running smoothly."

"Why not ask Nestor?"

"I don't trust him," don Carlos says, moving his head sideways as though to release a cramp in his neck.

Does he know what you know, that Nestor's dealing coke on the side?

"Count on me," you tell him.

"I also wanted to talk to you about Flaco."

"He called?"

"This afternoon," don Carlos says. "Left a message on the recorder. He's quit the band."

"No explanations?"

"Nope." A strand of don Carlos's brillantined hair falls like a feather across his forehead. He pushes it back with his hand. To get his hair this black he must dye it.

"What happened?"

"Your guess is as good as mine," you say. At one time Flaco was a great friend, at least since elementary school. But an argument about who'd have control over the band and the money the band made put a dent in the relationship. Flaco hasn't spoken to you for over two years. He comes, plays, and, when the night's through, he leaves.

"One more thing," don Carlos says, "I heard about what happened a couple of nights ago."

Trying to think that far back jerks your memory a little too hard. You, who have been living from day to day since V left, shift your weight on the chair.

"Because of your pirouette I lost my best customer." Don Carlos cracks a nervous smile. "A two-thousand-dollar-per-week account, gone."

A fat slob, a regular at the club, brought this knockout of a woman and you picked her up and took off with her.

"Stay away from my customers' pussy, will you?"

"She had it coming."

"I had a hell of a time apologizing," don Carlos says, his small eyes opening wider. "And *you know* how I am at apologies."

You laugh, then look away at the rectangular, tinted-glass window.

"Vanessa left me, don Carlos."

"What do you mean *she left?*" he says.

"She's gone. Since Wednesday of last week. I went to our apartment and she wasn't there. I don't know where she is and her mother won't tell me. Things are getting out of hand."

"She'll come back," don Carlos says and stands up. "What are you going to do?" he asks, removing a bottle of Rémy Martin and two glasses out of the top drawer of the desk.

"I don't know," you say. "Wait, I guess."

Don Carlos pours about an inch of brandy into the two glasses, puts the bottle down, and picks up his glass. "You'll find her," he says, raising his glass.

You raise your glass to his, then drink. "I think she's in Miami," you say, putting the shot glass down.

"Maybe you can come with me," he says. Don Carlos refills his glass, drinks, and puts the bottle on top of a stack of liquor-purchase invoices. "Nestor can stay with Berta."

"I wouldn't know where to start looking," you say. It's time to go back onstage.

"Maybe Vanessa'll let you know where she is," Don Carlos says, then he begins on the break-in again. "It's possible that the whole country is fed up with scarcity. Everything made over there goes to the Russians. That's not fair, you know. Those fucking bloodsuckers." He falls silent as though he were thinking about what he has just said.

"The band's waiting," you say and grab the knob and open the door.

Don Carlos looks toward the stage. "Let me know what I can do?" he says and sits down.

"I will. I will." You close the door behind you and descend the stairs.

Sweat trickles down your back and front. If you get your silk shirt wet before you start the next set, you'll feel miserable. Take the coat off and play that way. This is what you think of: Ask don Carlos for Flaco's telephone number (Flaco moved after the fight and you don't know where he lives now) and call . . . no, why care?

ESTEBAN / Having a beer at Coco's, a local bar, he watches the news closely on the TV on the other side of the room. The bartender, a skinny Mexican man with a cross tattooed on his hand, comes over and places a new napkin under the bottle.

"*Chingada madre,* all hell's breaking loose, eh?" the bartender says. "Doesn't Mexico have an embassy in Havana?"

"Listen," Esteban tells him.

The American woman on the screen, whom he's seen before, is reporting from Miami, where already large crowds of Cubans have gathered to protest and demand the freedom of those in the Peruvian Embassy.

There's something about her Esteban likes, her confident voice perhaps. She's got a friendly face and a quick smile. The clothes she wears. That's it, he thinks, it's the clothes. She is wearing a low-cut blouse. A lot of skin shows.

She looks to be in her forties. Her eyes are green and they are beautiful when she smiles. Esteban notices she isn't wearing a ring as she changes the microphone from one hand to the other. Means nothing, he thinks. She is interviewing a bald man. Her Spanish doesn't sound too bad. She translates what the man says, that the Peruvian Embassy must act with expediency, do something about this tragic situation.

"From Miami," she says. "This is Janna Douglas."

When he finishes the beer, he calls the bartender and orders another.

"Got any family in the old country?" the bartender asks as he reaches inside the freezer for the beer, uncaps it, and puts it in front of Esteban's hands.

"A son," Esteban says, then starts to tell the man about Hugo being in prison for political reasons.

"Is he getting out?"

"I doubt it," Esteban says. "He fought in the revolution, my son."

"No kidding?"

"Came home on vacation from the University and never went back. He ran up to the hills. I didn't even know what had happened. My wife kept it from me. Otherwise . . . " He stops to drink. "I would have stopped him. A fucking stupid move. It cost him. Cost us all."

DIEGO / Don Carlos jots down on a piece of paper Flaco's phone number, which you dial on the office telephone, but nobody answers. Let it ring a little longer . . . Nothing.

Call Flaco's mother tomorrow, and ask her if she knows where her son is. Tell her that if he doesn't show up day after tomorrow, tomorrow being a day off, you're going to put an ad in the paper for a new piano player. Is he doing this to screw you over?

On the way back to the bar for a drink, you spot Tictacs slow dancing with a tall blonde, a foot taller than he is. Poor sap, you think, and smile because he looks so funny with his eyes closed and his nose buried in her neck.

You walk up to Nestor's station and sit on a stool. He's working fast mixing his drinks, five, seven at a time.

"You look pissed," Nestor says.

"Flaco quit," you say, "and now I'm stuck with the piano."

"I can't hear the difference," Nestor says, squeezing a lime wedge into a tall glass.

"Piano's important, man, too important."

Nestor pulls a bottle of white wine from the rack, uncorks it, and pours two glasses full.

"Things haven't been the same since that day, remember?" you ask Nestor who, after finishing the drinks, collects the soggy napkins, then wipes the counter with a towel. "All because of a stupid argument over money."

"You know what they say about money."

"Fuck."

"Flaco's always been a greedy bastard. You know him as well as I do."

Somebody calls Nestor, so you take this chance to eat some maraschino cherries. Maruchi comes over; she's looking tired now, her hazel eyes lost in her tanned complexion.

"Customers treating you right?" you ask her, sliding your knees out of her way so she can squeeze in.

"Not too bad," she says. Her breath smells of peppermint gum.

Humm, those meaty moist lips, you think. "What do you usually do after work?"

"Ah, not much, go home to bed." She's not looking at you, instead she's writing down numbers,

"Maybe you'd like to join me for breakfast some time?" If you look hard enough you can see the tan line on her breasts.

"I've been warned about you," she says and looks at you from the corner of her eye. She smiles.

"Don't listen to what they tell you about me," you say. "Nobody here knows me *that* well." Nestor does, too well for his own good.

What could she possibly know about you?

"If you have any questions, come to me."

Trying to smooth out the dog-eared one-dollar bills in her change box, she says, "And you'd tell me the truth, right?"

"About?"

"Yourself," she says, then picks a cigarette out of her Virginia

Slims box and puts it to her lips. You reach over the counter for a book of matches, tear one out, and light it. She leans close and pokes the tip of the cigarette at the flame.

"Umm, you say not to ask anyone but you."

"That's right, you come to me first. I'm an expert on Diego Falcón."

She smiles. Nestor comes back; and when he sees you talking to Maruchi he smiles that wicked smile of his. You find it annoying.

"Nestor," you say, "what have you been telling Maruchi?"

"Me," he says, "nothing. Oh . . . " He catches on. "Only that you're rich and would love to spend every single penny on some beautiful babe."

"Seriously," you say.

Maruchi laughs. "Lunatics," she says then tells Nestor to hurry up and fill her order.

"Why don't you get off early tonight and let's go get breakfast?" you ask her.

"And you'll pay my monthly car bills when I get fired."

"Who's going to fire you? Don Carlos is a pussycat."

"Cats scratch."

"Look," you continue, "I'll go upstairs and arrange it with the man. We'll take off after the last set, all right?"

"Go ahead," she says. The slight smile on her lips reveals that she doesn't believe you'd go upstairs and ask don Carlos to let her go home early.

"All right, I will," you say. "As soon as I finish playing I'll ask him."

"How about her?" she says.

"Who?"

"Your wife," she says and places the drinks on her tray. "Won't she mind you having breakfast with another woman?"

Sure, somebody's been warning her about you. Lowering your voice, you say, "She left me."

Maruchi takes a last drag from her cigarette and crushes it in the ashtray.

"Got tired of my cooking," you say, pointing to your glass to let Nestor know you need another drink.

"Oh, that bad, huh?" Maruchi says, picks up her tray, and leaves you sitting there.

As she walks away you notice how good her legs look in fishnet stockings. Light reflects off the golden anklet on her right foot.

Nestor puts another Kamikaze in front of you.

"Hey, bro," he says, "I've come up with a good name for Susie."

Susie is the waitress Nestor's been dating. "Let me guess," you say. "Satanic Susie."

"Close, bro, real close. Silicone Susie."

This is a good time to ask him for some coke, but he goes away again. The liquor crawls like a slug in your stomach, it inches its way up to your brain. Numb. The faster each drink gets home, the better.

The timbales, in their mighty brilliance, stand in the middle of the empty stage. You were twelve when you first started playing, ten years ago. A sip to celebrate this fact; another for how long the other set of drums at the apartment has lasted.

One by one—Denim first, followed by Ramón (who plays the maracas and the guayo), Negro, Chucho, Godoy, Rudy and the entire horn section—the rest of the band returns to the stage. Time to start the last set.

"I'm in the mood for something slow, guys," you say as you climb onto the stage.

Negro and Godoy laugh.

"Don't forget to tip those bartenders and waitresses," Tictacs announces, then, "Again, ladies and gentlemen, the Toucan Club band!"

Ramón shakes his maracas, and the first tune of this last set is underway. Negro sings, *"Dicen las mujeres que a Paquito le gusta él baile, miren, señores, como el se menea . . ."*

Already the heat and the drinks and the pretty women dancing in front are enough to make anyone forget everything. Shed the troubles and play the rhythm on the keyboard.

Eyes closed, feel the music work through your body, jumping on the bones. The beat, that glorious beat.

Maruchi walks up to your spot and puts a note under your drink which reads, BREAKFAST SOUNDS GOOD! When she looks back you wink, then join Godóy behind the microphone to sing chorus, *"Paquito, el gallito del solar . . . "*

ANGEL / He reads the newspaper while Lilián watches a movie. They are waiting for the late-night edition of the news. Esteban left the house after dinner and hasn't returned. He wonders where it is the old man goes. Perhaps he's got a mistress. Why not.

"Did you write up the list of merchandise we need for tomorrow?" he asks his wife.

"Not yet."

"I don't think I'm going to wait up," he says and puts down the newspaper.

"Father hasn't returned."

"He's a big boy now, right?"

She smiles. "Big boys get into trouble too."

When his mother-in-law died, Angel felt sorry for the old man. Esteban took it pretty hard at first, he did and said very little. Eventually he snapped out of it, on his own. Now he seems to be enjoying himself more. Domingo helps. They go to bars and drink, or play dominoes.

"Let's turn in," Lilián says. "The news is going to be the same."

They get up and leave the den in which Diego sleeps on a sofabed. Angel goes straight into the bedroom, removes his clothes, then sits on the bed for a while, trying not to think of anything in particular.

In the kitchen Lilián takes some milk out of the refrigerator and pours it into a glass. A habit she's kept throughout the years. She heats some. Warm milk, she says, it makes her sleep better.

The bed feels cool to Angel, just the way he likes it. Lilián takes a long time to drink her milk. He thinks that maybe she changed her mind and returned to the den to catch the news, so he rolls over and tries to fall asleep.

Later, when he opens his eyes again, he hears Lilián and Esteban in the kitchen. They are discussing something about the embassy. News from Cuba always interests them because of Hugo.

HUGO / By the time I reach the city riding in the truck, the morning has turned gray and overcast. It's been years since I've seen this part of town. Old Malecón. The Capitolio. The buildings stand in need of paint and repairs. We pass by Plaza Máximo Gómez and scare the pigeons aflutter.

The driver looks at me and shows me his yellow, rotting teeth. His eyes are bloodshot. Hairs protrude from his nostrils. If he doesn't get some rest soon, he's going to collapse.

"Know any good places where I can hide until tonight?" I ask.

"Here?" he says and scratches an itch on his arm. "Can't hide here."

"I've got to get you the rest of that money."

"Who's got it?"

"Somebody in Mazorra." When I mention Mazorra the man opens his eyes real wide and his bushy eyebrows arch on his forehead.

"Mazorra's not on my route, too far," he says.

"Don't you want the rest of the money?"

"Sure, but I can't take you that far."

Murky and weathered, the buildings down the street look badly constructed. Balconies high over the sidewalks give the impression of instability. Rust and decay have found their way everywhere.

How many times had I the chance to come here with my father when I was a child and never did? The word *Havana* rang no mystery nor stirred any enthusiasm in me then. The only time besides this one that I've been able to visit Havana was when they relocated me from La Cabaña to Mazorra, and then I didn't get to see much through the back windows of the security car.

"I've changed my mind," I tell him, reaching for the gold chain. "Take this and give me back the money I gave you." My mother's dead, I think, so she won't know I'm giving her gift away. Besides, I'm going to need the money. The man doesn't hesitate to make the trade. I drop the necklace in his hand; he returns the money.

"Take me as close to the embassy as you can get me," I tell him.

He's still contemplating and feeling the weight of the chain in his hand. Dark semicircles bulge under the man's eyes.

"Take care of it," I say.

"Don't worry about it," he says and cracks a smile.

"You'll probably sell it, you bastard."

"We're not too far away from where you want to go."

The embassy compound stands behind a brick and wrought-iron fence, the kind with the SS designs and spearhead ornaments. From the rear entrance, it's very difficult to see inside because the mango trees are blocking the view.

"Get off here at this corner," the man says. "Just jump out and go."

The man drops me off at the rear entrance. I cross the street in order not to attract too much attention. My pants are torn at the knees.

Sentry posts surround the outside. Toward the front I manage to see the commotion: the rows of parked jeeps and crowd-control trucks, the soldiers, members of the foreign press, and behind them, the people crowded inside the embassy grounds. Those who are pushed against the fence and whose limbs hang out are shouting for space, food, water.

Barricades stand at opposite ends of the street. A soldier moves one out of the way to let a Red Cross truck enter and park in front of the building.

No wonder the city looks so desolate; everybody's here.

At the entrance there are no guards, only more people pushed against the fence. Looking out. Shouting.

"All those wishing to enter the embassy may do so!" a soldier shouts through a loudspeaker. Are they insane, the government? Doubtful.

A woman with two children clinging to her waist hurries across the street and they enter the embassy. They disappear among the waves of people. Why haven't they put a stop to this?

Wondering if it's going to be this easy when Lucinda and I come back, I stop at the corner and notice the large crowd gathering behind the barricades. They are carrying! ¡CUBA SI, YANQUI NO! banners and waving 26th of July movement flags and posters of Ché Guevara and Camilo Cienfuegos. This is all show; government supporters on parade. This part of the street is cordoned off.

The soldier with the loudspeaker repeats the message and this time I cannot believe what happens. One of the guards on the sidewalk drops his weapon and climbs over the side fence. Another soldier runs over, picks up the rifle, and heads back to one of the jeeps.

It'll be better for Lucinda and me to come during the middle of the night when the demonstrators have gone home.

The people inside the grounds shout. God, how do they know they are safe? Anything can happen to them now. Soldiers with flamethrowers can be ordered to set fire to everything within the compound.

But nothing like that can happen with the foreign press being allowed to witness the parade. This *is* a show then, packaged and prepared by some politburo genius. The people inside the embassy sense they are safer than ever and on their way to Peru, or wherever it is they are going to be taken.

The crowd behind the barricades keeps expanding, there are now people in front of the barricades.

I need to do three things: get clothes, send my father a telegram to let him know where I am and that I might be getting out, and get Lucinda out of Mazorra. All of which for the moment seems impossible.

Glass shatters behind the parked jeeps and the crowd goes wild. People start to push the barricades out of the way and they march down the street in front of the embassy. Time to get the hell out of here. Move!

The demonstrators shout obscenities and hurl bottles, eggs, tomatoes, stones and sticks, and anything else they can find, at the people inside the embassy. A man shouts that a woman has been hit on the head by a stone and needs medical assistance.

"BACK OFF!" the voice orders over the loudspeaker. Somebody fires a round of ammunition into the air.

The noise chases me down the street away from the embassy grounds.

Thirteen blocks away I find a post office. Before entering I check my appearance in the glass window. Dirty clothes. Need to wash my face, get the grime off, don't look healthy at all, what's Lucinda going to think? Let's give this a try. Shirt tucked in, I pull the glass door open and approach the counter behind which a man in a postman's uniform greets me. He wears thick glasses. Probably myopic . . . Blind?

"I'd like to send a telegram," I say.

"Address first," the man says, producing a writing tablet of lined yellow paper.

If the family hasn't moved. I give the man the address I remember.

The man stares at me, then tears a sheet and gets his pen from behind his ear. He writes *South Gate, California.* "Who to?"

"Esteban."

"Last name?"

No last name. I don't want to give it away, so I say Falcón, that's Angel's last name.

"Content?"

I spell out the following message: E-X-P-E-C-T / T-O / H-E-A-R / D-I-E-G-O / P-L-A-Y / L-I-V-E / S-O-O-N.

"What language is this?"

"Yanqui," I say and smile.

"What does it mean?" asks the nosy bastard.

"Let the censors translate it." I give the man twenty-five pesos and wink. "Signed your son."

"*¿Hablas inglés, eh?*" the man says.

"Learned it a long time ago, friend."

"I bet it's going to come in handy."

"I hope so." I wonder if they have a bathroom in the back I can use to clean up, but I shouldn't push my luck.

"It'll get there by tomorrow."

I tell the man to have a great day, then I leave. Next, a house to break into and change clothes. Wash up . . . seventy-five pesos left . . . enough . . . water to refresh the skin and help wounds heal . . . everybody's gone . . . nobody out on the streets . . . scared . . . at work . . . keep fingers crossed . . . Lucinda, love, watch over me . . . all you can, and soon we'll be together.

At the end of the street I turn and head east toward the university. Inside a Copelía's ice cream parlor a woman's mopping the tiled floor. She straightens up and sees me go by.

A light drizzle begins to fall and feels cool on my scalp. I see it, the house. It is one with limestone walls gone green with moss. The upstairs windows are open but no way to get to them. Under my weight, the three steps leading to the termite-ridden portico squeak. I knock gently. No answer. Say something, I think. Ask for water. Say you've been in an accident.

After a second round of knocks, I put my ear to the door. Nothing. I go around to the back where the kitchen door's locked and the windows barred. No one's watching so I kick the door several times until it opens.

Inside the air smells of mildew. Cobwebs hang from the kitchen cabinets. A leak has turned some of the ceiling panels brown. If somebody comes there are no excuses.

The house is empty. In the closets upstairs all I find are a couple of twisted nails, some screws, and a broken piece of mirror. Outside it has begun to rain hard, and the drops knock against the glass of the windows.

I check for running water in the bathroom but none of the faucets work. "Jesus," I say. No other alternative but go outside and stand under the rain for a while and hope my clothes and body get clean that way.

Instead of going out in the rain and risk being seen, I undress, open the window facing the back, and wash my pants and shirt. Once the shirt's soaked, I wipe my head, face, chest, and arms with it. A cool breeze comes in. It feels good to be naked.

I sit on the dusty, wooden floor and wait for my clothes to dry. Who knows how long it'll take? Thunder rolls in the distance. That and the sound of rain falling everywhere make me want to relax. I am safe here.

CONCHA / Mama Concha's medley, medley of past lives without which present life would be unbearable. Three days before she died at Saint Francis of Assisi Hospital, she sent for her grandson Diego. Not that he was the only person she wanted to see, but there was a particular reason why he had to hear what she wanted to say.

The boy (this is what she called him, this and sometimes Diegito), she knew the boy was growing up rootless, or, as her own mother—her soul rest in glory—would have put it, wild. Almost wilder than the negro children whose screams used to fill the cobblestone streets of Santiago, begging strangers to allow them to shine their shoes.

Before the stomach cancer, while she was still at home, she heard her daughter Lilián argue with him about forgetting the language, how little Spanish he spoke, his poor pronunciation. He showed no interest in his heritage or in knowing what had brought him here to this magnificent land.

He needed to relearn his background, Concha thought. This was the only way he could find identity and self-confidence. He had become too Americanized. Gringo. Rootless. And she also knew that anybody who grew up rootless eventually lost his or her soul to . . .

The past was all important.

Diego came on a sunny afternoon, shortly after her siesta and bath. One of the nurses combed her hair and put a little rouge on her cheeks, but no lipstick. She never wore lipstick, didn't need to. Her lips possessed that deep crimson she had always been complimented for when she was a young lady.

Already aware of what the doctor had told him, that she wasn't going to last more than a couple of weeks (the cancer was diagnosed too late), he stood by the bed, a one-hundred-and-thirty-pound weakling, large, hungry-eyed, sweaty complexion, not a boy accustomed to smiling, tall and wiry in his slimness. At seventeen he was as tall as his uncle Hugo before he ran up to the sierras and fought on the rebel side.

Hugo! What she wouldn't have given to have seen her son one last time.

She took a deep breath and gestured for her grandson to sit by her bed on the blue-cushioned chair. He, aloof so it seemed, dragged his feet as he walked over and sat next to the IV fork.

She wanted to know what the doctors had told him. Doctors, she knew, were capable of exaggerating, or making things sound a lot worse than they really were. She asked him to be nice to her because . . . she laughed at her melodramatic thoughts.

"Don't think I'm sad," she said to him. "I am glad I've lived the life I have."

Diego sat shrouded in silence, his fingers gripping the chair's armrest.

"I want to tell you stories, son," she said. "Some, I'm sure, you've heard before, others you—you were never told."

"What kind of stories?" asked Diego.

"Good stories. About the family," she said.

"The doctor says you should rest."

"To hell with the doctor," she said and paused to gather her thoughts. "What I'm about to tell you might not make sense, but one day . . . promise to remind them . . . once in a while . . . especially your grandfather. Don't let him forget why we came to this country . . .

"*Curunguango guango, curunguango guango curungua tere me aguano curo* . . . , which, according to Marcelina, the woman who cooked for us in Vista Alegre, meant, Pay attention, pay attention, attend to the extraordinary thing I'm going to relate."

HUGO / The rain stops. I wake up to its silence. The sun has come out and dried my clothes which hang awkwardly from the window. Not completely, though. The pockets of my pants and the inseam feel damp. Should have turned them inside out, fool. The shirt too.

I dress and go downstairs. Once on the street, I start to retrace my steps to the post office to find a taxi. The sidewalks are wet and muddy. A stream of water carrying leaves and newspaper flows in the gutter.

The shirt fits me more tightly now. Must have shrunk, but it doesn't look wrinkled. The pants do. Nothing can be done about that tear at the knee. Forget it.

The good thing about taxi drivers—at least this was true of them in Santiago—is that they never ask why you want to go where you tell them, but the one who picks me up does. He wants to know why Mazorra.

"My girlfriend works there," I tell him.

"Is it true that they're going to take the crazies to Mariel?" the man says.

"Where did you hear that?" I say. leaning forward.

"Somebody told me. It's probably a rumor."

Lucinda's waiting, I'm sure she is. She knows I'm coming for her. I told her I would first chance I got.

The taxi driver turns on the radio to music, Tejedor and his orchestra. The man sings along. When I lean over to ask him where I can buy a sandwich or something else to eat because I'm starving, I see that his right arm's gone. His shirt sleeve is safety-pinned to his shirt.

"What are you staring at?" the man asks, looking at me from the corner of his eye.

"Nothing," I tell him. "Know where I can buy something to eat?"

"*Por aquí nada*," he says. "Everything's closed. This city's been wild since the break-in."

"Forget it then," I say.

The tune ends and the man turns the radio off. The ticks of the meter sound loud in the cab. "Got it blown off," he says. "I didn't even feel it."

"Where?" I ask.

"Angola," he says and looks up at the rearview mirror.

"That's too bad."

"Not really," he says, "in a way I'm glad it happened. I knew a lot of other guys who lost more than an arm."

"I know what you mean."

"What? You were there?"

"No." How old does he think I am? "In the revolution."

"Revolution?" He lets out a short laugh. "Are you serious?"

"I fought with comandante Morales. Lobo Morales."

"That was a long time ago," he says. Then, "So you're with the Party?"

The taxi driver senses my reluctance to talk so he looks up at the mirror and smiles. He's got a big scar under his right eye which makes that eye look smaller than the other.

"You know," he says, "after this happened, I had a chance to join the Party but didn't. And here I am now, driving this piece of shit."

"It gets you around, doesn't it?"

"Whenever it wants to. Parts are scarce."

"It seems to work all right," I say.

"What have you been doing all this time?"

"In jail."

"You kill somebody?" the man sounds excited to have somebody to converse with in the car.

"See, when Fidel ordered Camilo Cienfuegos to arrest Lobo Morales in Santiago, I was Lobo's aide. When the soldiers came for him, they took me too. Everybody in our unit was taken in. They even arrested this thirteen-year-old girl—"

"Wasn't Lobo the one who said that communism was infiltrating the revolution?"

I say, "He was the smartest and bravest man I've ever known."

"He's dead?"

"A firing squad killed him."

They took Lucinda, so young, and I never saw her again until Mazorra.

We reach the corner of the dead-end street that leads to the front gate of Mazorra.

"Go to the embassy," I tell him. "You've got no future here."

"I'm afraid I can't do that," he says. "My wife doesn't want to leave. She waited for me while I was in Angola."

I understand his loyalty. "Drop me off before we get there," I say, reading the amount I owe him on the meter. Thirteen pesos. I drop twenty on his lap. "Keep the change," I tell him.

The man pulls to the side and stops the car. He looks back and thanks me. "Maybe we'll run into each other," he says.

"Good luck," I say. I step out of the car and close the door behind me.

Soon it'll be dark and I can move in and try to find Lucinda. The man makes a U-turn and heads back to the main road. I watch him go until the car turns and vanishes around the bend, then I cross the street, jump the fence upon which a NO TRESPASSING sign has been posted, and run around to the back of the building.

The new Havana zoo lies beyond the ravine.

The mangoes high up on the trees look ripe enough. I climb one of the trees slowly so as not to scrape the insides of my thighs on the thick bark. Once at the top, I knock a couple of mangoes down. Dinner.

In the ravine I find a place to remain out of sight, behind a tree stump. The grass surrounding me is really ivy.

Peeled, the mangoes are green and hard and taste sour. It'll be a while before they can be eaten. I eat a couple anyway.

The tall fence encircling Mazorra won't be a problem to jump over. Lucinda's window shouldn't be hard to spot. She's got all those plants on her sill. It's in the left wing of the building. Her window might be open, since she enjoys the cool breeze in the evening.

Judging from the darkness of the sky, I guess the time to be between five and six. One more hour and it'll be dark enough. Birds begin to nestle up in the trees for the night.

Still hungry, I contemplate knocking down some more mangoes. Something to do to kill time. If she only knew how close I am to her. A tiger roars and the sound strikes panic among the birds up in the trees.

Still May, 1958

Mamísima Conchísima:

This morning Lobo Morales returns from a recon-naissance mission. He sings a song.

In profile he looks young, too, too young to be in com-mand of this brigade. In his early thirties, he is handsome and tall. Around his men, he is the tallest. Short hair grows curly at the top of his head like a crest. He has large blue eyes, bright and smoky, and a thin mustache. From the descriptions I had heard, I expected him to have a beard, but his face is red, pinched a little by the sun.

His men flock around him as though he were bringing them gifts. He smiles an it's-great-to-be-back smile. The olive-green uniform he wears is damp, from either sweat or rain or both. (When it rains up here it pours, the drops pound on the leaves of the plants and trees like hammers falling from the sky.)

After he sits down and talks about what he plans to do—tomorrow we march another five miles deeper into this jungle—he looks my way and stares as if he knows I am new. What gives me away, I believe, is the look of awe on my face. The mouth-agape, dumb look I put on sometimes when I'm amused.

"Who are you?" he asks, picking the mud off his boots with a twig.

Feeling a bit nervous, I introduce myself. I tell him I ran away from the university to come join his men.

He wants his men to give me room, so that I can talk to him. This, I imagine, is what makes Lobo such a charismatic person—his interest in what others have to say.

So. I tell him where I come from and why I left the university.

"What were you studying?"

"Pharmacy."

The first thing he says is, "You shouldn't have left it. This game's almost over."

I am surprised when he calls the revolution a game, the great struggle, three and a half years in the making.

"We've got this island by the balls," he continues, then laughs. "Do you know where its balls are?"

"No," I say.

"Havana, my friend. That's where the big kick will hurt most."

I understand what he's talking about and I suddenly get excited. When Havana falls, the revolution's won.

He tells me he used to be a teacher in Matanzas—he taught farmers' sons and daughters in a rural school—but then he went off to Mexico and returned on the Granma. When he finds out I attended some of the best prep schools in Santiago, he says, "Lucky man. I need somebody like you to be a medic."

"Medic," the word escapes my mouth, wondering what I know about being a medic.

"Many have gotten hurt," he says, "and I suspect you'll have your hands full before this is over."

He looks at my rifle. "That doesn't mean you won't have to fight when the time comes, understand?"

I nod yes.

"The rifle comes first," he says.

I understand him loud and clear.

Then he stands up, shakes my hand, and welcomes me.

*As he walks away I notice that he isn't armed. No gun, no
holster, nothing. Only the uniform and the large, black,
and heavy-looking boots that leave deep tracks on the soft
earth.*

*Your Son
Hugo*

HUGO / The arrival of the night works on the zoo animals like a
muzzle, especially on the tigers and lions. Scratching a fresh
mosquito bite, I wait behind the tree stump. An owl sits overhead.
It scratches its wings, then sharpens its hook beak on the bark of
the branch.

Good hunting, I offer it as I stand to wipe the seat of my pants.
The night was made for creatures to prey on each other, for
fucking mosquitoes to bite and suck blood unseen. Unfelt. Night is
the perfect excuse for treachery. Let hunger feed itself.

I hear the sound of a helicopter approach. I run and hide
behind some shrubs until it passes and its noise fades.

Not one ray of light sneaks out from behind the curtained windows of Masorra. I jump the fence and near the patio entrance.
Everything's dark. What the taxi driver said about the place being
vacated comes back to me.

If they moved everybody out, where did they go? To the embassy? There is no room left there. I move quickly. There's no
sense in wasting time around here. Lucinda, wherever she is, can
take care of herself.

Instead of leaving the same way I came, I take a shortcut along
the zoo fence to the entrance where I might be able to catch
another taxi or the bus.

After a long wait, the bus arrives and I decide to take it instead
of wasting any more time waiting. I board, not minding that the
bus is full and that it stinks of exhaust. It's easy to blend in with
the crowd.

A young woman stands with her back to me. One look down
reveals what a big ass she's got. On a turn her body comes close to
mine and I can almost feel her pushing against me. My cock rises,
and I try to restrain myself. I turn sideways, because, if we come in
contact again, she will notice. The last thing I need is to get involved in a scene.

The ride is long. The downtown stop's not too far from the embassy, so I walk the rest of the way. What was once a mission, villa, or mansion in the rich neighborhood of Miramar is now the dark and crowded Peruvian Embassy.

All that remains of the earlier demonstration is the scattered trash and broken glass. Crossing the street quickly, I try to spot a gap through which to sneak in. Otherwise I'll have to jump the fence.

Faces peer at me as I move along; no one speaks until I'm almost at the corner where a jeep is parked.

"They opened the gate on the other side," a voice in the crowd tells me.

Sure enough, the gate's closed but not locked. I roll it back on its wheels wide enough for me to slide in sideways.

Once inside I move among tight spaces between bodies on the grass and walkways, bodies wrapped in colorful bedsheets, towels, and blankets. People on the ground, on top of upturned trash-cans, behind clotheslines from which wet diapers hang like flags of surrender, on top of the iron grating, on the roof. Tree branches.

I kick someone by accident and almost lose my balance. What are my chances of finding Lucinda here? If she *is* here.

Arms and hands there, torsos here, heads, legs, and not a place to sit. That's all I want right now, to sit. I move on, away from the fence. Havana has squeezed in here. I'm by the side of the building, moving toward the front porch.

A baby cries. Someone coughs up a mouthful of phlegm and spits.

Men, women, and children, young and old, half naked, hungry, restless, tired. I feel like screaming that I've come to save them. But save them from what? The damage has been done. Done twenty-one years ago.

At the front steps which lead to the entrance of the building, I hear a voice tell me not to come any closer, that there is no more space available. On the other side I find more people.

Toward the patio I spot a hole big enough for me to stand, or sit with my knees bent. Bodies wiggle next to me as if seeking warmth. They touch my feet.

A woman says to a man, "They're going to hand out safe-conduct passes tomorrow."

"I'm not setting foot outside," the man says.

In the dark the voices seem to be coming from nowhere.

"I haven't taken a shower in three days," the woman says.

"Who cares about showers?"

"I haven't eaten either."

There's a short pause, then the man says, "No way am I going outside. I've heard we are going to be taken to a port."

"What port?"

"Mariel."

It is now that hour when the children have stopped crying and men begin to snore, and their snoring sounds like the groans of a wounded pig. Then a pouring sound is heard of someone urinating behind a tree. Asleep, an old man next to me farts and all I can do's turn my face in the other direction.

Mariel's where Lucinda must be, I think. At least I know we're both headed in the right direction.

More room becomes available and I am able to stretch out my legs. I can sleep now, I think, but the mosquitoes have started to bite. Let them! I tell myself. Let them suck me dry.

DIEGO / How golden can a golden anklet be?

Blindingly golden, almost annoying. The anklet, this is what becomes visible when the eyelids part. Hold them open and stare until the braided gold anklet comes into focus. The ankle, a protruding bone because the foot rests in an awkward position.

The anklet attached to the ankle connected to the leg and the leg joined to the naked torso of a woman sleeping: Maruchi.

A tanned-skin woman. *Sabrosona!* a word from one of the songs last night meaning delicious. You appreciate the Levolor blinds on the windows. If it weren't for them, the sun would intrude and damage the gentle twilight in the room.

Completely still, you lie and begin to look upon the clothes on the rug. A red leotard with a couple of broken plumes. A coat, her high-heeled Giorgio Brutini shoes, scratched at the tips, pants, all in piles.

In the room the furniture seems to be crowding, a bookshelf and desk and director's chair and television and dresser and coatrack. All too close to the queen-size bed. A poster of what looks like flowers hangs on the wall in front of the bed.

Maruchi, asleep, lies next to you, but her face is hardly visible for it is covered by a fluffy pillow.

Why are you facing her feet?

Last night's, or rather this morning's, events return one by one. Don Carlos let Maruchi go early (what did you end up using as an excuse?) then she and you went to . . . the exact details blur. Hangover.

Another look up her naked leg half covered by a sheet reveals the dark V, a crevice (a telephone directory opened in the middle), where the line separating her buttocks ends. Her tan line forms a larger V on her ass.

You feel like a washed-clean conch, hollowed out, and when it's time to move the bed moves. When your sensory mechanism fails, stretching on the bed feels as though you are swimming, trying to remain afloat.

The anklet moves when the leg bends, when the torso sits up. Her sleepy face peers down.

Maruchi's first words make no sense. Is she yawning or speaking, and why can't you hear her?

The bedsheet slides from her chest and exposes her tits. Now the face draws near. She kisses you, and her lips tug at your own. A tongue searching for refuge inside your mouth.

"Good morning," she says and pecks your cheek.

The desire to know what time it is becomes urgent.

A cold hand crawls down your chest. Maruchi's small hand. Her face disappears behind her undone hair as she kisses past the navel. She takes your dick into her mouth. Christ, it feels as though she were sucking the nausea out through a straw. Is this the way you fell asleep?

Wet, her pussy lips part to let your tongue in. Her tits rest on your stomach and, as her head bobs, the nipples rub against your skin.

Once you get hard, she cradles around your waist and slides you inside her. She grabs her own tits and leans over for you to kiss them, suck them, bite the nipples.

Little sperm armies gather for the final charge.

"What's taking you so long?" she asks, her hair still in front of her face.

"I'm enjoying this," you say.

She laughs wickedly as though you had just told her a dirty joke.

Ah, Maruchi!

After you come, she bends over and kisses your neck. Then she stands and walks to the window, opens the blinds. Light darts into the room.

"Join me for a shower?" she says, opening her closet.

"No, no," you say. "You go ahead. I pass." If you take a shower with her, you'll end up with another hard on. Where do women get the energy after making love?

She finds a towel and leaves for the bathroom. Shortly, the jet of the shower hitting the bathtub becomes audible in the room.

While she showers, you call Flaco. Again, no luck. Try his mother.

Three rings and Fé, Flaco's mother, answers.

"Good morning, Fé," you say. "This is Diego."

"Diego!" She sounds surprised. How long has it been since you've spoken to her?

"Listen, Fé, I'm in a hurry. Is Danny there?"

"Uh," she says, "no. No. He hasn't been by."

"He's not at his place," you say and move away from the front of the dresser mirror. "Do me a big favor. If he comes by, tell him to call me."

"Sure, Diego," she says. Her voice sounds too distant. "I will, but you know how he is. Sometimes he doesn't show for days."

Why is she lying? You know, or at least that's the way you remember it, that Flaco always goes home to eat lunch. He's a lazy son of a bitch who can't even fry a couple of eggs.

"Diego?"

"Yes?"

"Everything all right?"

"Everything's fine, Fé," you say, picking your clothes off the rug and putting them up on the blue director's chair. "He didn't come to work last night, and—"

Maruchi comes out of the shower wrapped in a beach towel with ladybugs printed on it.

"Just tell him to call me, okay?"

"I'll do that."

As soon as you say good-bye and hang up, you walk over to Maruchi and hug her. Her skin is wet and warm, her hair smells strongly of henna shampoo.

"That wasn't long distance," you say and kiss her.

"Just as long as it wasn't to your wife." The smell of toothpaste emerges from her mouth.

"Smartass." You bend over, lift the towel, and bite her butt.

"Oouch!" she says. Maruchi presses the ON button on her portable radio and music comes on.

A commercial.

The news. That means it must be almost noon.

A deep, Henry Kissinger-like voice says something about the increasing number of Cubans that have gathered inside the Peruvian Embassy.

She unplugs the radio and plugs in her hair dryer. Bending over to push all her hair over the front of her face, she exposes her ass.

You sit on the edge of the bed and contemplate the view, admire the firmness of her body. No wrinkles or flabby areas behind her thighs.

She begins to fill in the details about last night. In her car she drove here after work because you got sick. Nestor asked her to take you home since he (Nestor) wasn't getting off until closing time. The Spitfire's still at the club.

"It was so funny," she says. "You stuck your head out the window because—let's see—oh, because you said, 'the air feels good.' You kept telling me to drive faster.

"Also, you said I was the best friend you had left in the whole wide world. You kissed me over and over again. Until we got here, then you got sick in the bathroom, came out looking pale and with this wild look in your eyes, and you said, 'I need another drink.'" She laughs.

Finished drying her hair, she opens a dresser drawer, grabs some panties and puts them on. They're like the lace kind V wears, except these are much more revealing, two narrow hip straps hold the front and back. An embroidered, tiny heart is attached to the front. She walks over, stands in front of you, and lets you kiss her belly button.

"What are you doing today?" she says and turns to face the dresser mirror.

"I've got to go home."

"I want to see you again." She hugs her tits as though to push them into a certain desired shape.

"You will," you say and stand. "Mind if I take a shower?"

"Go ahead," she says. "That'll give me a chance to get ready."

"Ready for what?"

"I have to take you to your car, right?"

"You can take me wherever you like," you say and pat her ass.

Maruchi turns and wraps her arms around you, puts her ear to your chest. "Something's loose in there," she says.

"It's always been that way," you say.

Naked, you leave the room and find the bathroom at the end of the hall. That you remembered the way is a good sign.

The intense light in the bathroom stings your eyes, tender still. Everything's blue: tiles, clothes hamper, shower curtain, and, as you pull the curtain open, the fish-shaped rubber stickers on the surface of the tub.

Afraid to slip and fall, you move about in the tub slowly. The spray falls over your head and it feels as though each squirt is a finger massaging a different part of your scalp.

Maruchi enters the bathroom to ask if you'd like something to eat. She's making a sandwich for herself. You shut the faucet, open the curtain, and get the towel on top of the toilet. "I'm really not hungry," you say.

"Some coffee then?" she says.

"Milk."

Maruchi leaves so you can dry and get dressed. Back in the bedroom the bed has been made and your clothes placed on it.

Getting dressed has always been a slow ritual. In this way you are like your grandfather who takes forever in the shower and even longer to get dressed. Except time's running out and you need to run a couple of errands.

What has happened to the suit brings on anger. A button is missing and there is a grease spot on the lapel. Grease? The shirt and coat reek of smoke and who knows what else. The tie, you roll and drop in your coat pocket.

In the kitchen Maruchi's eating her sandwich. She seems like a slow eater, nibbling and chewing. You sit at the other end of the table. "I like this place," you say, then drink the milk in front of you.

The kitchen is small but neatly organized: herbs and spices and seasonings containers lined up in a row on top of the stove. The framed posters of exotic fruit match the table cover and doilies and cookie jars.

"I used to live with my mother," she says, "but she and I don't get along."

"Your parents are divorced?" you ask.

"No, my father died when I was eighteen. An accident. After that my mother met someone else."

From the disgusted way she pronounces *someone else,* you try to recreate the whole scenario. This man whom her mother met tried to put the move on Maruchi. One night, you imagine, while Maruchi's mother sleeps, he sneaks out and knocks on Maruchi's room. This sort of thing happens all the time.

"I loved my father," she says and puts her half-eaten tuna sandwich down. "He was the kindest human being."

Maruchi, Nestor has told you, is Italian/American, but she's got a Spanish last name. Ruiz.

"Your father," you say. "He was Italian?"

"No, my mother is. She's the one with the hot blood." She stands to throw out her leftovers into the trashcan, then washes the plate in the sink.

Standing up and moving behind her, you put the glass in the sink, hug her, and kiss her neck. The softness in her voice carries a hint of honesty. What about other men she must have had? No, you have no right to that information. But you wonder. Suddenly you want to tell her about your misfortunes, but why plural? Misfortune, with a capital M. This you leave blank.

"Let's have dinner sometime," she says, drying her hands on a kitchen rag.

"That sounds good," you say.

On the way out Maruchi gets her purse, checks it for her keys, and closes the door after you. "Got everything?" she asks.

Smile.

To get from Century City where Maruchi lives to the club, she takes the San Diego freeway. The freeway, so desolate at this hour, seems like an intrusion upon the hillside. Only during rush hour does this freeway have a purpose. From the SanDiego to the Santa Monica, off on La Brea where she makes a right. La Brea leads to Sunset. Her Toyota Celica's faster than you thought, and Maruchi drives well.

The streets are busy and crowded and filled with people returning to work after lunch. Sunset Boulevard is not the same during the day. No hookers or pimps loiter outside motel entrances. The glitter subsides, but the traffic remains heavy. Cars everywhere.

In the club's parking lot, Maruchi parks next to the Spitfire which leans awkwardly to one side. "That's all I need," you say, "a flat tire."

"Where's the spare in such a small car?" Maruchi says.

"Sitting upright in the trunk."

"Want help?" she says.

"No thanks," you say and get out of the car. "Go on home. I'll call you later."

Maruchi takes a pen and a piece of paper out of her glove compartment and jots her telephone number down. "Don't forget," she says, handing you the paper.

You lean inside and kiss her good-bye. She drives away. Her handwriting is sleek, short, delicate letters. You slip the piece of paper into your shirt pocket.

The flat is not a flat but a slit tire. There, on the side of the tire, the jagged gash looks unreal. A Swiss knife must have been used for the job. Also, the same knife must have been used to scratch the word "maricon" on the side of the door. *Maricón* means faggot.

The insurance'll cover it, you say to yourself, don't get angry. It takes only ten minutes to change the tire, then you walk around the car and inspect it thoroughly. Nothing else seems to be missing or damaged. Putting the jack and tire iron back in the trunk, you find a bottle of rum—half empty.

You unsnap the top and pull it down. Start the car and let it warm up. The bottle of rum sits on the other seat. The way your stomach feels, booze is the last thing needed. Driving out of the parking lot, passing by a trash dumpster, you dispense with the bottle. It shatters on impact.

ESTEBAN / *Viola Lust Unzipped* is showing at the Pussycat Theatre on Pacific Boulevard. Something to take his mind off the embassy break-in, Hugo, and the troubles Domingo's having with Ruth.

Esteban studies the movie poster of a big blonde, her cherry-glossed lips sucking her middle finger, completely nude except her nipples and crotch have been masked over. She stands with her back to a mirror. What an Amazon, he thinks, her tits look too good to be real. Probably had them implanted. Viola Lust, porn starlet, XXX vixen, so, so "young and willing." *Playboy* and *Hustler* magazines have given the movie high ratings.

A couple of high school boys go by and laugh. Punks, he thinks, don't they realize that when they get to be . . . everybody needs something to pass the time. This is entertainment.

Viola, what other movies has she starred in?

He should go home before his daughter starts to worry. Walk home, the exercise'll be good. He can work off the three beers he's had.

Two men in raggedy clothes open the door and walk out telling each other what a good movie it was.

"Where do they get such beautiful whores?" the taller man asks. His faded jeans are torn and patched and repatched.

"I don't know, man, but those bitches certainly know what fucking's all about," the other says.

They laugh and turn out of sight.

That's it, Esteban says to himself, why not? He goes in, pays, and enters the dark of the theater.

He finds a seat toward the front, which he checks in case somebody masturbated and wiped their hands on the cushion. People tend to crowd at the back, especially the couples, but he doesn't care where he sits. Since Concha died, he's lost his shyness.

Previews of upcoming attractions start. He leans back and relaxes as a montage of erotic scenes flash on the screen: a woman on her hands and knees, two men inside her, a girl hanging upside down while a skinny black man comes all over her breasts, an orgy in the middle of a living room, a midget in the center masturbating . . . .

DIEGO / "A certain Mrs. Plater called," your grandfather says when you drive up and park in front of the garage. "Says for you to call her." He is drinking a Beck's.

"Mrs. Plater?" you say, opening the door and getting out.

"Your neighbor," Esteban says. "I wrote her number down and put it by the phone. It's in red ink."

"I remember who she is."

"You spend the night at the apartment?" he asks.

"No," you say. You've always told your grandfather the truth because he seems to understand, or you like to think he does. "At a friend's." You take your coat off and fold it over your arm. "Somebody slashed my tire, so I stopped over to report it at the Triple-A office."

He eyes the car from under the shade of the avocado tree where he's sitting on one of the patio chairs your father built out of scrap wood and a steel frame.

"Just got back from a matinee," he says.

It's afternoon. His hair seems grayer, almost ashen. In the shade, his face is dark and too serious.

It looks as if he has just finished watering his plants because the cement of the driveway is wet. The ice cream truck's gone, and there is a puddle of oil where the truck is usually parked. Too bad, you think, you wanted to see your mother. They work all day; you play all night. Tough schedules.

"Have you heard the news about the break-in?" he asks.

"Several times," you say. "Do you think Tío's coming?"

"I don't know," he says and removes his ivory hat from his knee. "Those sons of bitches won't let him go."

For a sixty-three-year-old man, Esteban looks in pretty good shape, except for the fat around his waist. It's all that beer he drinks. Esteban's cleanly shaven and dressed in his new, brown chinos and leather-strapped sandals. You ask if anyone besides Mrs. Plater has called and he, in an irritated manner, tells you that no, nobody else has called.

"Whose call are you expecting?" he asks.

A lawyer, you want to say, but this is only a fear best kept in the farthest reaches of your head for the moment.

He stands, puts his hat on, and walks inside the house via the kitchen door. You follow him. "Do you want me to take you somewhere?"

"I'm starving," he says. "I need a ride to Pacific."

If he can wait ten minutes, you let him know, long enough to call Mrs. Plater, find out what she wants, and for you to change, you'll be more than happy. You put your hand on his shoulder because you don't like the worried look on his face.

"Keep your fingers crossed," you say to let him know you're concerned about your uncle.

"I'm ready for whatever happens," he says.

Leaving Esteban in the kitchen, you walk to the phone, find the piece of paper with Mrs. Plater's number, and dial. The phone rings several times then a raspy voice answers.

"Mrs. Plater," you say, "this is Diego, your next-door neighbor."

"Yes, yes," she says. "I thought I'd call you, Mr. Falcón, because something has happened. I don't want you to think I'm a snoop, you understand?"

"I understand, Mrs. Plater," you say, trying to remember what she looks like.

"I think somebody broke into your apartment yesterday afternoon," she says.

You lean against the door of the hall closet and close your eyes.

"These three men. They drove a car similar to your wife's," she continues.

V drives a Ford Mustang, a wedding gift from her father.

"Did you call the police? Did you see what these men looked like?" you ask.

"Oh, please don't ask too many questions," she says. Then there is silence. "They took a lot of furniture."

"Mrs. Plater? Listen, I'll be over shortly, okay?"

"I'm not a busybody, Mr. Falcón," she says and her voice fades.

"Nobody says you are, Mrs. Plater. I'll be over soon," you say and hang up.

Esteban waits in the kitchen and when you walk in he asks what Mrs. Plater wanted. After you tell him, he says, "Go see what they took. I'll take the bus."

"No, no, I'll drop you off. It's on the way," you say and leave the kitchen to go change.

The room you change in used to be your old room, but, after you married V and moved out, your parents turned it into a den. The sofabed faces the giant-screen television console on which your grandfather watches the triple-X movies he rents. A dirty old man, your grandfather, and sometimes seems to be proud of it.

A lifesize poster of Clint Eastwood, rope tied, cigar in his mouth, hangs behind the door. The only possession brought from the apartment after V left, the poster was her birthday gift to you two years ago.

There on the wall next to the bookshelves sits V's picture. Don't stare at it. Try not to, please. Can't help it. The long blond hair, the killer-cat green eyes. That cruel smile. Ah, perfection, mother of vanity. Shit. As you move about the room, her eyes seem to follow you, as if she were saying, Poor Diego, poor baby.

Dressed in shorts and a sweatshirt, you shout at your grandfather through the sliding door dividing the den and the dining room, "Get the Monte Carlo keys from the drawer. Meet me by the car."

With a pair of tennis shoes and socks in hand, you walk outside. Esteban's in the car waiting. Your door's open. Barefoot, you get in, start the car, and drive away from the house.

"Drop me off at Thrifty's," your grandfather says and straps the seatbelt into place. "They have good specials."

Inhaling the thick exhaust from the RTD bus in front gives you a rush that makes you drive fast enough to make your grandfather hold on to the dashboard. He won't tell you to slow down, you know, because he's the only one who's never told you what to do.

For such a large car, eight cylinders, the Monte Carlo takes the turns gracefully. Your mother, you remember, liked it the first time she saw it on the sales floor of the dealership.

"Haven't heard from her, have you?" Esteban asks.

"Who?" you say and put the visor down because the sun's reflecting off the hood.

"Vanessa."

You shake your head no and turn the radio on to let the music do the talking.

In front of Thrifty's, your grandfather gets out and tells you to be careful. After he walks in through the sliding doors, you step on the gas and take a couple of red lights on the way to the apartment.

CONCHA / She remembered Esteban this way:

They were neighbors. Their backyards in Santiago were separated by a wooden fence which a storm had knocked down a year after the family moved to Santo Domingo. At night the breeze carried the scent of rotting wood.

Her house was more of a villa. Large earthen pots or *tinajones* decorated the brick walls by the kitchen entrance. WW patterns adorned the wrought-iron grill in front of the windows.

The paint on Esteban's house had flaked off during the last storm, and the wood had taken on a grayish color of decay. The paint covering the walls was imported from the States. The trim was ivory and the walls pastel yellow. The Laras' gardener kept the yard full of gladiolus and tulips and roses. Lots of roses.

This was after the summer her father took her to the beach chalet. She was almost fourteen. In the afternoons she would do most of her schoolwork out in the patio, on the iron table under the shade of a parasol. She would stay there until very late, always hoping that Esteban would come out of the house to talk to her.

He was shy, a little innocent, but she liked that in him. The way his earlobes turned pepper-red under the sun.

Whenever he spoke he charmed her with his voice. She loved the crispiness of it, the way he talked without stumbling for words.

"I came out to see you," she told him.

"What a coincidence," he said. Then, "Do I make you nervous?"

"Not at all," she said. "It's just that I don't want the maid to see us. She'd tell my mother."

"I enjoy our walks to school."

"Me too."

"You know what?"

"What?" she asked.

"Would you mind if—" He pauses.

"What?"

"I want to kiss you."

He took her hand and for a moment her legs trembled as if she were going to fall. Then, he drew close. She kept her eyes open. His smooth hand touched her cheek and it set her skin on fire. He smiled and kissed her.

The kiss created an avalanche of emotions in her. She felt like breaking away and running inside the house. What was she to do? One thing she was certain of, and that was that she liked the gummy softness of his lips.

It was the first time she had ever been kissed by anybody and her whole body tingled with excitement.

DIEGO / The Moor Apartments stand on the other side of the train tracks in Downey, a residential neighborhood where not too many Cubans live. Mostly Americans live here in stucco and wood houses with brick fireplaces and wrought-iron fences. Spanish tiles on the roofs. Except for the multitude of flowers and trees, there's nothing out of the ordinary about River Street.

At the end of the street, the apartments face a schoolyard that is now empty. Usually kids stay after school to play basketball and tag-football and make a lot of noise.

You park in the spot marked APT 3, put on your socks and shoes, get out, and walk to the back. Facing the swimming pool, you unlock the gate and climb the stairs to the apartment.

No visible scratch marks on the door or window. Both locks, you find by inserting your keys, are locked. Inside the living room, only certain pieces of furniture are missing. The ivory sofa. A glass-top coffee table and matching vases. A chrome lamp. Without these the living room looks bare.

Wild, you move from room to room and see that only certain articles have been taken. Then you make the connection, and it's startling. Only furniture Vanessa bought or liked a lot is missing.

She must have been here, otherwise . . . In the master bedroom, the set of timbales you use to practice lie in the corner. The drums are cracked as though they were thrown against the wall and their skins torn. The salsa record collection remains in its milk crate.

V's clothes have vanished from the closets. No trace of her anywhere. No leftover makeup in the bathroom cabinets. No scent. Nothing.

A voice calls from the living room. "Mr. Falcón? Are you here?"

You walk out of the bathroom and find Mrs. Plater by the door. She's older than you remember: pale face, wrinkled, and unkempt, light-brown hair.

"Please tell me everything, Mrs. Plater," you request, approaching the door.

"Three men, maybe four," she says and holds her hands together. "One of them was built like a football player. The other two were thin, one black and the other with your skin color."

"All they took was my wife's furniture," you say, "and her personal belongings."

Mrs. Plater looks on with saddened eyes, as though she were thinking poor boy, poor boy. "I figured I'd call you first before making a drastic move like calling the police."

"I'm glad you didn't call the police," you tell her and watch her let out a sigh of relief. But maybe if she had, the bastards might have been apprehended.

"I didn't know what to to," she says and her hands move up to check the back of her hair. "The big one said he knew you and that you'd appreciate what they were doing. He was rude."

"I appreciate you keeping an eye open for us. For me."

Mrs. Plater lives alone. She has a daughter who's a flight attendant, but who never comes to see her. The separateness of American families is alarming. It doesn't make much sense how a daughter can abandon her mother and never come to check on her. An aura of loneliness is visible in Mrs. Plater's eyes.

"I'm sorry," Mrs. Plater says.

"It's all right," you say and smile to make her feel better. "It's nobody's fault."

"No, Mr. Falcón, I'm sorry your wife has left."

Stand at a distance and turn away to look at the curtained windows.

"It was all a mistake," you say finally. "She wanted her freedom and I should've—"

"Mr. Falcón, that's a lot of bull," she says and gets an angry look in her eyes. "Please, excuse my language, but that's just an excuse women use today. Never in my life have I seen such irresponsibility. That's what they are, irresponsible. Women today are built differently. All these feminists' ideas, ah! It's all a pile of—they have no interest." She pronounces interest like *inner rest*.

"No," you say. "It's been my fault all along, Mrs. Plater. I've been the irresponsible one."

She doesn't seem to believe you. She looks at the emptiness of the living room with a no-woman-who-says-she-loves-you-would-run-away expression on her face.

"Are you moving out?" she asks.

"I don't know yet. Maybe," you say, then walk over to open one of the windows.

Light inundates this very room you and V cohabited once. Made love in. Ate. Watched television. Invited friends.

"Yes," you tell Mrs. Plater who moves closer to the entrance as if to leave, "most probably. I will move."

"Good neighbors are hard to find," she says.

"Thank you, Mrs. Plater." She leaves.

Alone again. Tired again. It's all over. V has left for good. Decide now what it is you want to do with the place. No sense keeping it and paying rent when you're not even staying here.

Try listening to the palpitations of the heart. They sound loud, as though your heart is about to leap out of your throat, but instead you hear past arguments forever caught within these same walls. Forever listening to the tail end of her sentences. V's voice, soft, always on the verge of cracking into sobs.

You seek coolness in other rooms, for this is home. Worked hard and struggled to buy half of the things that once covered walls or adorned the corner tables. The rug moves against the floorboards. Age cures everything, so you think, but it hasn't cured your restlessness. What do you want? What do you need? What are you looking for?

Bombarded by these questions, back in the bedroom, you put your fist through the thin wall. The skin over your knuckles cracks and blood flows over your hands, but you don't stop pounding.

The heat follows you. It works on your skin like the warm touch of her hands. Yearning has led you astray. God, how you want her—wanted her.

The closet in the other room holds the magazines and books she owns, but whoever came to pick up her stuff didn't take them. These are self-help books V used to read and reread. A yellow paperback you remember slightly catches your attention. You pick it out from the shelf and hold it in your bleeding hand as though it is an unfamiliar object. The book is titled *How to Catch Your Husband Cheating*. Use it now to wipe the blood off your hands, then you tear it down the middle and drop it on the bedroom carpet.

Fuck her, fuck her, fuck her, you repeat on the way out of the apartment. This is what you will do: sell the furniture (give it away?) and move out as soon as possible.

There seems to be only one alternative and that is to forget her. Therefore, you will call Maruchi and go out to dinner with her. One thing Diego Falcón never does is feel sorry for himself.

In the Monte Carlo again, you drive away. Then on impulse, you step on the accelerator and give the car all the gas it can swallow. Peel rubber at the corner, turn, and head homeward. Believing you'll be the first to get the divorce underway, you drive watching the sun behind a veil of smog.

ESTEBAN / Back on the street. His stomach is full, and now he's walking off the meal. The rush-hour traffic hasn't let up, and he knows it won't. It has always seemed strange to be in the flow of so many automobiles. From what he remembers, traffic wasn't as dense in Santiago. He never learned to drive, didn't need to. After Angel married Lilián and they opened their cafeteria two blocks from Esteban's pharmacy, Angel gave him rides to and from work in his '56 Chevrolet.

So much chrome, that's what fascinated Esteban about American-built cars. Now the Japanese have cornered the market. Their cars are nothing but plastic and aluminum. One wreck and the best that can happen is that you come out in one piece, he thinks.

Walking through the streets of Huntington Park can be damaging to his sense of dignity and respect. The floor of the Pussycat is cleaner than this.

The sidewalks are cluttered with trash and gum softened by the heat and torn pieces of pornography: a naked leg under a doorway, a black penis thumbtacked to a eucalyptus tree, and a pair of large breasts by a gutter. Viola's? whose specialty is putting the head of a boa constrictor up her crack.

Pussy, Esteban contemplates, can either mean cat or vagina. This doubling is what he likes about English. He's also heard Diego refer to people as pussies.

No shade under which to seek shelter from the sun. These streets seem like narrow streams which lead to the giant cesspool that is Pacific Boulevard.

Inside the stores and shops the men and women, owners or attendants, stand behind the cash registers in the cool of the air conditioners. Tired eyes.

It's good to be retired, Esteban thinks. Though legally he shouldn't be. The immigration department made a mistake on his citizenship application, made him three years older. When he applied, he was working at Frederick's Pharmaceutical, coating pills in the laboratory.

Four years ago when Concha was alive things looked better around here. Americans owned most of these stores, and took better care of them. Of the city.

Walking away from the heart of the boulevard, Esteban startles the pigeons on the sidewalk. He changes his mind suddenly. The walk's tiring . Instead, he decides to take the bus.

Why he keeps returning he doesn't know. Something about the murmur of these streets that reminds him of Santiago when he owned the pharmacy on José Martí Street. No, never mind, no way do these fucking streets have anything in common with Santiago's. Here the trees choke under the brown haze. Plants don't survive.

Wondering if he'll go back if something, well, if the situation in the island changes, Esteban steps off the curb to cross the street. The DONT WALK! sign's blinking. An approaching car making a right turn beeps its horn and the driver shouts "Get the fuck out of the way, old man!" out the window.

Esteban raises his middle finger at the car. "Son of a bitch," Esteban says under his breath, then notices a young lady next to him.

She wears a miniskirt, too mini. He can't help but look up her tanned legs and imagine where they lead. Nothing too tight or loose. The thought that at least Diego inherited his hot blood for pretty women tickles him and he grins. The girl greets his smile with one of her own.

He's at the corner of Gage Avenue. Shaped like a box, the Woolworth's stands across the street. The bus turns at the corner and he hurries to catch it.

Its door hisses open. As he lifts his leg to climb the first step, his knee pops—a silent explosion. Cartilage, tendons, bones, and muscles fail. An acute pain strangles his thigh and turns into a cramp that almost makes him fall to the sidewalk.

The bus driver, a black man in his early thirties, springs from his seat and takes hold of Esteban's arm. "Let me help you," he says in an accent Esteban has trouble understanding.

"I'll be all right," he says to the bus driver.

"Here," the bus driver tells him and helps him sit down on the bench. "Rest right here."

The driver climbs back in his bus, closes the door, and leaves.

He needs to call Diego or Lilián, someone to come get him. But who knows if they're home? Lilián and Angel are probably still out selling ice cream. It doesn't matter, whoever's home.

The pangs of pain bring muscle spasms to his leg. Something's torn, a ligament perhaps. Fingering the sensitive area over his kneecap, he feels his knee swell. At the rate his body seems to be deteriorating, who knows?

Spontaneous combustion, he thinks, got to keep the valves clean and the oil flowing, or, or else, what? When he goes, he goes, but he doesn't want to end up causing anybody any trouble, especially his daughter Lilián. If Hugo comes, maybe the two of us can rent an apartment, catch up on all these years.

A man approaches and asks Esteban if he's okay.

Esteban can't hide the fact he's in pain behind a grin. "I don't know what happened," he tells the man. "Damn!"

"I can call a taxi for you," the man says.

Do I have enough money for a taxi? Esteban wonders. "I'll be all right, thank you," Esteban says.

When the man walks away, Esteban tries to stand, but he finds out he can't put any weight on his right knee. Too fucking painful.

The exhaust from the passing cars rising in the air nauseates him. A wreck zooms by, its loose muffler rattling.

Are you with me, Concha? Is this how you let me know you disapprove of my having fun?

He starts to laugh at his own silliness. When is he going to start again? Get himself another woman and spend his days in bed, now that he doesn't have anything to do but live, live! something he hasn't been doing. He sees it now: a younger woman he can watch dress and undress in front of him.

Esteban limps across the street to a public phone from which he calls the house. The line's busy: At least somebody's home. Perhaps he should make an emergency call, but then he'll have to deal with the operator. His English is not that bad, but he doesn't feel comfortable with his heavy accent. He waits, then tries again.

The phone rings and rings, before Diego answers. He tells his grandson his location and what has happened to his knee.

Diego says, "I'll go get you right now."

"Come in the Monte Carlo," he says. "Your car's too low."

Ten minutes later Diego arrives, parks the Monte Carlo in front of the bus stop and gets out, emergency lights flashing. He opens the door and helps Esteban get in. "Easy, easy," Esteban says, groaning as he tries to bend his knee.

"What were you doing?" Diego asks, holding the car door open.

Once Esteban's sitting inside, Diego runs around, jumps in, and drives down the street. At a stop sign Diego tries to push the seat of the Monte Carlo back, but it's already as far back as it's going to go.

"Take me to Dr. Glase," Esteban says, massaging his kneecap.

"Do I know how to get there?"

"Dr. Glase was your grandmother's doctor," Esteban says.

"That doesn't tell me how to get there," says his grandson.

Esteban gives him directions.

Every time Diego stops and goes, Esteban feels pain all the way up his body to his forehead. It pangs there. "Slow, slow," he tells Diego.

"The faster we get there, the faster—"

A diesel truck cuts in front of the Monte Carlo and forces Diego to make an abrupt lane switch.

"*¡Leche Maldita!*" Esteban says and closes his eyes; then, after the pain subsides a little, "Tell me what was stolen from the apartment?" Anything to alleviate the pain.

"What happened to your hand?" Esteban asks.

Diego looks at his swollen hand, then shows it to his grandfather. "A little accident," he says.

Esteban listens to his grandson relate how all of V's furniture was taken from the apartment. "What are you going to do?" he asks.

Diego, looking ahead intensely, says, "Find out where she is. Have a husband-to-wife chat with her."

"She's trying to teach you a lesson," he says to Diego.

"I'll find her," Diego says, making a turn on to the parking lot.

Situated in a newish office building, Dr. Glase's office is the first door to the left. From what he recalls, Dr. Glase is a greedy bastard. A workaholic. He must be extremely rich, Esteban thinks, because he owns the building.

His arm around his grandson's shoulder, Esteban lets Diego help him into the office. Inside the coolness and fluorescent brightness of the waiting room, Diego takes charge. He knocks on the opaque glass of the window and explains to the young nurse's aide what has happened. She, in turn, asks for Esteban's Medicare or Medicaid card.

Sure, Esteban thinks reaching into his back pocket for his leather wallet, he can be proud of being another number of the Social Security herd.

"He's been here before?" she asks Diego.

"For all the wrong reasons," Esteban answers, giving Diego his Medicaid card.

The girl smiles, looking at Diego. "The doctor'll see you next, Mr. Carranza," she says. "Have a seat."

Esteban tries to sit down, but he can't bend his knee. He settles for standing between Diego and a potted fern whose leaves are drying at the tips. He pokes a finger into its dry soil. No wonder, it needs lots of water.

Diego seems restless. Dressed in white tennis shorts and a T-shirt, he looks skinnier, taller. He hasn't shaved, so the stubble makes his face darker.

"Flaco quit the band," Diego says.

Esteban remembers Flaco from when he used to come over and play basketball in the driveway and ruin the plants with the ball.

"Didn't have another argument, did you?" Esteban asks.

"He just quit, you know, didn't show up to play last night."

"Maybe he's found another job."

Sticking her head out of the window, the girl says, "Okay, Mr. Carranza, the doctor'll see you now."

The door buzzes and Diego opens it. Esteban limps as Diego guides him to the examination room she assigns. She walks in front of them, so Esteban gets a good long look at her flat hips. Pretty face; no body.

"Wait here," she says. "He'll be right with you."

He and Diego enter the room. The girl helps Esteban onto the black padded examination table and asks him to please roll up the leg of his pants. Why doesn't she do it for him? Esteban thinks.

"I'll wait for you outside," Diego says. "Unless you want me to stay and hold your hand." He cracks a smile and leaves the room.

There are bone and muscle charts hanging on the walls, a weight scale, and a glass cabinet in which he recognizes the names on some of the medicine packages.

His knee is swollen, that much seems wrong. No longer can he finger the cap without feeling pain. "What do you think?" he asks Glase's aide.

"Looks bad," she says and puts her fingers on his thigh.

She pokes, getting closer and closer to the pained area. Ringless fingers, unpolished nails. Her white dress fits snug around her bosom. Half of a gold heart hangs from her necklace. Who's got the other half?

"One X ray'll show everything," she says.

Glase enters the room and greets Esteban with a warm handshake.

The receptionist leaves. "Nice girl," Esteban says.

"Hard worker," Dr. Glase says and winks.

The doctor's dark hands stand out against Esteban's pale flesh.

"Overhaul time," Esteban tells him and smiles.

"Nonsense," Glase says. "Just a tuneup."

"Today the knee," he tells him. "What will it be tomorrow?"

"Does this hurt?" the doctor asks, feeling with the tips of his fingers.

"It hurts, it hurts."

"Got water in it."

Esteban tells him how it popped. Pain is hard to describe, easy to feel.

Dr. Glase manages to stay young, even though he is as old as Domingo.

"Umm," says the doctor. "No need to take an X ray, we'll have to drain the water out."

The doctor leaves the examination room for a short moment and returns with a plastic container. It's a syringe, a big one. Looking at all types of medicine and medicine containers Esteban can stand, but medical instruments . . . Since childhood, he has hated surgical instruments, especially syringes.

Glase prepares the syringe and long needle which gleams under the bright light, then he says, "Lower your pants, please."

Painfully, Esteban steps on the short footstool and unbelts his pants. He unzips and lets his chinos fall around his ankles.

"Angie should see this," the doctor says.

"My sexy legs, you mean," Esteban says and climbs back on the table.

With a smaller syringe he injects novocaine to dull the flesh around the knee, all in preparation for the big pinprick. He injects both sides of the kneecap as well as top and bottom.

The water is located in the joint above the meniscus and around the cruciate ligaments.

The small needle doesn't hurt.

"Have you heard what Peru and Venezuela have said?" Dr. Glase asks.

Esteban, leaning back with eyes closed, nods.

"Well, they won't take everybody at the embassy, just a thousand or two."

"Something's got to happen," Esteban says. "There are more than ten thousand people there."

Now he feels the big needle slide in, tearing through to get to the water. "Jesus," Esteban says.

"It's like a mosquito bite, that's all."

"Mosquito, my—"

The suction begins. Water drains slowly into the plastic syringe, slush-colored water mixed with blood and who knows what else.

Memories of when Concha was at the hospital come. She didn't want to see anybody but Diego.

"It's all under the kneecap here," Dr. Glase says and when he pronounces *here* he pulls the needle out and inserts it in through the side.

"A little cortisone and you can run the New York Marathon."

Bent over the knee, Dr. Glase once again removes the needle from one side and sticks it in through the other. "I'm almost done," he says and tries to move the kneecap around.

Esteban groans and sinks his fingers into the padding on the table.

"There, there, it's over."

Angie walks in and Esteban is glad to see her. A faint trace of her perfume floats over to him. "Ugly sight, eh?" he asks her.

She doesn't say anything, as though everybody who comes here comes to have water drained out of their knees.

"Look how much water he had in there," Glase says to Angie. Then to Esteban, "I'm glad you didn't wait to come see me."

"So am I," Esteban says, sitting up. "It's always a pleasure."

"I'll write up a prescription for Decadron. Angie'll give it to you. Come see me if it swells up again."

Esteban says good-bye to Dr. Glase and gets off the table to put on his pants. Already he can feel less pain in his knee, though he still can't put weight on it.

"Hold on, Mr. Carranza," Angie says. "Not yet."

"Oh," Esteban says, not buttoning his pants.

"The cortisone shot," she says and smiles.

He drops his pants again and turns around. "Let me warn you," he says, "the skin back there is tough."

"Don't worry," she says. "I'm an expert."

After the shot, she cotton-swabs his ass with alcohol and tells him to get dressed. If he were twenty years younger, he thinks, she'd be in trouble.

"Would you like me to call the man outside?"

"My grandson, he's my grandson. Sure, why not?"

Shortly after she leaves, Diego comes. "I heard you crying," he says. "What did he come at you with, a chainsaw?"

"No, just a rusty icepick."

In the waiting room, Angie hands him the prescription and his card. She and Diego exchange glances.

A woman and her son walk in. The child's got a broken upper lip.

Diego holds the front door open. With difficulty Esteban walks out and heads toward the car. Bless medicine, he thinks, for the painkiller—a tiny army of cortisone attacking his knee—has started to work.

"I called the house," Diego says. "Mother's all excited. A telegram from Uncle Hugo came."

CONCHA / For her fifteenth birthday her parents gave a party and invited all their friends, influential people from Vista Alegre, It was a long day because her mother woke her up early. Already there were strange people she had never seen in the house. A cleaning crew waxing the floor and dusting the curtains, caterers, flower arrangers . . . a lady brought the dress she was supposed to wear.

In the kitchen the maid was flirting with one of the cooks. At one point she saw the man pinch the black woman's behind. Conchita, as she was called in her youth, smiled at the both of them.

"Eat your breakfast," the maid said to her, "and don't pay attention to us."

"Teach me how you do it," she told the maid.

"How you do what?"

"Flirt."

The man laughed. He was slicing ham. The slices were piled up on a silver tray. The maid took a slice of cheese and one of ham and rolled them together, then put a toothpick through the middle.

"Who's your escort?" the woman asked her.

"I don't have one."

"You don't have one. What do you mean? This is an important birthday, you should have one."

"Well, I do, sort of."

"Who is he?"

"The boy next door."

"Does your mother know about this?"

"It's a surprise."

"She might not like it."

She was beyond her mother's likes or dislikes. Esteban would come to her party because it was her party and it was her wish that he come over.

When she walked upstairs and tried on her dress in front of the mirror, she noticed for the first time how pretty she really looked. Not that she had doubted it before. She was pretty, but pretty in the way children are pretty. Now she was a young woman and it showed. Her breasts looked fuller under the low-cut dress.

The whole day went by filled with commotion. By five o'clock she was exhausted, but anxious for Esteban to see her. Slowly, the guests arrived and she greeted them and led them into the dining room where there was enough food to feed one thousand people.

They brought her gifts and flowers, which, after saying thank you, she handed to the doorman. He knew where to put them. The women guests left lipstick on her cheek, and she had to keep wiping it off with an embroidered kerchief. The men complimented her, told her how utterly beautiful she looked.

Her confidence soared. She kept looking at the clock because Esteban was due any minute.

When he finally arrived she was returning from the dining room so she missed his entrance. How handsome he looked dressed in his suit.

"For you," he said and handed her a dozen white roses. "Happy birthday, gorgeous."

She kissed him on the cheek and made sure to leave her lipstick on it. Hand on his arm, she led him inside the dining room and introduced him to her mother and father. Her mother greeted Esteban with an edge of indifference, but her father, as usual, was warm and overly friendly because he had had more than a few drinks by then. "Have fun," her father said, then took her mother by the hand and went away to socialize. She knew it would take them awhile to get used to him.

There was music being played by a band, so she asked him to dance with her.

"I'm sorry I didn't bring you a gift," he said.

"I'm just glad you came."

He held her at a proper distance, but firmly, while they danced. "But I did come to ask you something."

"Ask me," she said, noticing how all the guests who were on the dance floor kept moving in their direction for a better look at her partner. To them he was a stranger. Because his father did business in Santo Domingo, they weren't familiar with the Carranza family.

"Not now, later."

She wondered what it could be that he wanted to know, but she didn't mind that he wanted to wait until later.

Later, they went out to the garden and they held each other. She removed what was left of her lipstick and she kissed him.

"I want to marry you," he began. "We can do it. It'll be wonderful. As soon as I finish at the university, we'll get married. I want to set up a pharmacy. My father said he'd help me."

She didn't know what to say.

Suddenly she felt so happy and lightheaded that she held on to him because she thought she was going to faint. "Kiss me," she said and embraced him as hard as she could.

ESTEBAN / "Expect to hear Diego play live soon," Esteban, sitting on a chair, reads out loud to Angel, Lilián, and Diego in the kitchen.

"Does that mean he's inside the embassy?" Lilián wants to know.

"Could be," Esteban says. "The telegram's out of Havana."

"He ran away from Masorra?" Angel says. He sits on the other side of the table.

"Maybe," Esteban says, folding the piece of paper and putting it in his back pocket.

"The knee, Father," Lilián says. "You've got to take care of it now."

"It's fine," he says. "The pain's going away. The Decadron prescription's working."

He knows what needs to be done. It's all a matter of having to wait for the American government to decide what to do. Castro's not stupid, he'll milk the situation for whatever it's worth.

Lilián is so excited she has started to bring food out of the refrigerator. Vegetables and meats crowd the kitchen counter.

"What are you making?" Diego asks her, leaning against the doorway.

"Oh," she says, "don't ask. I know what I'm doing. Eat a snack."

"Put some coffee on, please," Angel says and begins to count the change he and Lilián made selling ice cream today.

"I'll do it," Diego says, opens the cupboards and removes the Gaviña coffee can.

"Since when do you know how to brew coffee?" Lilián asks.

"I'll have to go get him," Esteban says. He lights a cigar.

"Marriage is the antidote for ignorance," Diego, getting the espresso maker ready, says.

Lilián to Esteban: "I'll go with you." She chops and puts the tiny pieces of carrots, onions, garlic, and potatoes on plates.

"Your father can take care of it," Angel says. A stack of dimes rolls off the table and the coins spill on the floor.

"Help me pick this up, Diego?" Angel says and bends over.

"I'm busy, Dad," Diego says. He fills the espresso maker with water, spoons the coffee in the funnel, and screws the top back on.

Angel picks up the coins making sure he doesn't miss any. Lilián stands by him. She says, "Sooner or later we need time off. A week or two."

The faded Sergio Valente blue jeans fit her too tight, Esteban notices. He wonders if Angel cares or likes it—doesn't mind, probably, because more men will come to the truck to buy ice cream.

Red in the face from being bent over, Angel looks up at her and shakes his head. "Diego can go with your father," he says. "You know how sales get this time of year."

"We don't know what's going to happen yet," Esteban says. Smoke floats in front of his eyes. He blows it away.

Diego places the coffee maker on the grill and lights the stove. "See, nothing to it," he says to his mother.

"Don't make a mess," Lilián says and moves away from the

stove as though the espresso maker is going to explode.

"Don Carlos is going," Diego says, "and he wants me to go with him."

"He's got a boat?" Esteban says.

"I don't think so, but he can rent one."

Lilián takes the pressure cooker from the cabinet under the sink and drops all the chopped vegetables in it. Adds water, a squirt of olive oil, salt, pepper, a square of chicken bouillon and carries the pot over to the stove. "Don't impose on other people," she says. "Fly down and rent a boat. We'll give you the money."

"I've got my own money," Esteban says, looking at how carefully and slowly Angel stacks the change. Esteban knows how to do it faster.

"Tell us how much you're going to need," Angel says. His fingertips are dirty from handling the coins.

"Come on, people," Diego says. "All this talk's bad luck. Don't jinx it."

Esteban thinks: I'll go to the bank and withdraw the five-six thousand and if I need more, I'll take out a loan. Before Concha died she wanted to go back to Santiago. She said it over and over.

"Diego," Lilián says, "hear that? The coffee's ready. When you make it you've got to stay on top of it."

"It won't spill, I got it," Diego says, and walks over to the stove, puts on an oven mitt and removes the coffee maker from the red-hot grill.

Lilián helps him by bringing out the espresso cups. "Mix two tablespoons of sugar in it," she says.

"A family with a sweet tooth," Diego says.

While Diego gets the coffee ready and brought over to the table, Esteban turns on the portable television set on the table. Because the news is not on yet, he watches the *Hollywood Squares* game show.

"I'm sorry, Esteban," Angel says and stops counting to drink his coffee.

"What for?" Esteban takes a small sip in case he burns his tongue, blows to cool the coffee, then drinks the rest.

"If I don't sound too enthusiastic about Hugo," Angel says. "But there's so much to be done."

Esteban can see it now, his son-in-law's afraid. I don't blame him, he thinks, he went through hard times in Cuba, but so did everybody else. "Stay," Esteban says and smiles." "You and Lilián can stay and work."

Diego collects the empty cups and takes them to the kitchen sink where he leaves them.

"I'm going out," Diego says and moves toward the door.

"Stay and eat with us," Lilián says.

"I owe somebody a dinner."

"Coming back tonight, or staying at the apartment?" Lilián says.

Diego tells his mother what happened with the furniture.

"Don't waste any more money," Angel says from the table. "Move out."

"That's what he plans to do," Esteban tells Angel.

Diego doesn't say anything and leaves the kitchen.

Something begins to smell good. Condiments and spices. Lilián has learned to cook as well as Concha. It's taken a long time though, a long time.

The news comes on. Cubans and other Hispanics have gathered at a rally in Echo Park in Los Angeles to protest Castro's treatment of the people seeking asylum in the Peruvian Embassy. For a clearer reception, Esteban tries to adjust the antenna.

On the screen a woman carries a banner that says ¡PERU Y VENEZUELA AYUDA A TUS HERMANOS! meaning help your brothers. Then the Cuban national anthem is sung by people marching by. Cut to the embassy in Havana. More people everywhere. The camera work seems haphazard, with too much movement, as though the cameraman is being pushed along. Esteban leans closer, but every face looks the same: dirty, tired, hungry.

"In other news today . . . " the anchorman says, "the release of the Iranian hostages has—"

Esteban turns off the TV, reaches for Hugo's telegram in his pocket, and reads it again while Lilián finishes the soup she's making. Our son's coming, Concha, this time he's coming.

ANGEL / The thing about money is that none of it lasts. It comes and it goes so easily. He's getting tired of having to count all the daily change. The bank won't take it unless everything's wrapped properly. He and Lilián deposit it at least once a week. People give them strange looks as they wait in the business-transactions line with the heavy bags.

But—one of the saddest truths about life being that in order to eat one has to make money—it buys the food Lilián cooks and serves.

For dinner tonight they are having black beans, white rice, fried pork, and boiled yams. Esteban drinks beer. Angel, milk. Lilián doesn't drink anything while she eats. It's supposed to make her lose weight. This is the food money buys. The kind of food that was hard to find back home, even with money. Glorious food that appeases their hunger.

Angel turns his mind off and settles down to enjoy the product of his hard work.

ESTEBAN / "Hello. Oh, hello?"

"Esteban, listen, this is Ruth . . . Esteban?"

He holds the phone against his ear and shoulder, wondering how long it's been since Ruth has called. "Yes, Ruth, how are you?"

"Disturbed . . . listen!"

"I'm listening Ruth, go ahead."

"I'm worried sick. Have you seen him? I came home and . . . "

"I haven't seen him in days." A lie he's enjoying telling her so that she can worry some more. Hers are like the worries of a scorpion.

" . . . wasn't here. Usually he leaves me a note." She speaks in a know-what-I-mean? voice.

"Yes, Ruth, I know how he is." He, woman, is a good friend who has decided to leave, but where? "Did he pack?"

"I don't know, I didn't check."

"Check, I'll wait."

She puts the phone down and Esteban can hear the television in the background. He tries to imagine her lazy movements from living room or kitchen where the phone must be to the bedroom. Through all the years he's known Domingo, Esteban has been to their house less than . . .

"He did pack," she says. "One suitcase is gone."

"Where can he go?"

"He gets these crazy ideas that I'm against him," Ruth says. Her voice cracks at the other end of the line. Fake despair. "I'm afraid his condition's getting worse, Esteban. It's ten-thirty and—"

"Calm down, Ruth," he says. "If he comes by, I'll tell him that you're going crazy, umm, that, that you're extremely worried."

"Please, please, tell him I need to see him."

"I'll be the first to tell him, okay?"

She hangs up without saying good-bye. What manners. Esteban returns to his room. The digital clock reads 10:33 P.M., time for the helicopters to fly over the house and spray the deadly malathion.

DIEGO / Maruchi takes you to Scallaris, this Italian restaurant down Wilshire Boulevard she says is the best. It's a small little place tucked in the corner of a shopping plaza. She knows the owner, had dated his son in high school. Pink, blue, and white neon lights adorn the walls. The maitre d' shows you to a table in the back. He pulls the chair for Maruchi, who looks ravishing dressed in black. "What would you like to drink, signore?" he asks.

"Bring me the best champagne you've got," you say. The maitre d' leaves. A waiter comes and brings the menus. "May I suggest the fettuccini scampi," he says.

"That's good," Maruchi says.

You take it.

"And for the lady?"

"The parmesan chicken and risotto, please."

The waiter collects the menus and leaves. Feeling a little awkward, you reach for her hands and hold them. She smiles and blows you a kiss.

There is so much you want to tell her, but the champagne comes. You settle for observing the action surrounding your table. The maitre d' pours the champagne, then puts the bottle back in the ice and leaves.

Maruchi lifts her glass and says, "Here's to—"

"Something special," you say and make your glass chink against hers.

She drinks quickly. "Take it easy," you say. "There's more where that came from."

"Good," she says. "Because tonight is my turn to get drunk."

Lean back against the chair and admire her face, her contented posture—she seems really comfortable with you. "I want to tell you some things about me," you say, "since I did promise to set the record straight, so to speak."

"Concerning her?"

"No, concerning you and me."

So begin at the beginning, all the good things you thought about her the first time you saw her. But conversation comes hard when it is this superficial. After all, she's a perfect stranger. Stranger with a nice smile, and some tenderness for . . . At the present moment you are not looking for anything serious.

"You know what is the most important thing you should keep in mind about me?" she says.

"What is that?"

"I'm not just a fuck."

The food arrives, but suddenly a valve has popped open—you want to talk, about everything. Go back to high school, to friends and good times, to . . .

ESTEBAN / The smell of bread burning comes like a woman's perfume to Esteban, who can't go to sleep. Sitting up on the bed, he looks around in the dark; then for a brief moment he believes Concha has returned. There, on the closet door, her shape evolves and holds steady.

But it is only the light from outside.

The notion that Diego, who sleeps in the den, left the gas on in the stove makes Esteban want to get up. The pain in his knee, numbed by the cortisone, has gone away and he doesn't want to get it started again.

He hears footsteps. Whispers.

His slippers are not where they're supposed to be by the side of the bed. He gets out of bed carefully, slowly, without having to move his leg too much, and walks outside into the hallway.

In the hallway closet he finds the flashlight he uses sometimes to go to and from the bedroom to the bathroom. He doesn't want to turn on the lights just in case what he smells is gas and not toast. He heard in a show once that naked copper wiring can cause a short circuit that, if met by gas, can produce an explosion.

Standing in the dark of the hallway, he hears giggles from the den, and they certainly don't sound like Diego's. With every step he takes he reminds himself that if he hits something in the dark . . .

From the kitchen he hears soft laughter now, crisper: a woman.

The television brightens the den from behind the wicker sliding door which divides the den from the dining room.

A strong odor of incense fills the dining room. Esteban clicks off the flashlight and walks across the kitchen to the dining room where he stops and stands behind the door. Through the little holes on the criss-crossed wicker he can see them.

Diego's got a young woman in the den with him. Both of them, completely naked, are playing some kind of card game. No, the woman's reading Diego his fortune from tarot cards.

"Wow," the young woman says. "The Lovers. What a coincidence."

"Sure you're not cheating?" Diego says and laughs.

"These cards don't lie," she says. A bottle of wine sits between them. Afraid he might be heard, Esteban tries to be as quiet as possible. He breathes through his mouth so that air won't whistle out of his nose. His heartbeats come quickly.

His grandson's got a girl in there, all right, but she doesn't look anything like Vanessa.

Thanks to the television light he can see them clearly. The woman drops the cards and lets Diego move her to the bed. Her back's to the door. Diego holds her by the waist. She wiggles on top of him.

She reminds Esteban of Iris Chacón, the Puerto Rican dynamite beauty who's got a show on channel 34.

The light glistens off the woman's back. Diego moves her off, then stands and approaches the door. Esteban hurries back to the kitchen, but on the way he almost bumps his knee against a dining room chair.

In the kitchen he switches on the light, hides the flashlight in one of the counter drawers and acts as if hunger got him out of bed.

Diego walks over wearing a pair of shorts, no shirt, no shoes. Hair mussed. "I thought I heard something," he says.

"Just me, I can't sleep."

"Pain? The knee?"

"No," Esteban says, checking the time on the clock radio by the boxes of Kellogg's cereal. "I thought I heard something, too."

"Want a sandwich? I'm making myself one."

If he says yes, he might have to prolong the embarrassment. "No thanks," he says, "I think I'll just have some milk and go back to bed."

"I'll be right back," Diego says and goes to the den.

Esteban hears the commotion and imagines the young woman trying to get dressed. Will she come out to meet me?

The den blacks out.

The milk begins to boil, so he takes the pot off the stove and pours the liquid into a tall plastic glass, and drinks. The front door opens and closes. A car starts. Closing his eyes he tries to imagine how the woman looks as she sneaks out, how Diego holds her one more time and slips his hand inside her pants or under her skirt. One last pat on the slat for good-bye. The car pulls out of the driveway.

Diego returns to the kitchen. His shorts are zipped but not buttoned. He sits on a kitchen chair and rubs his feet together to get the dirt off them, doesn't look up at him.

"Burning incense?" Esteban asks. He wants to break the ice.

"The air's a little too stale in the den," Diego says, stands up and starts to get things out of the refrigerator to fix his sandwich.

"Christ, I thought it was gas leaking."

"Incense doesn't smell like gas."

A pause gives them both a chance to finish what they are doing. Esteban drinks; Diego prepares his sandwich.

"I could've sworn I saw somebody behind the door," Diego says and slices the sandwich.

"It was me. I saw her." He doesn't like to pretend, besides he wants to know who she is.

Diego tells him Maruchi's one of the new waitresses at the club.

"She's a beauty," Esteban says.

Diego walks to the dining room table and sits down. Esteban leans against the refrigerator and looks at his grandson eat the sandwich, which he devours in a few bites.

"Does she know about Vanessa?" Esteban asks, regripping the warm glass.

"She knows everything."

Diego wipes his mouth with his fingers, sweeps the crumbs into his cupped hand and walks to the sink to leave the plate under the faucet. Out of the refrigerator he pulls the gallon of milk and pours a glassful, drinks it, pours another.

Esteban feels like telling Diego he shouldn't have married so young, but what's done is done. Not so young, though. Diego married Vanessa when he was eighteen, barely out of high school and with ideas about starting his own band. But his grandson doesn't need to hear negative comments, things he already knows.

Esteban nods and walks around the kitchen aimlessly. So much on his mind, too much. Diego says good night and returns to the den. Light on. Television.

Someone knocks on the kitchen door. Esteban moves over to the window, looks out, but cannot see who it is.

"It's me, Esté, Domingo."

He unlocks and opens the door to let his friend in. Green-plaid suitcase in hand. Domingo climbs the steps and enters the house. He is wearing a gray suit, red tie, and black shoes scuffed at the tips. Domingo drops the suitcase on the kitchen floor.

"Ruth called," Esteban tells him, moving out of Domingo's way.

"Ah, fuck her. Left just at the right time,"

Esteban asks where he has been since this afternoon.

"Fooling around," Domingo says, "trying to decide what I want to do."

"Sit down," Esteban says.

Both Esteban and Domingo sit at the kitchen table. The spandex band Esteban's wearing with Ben-Gay bulges under the leg of his pajamas. His friend notices and Esteban tells him what happened. "It feels better," Esteban says. Then, "Hugo's coming, Domingo. I got a telegram today."

"What wonderful news," Domingo says and lights a cigarette.

Diego sticks his head out of the den and says hello to Domingo, who gets up, extends his thin arm and shakes Diego's hand. "Glad to see you, Diegito."

"It's been a long time," Diego says.

"Yes, it has, hasn't it?"

Domingo sits down again, tips his cigarette to drop the ashes into the square ashtray, and tells how he packed up and ran away before Ruth got home. "I remembered the address here," he says.

"Of course you remember it," Esteban says.

Diego excuses himself, says good night, and returns to bed.

"Nice boy," Domingo says. "Too bad about—"

"You can stay here," Esteban tells him. "You look tired."

"I am."

"We can talk in the morning," Esteban says and stands up slowly. For now he needs sleep. The more he rests his knee the faster it will heal. Injuries last when one is old. He shows Domingo the way to his room, asks him to please feel at home.

"She'll call again," Domingo says.

"Don't worry about Ruth," Esteban says, sitting on the mattress. "Although she did sound determined to find you."

"And I'm determined not to be found."

In the room Domingo undresses and stands by the window in his underclothes. "If you go get Hugo, I want to go with you," he says.

"Sure," Esteban replies. "Tomorrow afternoon I'm going to the cemetery."

"To visit Concha?"

"No, to see about exhuming her remains. She's coming with us."

"I see," Domingo says and climbs onto the mattress as easily as a cat jumps from a windowsill.

Darkness. Esteban grabs one of the pillows and slides it over to his friend. After a while he warns Domingo that he snores, to which Domingo answers, "So did Ruth. I'm used to it." Domingo laughs.

Precious silence, a buzzing. The peace and quiet is broken by the thwap-thwap of the helicopters. They are late. "Damn them," Esteban says and looks at Domingo who has already fallen asleep.

Leaning back on his pillow, Esteban sighs. He shuts his eyes to the thought of this gooey and thick and useless pesticide falling all over Concha's miniature roses, of it settling gently on the petals, of it working decay: a burning gone unheard.

May, 1958

Mama Concha:

Later, when I run into Lobo again, he calls me Chester. His men laugh. The name comes from the make of my rifle. Winchester. Everybody, I find out, sooner or later is nicknamed by Lobo himself.

The next couple of days I find myself walking alongside the man. He walks with a quick step, even over rough ground. Though it's hot and humid, he doesn't slow down. We've been hiking for two days, each day climbing a little farther in order to escape any possible air raids and fire bombs.

He tells me that now that I'm part of the troops it gives him a chance to talk to an educated person. Most of his men come from holes in the ground, unlearned and un-civilized but anxious to fight for what they believe to be a tremendous, worthwhile cause.

"The uneducated are in tune," he says, "and the educated think too much, know what I mean? This revolution is being fought to educate everybody the right way." As we continue he brings me up-to-date on the advances of the revolution.

There are approximately fifty to seventy men scattered about. If you listen for a while you can hear the blades of their machetes cutting through the thick vines and bran-ches, clearing the way.

This part of the sierras is heavily vegetated. There are plants and flowers here. Lobo knows a lot of them by name, especially the ones with edible roots and those with wild fruits. I've seen earthworms a foot long, strange-looking lizards and chameleons, frogs and snakes.

The Scavengers are a team of five men assigned to scout the area for food, and snakes are what they usually find and bring back for supper. Sometimes wild hares and other large rodents. Birds and doves are delicacies but hard to catch without shooting them. Lobo doesn't want any shooting, to save ammunition, but also because he's afraid the reports will give our position away.

We hike during the day and set up camp at dusk. By setting up camp I mean that we gather around Lobo's tent, which he insists on putting up himself. The rest of us sleep where the night finds us.

The men build several fires in which to cook whatever's for dinner, then sit about and talk. Most of us are too tired and go to sleep immediately after the meal—snake meat is chewy and therefore hard to digest.

Some of us stay up and listen to Lobo speak. He adopts a different subject to talk about every night. But most of the conversation deals with the revolution. He wants to teach his men. His subject is language. If he had access to books he'd teach his men to read. But, really, most of what he discusses has to do with his plans to hike up the mountain and come down for an attack on the other side.

"The only way," he says, "of finding out information is to go down to a town or the city. People are well-informed because of the newspapers. Our movement has to be synchronized with that of the other troops in Camaguey."

Lobo, from what I've been able to observe, suffers from insomnia. At night you can hear him moving about the tent, sometimes a candle burning until dawn. Nobody knows what he does all night. That he reads maps to establish the troops' position and plan strategies are only guesses. I figure that he must like to be alone or that something is bothering him and he doesn't know how to deal with it, something that doesn't let him sleep.

In the morning his is the first voice heard. By the first light he already has water for coffee over the fire. The coffee comes from another raid that took place before I arrived. What's left of it is carried in backpacks or mochilas. Then the tent comes down. Lobo rolls it up and ties it to his backpack.

Morning, according to comandante Morales, is the ideal time to move, when it's cool and the sun hasn't become powerful. It's during this time that we advance rapidly, then at noon we stop to rest. The men nap for a couple of hours. By three in the afternoon we are on the move again.

It takes us one more day to reach the summit, and three more to hike to the foothills from where the houses look like miniatures of the real thing. Lobo says we are supposed to wait for the night, when we can attack.

Love, Hugo

ESTEBAN / Domingo is still asleep when Esteban wakes up. Sliding out of bed as carefully as possible, he sits up. Under the bed he finds his slippers. He yawns as he puts them on. Air makes a funny noise coming out of Domingo's nose. While he goes to the bathroom and takes a shower, Esteban starts to remember how their friendship began:

Scared, his son-in-law called at the pharmacy. Angel said he didn't know what was going on anymore. Somebody had spread a terrible rumor about him aiding the rebels.

With so much commotion the streets were unsafe, dangerous. People were being murdered. Innocent men and women. The closer the rebels drew to the city, the more panic the police tried to create. They arrested everybody who looked suspicious.

The house in which Lilián and Angel lived sat at the end of the street, overlooking the hills. Angel painted it light gray with white trim. There was a ravine that ran through the back and overflowed every year during the rainy season.

Lilián came to the door when he knocked; her teary eyes were bloodshot. Angel was in the kitchen. He looked pale, his shirt was dampened.

"It's all a lie," he said to Esteban, then sat down on one of those footstools.

"Calm down," Esteban said. "I know somebody who might be able to help us. He's a lawyer."

So he went to see Domingo Sosa, who had the most respected law firm in Santiago. Esteban knew his wife, Ruth.

The office was located not too far from Esteban's pharmacy. To get to the upstairs suite, he rode the elevator, which cranked and rattled. He tapped lightly on the opaque glass of the door and a voice asked him to please come in.

Inside he found Domingo's secretary hidden behind a couple of fresh bouquets of flowers. "Will you tell Señor Sosa that Esteban Carranza is here to see him."

"Do you have an appointment?" she asked.

"No, I have a problem I'd like to discuss with him," he said. "His wife suggested I come see him."

It didn't take more than a few seconds before the door opened and Domingo greeted him. The man in front of him looked tanned, just back from vacation. His hair was sleeked back with brilliantine, which was the style. A new double-breasted suit, pin-striped, and shiny black shoes, the kind with tassels.

"Come in, Carranza," he said. "Make yourself comfortable."

The office consisted of a large mahogany desk, wall-to-wall law books, art prints, and several pictures of his wife, Ruth. From the window behind the desk he was able to see the park's fountain.

"Eva," Domingo called to his secretary. "Please bring in some coffee."

Esteban told him why he had come.

Domingo listened intently, then reclined back in his chair and told him not to worry about a thing, that he'd have the problem solved by tomorrow morning.

"I don't want my son-in-law arrested."

"I'll speak to the mayor," Domingo said, "and ask him to have a little talk with the chief of police."

They shook hands, then Esteban asked about Ruth.

"She wants to leave the country," he said. "She's very nervous nowadays."

"The rebels are everywhere," Esteban said. "Havana's about to fall."

"Let's hope it's all for the best."

Esteban asked how much he owed him and Domingo said to consider the matter a consultation visit. No fee for consultations. They shook hands again, then Esteban assured him that if he ever needed anything from the pharmacy. . . .

"I've got a headache," his friend says when Esteban enters the bedroom.

"Take aspirin," he says, finding the clothes he's going to wear. "There's some in the bathroom cabinet."

"Been up long?"

"Just got up."

Esteban finishes getting dressed and stands in front of the dresser mirror to fix the collar of his red shirt. He combs his hair. Sleepy-eyed, Domingo sits up and scratches his chest.

Concha invited Ruth and Domingo to several parties. Domingo became a good friend. They would go out to the cafés together, or to a bar for a drink. Sometimes they played dominoes poolside at Domingo's house. Then after the revolution, his friend left the country.

"We have a busy schedule ahead of us," Esteban says, "so take a shower, get dressed, and come eat breakfast."

ANGEL / Warm flesh. He feels an erection. Lilián rolls over on her side and the bedsheet slides off her chest. Angel, who hasn't been able to sleep well all night, leans over and kisses her flesh. She stirs but doesn't wake up. Web pattern. Nervelike stretch marks on her breasts look like etchings on a drawing.

Angel slides his hand under the covers to rescue the fleeting sensations. It feels too wonderful, and it's been a long time since they've made love, he thinks. He moves closer to her back; her skin is smooth.

His hand stumbles upon the moist area between her legs. Sweat? Her legs part to let his hand in. A finger. Surely, she's feeling this, he thinks and enters her from behind.

She's awake. Her eyes are wide open and she's peering at the full-length, closet-door mirror. She turns over to face Angel, kisses his forehead, cheeks, lips.

"We don't do this often enough," she says, caressing his chest. Hairs grow only in the middle of his chest, long and curly.

Her hands cup his balls and she squeezes gently. Stiff as a broomstick, but can't come. Years of intimacy have shown Lilián what he likes, what makes him feel good.

On top, she takes his cock, massages it, and slides it into her mouth.

Eyes closed, he concentrates. The walls of her mouth close in. Tongue. Lips. He comes . . . .

Lilián holds him until the last drop, until he grows limp, then she moves up and kisses him. Her small lips are burning. Angel runs his fingers through her short hair and kisses her neck. "I'm sorry I woke you up," he says.

"I wondered how long you'd be able to," she says and puts her head to his chest.

"To what?"

"Hold back."

"I wasn't holding back," he says. Then, "Too many things on my mind."

She smiles and rests her body on top of his. Lilián is thin—if he feels above her stomach he can count her ribs. She isn't too attractive—skinny. At thirty-nine, her body remains young. He doesn't have the slightest clue what has happened to her breasts. He can't remember whether she breast-fed Diego.

Still dark outside, and the pigeons cooped up on the palm tree next door start to flutter and make noise among the fronds. "I heard strange voices last night," Angel says.

"It was probably Diego," Lilián says, moving over onto the mattress.

"He's got me worried."

"He'll be okay. These things happen, you know. Kids today get married out of boredom."

"You sound like your father," he says and looks at the digital clock which reads 5:51 A.M.

"He should be glad it happened now and not later. Things could be worse. Children—"

"The way I see it," Angel says, "he's taking it well."

Her hands are massaging her breasts as though she were checking herself for cancer. "Diego avoids me," she says.

"You've been a good mother."

"We hardly talk."

"Nobody's going to solve his problems, but him," he says. "He's got to learn that about life."

Lilián gets out of bed and walks inside the bathroom. The faucets screech when she turns them on. The house is falling apart. Nothing has been replaced or repaired since Concha died.

If Angel weren't selling a lot these days, he'd take a day off and fix a few odds and ends.

He hears his wife brushing her teeth. On the nightstand next to the bed sits an old photograph of his mother. The black-and-white snapshot has faded to a blurry yellowish-gray. His mother's hair no longer has any resemblance to the shiny black hair she used to have. Her blue eyes, if he moves, seem to follow him. There's a brown birthmark on her chin. When he was a child, he recalls, she told him that the birthmark was a pillbug and that if he stared at it hard enough he'd see it move.

In the bathroom, while Lilián showers, he sits on the toilet and urinates, turns the handle to flush and gets up in front of the cabinet. Last time Lilián cleaned the bathroom she reorganized everything. Now he can't find the cotton swabs to clean the wax out of his ears.

Another thing, she never turns on the air vent to let the steam out when she showers.

"What are we going to do when Hugo comes?" he says, looking at the shape of her body behind the steamed glass on the cabinet mirror.

"I don't know," she says, shutting the water off and sliding the door open. "I've got to get used to the idea first." She reaches for a towel with which to dry herself.

"Hugo's a sly fox. He'll come." Angel squeezes a tad of new green-and-red Colgate toothpaste onto his brush and brushes his teeth. Smoking a pipe all these years has turned his teeth yellow at their roots.

"We'll have to tell the back tenants," she says, drying herself and stepping out of the tub.

"He can live with us, can't he?" He leaves fingerprints on the cabinet mirror as he puts the toothpaste and brush back.

"I guess he can," she says. "In the spare room. Diego can keep using the den." She unrolls some toilet paper and wipes the mirror clean.

When Diego comes late, he often stays in the den. For some unknown reason his son likes to sleep in that room. Angel turns to embrace his wife whose breath smells just like his, of toothpaste. Water from her hair drips on to his hands and arms.

The last time he saw Hugo was when he accompanied Esteban and Concha to La Cabaña, and even then he didn't get to see his brother-in-law because they let only one person in at a time. Concha went in first, followed by Esteban. By the time it was Angel's turn, the visiting hour was over.

"I'm taking the day off," Lilián says. "Father needs me."

Lilián leaves the bathroom to blow-dry her hair in front of the dresser. The truth of the matter is he enjoys her company. The day seems to glide by a lot faster when she's in the truck with him.

While Angel takes a shower, he figures out what he needs to sell today in order to beat yesterday's sales record, which came close to three hundred dollars. All he has to do is sell the following: ten boxes of Jumpin' Jiminys, Frooty Patootys, Blue Ghosts, Frozen Toes, Deluxe Drumsticks, Popsicles, and Carnation ice cream sandwiches. The Neapolitans sell faster, must be the three flavors. Selling out most of the merchandise keeps him making daily trips to the wholesale ice cream warehouse.

But now, without Lilián's help, who knows? He's not as confident. Finished showering, he steps out of the tub, dries himself, and walks back to the bedroom to dress, and comb his hair. It's almost seven. Lilián is writing a grocery list with a pen that is running out of ink.

She is wearing a white flower-print dress he's never seen.

"You look nice," he says.

She tells him that she bought the dress not too long ago, that V picked it out for her, of course this was when they . . .

The top of her dresser is covered with check stubs and pennies, Lilian's earrings and bracelets, her perfume—very little of the mess is his: his comb and a bottle of Brut cologne she gave him for Christmas last year.

His work clothes consist of a pair of ragged blue jeans and a red cotton shirt comfortable only when it doesn't get too hot in the truck and he sweats. If he wears the white tennis shoes Diego let him have, he'll be dressed in patriotic colors.

Angel Falcón is proud to be an American citizen, no more no less. But instead of the white tennis shoes he chooses a pair of deck shoes, which he finds are not as rough on his feet. Though Diego has told him not to wear the deck shoes with socks—fashion can go to hell—he does. His feet sweat profusely so close to the heat of the motor.

"You have enough pipe tobacco?" Lilián asks, finishing the list and folding it into her purse.

"Are you going to the market now?" he asks, checking his hair in the mirror.

"After breakfast I will," she says and moves over to the bed and starts to fold the sheets.

Yes, breakfast, he thinks, making love has made him hungry. He needs coffee to revive the palate, to appease the sting of the toothpaste. First a piece of toast with strawberry preserve and a slice of American cheese and milk for his ulcer.

In the kitchen he encounters Domingo and Esteban eating at the dining room table. Esteban in his brown slacks and red shirt and Domingo in a pair of khakis which fit him big and a dress shirt.

"What are you doing here this early?" he asks Domingo.

Esteban tells Angel that Domingo's going to be staying in the house for a while.

"I hope," Domingo says, "I don't inconvenience you in any way."

"Stay for as long as you wish," Angel tells Domingo. Then to Esteban, "How's the knee?"

"The Decadron's working fine."

Angel looks down at Domingo's bare feet. The contorted veins so dark stand out on the instep. Long toenails, crooked and the color of a nickel. Maybe with this many people in the house, Angel thinks, he won't be expected to return early.

From the kitchen he hears the conversation between Domingo and Esteban. They are talking about going to the cemetery, something about exhuming Concha's body. Esteban's voice has a high pitch of excitement as he discusses the probable trip to Miami.

While he prepares his breakfast, Angel sees sleepy-faced Diego, pillow in hand, pass by the kitchen door on his way to the back bedroom. The noise probably woke him up, Angel thinks, and hears Lilián saying something to him.

After eating his breakfast Angel leaves the kitchen and steps outside. A foggy morning greets him, and the dew prickles on his forearms. A bit chilly.

SUPERSTAR: the black elongated letters painted on the sides of the ice cream truck seem to be fading. The stickers advertising the different kinds of ice cream he sells are peeling off. Sooner or later he's going to have to stencil the letters back on and get new stickers. The truck, his Rocinante, a '68 Dodge, still looks good after he had it painted and the motor overhauled and new tires put on. White walls. This is his home on the road, what keeps the harsh sun and rain and cold off him.

Unlocking the door, he notices a crack on the glass display. Nothing's missing from it, though there are pry marks on the metal case. Inside the truck most of the toy merchandise and candy lies strewn all over the floor. Somebody did break in.

The side window out of which Lilián sells when she's with him is broken. There are pieces of glass everywhere. "Goddamnit," he says under his breath. Now he's going to have to take inventory, something he enjoys doing but not under these circumstances.

He counts most of the merchandise as he puts everything back and finds out only his Snickers and M & M's and Mars bars are missing. Somebody with a strong craving for chocolate.

This is the second time this past year that somebody has broken into the truck. How can they do it? He's taken every precaution. Keeps his bedroom window open so that he can hear. If he ever catches the culprit breaking in, he . . . the window's going to cost at least thirty-five dollars to replace. Damn! Cleaning up and rearranging the merchandise, he thinks that it's now unlikely he'll have a good day.

June, 1958

Conchita:

The night comes. Only ten men get to go down and attack. I stay behind with Lobo, who seems confident his men will succeed. All they are supposed to do is create havoc, let people know that there's fighting going on. Hit and run, that's all. Of course, they must search for ammunition and whatever other supplies they can find.

Thus far nobody's gotten killed or hurt during these

nocturnal attacks. The only result of these attacks is that more men join the troops. Word about the revolution has been out for a while now. People are aware of what's going on, and they seem to want to take part.

"They aren't scared anymore," Lobo says. "They are also tired of being abused and exploited."

Commotion starts. The shots fired sound hollow from so far away, like a piece of wood going cra-aack. A couple of flares go up and descend slowly, burning out.

"Here they come," Lobo says. "That's what the flares mean. That they are retreating."

And in fact the men do return, none of them in need of my assistance. Lobo stands in the middle of the group and asks questions about what they did or what they had seen. Most of the men are still trying to catch their breath.

But with them comes a new face. A young girl. Dirty-faced and sweaty. She, too, is short of breath. She reaches into a sack and produces a newspaper. She hands it to Lobo, who, smiling, takes it and goes inside the tent. Lights a candle. While he is inside, the men gather around the girl.

When Lobo comes out of the tent, they hush up and listen.

"Air attacks will be increased," he says, "to four missions during the day and two at night. No more fires during the night. We don't need to be spotted by airplanes."

"The girl wants to stay," somebody says.

"What is your name?" Lobo asks the girl.

"Lucinda," she says. "I want to fight."

Lobo smiles, then asks her to step inside the tent so she can answer some more questions. The men laugh. Lucinda walks toward the tent, stops and turns around to look at everybody, then disappears inside it.

Your Son,
Hugo

ANGEL / After a quick stop to have the truck's window replaced—it cost $29.95, cheaper than last time—he drives to the ice cream warehouse to replace the stolen merchandise. He drives to the rhythms of his own silence. The fact that the portable TV/radio wasn't taken leads Angel to believe that kids broke into the truck.

There should be twenty-five hours in his day, fuel-injected, turbo-charged time. Smoke from his pipe rises up and wisps of it cling to the air in front of his eyes.

Maybe Lilián is right, it's time for a vacation. But, though he likes to stay at home, he is constantly reminded of how things used to be in Santiago. When Lilián isn't talking about it, Esteban is. Esteban reminds him of old age; and if he so much as eyes his son Diego, he sees failure at its prime. Diego, who at his age knows what failure means better than anyone else Angel has ever known. Instead of going to college as Angel thought his son would, Diego, after he graduated from high school, decided to form a band. Then one thing led to another: Diego got a job playing at the club, started to make money, met V and married her. His son has failed at marriage, but maybe the way he measures failure is not the same way Diego judges it.

He remembers a year ago Diego was scared—he thought he'd have to enlist to go fight in Iran. Maybe that's why his son decided to return to V after he had left her. Angel doesn't approve of his son's restlessness. Hell, when he was Diego's age, he was already married, had a son, and two businesses to take care of.

Now Hugo is coming. Angel wonders how much sense this many years of prison could have drilled into his brother-in-law's head. Stubborn bastard. Lilián loves her brother, worships him.

Angel tries to assess the damage done so far this morning. Each of the boxes stolen cost approximately eighteen dollars. Three stolen. That's . . . let it go. He wonders what else has happened at the embassy.

There is no news on the radio until ten o'clock, so he listens to Radio KALI, which is playing Puerto Rican salsa, the kind of stuff Diego plays. ". . . *Dame un besito, mi negra, dame un besito . . .*"

He makes a left on to Long Beach Boulevard, then a right to the entrance of the ice cream warehouse. He parks the truck next to another which he recognizes as his competition.

115

The engine dies to a blrrrrrrrrrr.

Eloisa, the proprietor's wife, is serving behind the counter, while Bebo, dark-skinned and with a crewcut, talks with the owner of the other truck. They laugh when Angel walks in. Eloisa greets Angel.

To make friendly conversation, Angel asks her if she's heard anything about the embassy, to which she shrugs her shoulders.

Angel fills out an order sheet for the merchandise he needs, both ice cream and candy, and hands it to Eloisa. She walks over to the back entrance, calls the Mexican boy who works the freezer and gives him the order.

She returns to the cash register, checks the total amount on the carbon copy, and rings it up. She overcharges him seventy cents. This is not the first time she's done it, so Angel suspects her error is intentional. What bothers him is that they never make mistakes in his favor. He points out the discrepancy and Eloisa smiles and corrects it.

He pays the $95.10 for his order, walks around the back where the merchandise is waiting on a pushcart, and begins to check the number of boxes. At the end of the count, he finds that there are four boxes of Popsicles missing.

As soon as the Mexican boy comes out of the freezer dressed in a thick winter jacket, Angel shows him his copy of the purchase order. The boy goes back in and brings out the rest of the Popsicles.

The boy doesn't say anything, doesn't apologize. While Angel checks the rest of the merchandise, Bebo comes over and says hello.

"You should hire extra help," Angel suggests.

"We do all right," Bebo speaks in a low voice.

"This is the third mistake your wife makes on my order this week."

"I'll go inside and spank her," he says and smiles.

Bebo calls the Mexican boy over and asks him to bring Angel a box of the new Fudge Bombs that have just come in.

The Mexican boy looks *mojado*, meaning an illegal immigrant, and is probably working for rock-bottom wages.

Bebo, while Angel waits, tells him about an accident.

"It happened about a week ago," Bebo says.

"In my area?" Angel asks.

"A car ran over a kid. He didn't die, but he's still in a coma."

Angel tries to think where he was that day, in what part of his zone. Lilián might remember.

"There was a police report," Bebo continues. "The parents are suing some of the ice cream trucks."

"No shit," Angel says. "Why do we get the blame?"

Bebo smells of cardboard and sweat. The Mexican boy steps out of the freezer, smoke rising from his moppy-looking hair, with the box of ice cream. He gives it to Angel.

"On the house. Try it out. You know how it is, Angel," the proprietor says, "the insurance companies can blame the trucks for just being in the area. For baiting the kids out of their houses."

"Insurance companies can go fuck themselves."

"You have a lawyer, don't you?"

Angel remembers the trouble Domingo kept him out of in Santiago. He's always been grateful to Domingo. "I'll get one when I need one."

"Maybe you won't get called in," Bebo says and walks back to the office.

Angel carts what he bought back to the truck, carries it inside, and places the boxes neatly in the freezers. If the kid's parents want to they can sue all the ice cream trucks working Angel's area. They can get witnesses to say that Superstar was in the area the day of the accident.

July, 1958

Mama Concha:

Lucinda has been doing night-watch guard duty since she got here. Some of the men have made bets that she'll fall asleep and that we'll find her sleeping before dawn. Not the case. And part of why this hasn't happened is because I've been staying up with her.

Yes, she has made an impression, deep and devastating on me.

We don't get to talk much during the day when the troops are moving through the jungle. Night is our chance. We seem to have a lot in common, mostly reasons why we

117

decided to change the mundaneness of our lives and join the revolution.

Her hair is short now, cropped evenly at the front and back. Whenever there is a full moon, like tonight's, you can see the whiteness of her neck. Her arms are tanned, caramel color.

"Lucinda," I call out in order not to sneak up on her and startle her. For all I know she might pull the trigger.

"I'm over here," she says in that soft, scratchy whisper I like so much.

She's sitting on the fallen trunk of a tree, holding her rifle on her lap. The boots she is wearing are big, awkward-looking like mine.

"Can't sleep, eh?" she says.

"The only time I'm able to sleep is when it rains," I say.

The night can't get any hotter and muggier, the humidity becomes a warm breath that seems to follow us everywhere. Mosquitoes swarm about unseen, biting like crazy.

I sit next to her on the trunk.

"Want a cigarette?" she says and reaches into her shirt pocket.

"I didn't know you smoked," I say.

"Only when I find myself alone."

"You're not alone now."

She looks at me and smiles, then she asks me all about being a medic.

"Lobo thought that it would be the thing for me to do. I was going to study pharmacy at the university."

"I like Lobo," she says and lights a cigarette.

"I guess you got to know him real well," I say.

Suddenly she looks cross, upset at what I've just said. "What are you insinuating?"

"I'm not—nothing."

"You think I fucked him, don't you?"

"I don't think anything."

There is a great silence between us before she speaks again. "He reminds me of an uncle who used to come visit my mother every morning. He'd sit on this worn-out rocking chair and drink coffee and chainsmoke. He's dead now. Everybody's dead."

The smoke from her cigarette is invisible in the dark, but I can smell it, what little of it she exhales.

"Lobo's confident that we will win," I say.

"I don't doubt it. Do you?"

I shake my head.

She tells me that she's been getting the shivers every night. "It's strange," she says.

I reach over and feel her forehead.

"It's not fever," she says.

The skin on her forehead feels smooth, a little moist but that's normal. "I don't know what it could be," I say and stand to go.

"Where are you going?"

"It's going to be daylight soon and I don't want anybody to—"

She gets the shakes. A violent trembling as if somebody had her strung up like a puppet and kept yanking on the strings. She falls off the trunk and hits her head against the ground.

Immediately I jump on top of her and try to keep her from hurting herself. I never thought she'd be this strong, but twice she throws me off. When I realize that what she's going through is an epileptic attack, I tear the front of my shirt and put it across her mouth to keep her from gagging on her own tongue. She's kicking and flapping her arms wildly now. Her fist finds my face and lands on the bridge of my nose. The bone breaks.

I pin her to the ground with my hands and knees, being able to keep her steady, feeling her upper torso sliding.

The attack leaves her and she goes limp as though she has died. She's still biting on my shirt. I pick her up and carry her back to Lobo's tent. I don't have to wake him up.

"What happened?" he says, lighting a candle because it's dark inside the tent.

"She's had an epileptic attack," I say and put her down on the ground.

He kneels next to me and for the first time I see a

119

puzzled look on his face. "Will she be all right?" He is looking at my nose.

I confess I don't know. "It all depends on whether she's just had a petit or grand mal."

"You stay with her," he says and stands.

"What do you mean?"

"Stay and look after her," he says. "I'm leading the troops to Santiago. Keep the tent. As soon as she recovers, you can catch up. Meet us. You know the way."

"Couldn't we take her down into town and leave her?"

"They'll find her and arrest her," he says. "Or worse."

Lucinda comes to, her eyelids open and close slowly, still a little groggy. She lifts her arm and tries to touch my face. I turn to keep her fingers from my nose. It's hurting now.

"Do as I say," Lobo says.

He walks out of the tent and I can hear him getting the men up and moving.

"Hugo," she says.

"Sssh, rest, okay," I tell her, caressing her forehead. "How are you feeling?"

She doesn't say anything. Instead she seems to pay attention to the commotion outside the tent.

"They're moving on," I say.

"Let's go . . . ," she says and closes her eyes.

I leave the tent and go outside and watch the men start to move out. Before heading out, Lobo approaches and tells me to join them in the cane fields outside the city limits in Santiago.

We stay behind the whole morning and part of the afternoon, then Lucinda gets out of the tent. She is holding her rifle. Looks ready, as though nothing had happened to her. She smiles when she sees me sitting under a tree right in front of the tent.

"You need a doctor," I tell her.

"He'll have to wait," she says, "until we get to the city."
Then she asks what happened to my nose.

I tell her about the attack and how she hit me.

"Pretty good hit," she says, studying my face.

I laugh, then tell her she's ready to get in the ring with Dempsey. She doesn't know who Dempsey is, so I tell her he was one of the best heavyweight gringo boxers.

She comes over and puts her hand under my chin and lifts my face to have a better look at my eye. "I'm sorry," she says.

Right then and there I kiss her. I couldn't wait anymore. Though I expected her to move away, knowing how feisty she can be, she doesn't. Instead she holds my face and kisses me back with a vengeance, her tongue turning in my mouth.

"We are all alone," she says, then stands up and takes off her pants.

Oh, Mother, I wish I could tell you what happened next, but I must respect you.

Lucinda and I spend the rest of the day together. Before night comes, I go out and scout the area and find a couple of roots, bring them back and boil them. After we eat, we fall asleep like babies until the morning.

All this time I keep thinking about how happy I am. Sure there's struggle and hardship involved, but there's also a bond, a great feeling of belonging and camaraderie.

She helps me take the tent down, pack it, then we move on. What I figure is that we are only a day or so behind Lobo. By tomorrow we should be upon them, ready to rejoin the effort and attack Santiago together.

Muchos Abrazos,
Hugo

PART III

Book of Departures

ANGEL / He drives the truck looking out of the windshield at the houses across the street. They are in desperate need of paint and repair. Their lawns are dry, patches of weeds growing everywhere. Driving around, he waits for kids to signal or shout to stop while he combs the streets at a slow pace, 15 mph, slow enough to give everyone a chance to hear the music on the loudspeaker. "Raindrops Keep Falling On My Head" sounds scratched.

The music plays over and over but he doesn't turn the volume down even though he knows the static in the speakers hurts the retirees in this part of the city. The louder the music, the more people will hear it and the more he'll sell.

He checks the mirrors now. A CAUTION CHILDREN sign has been stenciled in fluorescent-red letters on the dashboard. This is the most important rule about selling ice cream: Always check all the mirrors before pulling away from the curb.

Be always on the lookout for babies. He has taught himself this for all the years he has been selling. If he were to run somebody over, a little one still in diapers, he might as well go bankrupt.

In a vacant lot at the end of the street, the oil pumps rise and fall like iron rocking horses, sucking oil out of the dry ground rapidly with the creaking sounds of iron biting iron.

The blue change box by his knee remains half filled with overlapping coins. He hates to admit he loves the coins' silveriness, the contrast the ridgy copper edges makes against the bas-relief faces and backs. Presidents in profile. They'll never put President Carter on a coin. God knows the man doesn't know what else can go wrong with his presidency: the Iranian hostage crisis, his big-

125

mouth, fat brother Billy, and a giant killer rabbit.

A glance up at the rearview mirror reveals the inside of the truck: a bona-fide example of neatness and cleanliness. There isn't a flake of paint peeling or rust spots anywhere. No trace of melted ice cream on top of the chrome-plated freezer lids. The bags of potato chips are stacked on the shelves domino style. According to Angel, appearance and cleanliness are important. Without them, he wouldn't be able to pass the city's health department inspection; and if he doesn't pass inspection, he can't obtain the sales license, and without it. . . .

Trees and houses track the street on both sides. The trashcans in front of all the houses overflow with garbage. Another ice cream truck stands parked up the street, selling to a group of children. Children, Angel thinks, have no sense of loyalty. They buy from whichever truck goes by first.

He drives by and gets a glimpse of the man selling behind the window. White haired and skinny, the man grins up at Angel. Why can't this truck stay out of his zone, the area he's worked so hard to keep? Usually, if the truck doesn't have a permit sticker on the back, Angel calls the city inspectors.

One thing, if the economy of the country doesn't improve soon, these streets will be bumper-to-bumper ice cream trucks.

"Stop!" a kid screams, slamming the screen door of his house open. He runs to the grass next to the sidewalk.

Angel thinks of all the questions he has learned to ask and answer in English: How are you? How much? What do you want? What else?

The kid's hand comes up over the edge of the window with a dollar bill forked between his fat little fingers.

"What do you want?" Angel says, putting his pipe on the window counter. The kid looks at it in awe.

"A Froze Toe," he says, jumping up and down, showing the white of his teeth behind a Kool-Aid–stained smile. He wets the corners of his mouth while exposing a dirt ring under his neck.

Angel reaches inside the freezer and takes out a bar with the picture of an orange foot with a blue bubble-gum ball on the big toe from among the cardboard ice cream boxes. The ice creams seem to smile with their red-orange-yellow-blue-green colors, each wrapped individually in paper.

See what else he wants, make sure they always leave the dollar. He gives the kid the ice cream, and the kid smiles. "What else?" Angel says.

The kid shrugs his shoulders, then shakes his head biting the wrapper off and spitting it out. The piece of paper falls onto the grass. He hands the kid his change.

"Pick that up, will you?"

The kid ignores him.

Angel sits behind the steering wheel and drives away from the curb. The day might improve after all. Up ahead a group of kids jump and skip around a short man. The smallest of the kids hangs from the man's thighs.

The mans signals Angel to halt. When he stops, the man walks up to the window, the children screaming excitedly all around him.

"I want this one, Daddy," one of the girls says.

"This one!" a boy shouts.

The smallest kid jumps, pointing his finger at the case display of all the toys and candies.

"No, José," the man responds, taking the kid by the arm, "no candy."

The kid turns to look up at his father, not fully understanding, and then starts to pout.

"Give me six Popsicles," the man says.

"I don't want no Pop—"

"Popsicles or nothing. I don't have the money to buy you what you want. Be quiet!"

"A Blue Ghost. I want a Blue Ghost."

"I said no."

The smallest kid begins to cry.

"Be quiet, José, or I'm not gonna buy you nothing. I'm gonna tell the man to go away."

Angel places the six Popsicles on top of the counter. Counts them. Six. Twenty-five cents each, that's a dollar fifty. "Dollar fifty," Angel tells the man.

The skin around the man's eyes is of a darker brown than that of his cheeks and nose. His eyebrows curl upward, as tough-looking as thin wires. The man digs deep inside his pockets and produces two wrinkled green balls with lint sticking to them. He throws them like dice on top of the counter, and the two dollar bills roll. Angel unfolds the bills, smooths them out, and goes to the front to get change from the change box. He drops the two coins into the man's hands.

Angel thanks the man out of the front window.

The man gives each kid a Popsicle, then he walks away with his hands in his pockets. José takes his, holds on to it as though it is something precious, but he's still sobbing. He follows his father back to the house.

The bastard doesn't want to spend his beer money, Angel thinks, moving onward.

After this he has no more customers for quite a while. He begins to count the passing of time by how many ice creams he sells. August is the best month. Sales skyrocket then. It is during the hot days in August that he comes close to setting new sales records. Last August, he remembers, he sold close to four hundred dollars one day.

Wondering how much money there is in the box by now, he spots a customer waiting up ahead. "Make the kill fast," he says.

A barefoot woman holding a little girl to her breast comes to the window. She has dirty fingernails, very short and jagged, as if she bit them all the time.

"Give me four ice cream sandwiches," she says.

"Vanilla or Neapolitan?" Angel asks. Pronouncing *vanilla* bothers him because he always says it *vahneeya*.

"Vanilla," she says.

He takes the four ice cream sandwiches out of the right freezer and puts them next to the young woman's blue-veined hands. "Two dollars," he says.

She takes the money out of her yellow-stained brassiere and hands it to him, then walks away. Yellow blisters cover the back of her heels.

He turns to the sound of distant music on a loud-speaker—coming from the next block?—Angel moves on.

The truck is working well today. On the same street, another kid stops him. Angel pulls over to the curb under the shade of a tree. The kid holds his tongue out. His eyes seem to be too small for his big face. Big head; small, frail body.

"Where is your money?" Angel asks.

The kid claps his small hands quickly, walks over to the truck, and hangs from the edge of the window.

"No, no," Angel says. "Get away from there!"

"Wan icleam," the kid says.

"You'll fall and hurt yourself. Come on."

"Wanicleam! Wanicleam! Wanicleam!"

He tries to unstick the kid's red fingers from the metal edge of the window, but the kid refuses to let go. If Angel removes one hand, then the kid hangs on with the other.

For a moment Angel believes that the kid's cutting his little fingers while trying to reach for a penny candy.

"Don't take," Angel says. "I give it to you, okay? Just let go."

The kid doesn't let go.

Angel climbs out of the truck, comes around to the window and the kid, pulls him away from the truck to the sidewalk and sits the kid down on the cement. He drops a couple of candies on the kid's lap.

Back in the ice cream truck, Angel pulls away. He sees the kid grow smaller and smaller and then disappear as the truck turns the corner.

Close call, Angel thinks. Can't give his merchandise away. If he does, there's no profit to be made.

The sun sets slowly, and, descending, it spreads Popsicle orange on the sky. Darkness creeps as slowly on the other side of the city. The temperature gauge reads hot; time to go home.

On the radio he hears more news about the embassy. Castro supporters are planning a big demonstration against the anti-social elements seeking asylum in the Peruvian Embassy. Things can only get worse, Angel thinks, driving home, before they can get better.

HUGO / In the dream I am back at La Cabaña, the pisslike smell of mildew is too pungent on the lime walls. The scratched graffiti on the walls blur. Sweat covers my face and arms and my whole body. The heat feels as though everything around the cell has been set on fire. The cell is nothing more than a cubicle with a hole in the ground for a toilet and a rusty bucket for a sink.

The bunk bed has been stripped bare. No pillows or sheets or mosquito net, nothing. The sound of water dripping echoes between the thick walls. A dizzy fly flies around looking for a way to get out. Now everything grows quiet. A great stillness. I think I can hear the blood rushing through my veins, in and out of my heart. Pump!

Voices rise above the rattling of the wall fans. Two guards dressed in khaki-blue walk by dragging a plastic body bag behind them. A trail of blood is left on the broken bricks of the narrow corridors. The sound of someone digging a grave grows louder and louder. Pig squeals echo and succumb to the silence. A shovel scrapes the dirt and rocks and pebbles.

A harsh rain pounding on the iron grating of the roof awakens me. I realize I'm still at the embassy. People are huddled in tight groups. When I try to move I find that the space around me has been taken. To my right sits a man who is looking at me gravely, and to my left there is a small boy who has fallen asleep under my arm. The boy's breathing is heavy, his hair fallen over his small eyes. His shirt is torn at the pockets.

"Bad dreams," the man says and smiles. His lips are pale, a bloodless pink.

"How long has it been raining?" I ask, trying to move my legs which have fallen asleep.

"Just started."

I try to move without waking the little boy up. His drool has soaked my shirt sleeve. The tiny humps of endless mosquito bites stand out on his thin arms. They crucified him last night. I look around for the boys' parents, but next to the boy is an old man and a body covered by a sheet of plastic.

Blood circulates through my legs for I can feel the prickling sensations. The boy stirs while I try to move him but he doesn't wake up. I lean him against the wall of the mansion.

"There's no place to go," the man next to me says.

In a nearby tree two young men sit on a thick branch with their legs dangling. They are lucky the rain has not touched them. Everybody on the ground is drenched.

The rain increases to a quick downpour, then lets up and slowly ceases. I'll find Lucinda wherever she is, I think, and move away from the wall, inching toward the front gate.

There are bodies everywhere. Wet and muddy and sprinkled with broken leaves and grass and twigs. They stir slowly. They writhe like snakes. Toward the front gate a woman has removed her blouse to cover her infant.

Outside a caravan of troop carriers arrives and the trucks park on the other side of the street. Soldiers in riot gear climb out and surround the embassy grounds. Down the line, every fifth man or so, stands a soldier with a semiautomatic AK-47.

People hear the commotion and begin to stand up and walk closer to the fence.

A voice through a loudspeaker says, "Form a single file behind the gate! Only groups of ten will be allowed to board the trucks!"

This is when the crowd stirs and a crickety murmur starts throughout the embassy grounds, people asking questions.

I walk away from the fence. In groups of ten, I repeat to myself, it's going to take a hell of a long time to empty this place.

As I move inward, people keep heading toward the gate. A huge clot has formed there. A multitude of heads swaying and bobbing. I stare at everybody and everybody stares back as though I were some kind of madman. It surprises me how well I blend in. Everybody looks haggard and worn out, filthy and tired.

"Make room, people!" the voice says in the distance.

On the other side of the building two men are arguing over a cigarette butt. For a moment there I think they are going to tear each other's eyes out, but another man intervenes. No doubt, this is madness at its best. I bump into people eager to leave.

If my Lucinda's here, I'll find her. "Lucinda!" I shout over the crowd.

I circle the grounds twice without success; but I keep trying for something tells me I'm going to find her. I step in a puddle and water gets in my shoes. My toes swim in mud.

No use. She's not here. She could have been brought here or taken directly to Mariel. It's only a matter of time before I make it there. At the rate they are emptying this place . . .

A convoy of trucks leaves full and more drive up and park and the process begins all over. Where do they get the trucks from? I've never seen so many of them. All Soviet-made.

The gray sky over Havana cracks and the sun comes through with a vengeance. It forces people to squint or use their hands as visors.

By noon a crowd of government supporters gathers outside the embassy for a rally. Once again they begin to shout obscenities and throw things. More crowd-control personnel arrive and take their places across the street. They make sure nobody steps out or gets near any of the trucks. People board the trucks panic-stricken.

Another line is formed and now there are people being processed to the left and to the right. More trucks come.

I keep waiting and waiting until I realize that if I'm to spot Lucinda I can probably do so by the gate. Within the crowd now, I get pushed and shoved closer and closer to the gate entrance. I'm too close. I try to push my way back toward the mansion, but it's too late. I'm caught in the middle and going with the flow.

All that's really going on is this: A lieutenant asks the people in line to keep quiet and board the trucks. Destination unknown, but rumor has it the trucks are going to the port of Mariel.

Lucinda will be there.

I get pushed in line and soon enough I'm at the gate facing the lieutenant and a dog-faced soldier with a machine gun.

The lieutenant eyes me slowly. He must not like my smile, I assume, and smile some more. I'm taking my chances, I know, but he can never guess who I am in a million years.

He counts ten more people in front of me and lets them go toward the truck.

The crowds on the other side of the street with banners boo and scream the following: *"Viva Fidel! Viva La Revolución! Escoria, escoria pa fuera!"* *Escoria* means filth. Filth get out.

My turn comes up and I get to board the truck. There are ten people in the truck already and after I climb in nine more follow, then ten more. There are thirty total.

The heat is intense. When five more people are pushed in, someone complains about not being able to breathe. I'm pushed and crowded toward the back, my head pressed against the canvas. It is as though I were sitting inside a tunnel. Of the outside there is little that can be seen.

When the truck starts I bang my head against the metal rib of the cover. Nobody's talking except to complain about not having enough room. This reminds me of Cochiquero and I wonder if it's a lie that they are taking us to Mariel and not to a camp to exterminate us, the way the Germans got rid of the Jews.

DIEGO / Nestor calls during practice. You are rearranging the new song list and drumming on two ice cream boxes you brought inside the house from the garage. He wants you to meet him this afternoon at the Redondo Beach Pier. Important information he just found out about today, he says and hangs up.

Leaving you on the edge like this is part of Nestor's hurried, if-you-want-me-come-see-me style. Maybe you can score some coke, that's the least he can do for making you drive such a long way.

Once again the house is empty. By the time you woke up everybody was gone. This morning you feel rested, clear-minded, and ready to start afresh. The good thing about living here in Los Angeles is, if you don't like the way the events in your life are turning out, stick around and they'll probably change.

After a quick shower you get dressed and drive out to meet Nestor. The Long Beach Freeway leads to 91 West, which, starting with the on-ramp, is congested with traffic. There has been an accident. Quickly, all the other cars close in, blocking the lanes. Squeeze into the middle lane from where the commotion up ahead becomes visible. The tow truck's flashing lights, the police cars, and a helicopter circling overhead.

The traffic moves slowly; it is being funneled right by a state trooper. The ambulance arrives, the injured are carted into it, and driven away to a nearby hospital. People like bloodshed, otherwise why would they stop to look? Carnage on the freeways of L.A. is as common as smog. The state trooper signals to go.

You pass as the tow truck cranes the smashed car up on its rear tires. Glass breaks. Now the traffic moves at a normal speed and in no time you arrive at the beach where the air is thick and salty and a cool, strong breeze sweeps inland from the expanse of the ocean. The ocean, so blue, looks like a reflection of the sky.

The beach seems like a completely different world. No smog, but lots of graffiti. At a corner stand a group of surfers holding their boards under their arms as though they were as light as loaves of bread. They wait for the light to change so they can cross the street.

The pier stretches out in the distance like a sea serpent, a giant millipede with black pilings for legs. You hope there'll be parking space available, as you drive under the six-foot clearance sign of the lot. This is a new parking lot they built. On the third level there is a spot. Third level, green color code, you make a mental note as you park, climb out, and put the top up.

It's chilly in the shade, so you hurry to get to the boardwalk and under the sun. On the boardwalk people move slowly, laid back, as though worry and time are completely alien to them. A woman wearing a yellow scarf on her head walks her two poodles. The ash-colored one stops, squats, and moves on. The woman takes a Kleenex out of her beachbag, picks up the turd and throws it into a garbage can. With another Kleenex she wipes the dog, then she gets a contented look on her face.

Groups of fisherman move up and down the pier where apparently the fish aren't biting. Frustration is written all over their bloodshot eyes, induced by either beer or weariness. Tourist shops, where everything from intricate kites to breast-shaped coffee mugs are sold, skirt the entrance. The smell of Kikkoman soy sauce and sautéed beef emerges from the oriental restaurants.

Nestor said to meet him by the entrance of El Torito, the Mexican restaurant you and V used to frequent. They serve great shrimp cocktails here. You stand by the stairs waiting when all of a sudden a drop of something cold lands on your head. One look up and the culprit reveals himself. Nestor stands behind the veranda of the terrace, smiling, ice cube in hand.

"Come on up here, bro," he says and removes his sunglasses.

You walk up the spiral wooden stairs and meet him under the canvas awning from which the painted face of a little bull hangs. He shakes your hand as though he hasn't seen you in years.

"Scared me there for a minute," you say. "I thought a seagull—"

Nestor laughs and leads the way inside to the chiaroscuro of the lobby. He has reserved a table by the window overlooking the beach.

"Is it romantic enough for you?" he says and sits on the side from which he can see the people enter and leave.

"Don't tell me," you say. "I'm going to find an engagement ring inside an oyster."

"Did you eat lunch?"

"No, I'm starving."

A pretty, sun-bleached-haired waitress comes over and asks, "What would the gentlemen prefer to drink?" Nestor, in a jovial tone of voice, says, *"Sí, por favor, una cerveza bien fría."* Then, *"Tu eres una gringa muy linda."*

"Now in English," she says and smiles.

"I thought all the waitresses here spoke Spanish?" Nestor says.

The waitress stands at ease. She is wearing a necklace with a big emerald—too big to be real—which matches the color of her eyes.

"A G and T please," you say and open the cloth napkin over your lap.

"A Carta Blanca for me," Nestor says.

"We don't have Carta Blanca," the waitress says. "Just Corona and Dos Equis."

He opts for Corona.

The restaurant is rather empty for this time of the afternoon so the waiters and waitresses stand around chatting with each other, smoking. Once in a while a cook sticks his head out of the swinging doors for a breath of fresh air.

The waitress brings the drinks over and sets them away from Nestor's hands. She pours the beer into the frosted glass and puts the bottle on top of a napkin. The G and T is a little on the thin side, not enough gin in it.

Nestor reaches over and turns her tag down so he can read it. "Ginger," he says, "just like the bread."

"The special of the day," the waitress says, "is chicken fajitas."

"Chicken fajitas," Nestor says, turning the rings on his hands upside down. An old habit. "What do you think about that, Diego?"

"That sounds good," you say and take a long sip from the drink. Then, "But I'm in the mood for a shrimp cocktail."

"Jumbo or regular?"

"The bigger the better."

Nestor says, "We'll have the fajitas."

The waitress writes the order down on her pad and goes away. Nestor drinks his glass of beer and pours in the rest. "God," he says, "this beer's heaven."

For somebody who gets so little sleeep, Nestor looks great. His black eyes are deepset and their whites clear. Not one hair longer than the other on his mustache. Nestor is the kind of guy who, if he thought a scar would improve his looks, he'd be the first to start a barroom brawl.

"Big C called me today," he says and looks away into the distance. The surfers, paddling out, away from the pilings, wait for a wave and jump up on their boards.

Big C is what Nestor calls don Carlos.

"He found out about me dealing at the club," he continues.

"Shit," you say. A bed of kelp floats on the surface of the water. "What does he want you to do?"

"I don't know," he says. "He's giving me a choice. Quit dealing or quit work."

"Quit dealing," you say and suck the liquor from among the ice cubes at the bottom of the tall glass.

"Come on, bro, it's not that easy."

"He's going to fire you."

"I knew I could count on you. Boy, you're a ton of help. A regular Dear Abby."

"There's not much I can do, you know."

Nestor looks you straight in the eyes. He smiles and says, "Why do you think I called this meeting?"

"Let me guess, you cherish our friendship?"

"Close enough," he says. "I need you to put in a good word for me. Just an 'Isn't Nestor a great worker? It's because of him that people come to the club.' Something like that . . . you know."

"I thought people came to the club because of the music."

"Precisely," he says. "That's why he'll listen to you. Look, I need some time. I just can't quit dealing right now. You know how the business works. It's easy to get in; hard to get out. All I need is a little more time. Once I get rid of some debts—"

The waitress returns with the cocktails.

"Could we have another round, please," Nestor says.

She collects the empty bottle and glass and once again leaves.

"How are things working out with Maruchi?" he asks.

"Pretty good," you say. Nestor likes details, but you don't feel like revealing personal things.

"I knew you two would hit it off." He takes his fork and pinches a shrimp from the platter, dips it in the sauce, and eats it whole.

"Don Carlos wants me to go with him to Miami," you say and pour extra ketchup and Tabasco in the sauce. Some pepper, salt, and lemon. . . .

"Big C mentioned something like that."

"Yes, he wanted you to stay and help his wife run the club while he's gone."

"I fucked up," Nestor says.

"How did he find out?"

"Somebody must have known and snitched on me."

The rest of the food and drinks arrive. About time, you think, the Tabasco is burning your tongue.

"Careful," the waitress says. "The plates are hot."

"Thanks," Nestor says, turning to see her walk back to the bar. "She's probably a sweet girl. Most gringas are sweet."

You tell Nestor about the slashed tire and he says he doesn't know how it could have happened unless . . . "You ought to know something, Diego," he says, putting the fork down. "I called this meeting for a reason."

"What reason's that, bro?" Nestor, from the way he cuts his chicken fajitas into tiny bits, is a meticulous son of a bitch. He takes the napkin and wipes the corners of his mouth, then folds it neatly under his plate.

"Your ex-best friend Danny, better known as Flaco, has run off with a certain V, better known as Mrs. Falcón."

"Bullshit," you say. "Who told you that crap?"

"Somebody broke into your apartment, right? Took all her furniture, right?"

"Get to the point, Nestor," you say and spear another piece of chicken.

"Let's start at the beginning," Nestor says. "Make the connections as I go along. First, V leaves you, right? Second, Danny doesn't show up to play. Third—this one's the killer—Flaco,

Pelican, and one of his friends who valets at another club, go to your apartment and move her furniture out. Which adds up to one thing."

"I want to know how you found all this out?"

"I hate to be a bastard about these things, but—"

"All right, all right, I'll talk to don Carlos, just tell me."

"Forget it, all right? Just take my word for it."

You finish your drink slowly to let the news sink in. Never in a million years would you have guessed it. No wonder Fe, Danny's mother, sounded so jittery over the phone.

"That's all I know, bro," he says.

Did Pilar know, you wonder.

A group of kids play with a Frisbee on the beach. They have a dog with them. Every time the Frisbee goes in the water, the dog jumps in and fetches it.

"Hey," you say, "don't worry about don Carlos. I'll talk to him."

"Thanks, bro. Sorry I had to be the one to break the bad news."

Nestor calls the waitress. She comes and asks if everything was all right.

"Everything was excellent," Nestor tells her and smiles. He wants the check.

When she brings the check, he takes it, looks at it for a while as though he were adding up the figures, then puts it down. "This one's on me," he says to you.

He reaches for his wallet in his back pocket and takes a fifty-dollar bill out of it and puts it under the check on the tray.

After the waitress picks up the tray and he tells her to keep the change, he takes a little plastic bag out of his shirt pocket and slides it under your hand. "This might help," he says and winks.

Without looking at the bag you take it and put it away; then you finish off your drink, wipe your hands, and stand up to leave.

"Catch you later at the club."

"Hey, Diego?" he says.

"What?"

"Take it easy, okay? Don't lose your head." He puts his hand on your shoulder.

As you pass by the waitresses' station, she wishes you a nice day and smiles. Outside you check your front pocket and feel the shape of the bag. A couple of grams? This might not be enough for what needs to be done.

ESTEBAN / Not all chameleons seek the shade, Esteban thinks as he, Domingo, and Lilián drive to the cemetery. By this he means that all his life he has taken risks and he is proud of the fact. Chances spice things up. He took a big one the day he borrowed the money to start the pharmacy, another when he helped Angel start the cafeteria on José Martí Street, and an even riskier one when he decided that it was time for the family to leave the country. The way he figures it is, if he wouldn't have done the right thing at the right time, who knows? By then Hugo had been tried and sentenced to prison for treason. *Treason,* what the hell do they know about treason?

On the radio José Luis Rodriguez, the Venezuelan Valentino whom Lilián is enamored of, sings a new song.

On the way Lilián and Domingo chat about the ice cream business. So far, according to her, it's been a good year. To his daughter a good year means lots and lots of money. She's become greedy, partly because she's been married to Angel too long. All Angel knows how to do is work, work, work. No time for leisure or fun.

Sure, there is nothing wrong with working hard, but not all the time. Esteban worked hard, but he always knew when to have fun. He and Concha used to do so many things together whenever they got the chance, which was often. They'd go to the beach on cloudy days because she liked the way the ocean got rough and the waves would crash against the rocks and their spray would shoot upward. She had a little of a poet in her.

Concha liked to have as much fun as he did—and still does. Lilián is different, or, rather, has grown different. When she was younger she liked to go with her friends to catch the new movies that had just come out.

The cemetery lies at the end of the city limits, a wrought-iron fence under a marble arch at the entrance, a road outlined by eucalyptus trees and large tree ferns under which, in the shade,

Kaffir lilies and azaleas grow lusciously. What Esteban likes about this place is that it doesn't look anything like a cemetery. There are no tombstones, just marble slabs on the grass which make it easy for the gardener to mow the lawn. Practical and beautiful. Silence hangs in the air like the buds on the forget-me-nots.

Here crows stand out in all their blackness against the speckled flowers.

The caretaker's office is situated behind the fountain which contains goldfish and water lilies. It is a wood house with a brick chimney and metal awnings rusty at the edges and red tiles on the roof in which the insides of sparrows' nests hang like bushy beards.

Lilián parks in the visitors parking lot. She is wearing a pair of sunglasses more appropriate for Angel. Esteban observes how her face retains an expressionless quality. But he knows that his daughter's silence can mean only one thing: introspection. She doesn't like cemeteries, this much he can tell from the way she has always approached Concha's grave. A bit aloof and distracted by other things in her mind. What, he doesn't know. Diego's problems perhaps.

Domingo's also extremely quiet. Esteban wonders what his friend must be thinking. No, he knows exactly what Domingo is thinking, that, if he can help it, he doesn't want to die and be buried anywhere, no matter if the place is as peaceful and beautiful as this one. Death's finality doesn't scare Esteban, just worries him enough to motivate him into living the best way he possibly can.

"Why don't you go to the grave?" he says to Lilián.

"How long is it going to take?" she says.

"I'll go with you, Lilián," Domingo adds, "if you don't mind the company."

"Not at all," she says. Then to Esteban, "Don't take long."

He looks on as his daughter and friend cut across the lawn and stop at the grave. At this time of the afternoon the trees cast shadows on this side of the chapel in the courtyard. A gravel path winds up through the lawn up to the front steps of the office. The sprinklers come on and in no time puddles of water and loose debris form in the rose and tulip beds.

He enters the office. Inside, the caretaker, a skinny Mexican man, greets him with a reserved smile, a smile more appropriate for a mortician.

"What can I do for you, Señor—" the man says. The man's desk plaque reads Héctor J. Quiñónes.

"Carranza," Esteban says, "Esteban Carranza."

The man gestures Esteban to have a seat on the cushion chair in front of the desk.

"I come to ask you a few questions concerning my wife." He sits down.

"Is she ill?"

Shifting his weight on the chair, Esteban says, "She's buried here."

"My mistake, I'm sorry," Héctor says. His clay-colored hands rest on the desk.

"She passed away four years ago."

"I understand."

The caretaker leans back in his chair and lights a cigarette. He lifts the pack from the surface of the desk pad to offer Esteban a smoke. Esteban refuses; he's got a cigar in his pocket. He couldn't smoke it in the car because cigar smoke bothers Lilián.

"What do you want to know?" Héctor says.

Esteban inquires about exhumation procedures, the litigation involved, and how quickly Concha's remains can be removed.

"Is she not happy? I mean, are you not happy having her here?" Héctor says and places the cigarette on the ashtray.

This throws Esteban off. Of course he's not happy having Concha here. She died. If it were up to him, he'd much rather have her alive.

"The family is moving to Miami, you see," he says and pauses to let the lie settle in his mind. "I plan to take her with us."

"I see, I see," Héctor says.

"I was hoping you'd be able to tell me what to do."

"Gladly, Señor Carranza."

"Call me Esteban."

"Well, in order for the body to be transported, that is moved, you have to file a petition with the coroner's office at City Hall. They'll issue you a court order. We can put the petition through for you, if you'd like."

"Wonderful."

"When were you thinking of moving?"

"Soon, soon. I hope, by Friday of this week."

"Friday," Héctor says and scratches his chin. "I'm afraid that's too short a time."

The man goes on to tell Esteban all the prerequisites. The coroner's permission, the court order, the necessary fees that have to be paid, coffin transport charges.

"How long will it take?"

"Depends, sometimes as long as six months."

Six months is too long. "There's no other way, eh? Like—"

Héctor gets an incredulous look on his face. Esteban thinks he has just insulted the man. He tries to explain that he is willing to pay something additional to speed up the process. Héctor grows more uncomfortable.

"I'm afraid there's only one way to go about this, Esteban, and that is in a legal manner, you understand?"

"I understand," Esteban says, but not really. All he wants is to take Concha with him to fulfill her wish to be buried back home.

The caretaker crushes his cigarette in the ashtray among the half-finished, twisted, broken cigarettes, then continues. "Would you like us to proceed?"

"There's no other way, is there?"

Héctor shakes his head and says, "No other."

"Then go ahead and put the petition through."

"Very well," Héctor says. "I'm going to give you my card in case you have more questions."

He opens the middle desk drawer and produces a card, reaches across the desk and drops it in front of Esteban. Esteban takes it, looks at the office hours, then slips it into his shirt pocket.

In less than fifteen minutes, Esteban answers all the questions necessary to complete the application. "This should get things rolling," Héctor says.

Esteban thanks the caretaker for his help.

"That's what I'm here for."

Esteban stands carefully, though his knee hasn't been bothering him, and walks to the door.

"Not many," Héctor says, "Señor Carranza, not many people

move and care to take their loved ones with them."

Esteban tells him that Concha goes wherever he goes. They had been married for forty-seven years.

"Something to be proud of. Marriage seldom lasts that long. Nowadays . . . I should know. I just lost my wife."

"I'm sorry."

"No, no, she didn't die," Héctor says and smiles. "She left me. Wants a divorce."

Esteban thanks Héctor one last time and leaves the office. Thinking about Diego and where couples go wrong, about the things Concha and he never did, he begins to walk toward the grave.

In one of the flower beds a snail struggles to get out of the water. He bends down, picks it up, and puts it down on dry earth, in the shade away from the roses. Everything has the right to live, he thinks.

Work, he thinks, that's the problem today. Young people don't have time for each other and, even more important, for themselves. They lead hurried lives. That's why he dislikes big cities like Los Angeles. Angel didn't want to stay in Miami—not many job opportunities there ten years ago.

Graveside, Lilián and Domingo are silent as though they are praying. The last time Esteban came was Concha's and his anniversary.

Old age, old age, he mutters, mother of a great whore. Maybe his is an absurd idea. What good might it do to keep his promise to her, the promise to take her with him if he ever went back to Cuba?

Domingo notices him and walks away from the grave. "How did it go?" he asks.

"There's no time to waste," Esteban says and stops in front of the marble plaque with Concha's name on it.

"It's going to take too long, isn't it?" Lilián says. The tip of her nose and cheeks have turned red under the sun.

"At least you tried," Domingo says.

Lilián leads the way back to the car.

In the car they fall silent. Lilián drives with caution. Domingo has his eyes closed because he says the sun's too strong.

Esteban is thinking of what needs to be done. He tells himself that the Esteban Carranza of the past, *the* Esteban Carranza everyone knew and depended on, is dead and will never be resurrected. Must he keep his promise to Concha?—He's obliged to.

ANGEL / A man approaches Angel on the street. Angel, who is now anxious to get home, is selling ice cream to an old woman who always orders the wrong thing and asks for credit.

The man stands behind the old woman waiting. He has shoulder-length white hair which gives his face a distinguished look. Eyes the color of light coffee. No doubt, Angel thinks, he is Mexican.

"Frooty Patooty," the woman says. "My lover likes the way that sounds."

"No credit today," Angel says to her.

The woman looks at her ice cream, turns it in her hand as though she were reading the list of ingredients.

"I'm sorry," Angel says, "but—"

"Let me help you, doña Alicia," the man says and drops a five-dollar bill on the counter, then to Angel, "Let me have a vanilla malt."

"Gracias," Alicia says.

Angel gets the ice cream out of the freezer and hands it to the man. Alicia walks away to her dilapidated house across the street.

The man stands in front of Angel now. With the wooden spoon he scoops out large gobs of vanilla and eats them.

"Anything else?" Angel asks.

"Let me ask you something," the man says. "How often do you sell in this area?"

"Oh, I don't know," Angel says. "I always stop here before I head home. I live around the corner."

"Were you in the vicinity March twenty-second, around two in the afternoon?"

Angel knows that what the man is trying to get at has something to do with the accident, about the child who got run over by a car. "I never sell in the area before this time." He checks his watch. "Five-fifteen, five-thirty."

"You have your sales license?"

"Who are you? A health-department inspector?"

"I'm sure you've heard about the accident."

"What accident?"

"A car put my nephew in the hospital."

"Sorry to hear that," Angel says.

"It's your fault," the man says.

"Wait a minute. What do you mean 'my fault'? I told you I wasn't in the area."

"Somebody was," the man says.

"It wasn't me."

"Oh, it doesn't matter. All I can say is that whoever was selling here that afternoon better get himself a damn good lawyer."

If there is one thing Angel hates it's to be threatened. He starts the truck and pulls away. Never, he thinks, has he ever been in this area before four o'clock in the afternoon. Lilián is a witness to that.

Another thing, he's not about to spend any money on a lawyer for legal advice. Things are getting rough for ice cream vendors. God knows there are enough problems, to make a living selling ice creams can't get any harder.

At home, Angel finds the house empty. There's a note from Lilián stuck to the refrigerator door. It says Esteban, Domingo, and she went to the cemetery. In the thermos he finds a squirt of cold coffee left. He drinks it, then picks up the change box and a newspaper and goes to the kitchen table to count and stack the change. Today's earnings.

On the table the new can of Sir Walter Raleigh tobacco sits by the portable television. Lilián has already unsealed and opened it. Angel gets his pipe out, fills its bowl with tobacco, and lights it.

All he has to do now is count the change, stack it, and wait for Lilián to get home so he can get something in his stomach.

He turns the television on. On the screen they show a very crowded port in Key West. Boats everywhere. Esteban better move fast, Angel thinks. Otherwise he's going to have a hard time trying to find Hugo.

HUGO / Darkness falls on the road. Nobody inside the truck talks, but I can tell people are restless because they keep moving. We don't know where we are being taken. Mariel Port is only a guess. The heat inside has become intense. No way to pull the canvas up from the frame to let the breeze in.

I sit in the corner, knees close together with my arms around them to keep them in. Every time the truck goes over a bump I can feel it on my back. The wheels hum underneath the floorboards.

My father must be doing something, he must be. I trust him. The sun rises in the east and sets in the . . . three hours difference. What time is it here? There?

Questions keep coming like a steady cadence, a rhythm being maintained by invisible drums . . .

"Does anybody know where we are going?" somebody asks in the dark.

I can see your eyes staring, a firefly luminescence.

"Relax," a man answers. "We should be getting to the port soon."

A groan. A sneeze. Someone keeps clearing his throat. Nervousness causes all this. I stay calm, trying to concentrate on keeping my mind blank. No thought should invade my . . .

The stories start flowing now. No reason why, just restlessness. A man is telling one. He worked at La Faraya Restaurant when two G-2s, secret police, came and arrested him. The man did not want to leave. They forced him to come along. He didn't know where he was being taken.

The dark is like a ghost, all voice and no body.

"Later," the man continues, "I find out from a friend that my wife was behind it all. The bitch cheated on me. We were having problems, you know, what man and woman don't? . . ."

I must find you woman of my soul, my heart, my essence . . . I must find . . . where could you be?

" . . . the kids wanted to come and she didn't let them. I don't want to leave them here. I don't, Christ."

The road, invisible, narrow, winding, never-ending road that leads somewhere yet to be seen. The dark swallows everything. It works like a vacuum and sucks despair into itself and voices and lost dreams, and spits back agony and frustration. The question remains: where to?

* * *

ESTEBAN / "Can you drive?" Esteban asks Domingo soon after dinner, after he had excused himself and gone to the garage to get something and put it in the trunk of the Monte Carlo. Diego hasn't been home all day, otherwise . . . Domingo doesn't say anything at first, first he finishes what's left of his coffee and smiles.

"Of course I can drive," says his friend.

Lilián is talking to Angel in the kitchen about an accident and a lawsuit. They both appear distracted.

"I say we go buy a couple of six packs and sit outside on the patio for a while," Esteban says.

"Drink this late."

"Time has nothing to do with it."

"Whose car were you planning to use?"

"The Monte Carlo. Diego is probably at the club by now."

Domingo takes a toothpick from the dispenser on the center of the table. He starts to pick his teeth. Once in a while he looks at the tip of the pick carefully as though to find something there.

"Where are we going?" Domingo wants to know.

"The store, get some beer and a couple of cigars," Esteban says. "Listen, when Lilián asks you why we need to use her car, you agree with me, okay? I'm going to tell her we need the car to go talk to Ruth, all right?"

Domingo understands.

"Lili," Esteban calls.

Lilián interrupts her conversation with Angel and comes over. She looks at Domingo and, from the wry smile on his face, it is obvious Domingo is embarrassed.

"Lend us the car," Esteban says.

"Are you driving?"

"No, Domingo."

She knows Esteban hasn't driven in years and with his knee the way it is . . .

"Humm," she says. "I don't know. Where are you going?"

Esteban tells her the plan about going to see Ruth.

"This late? Doesn't she work late?"

This is where Domingo should step in, Esteban thinks. "She's off today, isn't she?" he says and looks at his friend.

"Yes, off. To tonight. She is," Domingo says.

147

"Leave it for tomorrow," she says, "and I'll take you."

It's not working, damnit. Esteban decides to do something else.

"The food was excellent, Lilián," Domingo says.

Lilián thanks him and takes the plates from the table to the kitchen sink. Angel has left the kitchen, so she starts to do the dishes.

Esteban lights a cigarette and smokes it slowly, savoring every drag. "How about a game of chess?" he asks his friend.

Domingo gets this I'm-not-in-the-mood look on his face. "What are you going to do about Concha, Esté?"

Esteban crushes his cigarette out on the ashtray, stands up, and leaves the dining room. He goes to the hall closet and gets the chess game from the top shelf. The box is so old and used that a couple of pieces slide out of it and fall on the floor. He knows he can't bend over, so he leaves the pieces strewn on the carpet. They won't need them for the game they're about to play.

Back in the dining room, he puts the game on the table, opens the board, and starts setting the pieces in position. Domingo looks at him for the longest time. Esteban glances over at Lilián who's almost finished with the dishes.

"What happened to the rest of the pieces?" Domingo says.

Esteban makes a gesture to Domingo to be quiet. "They are all here," Esteban says.

Lilián doesn't like games, so she usually leaves the kitchen which is what Esteban wants. Domingo is dumbfounded; he doesn't have the slightest ides what's going on. He'll get it, Esteban thinks, he'll know what this is all about soon.

They start to play and Lilián does leave the kitchen. The only person he has to worry about now is Angel. He's bound to come back to the table to fill out merchandise orders for tomorrow.

After a while Esteban stands and moves to the kitchen sink. In one of the cabinet drawers he finds a spare set of car keys which he picks up slowly so they don't jingle. They have to move fast now.

"Let's go, hurry," he tells Domingo.

Domingo follows Esteban outside to where the car is parked. He opens both doors, climbs in, and slides the key in the ignition. Domingo sits on the driver's side and starts the car. He repositions the rearview mirror, the side mirror, puts on his seatbelt, stares at the dashboard.

"Let's go," Esteban says. "What are you waiting for?"

They move out fast. Once on the street Domingo puts on the headlights and drives away from the house. "She's not going to like this," Domingo says.

"She won't even know we left. Lili thinks I'm a child, you know."

"Okay. Where are we going?"

"Nearest liquor, my friend," Esteban says and smiles, "and then we're going to do a little exercising."

"Exercising?"

"Digging."

This catches Domingo by surprise. "You've got to be crazy," he says. "What about your knee?"

"Keep your eyes on the road, will you!" Then, "Come on, it's the only way. There is no time to get her out any other way."

The lights from the oncoming cars make Domingo squint. "You *are* crazy!"

"It runs in the blood."

"What if we get caught?"

"Trust me," Esteban says.

If they get caught they get caught. Nobody's going to put either of them in jail. What good are two old buzzards like them in jail?

"It's going to be a long night," Esteban says and turns the radio on loud.

DIEGO / Pelican sits on the stool inside by the entrance. You don't look at him because you don't want him to know that you know he helped Flaco break into your apartment and take V's furniture.

You go straight to the bar to find Maruchi, but she's working the champagne lounge tonight. Nestor is behind the counter and when he sees you he comes over.

"You gonna talk to the man, right?" Nestor asks. He pours two shots of fire water and slides one your way. He drinks his quickly without making a face. A shot of fire water is like a shot of ammonia, except there's no smell to it.

"I gave you my word, didn't I?"

On stage Ramón has the claves in his hands. They go tic-tic, tic-toc. Upbeat music for the souls on the way to drunkenness. This woman approaches the stage and says something to Ramón. It makes him smile.

When you go to Miami, if you go, you'll leave him in charge of the band, He's the most reliable because he's not a fuckup, in other words, he doesn't drink or do drugs.

Maruchi walks over and pulls you aside toward the ladies' room. She looks beautiful. Nestor cracks a smile. The fire water makes your stomach feel like a volcano about to erupt.

By the public telephones she hugs you hard and gives you a kiss that gets a rise out of you. She pushes against you.

"Jesus," you say, "what a welcome."

"I've missed you," she says. "I really have."

You hold her face with both of your hands and plant a long kiss on her lips. Her tongue is warm and restless in your mouth.

"I have bad news," she says and looks behind you in case someone comes.

No wonder she seemed so anxious to see you. You stand there with what you hope is an interested look on your face, having heard enough bad things already.

"Shoot," you say.

"Somebody told me what happened to Flaco."

"Who told you?" You want to find out who else gets involved in gossip around here.

"Susie," she says.

"Well, what happened to him?"

She pauses to look behind you once again. A man, already on his way to getting drunk, approaches the telephones and picks up a receiver. He can hardly dial, juggling the receiver from one hand to the other.

"Fuck," he says.

You take Maruchi's elbow and lead her back to the bar. Whatever she's going to tell you she can do so in the open.

Nestor looks over at you and points at his cheek. He's trying to let you know that you have lipstick on your face.

"What happened to Flaco?"

"He and your wife . . ."

The way she pronounces wife, almost spelling it out, tickles you and you laugh.

"What's so funny?"

"Ah, baby, I know. What I don't know is what I'm going to do about it."

"Forget her," Maruchi says. "She's a—" She stops herself.

A bitch? She wasn't like that all the time. No, V's a strong woman. She knows what she's doing and is certainly doing it for a reason, whatever that reason might be. If she's doing it to hurt you, then she can . . . get even.

"I've got to go," Maruchi says.

At the other end of the bar Nestor lifts the bottle of firewater, then pours another two shots. After Maruchi walks away, gravity pulls you toward the end of the bar.

Shot number two down the hatch, you recover and decide to go upstairs to talk to don Carlos. Before heading there, you check your watch. It's eight-thirty, you are early. The first set starts at nine.

In the bathroom Jorge is sitting by the hand dryer. He looks bored.

"You should bring something to read," you say.

"Those guys out there must have kidneys made out of lead."

"Give them time to drink."

You stand in front of the urinal and watch how the stream of yellow whirls next to the pink pill of odorizer. "Tell me something, Jorge," you say.

"Ask," Jorge says.

"When Pelican comes up here, does he—"

"He doesn't come up here." He picks up a towel and shines the mouth of the hand dryer.

"What? He doesn't piss?" You move in front of the mirror and check your tie. It's fine.

"If he does," Jorge says and moves on his seat, "he comes in and out. Poof! Just like that. You know how busy it gets in here, bro."

A sorry look in his eyes reveals he's telling the truth. Maybe he doesn't know anything. Forget it, you think. "I'll see you later."

Jorge just looks at the sink where his towels and combs and colognes are. On the way out of the bathroom, you run into the same man who was using the phone downstairs.

When you enter the office, don Carlos is standing by the window. He seems to be looking at Nestor's side of the bar. He is dressed in a white suit with a red tie and a gold tie clip that keeps his collar straight.

"Diegito," he says and turns around, "I heard the bad news."

"Amazing," you say. "News travels faster than the speed of light in this place."

Don Carlos moves behind his desk and sits down. He reaches to the shelves behind him and picks up an autographed Dodgers' baseball. The ball is encased in plastic to keep fingerprints and smudges from the signatures.

"I've decided to fire Nestor," don Carlos says, throwing the ball from one hand to the other.

"That's what I came up here to talk to you about."

"I've made up my mind, Diego."

"Don't let him go now," you say. "we need him. He can help your wife while we're away. I'm leaving Ramón in charge of the band."

"Nestor's a fuckup."

"He gave me his word that he'd stop."

"His word means nothing. Nothing means anything when you're dealing. And he's dealing in here, goddamnit!"

"I'll be responsible."

"This has nothing to do with you," don Carlos says. The ball falls out of his hands and rolls under his desk. You bend over, pick it up, and put it on the desk. Don Carlos leaves the baseball alone.

"Look," you say, "he asked me to talk to you, to tell you he'd stop dealing. He's got problems."

"He's a big boy, Diego, and big boys have to learn to get out of holes they dig for themselves."

Maybe if you change the subject, don Carlos will forget about Nestor for a minute. "Flaco and Vanessa are in Miami."

Don Carlos doesn't say anything, but sighs as he leans back on his chair. "Are you going after her?" he asks.

"I don't know," you say. The faster you get over her the better for everybody concerned.

Now you tell him about Pelican helping Flaco break into the apartment.

"What do you want me to do?" don Carlos asks.

"Nothing," you say. "I'll handle it. All I want to do is have a little talk with the motherfucker."

"Don't have it here," don Carlos says.

"I wasn't planning to."

Don Carlos smiles and says, "But I don't see any reason why you couldn't chat outside in the parking lot. After the club closes, of course."

It's almost time to go down and start playing.

"So when do we go to the Sunshine State?"

"As soon as I get the van ready and find out about renting a boat."

"How much room do you have in the van?"

"Plenty."

"My grandfather and a friend want to come."

"I can use the company. I hate to drive alone, you know."

Driving alone is one of your favorite pastimes, but you agree anyway. Don Carlos stands up and walks to the door. "Let's go down and have a drink," he says.

"I can use another."

"Nestor gave you his word, eh?"

"One last chance."

"I'm going to set that fucker straight once and for all," he says and leads the way downstairs.

Nestor pours two shots of Cuervo Especial. Don Carlos guns his and asks for another. You wink at Nestor as he puts the bottle away.

"You look good," Nestor says to don Carlos.

"Thanks," don Carlos says,

"A Ricardo Montalban," you say and laugh. Don Carlos and Nestor join in the laughter.

A tall blonde full of savvy strolls by, leaving behind her a faint scent of perfume.

"Jesus Christ," Nestor says.

"Keep your dick in your pants," don Carlos tells him.

"Well, gentlemen," you say and drum out a beat on the counter, "it's time for some music."

The band is ready and as soon as you climb on stage Tictacs stops the music and introduces the band. People applaud. You take the mike in front of the pianola and say, ". . . this first song is dedicated to all the beautiful women in the audience tonight."

This first tune is a *dansón,* slow enough to get the couples in love out on the dance floor. From where you stand you can see don Carlos and Nestor talking. After don Carlos leaves, Nestor raises his hand and flashes a thumbs-up sign.

ESTEBAN / The gate to the cemetery is locked with a chain, nothing handy wire cutters can't fix. Esteban returns to the trunk of the Monte Carlo. The wire cutter is big and heavy. He also grabs a pair of work gloves and puts them on. Domingo stands by, a scared look on his face.

"Don't just stand there, will you?" Esteban says walking past him. "Give me a hand."

"I don't think this is the thing to do," Domingo says.

"Oh, no, what do you suggest then? That I wait for six months?"

"I didn't say wait—"

"There's no time to waste, come on."

At the gate, Esteban places the chain between the blades of the cutter and pulls the handles down with all his strength. It works, he can feel them biting deeper and deeper. Harder, he thinks, pull down harder. The cut is accomplished, the chain falls with the heavy-duty lock hanging from one end.

"While I carry the stuff in," Esteban says, "you get the car out of here. Meet me at the grave."

"Straight ahead?" Domingo wants to know.

"Right down the path. Make sure to close the gate and place the chain right so it doesn't give us away."

"Got it," Domingo says and gets in the car and drives away.

Esteban picks up the sack with the shovel in it, the twelve-pack of beer, and another pair of work gloves for his friend. He holds it with his left hand so that the weight doesn't rest on his right leg.

Moving quickly, he searches for the grave site in the dark. In no time he finds it for he's been here so many times he can even find it blindfolded. He hopes Domingo has better luck finding the grave in the dark.

A deep silence surrounds him, and he doesn't like it. Somebody might hear them once they start to dig. In the sack he finds the twelve-pack, places it on the moist grass a bit away from where he will start to dig, twists off the cap from one of the bottles, and takes a long drink. He puts the bottle on top of the marble slab, spits on the palm of his gloved hands and takes the shovel.

With his foot he pushes the blade of the shovel into the grass. It cuts through the roots which make a tearing sound. This, he knows, is going to be the most time-consuming part: removing the top layer of grass without damaging it so that they can place it back after they finish.

The good thing is that the grave is between the shadows of two trees. It's hard to see it from the road. Anyway, the later it gets the less he's got to worry about. Very little traffic in these parts at this time of the night.

Sure enough, Domingo appears. He says he parked the car in a lot behind the corner Exxon station. "I'll go get it when we're done here," he says.

"I'm cutting blocks of grass," Esteban says, feeling the sweat starting. "Move them out of the way and pile them carefully."

Domingo finds the extra pair of gloves and puts them on, takes a beer, and stands by.

In the distance a siren starts to wail and slowly fades. Domingo drinks fast as though all he wants is to get drunk quickly, after that nothing matters.

"Let me know when you get tired," Domingo says.

"How deep do you think before we strike gold?"

"Like the saying goes, six feet under."

"That's a lot of dirt."

"Just remember your knee."

"Fuck my knee."

Once all the grass is removed and Domingo stacks it to the side, Esteban starts to dig deeper and deeper. Domingo begins to chat about Cuba. The more he drinks, the more talkative and explicit he becomes. He tells Esteban about all the women he had slept with in Santiago before he married Ruth, and how those days are gone now. All the fun he had before the revolution, then things gradually started to get worse and worse.

Esteban gets lost in thought and work; he is no longer paying attention to Domingo, only to tell him to hand over another beer. He's sweating profusely. Triumph comes with sacrifice. Soon, soon, it'll be done. He's reluctant to look at his watch. Time doesn't matter. Even if the digging takes all night, he knows they've got to be done and out of the place before dawn.

" . . . Where it all ends," Domingo is saying.

"What?"

"I said this is where it all ends, right here." Domingo kicks the dirt with his heel.

"Not if you don't want it to."

This makes Domingo look away as though he were thinking about it.

"It's your turn," Esteban tells him. "I've got to take a little break."

"The knee bothering you?"

"Can't feel it."

His friend takes over and starts to dig. Esteban watches as Domingo's arm muscles tense up. He's really strong for somebody so skinny.

The dirt is cooperating. He figures it was going to be hard-packed after so many years, but it isn't. It gives under the shovel, turns, comes up in chunks. Soon, Domingo's down in a pit that reaches up past his knees. Two or three feet, Esteban contemplates. Just a little more to go. Patience.

In two more hours, only two beers left, they're almost there. Esteban is shoveling now. Domingo is sitting on the grass nursing a beer he hasn't taken a drink from in a while. Is he snoozing? Esteban thinks about how easy it is going to be just to kick the dirt back in once they are finished.

He gives what he might find very little thought. It's been four long years, so by now all that remains are . . .

"I'm drunk," Domingo says.

"Well, here, take over. You've got to sober up."

Domingo stands up and walks over and jumps into the pit. Esteban hands him the shovel, wipes the sweat off his forehead and the back of his neck, and climbs out to fetch himself a beer, the last one.

He doesn't feel the beers the way Domingo does because he's used to drinking. Alcohol works differently on different people. The more you drink, the more resistance you build. He begins to rub his bad knee, feeling the bulged spandex under the leg of his pants. Nothing a little Ben-Gay won't fix.

Domingo started this turn slow, but now has caught momentum and is shoveling fast. He wants to get it over with quickly, Esteban thinks, so he can rest. So do I, my friend, so do I.

A pyramid of dirt has formed behind them.

"Esté," Domingo calls, "I think I just tapped something. Come see."

Esteban hurries over and slides in. On his hands and knees he searches for the top of the coffin.

"It's still a while before we can get it out," Domingo says.

"We're not getting it out," Esteban tells him. "Just clear the surface here. I got an idea."

Domingo, tired and worn out, looks at him with a strange expression.

"I'm using my head," Esteban says, then tells his friend how he plans to break the top of the coffin with the shovel and remove the remains.

"Brilliant," Domingo says and leans against the side of the pit. He no longer cares about getting dirt all over himself.

In no time at all they find what they worked so hard for, the surface of the coffin. With all the dirt cleared out of the way, Esteban starts to pound on the coffin with the shovel. It gives quickly, as though it is rotted. He uses the wire cutters to break parts.

Both he and Domingo are in the pit now. Esteban breaking the surface; Domingo removing the broken pieces.

"We're going to need the sack," he says.

"Get it," Esteban tells him.

Domingo climbs out of the pit and reaches for the empty sack. Once the top is broken off, Esteban reaches in without any fear whatsoever and grabs Concha's bones without looking at them. He puts them in the sack and when he's through he hands Domingo the bag.

They don't say anything to each other. It is as if, now that they have her, they don't want to acknowledge the fact. Now all they have to do is put the dirt back in and the grass and the job will be done.

"I'm going to need another drink," Domingo speaks first, standing over him at the edge.

"I'll buy you one as soon as we get this done."

"What time is it?"

"Don't ask."

"Bars close at two.

"I've got a bottle of rum back at the house."

"We can't go back to the house, not dirty like this."

Overhead comes the sound of helicopters returning from another spraying mission. They don't make Esteban stop. After making sure he got all of his wife's remains, he climbs out for the last time and starts to push the dirt in. Domingo joins in.

The dirt returns from where it came, it is uneven at the top. Most of it, Esteban figures, fell inside the coffin. Where can they get enough dirt to even out the pit? Esteban tells Domingo to look around.

Maybe once they replace the grass no one will be able to tell the difference, but that, he realizes, is a long shot. The gardener'll be the first to notice the indentation. So what if he does? By then we'll be on our way to Miami.

Esteban calls after Domingo to come back, to forget about the rest of the dirt.

Domingo returns and helps Esteban replace the slabs of grass. They work quickly, and when they finish they stomp around the surface so the cut roots will catch again.

They gather everything they brought, making certain not to leave any beer caps behind as evidence, and leave. Domingo carries the shovel, wire cutters, and the empty twelve-pack; Esteban the sack with Concha's remains. They close the gate behind them. Domingo goes to get the car and leaves him at the entrance. While waiting Esteban holds the sack close to his side as though to assure his wife that everything's going to work out fine.

* * *

ANGEL / A rattling noise comes from the backyard, from where the truck is parked. Lilián, who's been asleep since eleven, stirs but doesn't wake up. It's up to him to find out. This time he'll catch whoever has come to rip him off, no doubt about it. The noise comes again, this time it sounds like the garage door opening.

The digital clock reads 2:43 A.M. He slides out of bed slowly so as not to wake her—she'll want to know what's going on out there. On the arm of the bedside chair he finds a pair of pants that he puts on while looking out the window. The garage light sneaks out through the cracks in the wood. Somebody's there. First the truck gets broken into, now the garage. Incredible, he thinks.

On his way out he stops in the kitchen to get the baseball bat he keeps between the washer and dryer just in case. The bat is heavy, the metal kind, and had once belonged to Diego, who used it when he played baseball in high school. The kitchen lock is easy to unlatch without making any noise. The bastards are going to pay, he figures, but first he's going to scare them. Maybe lock them in the garage and call the police.

What he keeps in the garage is all the expensive merchandise to resupply the truck those days when he doesn't feel like taking another trip to the warehouse. The extra ice cream is in two freezers. Is that what they came for this time, the ice cream?

The Monte Carlo is in the driveway. He goes around the other side of the ice cream truck, regripping the handle of the bat. One good solid hit's all he needs.

Water is flowing in the garage sink. Footsteps . . .

"Hurry it up, will you?" he hears a voice whisper.

"I've got it all over, for Chrissakes!" another says. "I don't want to make a mess."

Two men in there, Angel thinks, better to lock them in.

When he reaches for the door handle to close the door, he peeks through one of the cracks and sees Domingo standing in front of the sink washing his forearms and hands. Esteban's got his back to the door.

There is caked mud on the garage floor. Angel loosens his grip on the bat and relaxes. Domingo removes his shoes and with a spatula he gets from the top of the freezer he scrapes the soles of his shoes free of mud.

"That bottle," Esteban says, "is calling us."

"For a celebration."

Angel stands in the doorway, still holding the bat. He doesn't say anything at first because he doesn't want to startle them with Domingo's bad heart. But when they go about their business and don't notice him, he clears his throat.

"Good morning, boys," Angel tells them. "Mighty late to get home, isn't it?"

They all laugh, but Esteban's laughter is louder.

Angel walks over to an old kitchenette chair and sits down, the bat resting between his legs. He notices the sack leaning against the garage door behind Esteban. A muddy shovel next to the sack and a pair of gloves.

"Did you both get lucky?" Angel asks Domingo, who turns to look down at his hands. The old man uses a rag to dry his hands.

"Boy," Esteban says, "did we ever." He moves in front of the sack as if to hide it. His eyes are bloodshot.

"From the way you both look, I'd say—"

"We went to the cemetery," Esteban says finally and sighs. Domingo appears really nervous, as though the area around the sink is too small and keeps getting smaller.

"To the cemetery, eh?" Angel says. They were up to something all right, and an idea plummets deep inside of him. He doesn't want to guess what's in the sack.

Domingo says that there was no time and moves away from the sink.

"We had to do it quickly, Angel. In and out," Esteban tells him and approaches one of the freezers to rest against it. "I kept my promise."

"It's a sacrilege," Angel says, putting the bat on a shelf behind him.

"That's what she wanted."

"I think I'm going inside now." Domingo says and walks to the door.

"Let's all go inside," Angel says and looks at Esteban as if he were waiting for a response.

"Not much to tell," Esteban says, "Just spur of the moment planning and three hours of hard work."

"I need that drink," Domingo says, raising his hands in front of him. Then, "Look."

His hands are aflutter, really nervous, making his wiry-looking fingers shake uncontrollably.

"Let's all have a drink." Angel needs one, or a smoke or something.

Domingo leaves the garage. They can hear him walking away. Esteban takes the tied-up end of the sack and lifts it off the ground.

"What are you going to do?" Angel says.

"She wanted her ashes—" Esteban pauses to put the sack on top of the corner tool cabinet. "Scattered."

"Why didn't you ask me for help?" Angel says.

"Like Domingo said, there was no time. Besides, I don't want to get you involved in any trouble."

"There's going to be trouble, all right."

Esteban tells him what a great job they did on the grave, how they replaced all the dirt and grass. Only the gardener will be able to tell, and maybe, just *maybe*, he won't notice. And if he does, it doesn't matter.

"When are you preparing to leave?"

"As soon as I get word from Diego. He mentioned this Friday."

Sack in the right place, Esteban moves away from it and toward the door. Angel follows him out, turns off the light in the garage and they both leave.

In the kitchen Esteban opens the cupboards and gets the bottle of Bacardi and twists the cap off. The seal is broken. Angel gets three shot glasses and lines them up in front of his father-in-law. Little does he know, Angel thinks, how much he respects him. He would have helped, if, as Esteban says, there was no other alternative. His father-in-law has always come through for him. The old man loaned him the money to open the cafeteria in Santiago.

With a steady hand, Esteban pours the dark rum into the glasses, then puts the bottle down. Domingo is sitting on one of the dining room chairs. Under the light he looks haggard and worn out.

"Come get it," Esteban tells him. "This is going to make you have nice dreams."

Domingo stands up and comes over and stands by the refrigerator. Esteban gives him the shot glass. He proposes a toast to the fine job they did, then they drink. Angel hasn't had rum in a long time so he cringes once the stuff hits his throat.

"Holy water," Domingo says.

"Another?" Esteban asks.

"No," Angel says. "I'm going back to bed."

"What's Lili going to think?"

"What do you mean?"

"She's going to smell your breath and think you snuck out," Esteban tells him. Domingo smiles.

Angel tells them they better turn in early and rest, tomorrow's another day. "Don't forget to lock the door," he tells Esteban, as he leaves the kitchen and returns to bed.

Lilián is still sound asleep. Feeling the rum in his stomach, he removes his pants and drops them on the chair. In the dark everything's easier. Things are easier to hide.

Thoughts of when Concha was alive come to him now as he searches for the warm spot on the bed next to Lilián. Concha's devotion was unlike any he's ever seen, that's why the old man struggles to fulfill her wishes. He'd do the same for Lilián, anytime.

Sleep comes slowly, in drops, like a faucet dripping. That's what he thinks about now: a faucet dripping. That's the thought he finally surrenders to.

HUGO / If the night could speak, what would it relate? Whisper, chant, groan, and moan. Ah, darkness, divine mother of treachery. I can't tell if I'm awake. Being numb, I can't move an inch. Everything's so stark and black. Faces turn and stare and the whites of their eyes dance suspended in the darkness.

Little throbs and tingles pass through my body; lonely is the heart's job, which is to keep the machinery working, the proper juices flowing. The constant heat and sweat makes it impossible to sleep, though I'd like to very much, unlike anything I've ever wanted before in my life. Hunger keeps my stomach on the edge. I feel as though I were on a roller coaster of vertigo. Feverishness . . . reminds me of being in the jungle.

Two hours ago the truck made a stop and waited for who knows what and the wait lasted for what felt like another two hours. Nobody came to let us out, so we wondered if in fact the slaughter would take place. Uncertainty is a killer in the dark. But then we started off again, down an unseen road.

There is a man sitting somewhere toward the front who on the hour, every hour, calls out the time. I don't know how he does it, see in the dark. His voice soothes me, it reminds me of Lobo's.

Lobo Morales, man of great charisma. His energy always impressed me. Even when we were up to our eyes in foliage and the heat was intense and there was no water or food, he kept us going. Where are you now, Lobo?

In the jungle we had no food . . . nothing. But we had cover from the sniper attacks in the foothills and from the frequent reconnaissance planes. Batista knew where we were, but he had no means by which to get at us. His men were afraid to enter the emerald. The jungle. It is the most beautiful place on earth. I remember this morning I stood in the clearing on top-of the mountain we had camped for the night.

It was a grand sight, all right, and I wrote what I saw and felt in my journal, which, before Lobo was arrested, I sent to my mother. There I stood, on the highest ground, and felt that no matter what had gone on in the past or what would go on in the future, this land would remain glorious. The night withdrew from the trees and revealed a valley of the most luscious green I had ever seen. It had rained all night and the water gave the vegetation a shiny sheen. The mountain overlooked a coffee plantation which was surrounded by tall palmeras and almond trees. The *campesinos'* bohíos or thatched huts looked like growths built on the slopes. A dirt trail wound like a snake from bohío to bohío, and there were a couple of horses grazing. Suddenly a noise scared a flock of doves into the air and I was tempted to shoot a couple because I was hungry; but I didn't want to disturb the silence.

The following night Lucinda joined our group, and from that moment on my whole life changed. Surely, I think, I will find her.

I can't take this ride anymore. The air in my lungs feels warm and heavy, thick with the thousand smells of the others in the truck with me. With my fingers I pinch some slack from the canvas of the truck and bite it. It's hard to do because the canvas is taut over the metal ribs of the truck. Once the material's between my teeth I chew and chew until my teeth tear through, then I poke a finger in and rip a wide gash. It is as though we were cooking inside a casserole and somebody removed the lid to let out the steam.

It grows steadily cooler in the truck now. Somebody in the truck says something about the air being able to circulate. I rest my head against the hard rib and breath in the air coming from the outside.

The waiting is the hardest part. It is similar to the waiting I endured for six months in Sierra Maestra. There we had no provisions. When it rained we had to put out old buckets and cans and any other containers we were able to get our hands on so that we could boil the water and have something to drink. Every process has a waiting period.

The gears of the truck grind, and the truck takes a quick turn. How long has it been since I've slept? The truck slows down. The air stops coming in quickly, the way I like it.

In the distance a ship's siren wails and this alarms people in the truck. They seem to know we have arrived; or, if not, we are close to the port. We are going over a gravel road, for I can hear the tires making a crunching noise as they turn.

The truck comes to a complete stop. I peek through the tear in the canvas, but it's hard to see out because there are no lights where the truck has stopped. The cab door opens and the driver climbs out. He slams it shut. His footsteps come around the truck and move away.

A hush overwhelms us inside the truck. I am not sure what it all means. All I feel like doing is stretching my legs, but I can't because there's a man with his back to them.

"One o'clock," the time caller says.

The footsteps return. The back canvas flap is untied and the tailgate lowered. "Get out, one at a time!" somebody commands. "Form a single line!"

A steady, cool seabreeze sweeps the inside of the truck like a godsend. I slide toward the tailgate.

There are three men overseeing the operation, two soldiers

with machine guns, and the driver. When my turn to jump out comes, I am able to see where we are being led. Into an empty berth warehouse. A naked light bulb hangs over the entrance.

Moths and other smaller insects swarm around the light and blindly fly into it.

We enter the dark warehouse and somebody tells us to move to the back, to leave room for the people to come. "The exodus is underway," a voice says behind me.

Bodies bump against me, and I don't even try to look at the faces. All I'm looking for is a spot in which to sit or lie or stand. I'd rather stand for a while, to stretch my legs, get the circulation going again.

Nobody knows how many people are in here, but from the noise, it is easy to guess: many. Once all the people are in, the door is shut and locked. The noise subsides to a tolerable level.

If only there were lights in here, my search for Lucinda would begin. The only light comes from the night outside the opaque windows on the ceiling. But it doesn't reach far down enough.

More agony to endure. And endure it I must, for I have a goal. I must find you, woman. Give me a sign, please, if you're here, walking among us, the weak and the tired, the forlorn, and even the hopeful.

DIEGO / Sets begin and end, and closing time's still a couple of hours away. Between sets, instead of going to the upstairs bathroom you go outside to the parking lot and finish the rest of what's brutal. You promise yourself no more. No more. What would don Carlos think? If he doesn't suspect it by now . . . This stuff's good for nothing, nothing but building a high level of alcohol resistance. Also, it makes the heart race, turn tricks like a hamster in a wheel.

Outside the night is overcast and there is no way to guess where the moon is. Invisible, a jet roars across the sky. This bad weather's bound to upset plans.

The traffic on Sunset Boulevard moves along slowly, the streetlights reflecting off the hoods of the fancy cars and lowriders. This here is the clot of the universe. Tictacs' music sneaks out of the club and follows as you go check the Spitfire. The car, parked in the far corner of the lot, seems to be all right. No broken bottles or cans under the tires. The tires, the way they lean out in the back as though they were going to pop out, look strange.

Why not have an alarm installed?

The word rootless comes to mind as you head toward the entrance. Mama Concha told you once you were rootless and then you wondered what she meant, but now you know. It's simple. There's no ground on which you can feel any attachment, passion, and this is exactly the origin of the restlessness, that need to get up and go and see new places and meet new people. Tired, that's what you are, tired of the amplitude of this coast. Here's the rat race at its best and quickest. Live from day to day, bumper to bumper, and one fine smoggy morning, boom! you wake up dead.

Things used to be better. What happened? To everything. The friendships are gone. Only Nestor's still around. The marriage to the women you thought you loved has become a flooded sand castle. Now Maruchi wants to get to know you better. Wants the particulars about the past, that strobe light you'd rather keep from flashing.

Inside by the bar, Susie's chatting with Nestor who acknowledges your presence by wiping his nose on the sleeve of his shirt. He smiles, the bastard. No more, bro. Susie doesn't look, as though she were embarrassed. She picks up her round tray and walks away.

Nestor's in a weird mood, too, maybe he's drunk too much. His fingers keep drumming on the counter. No one, except for Danny and V, knows you better. He's been there through the bad and the good, the thick and the thin, and the thin has been thinning so that now there's nothing holding you between this and that. Rootless.

It's all the moving your parents have put you through. Santiago, Havana, Miami, L.A. . . . Can't blame them. If life means anything, it means movement. Start at point A never to return, then die at point U. The unknown.

Better leave Nestor to his job. Besides, there's no sense in talking to him when the two of you have nothing to say to each other. Away from the bar, the dance floor is packed with couples. Tictacs has been playing a medley of slow songs.

Don Carlos is standing behind the upstairs window looking at how well his business is doing.

Maruchi's nowhere to be found, and you seek her out, but can't see her over the crowd. She's not tall. Finally, when you spot her, she's in the champagne lounge waiting for an order to be filled.

She sees you approaching and smiles. There's always a smile on her lips for you.

"Let's dance," you say and hold her arm.

"Oh, babe, you know I can't."

"Sure we can, come on."

You lead her out to the dance floor and hold her close, too close to be proper, but you don't care. The feathers of her uniform tickle. This is the time to have somebody next to you, whose warmth is comforting. She coos in your ear. Don Carlos is no longer looking out of his window.

"Tell me something," she says, her breath moist against your cheek.

"I love the way we move together," you tell her and she hugs you a little tighter.

"I'm sorry," you continue, "if I'm misleading you."

She looks deadbolt into your eyes. "You're not leading me anywhere I'm not willing to go."

"I'm going away soon."

"So?"

"So. I don't know what's in store for us."

"You're going after her?"

"I'm not asking you to wait."

She doesn't say anything.

"I don't know when I'll be coming back," you say.

The medley ends and Tictacs spins a fast, upbeat tune. The couples separate and start to dance to the beat. Who says there's no room for two music styles under the same roof? Maruchi goes back to the bar and there, in the dark of the corner, she kisses you.

"Let's spend the night together," she says.

"We don't have to," you tell her, "if you don't want to, you know."

"Would I ask if I didn't want . . . ?"

She picks up her tray and goes to deliver. A pot of gold, that's what she is.

The bartender taps you on the shoulder and asks if you'd like a drink on the house. Sure, why not. "How about something sour?" you say.

"I've got just the thing," he says and walks away to mix the drink.

The drink he brings is orange and has a sprig of mint in it. "What's it called?" you ask.

"Taste and see. Guess?"

There's gin and vodka and triple sec in it. The color comes from the cranberry juice. "A Rusty Stab?" you ask.

"No, a Blind Weasel," he says, and proceeds to tell you the story of how he saw a weasel cross a road when a truck came and. . . ."

"What makes it blind?"

"The mint." The bartender laughs.

You thank him for the drink and go away. This place is getting too crowded. As you walk back to the stage, climb the steps, and take your place behind the piano/pianola, the drink begins to take its effect, and it takes you. Eyes close, relax. There's still time before the next set.

Like the beat, the drink brings you back to the beginning, to where the disconnection took place. The life you've led is like a movie that's been rerun too many times, a little scratched and out of focus.

HUGO / Hours locked up in the berth warehouse. It's the kind of place I've learned to hate just from the smell, a rancid fishy smell better suited to a fish market than a storage warehouse. The opaque windows stand high up on the whitewashed walls. No light sneaks through. No air. With so many restless people inside the heat's hard to stand. From the ceiling hang pipes and air vents that look like the insides of a pig. That same intestine gray. I-beams crisscross the whole length of the roof.

Nobody knows how long we've been in here. I don't remember coming in last night. I haven't slept a wink and the lack of sleep is getting to me. A fly stuck in a jar, that's what I think of now.

* * *

DIEGO / At closing time, don Carlos announces that he's going to Miami and that he plans to leave Nestor in command. Whatever Nestor says goes or must be done, no ifs, ands, or buts.

Everybody is gathered around the bar, having a drink on the house. Tonight also happens to be payday and don Carlos hasn't distributed the checks so he's got everybody's complete and un-divided attention. Not for the band, though, the band gets paid every two weeks and the check is usually made out in your name, so you have to cash it and distribute the money accordingly.

Don Carlos promises, if everything goes well by the time he comes back, a raise in pay. Now he starts to hand out the checks.

Pelican, whom you've been keeping your eyes on, is sitting at the other end of the bar. When Big C calls his name and he goes to get his check and leaves, you follow him out to the parking lot.

He doesn't look back.

This late the lot is empty and most of the cars that remain belong to the employees inside. Nestor's Karmann-Ghia is parked in the middle of two spots. This way Nestor makes sure nobody parks close enough to do any scratching.

Pelican approaches his car, removes his coat, and is just about to get in when he sees you coming after him. He stops and waits.

"Hey," you say and walk around his car to where he is standing. "What's the hurry, man?"

"What do you want?" he says. His voice is soft and calm.

"I thought I'd ask you a few questions, you know."

"I'm fucking tired and worn out, man. Can it wait?"

"These are easy questions. I think you won't have any problems answering them."

"Cut the bullshit," he says and unbuttons the cuffs of his shirt and starts to roll up his sleeves.

"It's no bullshit, asshole, it's fact."

"Leave me alone, man."

You draw closer. He tries to open his door, but you kick it shut.

"A little bird told me everything."

"I don't know what you're talking about."

"You don't know, eh? Don't know. Suffering from short-term

169

memory loss, or something? Let me remind you."

He turns and swings. His fist misses its target by about an inch. You back away and let him be the aggressor. Then he lands a hard one and knocks some of the air out. In any confrontation, the thing to remember is this: The faster you make your point the better. So. When he least expects it, you kick Pelican in the balls. Quickly, he falls to his knees.

Now you squat in front of him and look straight into his pained face.

"What did you expect?" you say. "Not only do you break into my house and steal all the furniture, but then you mess with my car. There's so much I'm willing to take, know what I mean?"

"It wasn't my fucking idea, bro," he groans.

"No, Flaco just asked you to give him a hand, right? And you said, 'Sure, bro, anything for a friend,' right?"

"Go fuck yourself!" Pelican says.

Tsk-tsk. "Tell me where Flaco is in Miami?"

"I'm not going to tell you ape shit, man."

"Ah, come on, bro, don't be such a sore-ass. Let's say we're even." You help him get up and sit in the car.

"Get away," he says, holding his crotch.

"All I want is a chance to settle things, that's all."

He starts the car.

"Tell him that, if you talk to him, okay?" you continue. "And another thing, don't think of doing anything stupid, okay, nothing you might not be man enough to do by yourself or with your own two hands."

Pelican backs out of the slot and drives away. He doesn't even bother to put his lights on or signal when he turns on to Sunset Boulevard.

When you turn around to return to the club, Nestor, Susie, and Maruchi walk out and approach you.

"We're going out for some breakfast, bro, want to come?" Nestor asks. He puts his arm around Susie.

Maruchi looks over and winks. "Breakfast sounds good," she says, looking at Nestor.

"All right," you say and try to straighten out your shirt and tie.

"What happened?" Maruchi asks.

"Nothing," you lie. "Just tying up some loose ends."

Nestor smiles because he knows what you were up to. "Follow me," he says and he and Susie walk over to the Karmann-Ghia. He's done a great job fixing up the car, painting it. And it's got a terrific Alpine stereo system.

Maruchi and you get in the Spitfire and follow Nestor to Denny's, the only place open at this hour. She's quiet. You ask her what's the matter and she says she's tired.

"We don't have to eat," you tell her.

"No, I'm hungry."

"The sun's coming out," she says and the both of you drive into the parking lot and park next to Nestor's car. He and Susie are kissing.

Maruchi looks overs and smiles.

"This," Nestor says, getting out of the car, "is the beginning of a beau-tiful relationship."

You all laugh.

The morning feels cool, and across the street the sidewalk sweeper is making a lot of noise brushing the sidewalks clean. The man driving it has earmuffs on to keep the noise away.

This is the best time of the morning, you think, walking between Nestor and Maruchi, when there is no heat and the wind sweeping inland carries the smell of the ocean. Surely, the best time for cleansing and new beginnings.

ESTEBAN / A well-dug pit. The bed of rocks and pebbles at the bottom will keep the heat in. Mesquite charcoal and chopped pine blocks. Once everything is ready, then a little gasoline to get the fire started, and it does, quickly, and the fire blazes out of the mouth of the pit. At first the tongues of the flame emerge black and smoky gray; then, once the gasoline burns, they clear and only the wood and the charcoal remain burning.

Esteban lowers Concha's remains into the fire. Bones burn slowly and it takes intense heat to turn them to ashes. The sack catches fire quickly, tiny fingers poking through. The heat laps at his forehead. He moves back out of the way, but not so far back so he can't look in.

Behind him lie the cut miniature roses. He takes them and

throws them in. These belonged to her, she loved them. He covers half the pit with a sheet of corrugated tin. Keeps the heat in.

This is what she wanted, and I'm only granting her her wish. Esteban walks to the other side of the avocado tree, away from the heat and the flames and the sparks, and sits on a chair. From his shirt pocket he fishes out a cigar, bites the end, spits the cut piece out, and lights it. The thick smoke fills his lungs and makes him relax. He hasn't been able to sleep, doesn't need it when things are moving this fast.

Domingo must still be sleeping.

Angel and Lilián are gone, out to sell their ice cream, and Diego hasn't been around, hasn't bothered to call. It's better this way, with nobody around to ask questions, to pester him with *what ifs*. This is the way to get the job done, just you and me, Concha.

The cigar burns evenly, slowly. It's a Partagas, the best money can buy in the States. He makes a mental note to get some more for the trip. The trip. No word from Diego.

It's around ten-thirty, he guesses, and the sun is hiding behind overcast skies. The last thing they need, bad weather. When it rains here, it rains.

Sitting back on the chair, he starts to think of the rain and how it used to fall in Santiago, so long ago, so far away. One thought leads to the next: Hugo.

Hugo as a young man in Santiago, attending the university, trying to get his degree in pharmacy. Then one fine day Esteban gets home and Hugo's gone. Concha tells him that his son has taken off to the sierras to join the rebels. She tells him that Hugo said he'd write. Gone, gone to the hills, not to be seen again until three years later in prison.

One day, Esteban remembers, a black boy knocked on the back door of the pharmacy and delivered a package addressed to Concha. A package wrapped in brown butcher paper from Hugo. In it she found Hugo's tattered and dog-eared journal in which he tells of his life as a rebel.

At first Esteban blamed himself. The decision to go to Sierra Maestra was Hugo's, Concha said. Gone for two long years and not a word from him.

Esteban remembers how poorly he slept at night. Whenever he

heard gunfire in the distance, he started awake. Every shot was a shot he thought had killed his son.

Smoke whirls out of the mouth of the pit and is taken by the breeze.

He hears the kitchen door open and close, and suddenly Domingo appears around the corner of the house. He looks scared out of his wits.

"Esté," he says. "I've got to go."

"What's the matter?"

"Ruthie," he says. "She's out there."

"Out there?" Where?" He wonders if a nightmare woke his friend up.

"I took a peek out the window. I saw her park the car. She's headed this way."

"Calm down, all right? I'll handle it."

"I've got to hide."

"Hide in the garage. I'll come get you when she leaves."

Domingo opens the garage door, gets inside, and closes the door.

Wondering why Ruth has come, Esteban leaves the patio and walks to the front of the house to wait for her. He waits by the empty garden, empty because the miniature roses are all gone. The malathion was killing them anyway, he says to himself.

Sure enough, Ruth appears down the street where she has had to park. Today the street sweeper comes by so cars can park only on one side.

She is a short woman, but makes up for her shortness by being so energetic. She walks quickly, with sure steps. Her hair is brushed back and Spanish combs hold it down behind her ears.

"Don't say anything," is the first thing she utters. "I know my husband is here."

"What are you talking about?" Esteban asks.

"Don't try to fool me. Jesus, I thought about it and thought about it and then figured that the only place he could've gone to is this one. Your house."

"You better think about it some more."

"He came to you. His friend."

"All right, all right," Esteban says and takes a drag from his cigar. "He came to me. I'll admit it, but I turned him away. I know. I should've called you, but I have so many things on my mind."

"Where is he?"

"He spent the night, but he's gone now."

"Don't lie to me, Esteban."

"Ruth, I don't have to lie to anybody. Believe me, he's gone."

"Well, I don't believe you."

Her stubbornness rubs him the wrong way and he gets a mean look on his face, as though she is insulting him. "You want me to show you the house, eh? If it'll clam you up I'll show it to you."

"I'm going to go to the police with this," she says. "I'm going to file a missing person report and—"

"He's not missing, see," he says. "He's running away from you, Ruth. You and I know that. You know it better than I do. He's running away." Even if the truth hurts, Esteban thinks, I'm going to say it.

Ruth stands in front of him, looking at her hands.

"He's tired of you and the house and everything," he continues.

"That's what he tells you?"

"He doesn't have to tell me, Ruth. I've seen it with my own eyes."

"It's a two-way street, you know."

"Except his keeps getting narrower and narrower. He feels cornered, used . . . the list can go on."

"You don't know what you're talking about."

The quickness of her grimace, the harshness in her eyes won't mislead him. He sighs. Is she looking for a comeback?

"You're right," Esteban says. "Okay. But believe me when I tell you he's not here."

"Uh-huh," she says and looks beyond him.

Esteban turns around and is surprised. Coming down the driveway, Domingo approaches, determination tangled around his legs.

He stops in front of Esteban and looks at him. "I'm not a coward, Esté," he says and smiles faintly. Then to Ruth, "Turn around and go back to where you came from."

"No," she says. "You're going to come with me."

"I'd like to see you try and take me."

"I'm going to call the police."

"What are they going to do? You're so stupid, you know that."

This is when it gets uncomfortable for Esteban. He doesn't like to get stuck in the middle of two people arguing, but he feels he must stay put and offer his friend moral support. He admires Domingo.

"There I was," Domingo says, "inside the garage. Hiding from you. Then, all of sudden, I said to myself, I said, 'What the hell am I hiding from you for?' I'm not hiding anymore, not from you or anybody, goddamnit. You hear me, Ruth? You understand me?"

That's it, give it to her.

"You're not well," she says. This is her way of punctuating everything, that final tiptoe from the matador before ramming his sword into the bull.

"I'm not going back."

"See, he's crazy," Ruth says to Esteban.

"Not so crazy," Esteban says.

"I'm going to Miami," Domingo says. "I might stay there."

"But there are so many things to take care of, so many. I can't do everything."

"Sure you can. Keep everything. Handle it. You've always been a terrific meddler."

Esteban heads back toward the backyard. He turns around to see Domingo point in the direction of her car down the street. Domingo follows, leaving Ruth at the end of the driveway. His friend smiles, then wipes his brow.

"Sit down," Esteban tells him, pulling up another chair close to his. "I'm going to get you a beer."

"When are we leaving?"

"As soon as I hear from Diego."

Domingo looks at the pit and at the smoke rising out of it. "She was a great woman, Esté," he says. "Concha was one of a kind."

Esteban doesn't know what to say. He goes inside to the kitchen and grabs a couple of beers out of the fridge.

The phone rings. He walks to the hall, places the beers on top of the telephone directory, and lifts the receiver.

"Hello," says the voice at the other end. He recognizes the scratchy deepness in Diego's voice.

"Where are you?"

"At a friend's house."

"Just got up, eh?"

Diego clears his voice, but it doesn't do him any good. "Listen," he says, "I spoke to don Carlos. He tells me everything's fine. You and Domingo can come. I'm going too."

"When do we leave?"

"In two days."

"Why not tonight?"

"We can't. He's got to find out about this boat."

"Two days is a long time to wait."

"He knows what he's doing," Diego says and his voice trails off.

"Male or female?"

"What? What did you say?"

"Your friend."

"Maruchi."

Esteban remembers her. "Then I imagine you must be all right."

"In heaven," Diego says and laughs. "Listen, I'll see you later, okay? Got to go now."

"Take care."

"You bet." He hangs up.

Esteban returns to the backyard with the beers and gives his friend one. "Diego just called," he says to Domingo. "We leave this Friday."

"Good," Domingo says and drinks from his beer. "I'm anxious to get going."

They both sit under the shade of the avocado tree and drink and look at the wavering heat hovering over the pit. Esteban can't help wondering where his son is by now and what he's up to.

HUGO / Drops of sweat run down my sides and back.

Everywhere there are men, women, and children. Their steady humlike voices echo inside the warehouse. There are cries and whispers and prayers and broken voices gone unheard here. Nothing to do but wait.

Someone's yelling he needs a cigarette.

At the other wall a young man tries tó climb up to the window by using a stack of empty crates. Each time, the crates begin to sway and he ends up climbing down.

Lucinda, I don't have to try hard to remember what she looks like. Her face is branded somewhere on my mind, and in every face I see I look for her. Hers is like a superimposed image that doesn't seem to fit any other face.

Judging from the brightness behind the windows, I guess the time to be almost noon. If there's a thing one becomes an expert at in prison, it is time. Time can be a friend or the worst enemy, either way you've got to deal with it.

A commotion starts toward the front, where the door is, and people crowd around as though plates of food were being thrown in. From behind the door comes the loud muffled sound of a bullhorn, "Stand back!"

"Stand back!"

The door slides open and the sunlight rushes in and makes everybody turn away from it.

There is no way I can get close enough. Like everybody at the back I must await my turn.

"Only groups of twenty will be allowed out to be interviewed," says the barklike voice. "Twenty at a time. Stand back!"

I wonder what kind of interview they are talking about. The worst kind is to be expected.

Slowly, but steadily, the crowd at the front trickles out. Each time, the door is closed, then opened and twenty more people are counted out. Families, I imagine, must have a hard time trying to stay together. Plenty of those all around. Mothers with two, three, and four children. Children alone. Young boys and girls, old enough not to cry or be afraid of anything.

A soldier opens the door, counts twenty of us out, and closes the door behind us. The group I end up with is all males, young and old. There are three jeeps to the left, a line of soldiers with machine-guns in front of us, and a row of desks with high-ranking officials behind them.

We are led to the desk at the very end and told to wait in line. Not to speak until spoken to. Something's jumping in my stomach and it isn't until there are only two men to be interviewed ahead of me that I realize that what's jumping are my nerves. I can feel my stomach recoil, twist, and turn.

The interview is more like an interrogation. Hardly audible questions are asked by the officials, then when the man being interrogated answers, the official shouts out something like, "¡Prostituta! ¡Maricón! ¡Escoria! ¡Vago!" And so on down the line.

I catch a glimpse of the ocean in the distance. It is full of boats and yachts and sailboats and speedboats. The water is hardly visible. Boats arrive and leave full. Boat after boat after boat. They navigate toward the horizon and dip out of sight.

There are people hanging out of the sides of the boats at the dock. The hulls of the boats push against the rubber tires tied to the pilings. The impact is overwhelming, so many people, so many boats.

"¡Contrarevolucionario!" shouts the officer.

A mans steps over to the side and joins the group.

I sigh and take a step forward.

The official, a man in his late forties, balding toward the front and whose scalp is sunburned, looks up at me. "Why do you want to leave?" he asks.

I choke.

"Answer me!"

"Because I'm a thief," I say.

"¡Ladrón!" the man shouts. "We don't want thieves."

Whatever I have to say or do in order to leave, I'll say or do. I opt to agree with this bastard. That's right, I want to say, this society doesn't need thieves like me around, but instead I say, "I'm also addicted to painkillers."

"Drug addict!" he shouts.

In front of him is a clipboard with official-looking papers. "Sign here," he says.

I sign.

"Where do you come from?" he says.

By this point I tap into the game being played: confess your way to freedom. Confess your heart to all the crimes imaginable.

"Embassy," I say. "I stole a car and drove there."

"When did you enter it?"

"A day after I heard the news."

"Any family?"

"No family."

"Okay," the man says. "Stay with your group."

I walk away from the desk and go to the end of the line. A soldier comes and walks us to the end of the dock where we are supposed to wait for the next boat.

Looking all around, from boat to boat, to see if I spot Lucinda, I follow in line. What I see has no meaning. Only a sea of bodies waving, like the ribboned tail of a kite, crowding behind the fences. Behind the people, the boats rock, waiting. Anchored. Boats of all colors and sizes.

In the distance, the warehouse we came from blends with the overcast sky. Bad weather on the way, that's what someone is saying. Back there, the street ends. Multitudes of people gather behind the checkpoint. The roofs of the buses glow under the sun as they drive around and park and wait for the people to get off before driving away. Caravans of buses. Out of their windows faceless torsos hang, arms wave, fists bang on metal.

I feel faint, but the bodies behind me keep me propped up.

"Jesus Christ," the man behind me says as we walk. "Look at all these people. Everybody is leaving."

Nearby a horn blows.

"That's the one," the man says. "That's the one for us."

But the man is wrong and we wait under the sun for a long time before the boat for us comes.

When it does it is a blue-and-white fishing boat which has a hell of a hard time pulling up to the tires and docking. It's called the *Lady Sara*. No sooner does it dock then we are pushed up the gangplank and on to it.

I don't want to board without Lucinda, but I have no other choice. It's my word against the bastard's whose machine gun is pointed at my back. Where to from here, *compañero?*

More people come and board the boat, and the more that come the farther back I'm pushed on the other side. A young boy follows me. He looks scared.

"Never been on a boat before," he says.

"Me neither," I lie. I have been on a boat before, not a fishing

179

boat, but a sailboat. A long time ago. In Santiago. With a friend from school who invited me to go snorkeling for lobster one weekend.

"It's going to rain," the boy says and looks up at the sky. "I don't like the looks of it."

"We'll be on our way soon."

"Yeah, but this storm looks mean. It'll catch up."

"You know how to swim?" I ask.

The boy doesn't answer. His hands grip the deck rail.

A flock of seagulls flies in a circle overhead. One dives and lands on the roof of the cabin, right next to the radar. When the satellite dish turns, the bird gets scared and takes off.

"You have family?" he asks.

I nod yes; he tries to smile. "How about you?"

"An older brother, but I lost track of him last night. I don't know where he is. We got on separate buses, see."

"He'll find you."

"I don't care," he says. "We didn't get along that well anyway."

We turn and look out at the expanse of the ocean, which is crowded with boats. Foam forms on the crest of the dark waves. A skiff, tied to one of the pilings, rocks violently and moves out of sight under the dock.

ANGEL / The rain has a way of arriving unannounced. The sky, otherwise, turns purple and heavy with rain. Angel knows because he *makes* it his business to know. Usually, too, his bones ache, but not this time. In Los Angeles it's hard to tell because of the well of smog, all that shit in the air.

A few drops hit the windshield at first, then their pitter-patter begins. Lilián hurries to the back of the truck to close the window. They hadn't even started to sell this morning.

"That's all we needed, damn!" he says and bangs his fist on the steering wheel.

"Maybe it'll stop soon."

Doesn't look that way. The rain is falling hard against the windshield. It knocks on the roof of the truck. It glazes the streets. At the next intersection he turns left and goes around the block to return to South Gate. No sense staying out.

"Let's go to the warehouse," Lilián says.

"What do we need?"

"A little of everything. Ice cream sandwiches, Pushups and Big Sticks."

"What about sodas? Do we have enough?"

"We need some of them too."

They head to the warehouse under the rain. The streets get dangerous for such a big truck. It'll get clean now, he thinks. It hasn't rained in a while.

All morning Angel has been meaning to tell Lilián about her father bringing Concha's remains home. "Did you hear the racket outside last night?" he asks.

"You know how I sleep."

Angel looks up at the rearview mirror and smiles. "Domingo and your father in the garage."

"Up to no good."

"Worse."

"Oh?"

An approaching car's got its brights on, so Angel flashes his on and off to let the driver know. Angel thinks hard for a way to start telling her and settles on the quickest and most honest: the truth. He tells her they went to the cemetery and dug up her mother's remains.

She moves to the back of the truck and leans against the freezer. "He's lost his mind, Angel," she says. "How could he?"

"He says your mother made him promise."

"She made me promise too, you know, but I'm not about to do it, not that way anyway."

He tells her they really didn't have much time to petition for an exhumation.

"I wonder how he's going to take her."

"Your father knows what he's doing," he says.

They drive into the warehouse lot and park next to the freezer/storage.

"I wish I could go with them."

"There's not enough room," Angel says and turns the key in the ignition.

The rain gets louder on the roof.

"You're right," she says. "I'll just be in the way."

They climb out and hurry inside the office. Eloisa is sitting on a counter stool using a calculator. She's adding all the ice cream orders. She greets them and stops pushing buttons.

"Where's Bebo?" Angel asks.

"Oh," she says, "he's gone. Haven't you heard?"

"No, what?" says Lilián.

Angel grabs an order sheet and fills it out.

"He's gone to Miami," she says. "A big caravan left from Echo Park last night."

"My father's getting ready," Lilián says.

"Better hurry," Eloisa says.

Angel hands her the order sheet and takes a Kleenex from the dispenser by the cash register to wipe the rain off his face. "Things are happening fast," Angel says to Lilián, who walks over to one of the cushioned chairs and sits down.

Eloisa returns and sits down again. "I'm worried because of the bad weather," she says. "I told him to call me every stop on the way."

Angel sits on the chair's armrest and leans his back against the wall. He doesn't want to think about anything except the weather improving. Somebody's got to man the fort, he figures. Tomorrow the house will be as good as empty.

"Bebo's thinking of selling out," she says.

"Selling out?" Angel asks. "Now? This is not a good time to sell. Business's doing well."

"He wants to relocate to another place downtown. Business is better that way. He wants to have a larger place for when his father and two brothers come."

"How much, or has he not thought about it yet?" Angel says. Lilián looks at him.

"He's going to wait until he gets back."

"I'm interested," he says. "Tell him that."

"Tell him to think about it," Lilián says. She crosses her legs and touches her hair lightly as though there is something tangled there.

This is what Angel is thinking: If he owned this place, he'd know what to do to improve the business. The first thing he'd do is give that Mexican boy filling the orders a raise. Yes, sir.

Paradise Flavors, that's what he'd call his place.

The Mexican boy sticks his head in to say that the order has been filled.

"Never seen a faster worker," Eloisa says.

While Lilián stays inside, Angel goes outside under the rain and checks his order. Everything's fine. The Mexican boy carts the merchandise over to the truck and helps him load it. Angel gives him a two-dollar tip. "Stick around," Angel tells him.

"You plan to buy?" The boy asks.

"I don't know. Only if the price is right. You tell Ramón I'm interested, okay?"

"Okay, señor."

Angel stays in the truck and arranges all the boxes of ice cream inside the freezer. He cuts and removes the lids of the ones on top for easy access. The idea of owning his own place excites him. He's given it a lot of thought, because in the wholesale business people come to you, not the other way around. The trick is to get the customers to come to the store.

Once he's ready he honks to let Lilián know. She comes out of the office and hurries to the truck. She climbs in and takes her place in the back.

"What do you think?" he asks.

"About?"

"Buying this place."

"Depends on the price."

"I think it can really work out for us. This is the break we've been waiting for."

"We can rent the truck," she says.

"That's an idea."

He feels the excitement working in him, the way his fingertips tickle. All these years of constant hard work, daily running the risk of getting into an accident. It's time to move on to better things.

He remembers when he had the two cafeterias in Santiago. Even though it was hard work, he liked it because of the ambience. The people knew him, and Angel managed to make a lot of friends.

Lilián is lost in her own thoughts, too.

There were also people who envied him, who wished him the worst kind of luck, and who later took local government positions and made his life impossible. A year after the triumph of the revolution, two punks—he recognized them because they used to come to drink coffee in the afternoons—arrived in uniform to close down his cafeteria. That same day they closed down the one Lilián managed.

But none of that would happen here. No mistake, for this is the land of . . . when they drive to the end of the driveway and stop in front of the garage, Domingo and Esteban are standing under the avocado tree. Wearing long raincoats, they lift their hands to greet Angel and Lilián.

Smoke comes out of the pit covered against the rain by a piece of corrugated tin propped on four two-by-four boards. Both men are drinking. Esteban holds a beer in one hand and a cigar in the other.

Lilián climbs out of the truck. Angel gets out and plugs the freezer in. Now its motor starts turning, the fan turns.

Esteban takes Lilián under his arm and hugs her. From the angry look on her face, Angel thinks she's going to push her father into the pit, but she doesn't. She holds on to him.

"Ashes," the old man says.

"Why didn't you tell me?" she says.

"I didn't think you'd want to know."

Domingo steps to the side and props up one foot against the trunk of the avocado tree.

Lilián tells him that it was good of him to keep his promise.

"Don't I always," Esteban says and smiles at Angel.

"You helped him, didn't you?" she says to Domingo.

"He didn't want to at first," Esteban says, stepping in for his friend.

Angel can tell his wife doesn't even want to look at the pit. Just standing so close seems to make her uncomfortable, with all that smoke rising out of there.

He thinks that the best thing to do is to call her inside the house. Esteban needs room to work in, especially with the rain. Angel knows that the old man only drinks when something's bothering him or has him worried.

"We'll be on our way soon," Esteban says as Lilián walks away.

"Let's see if we can all get together for dinner," she says. "Is Diego around?"

"No," Esteban says, "he won't be here until later."

Lilian walks inside the house. Angel locks the truck and is about to follow her in when Domingo calls. "You want a beer, Angel?"

Angel doesn't think about it long. "Where are they?"

"Right here," Esteban says, pointing at the cooler next to the trunk.

"Hold on, let me take the change box inside," Angel says. He hurries to the kitchen door, opens it, and leaves the box on the kitchen counter. The refrigerator door is open and Lilián is getting some vegetables out to start on dinner.

When he returns to the back, Domingo hands him a cold beer which he takes and twists off the cap.

"That's a steady heat," Angel says and drinks.

"Steady enough," Esteban says. He bends over, picks up a piece of wood, and throws it in. "Bones burn slow. The heat needs to be maintained at a high level."

"You realize Hugo's not going to get to see her," Angel says.

"What's the use of seeing someone's grave," his father-in-law tells him.

Domingo sits on top of the freezer and stretches his legs. "He'll be happy to know Concha got her wish," he says.

All this commotion because of a little island in the middle of nowhere, Angel thinks. But he's glad things are happening this fast, it puts an end to the routines, for a while.

Under the avocado tree they stand and wait for the rain to let up, and while they wait, Domingo starts to talk about better days in Santiago. Angel makes him stand up so he can get another beer out of the cooler, then Domingo sits down again and continues. Esteban kneels on his good knee and keeps the fire going. Angel feels every drink go down while he listens to the drops fall on top of the metal roof guarding the pit.

Why work so hard? he asks himself, knowing that he tends to get pessimistic when he drinks. He kicks the ground with the tip of his shoe. So the saying goes, out of a hole we come and into a hole we go.

* * *

HUGO / When the boat pulls away from the dock, this great feeling of joy washes over me and I feel like shouting something at the sky, but instead I let out a sigh of relief. I'm free. Free, and there's nothing that can compare to it.

And it seems as if the feeling has taken over everybody because there are people shouting and crying and holding each other.

But everybody seems to know that nothing is certain until the boat has passed the twelve-mile limit and has gone into free waters.

The horn blows and everybody cheers.

DIEGO / In her bedroom Maruchi says that she plans to enroll in an advance-photography seminar she's been meaning to take at Cerritos City College. The phone rings.

She reaches over and answers. "Yes, he's right here," she says and hands you the receiver. "It's don Carlos," she says.

"Don Carlos," you say.

"Surprised?" he says. "I called Nestor at home and he told me where you were."

"No problem," you say.

"I just got a call from Miami, Diego," he says, "we got a yacht. A big one."

"When do we leave?"

"Can you and your grandfather be ready before noon tomorrow?"

"Before noon," you say.

"Yes, what's wrong with noon?"

"Nothing, except the desert heat's a bitch at that time."

"What's the problem? Haven't you ever heard of air conditioners?"

"And the rain—"

"Fuck the rain."

"All right," you say, "we'll be ready."

Don Carlos hangs up and the line goes dead. You reach over and dial your house.

The phone rings and rings and nobody answers. Let it ring some more. Somebody's got to be there. It's raining hard outside.

186

Maruchi's got her head on your chest. Finally somebody answers. It's your mother.

"Diegito," she says, "where are you?"

"At a friend's house."

"I'm making dinner," she says. "Why don't you come and eat?"

"I'm spending the night," you tell her in a smooth tone of voice because you don't want her to be disappointed.

"Everything all right, Diego?"

"Fantastic, " you say. You stroke Maruchi's hair. "You guys are home early."

"The rain."

"I know," you say. "I hope it doesn't last."

She tells you all about what your grandfather did at the cemetery. It doesn't shock you that the old man would do something like that. He's got *cojones*.

"Put him on," you say.

She asks you to hold while she goes and gets your grandfather.

Maruchi is kissing your chest now, licks and bites your nipples. It tickles.

"Diego," the old man says at the other end.

"I hear you've been playing thief."

Esteban laughs, then tells you what happened. Domingo gave him a hand. "The job was easy," he says.

"Listen," you say, "don Carlos just called. He's ready to go."

"When?"

"Wants to get under way by noon tomorrow."

"Noon tomorrow?" The old man sounds excited. "That sounds great. Did he find a boat?"

You tell him don Carlos found the biggest boat money can rent.

"Wonderful."

"So pack whatever you have to and wait for me. I've got a couple of errands to run. Wait for me. I should be there no later than eleven."

"Fine, son, fine. I'll be waiting."

He hangs up. You put the phone down and roll over to give Maruchi a big hug.

"Things are speeding up," you tell her.

"What errands?" she wants to know.

You tell her that you must get in touch with Nestor so that he can help you move out of the apartment tonight. Nestor's father owns a van you can use. "I'll be back tonight," you tell her.

HUGO / *Lady Sara* rises and falls, too small and crowded, on the rough sea. The spray from the waves that crash against its hull shoots upward and gets caught in the wind. The sky keeps getting meaner. The boy was right, I think, standing next to a black man who suddenly bends over portside and vomits.

Everyone in the back of the boat is getting soaked. Water runs out of the scupper. Sitting on the crate to the right is an old woman praying. She crosses herself and holds on to the edges of the crate.

"*Vírgen de la Caridad* save us!" someone shouts.

The stern dips too low and a lot of water rushes in.

The captain of the ship sticks his head out of the cabin and orders everyone to move to the center of the boat.

No one moves because there is no room to move. Two men climb on top of the cabin and hold on to the nets that hang over the edges. The boat slices the water slowly. Struggling.

The boat dips low one more time and this time it doesn't rise.

It sinks.

In the water heads bob up and down all around me. Some of the men try to help the old people who can't stay afloat. The sinking boat creates a vacuum which pulls me down. I kick and flap my arms to stay on the surface.

I swallow a lot of water, and choke, but I don't fight it. What I do is give into it, let the suction take me down. I submerge and begin to swim under the water and when I resurface the boat has sunk.

Debris floats by, none of it solid enough to grab a hold of to keep afloat. The boy is nowhere to be found. I try not to swim close to anybody just in case somebody decides he's too tired and doesn't want to stay afloat.

Other boats speed by, none of them stopping because they are just as crowded. A couple of them stop, though, to throw yellow lifesavers overboard. Surely, I think, somebody's bound to come to the rescue.

DIEGO / "Sure this is what you want?" Nestor asks while driving the van on the way to the apartment.

"Positively," you say and prop your legs up on the dusty dashboard.

On Gage Avenue the van drives by the junior high both of you attended. The buildings hide in the shadows behind a tall fence. "Remember that jail?" he asks.

Boy, do you remember. Nothing good came out of the three years in that hell hole. To think back to that first day, the very first class—it was gym—hurts. You didn't want to get naked in front of so many other kids. The teacher, a tall gringo with a thick broom for a mustache, made you strip and take a shower. Coming out of the shower area, you slipped and fell head first against the tiles.

"Umm," Nestor says, looking out behind his night-vision glasses, "all those pretty Messy-can girls."

He remembers the girls, you remember the torture. The gangs, the lazy unprepared teachers, and the dirt and graffiti on the walls everywhere . . . "You pervert," you say.

"Me? A pervert? Nah."

"Of the worst kind."

"All right, fine, I'm a *good* pervert then. Jesus."

He drives with both hands on the wheel and once in a while he reaches over to switch stations on the radio.

"You gonna take good care of the club," you say, "don't fuck up. This is your chance."

He says thanks for setting him straight with Big C, then, "Tell me the truth, bro, are you really gonna go find her?"

"I have no idea. Yeah, maybe. It all depends how I feel when I get down there. I might just give the whole thing up and say 'fuck it.'"

"You give up," he says and smiles.

"I can do it."

"That woman meant too much to you and you know it."

Nestor catches every light on the way. "I wouldn't know where to start looking," you say.

"Start simple," he says, "with her father, eh?"

"She wouldn't be at her old man's, not if she's with Flaco."

Nestor grows quiet as though he were thinking of all the places V can possibly hide in Miami.

"Ever been there?" you ask.

"Once. A long time ago. I stayed with a cousin who lived off Biscayne Boulevard. It's no big deal."

No big deal. Nestor tells you what little he remembers, the humidity, the flat, piney stretches of land, and the banyan trees.

Pass the Downey city limits sign, you ask Nestor if he remembers the way and he says yes, but he ends up turning on Old River Road instead of MacArthur. He shrugs to admit his mistake.

"Just turn right at the next corner."

Soon enough the apartments come into view and Nestor drives the van up and parks in the driveway. Both of you climb out of the van; Nestor goes to the back and opens the door.

"Everything should fit in," you say.

"One trip."

"Tell me something?" you ask, "and I want you to be honest, all right?"

"Lay it on me, bro."

"How much money do you owe?"

Nestor hesitates, then wants to know why you are asking him that particular question.

"Don't ask, just answer me."

"Oh, I don't know, two, three thou."

"If you pay it off, you'll stop dealing?"

"Don't lose me."

"This is what I'll do if you give me your word that you'll stop and get your ass set straight."

"I can take care of myself."

"Sure you can. Listen. Take the furniture and sell it. The washer and dryer, the TV and stereo. I don't want that crap. Once I get back I want to start clean, you understand?"

"I understand," he says. He leans against the door of the van with his hands in his pockets.

"Pay off what you owe."

"Why are you doing this, man?"

"Oh, I don't know. It's the Mother Teresa in me."

You both laugh and head upstairs. Inside the apartment the air smells a little stuffy. "Let's start with the heavy stuff first," you tell Nestor, who stands behind you with his arms crossed as though he were assessing the beach on D-Day.

It takes a little less than two hours to load everything into the van. No disagreements as to how the furniture should be arranged inside the van. Nestor works quickly, efficiently, almost as if he can read your mind. Something funny happens while he helps carry the heavy oak desk out of the back room. He asks what all that blood is doing on the wall.

You remember punching the wall that afternoon Mrs. Plater called you to tell you somebody had broken into the apartment. "I killed a roach," you tell him.

"Big roach. What did it do, eat a mouse?" he says.

Desk in, you close the door and you and Nestor give each other a high five. "Good work," he says, "we should do this for a living."

"Wait here," you say, "I've got to drop the keys off."

You go upstairs and knock on Mrs. Plater's door. She opens the door wearing a heavy-looking robe. She doesn't recognize you at first and when she does she doesn't say anything.

"I decided to move out, Mrs. Plater."

You take the keys and hand them to her. "It was a pleasure having you for a neighbor," you say, "please give the manager the keys."

"What about your deposit?" she asks.

"He can mail it to me. Tell him that, please."

She stands in front of you, her thin fingers clutching the keys, and doesn't say anything.

"Take care of yourself, Mrs. Plater."

"I'm moving out too," she says and smiles.

"You are. Why? What happened?"

Her smile broadens. "My daughter asked me to move into the house next to her."

"That's wonderful."

"Her children are older now. She wants me to take care of them while she's away."

You extend your hand to shake hers. She holds yours and

pats the back of it with her other hand. "Don't worry about anything," she says, "I'll make sure to hand the keys over and tell the manager about the deposit."

Once again you thank her. She wishes you good luck and closes the door.

Nestor's already in the van. The minute he sees you open the gate and walk out he starts the engine. "I was saying good-bye to a friend," you tell him.

"It's not like you're going away for good, is it?"

"Just somebody I probably'll never see again."

On the way back to Maruchi's house, Nestor tells you that you can count on him. He's willing to help you out any way he can. "Why don't you get in touch with your mother-in-law?" he asks. "She might be able to—"

"She won't help me at all."

"Forget her then," he says.

The drive back doesn't take as long on the freeway, though you'd expect the van to move slower with all the weight. The rain finally lets up, leaving a lot of the side streets flooded. Nestor mentions something about hydroplaning. He makes it sound interesting, like skiing.

He pulls up in front of Maruchi's house and stops the van. "Thanks for the furniture," he says. "Maybe I should put it to good use."

"Get rid of those debts."

"Get married or something."

"You want to come inside and have something to drink?" you ask and climb out of the truck.

"No, bro, gotta run," he says. "Besides, you guys need some time alone, know what I mean?" He smiles and arches his eyebrows a couple of times.

"We've had plenty of that."

"Call me cupid."

"Nice aim, Cupe."

Nestor waves good-bye and backs out. The van moves down the street and you stand there and watch the reflection of the red taillights on the wet pavement until you can't see them anymore, then you go inside and find Maruchi asleep. She stirs and says to get naked and jump in bed with her.

"I had no other intentions," you say and do as she asks.

The bed is warm and soft, and from it, the photographs on the walls, in the dark, look different. The objects in them seem to take on different shapes, shifting, moving.

Maruchi whispers she wants to give you something to remember her by in your ear. "Something," she says, "to keep you company during that long lonely ride."

In the morning you get up before Maruchi and decide to do something nice for her. In the kitchen, careful not to make too much noise, you brew some coffee and start on breakfast. The only thing you make well: a ham and cheese omelet with toast and a glass of orange juice.

Planning to take it to her in bed and surprise her, you move about barefoot in the kitchen. Naked. In the Budweiser mirror-sign hanging on the wall, you catch a quick glimpse of yourself. Disheveled hair, dumb morning eyes, askew expression on your mouth. Make a face, see if it scares you any.

"Interesting," Maruchi says, standing at the kitchen entrance. "You do this often?"

"Not often enough."

She smiles and pulls a chair out to sit down. "I don't look any better."

"Hungry?"

"Some," she says. "Nobody's ever made breakfast for me naked. I should take a picture."

"Don't you dare," you say. "Knowing you, you'll sell it to *Hustler* or something."

"That's an idea. Maybe they can use it in their 'Beaver Hunt' section. One for the ladies."

"I've got to eat and run," you say and put the plate in front of her.

She turns to face her omelet. "I'm glad you don't do everything in a hurry." With her fork, she cuts a piece of the eggs and eats it. "I like it."

You sit down to eat and the vinyl of the chair sticks to your skin. It makes you feel strange. "I chased the chicken for the golden eggs."

"Sure you don't mean goose?"

"I caught the goose."

Maruchi looks down at her food with a saddened expression on her sleepy face. "I want you to do me a favor," she says. "It's the only way I can do it. I thought about it last night."

The eggs need a little salt, so you get up and get the shaker from the windowsill and sit down again.

"Pretend you were never here," she continues, "and go."

"But I was here."

"Please. Just go. No need for me to see you go, okay? So just give me a kiss now—" She chokes a little, then, "Good luck, understand?"

You understand, or at least you think you do, so when you finish eating, you wash all the pans and silverware and put everything back where it belongs and shower and dress and leave, pretending, the way she wants, that you were never there.

A gray morning greets you outside as you get in the Spitfire and drive away. On the radio the weather forecast calls for more rain. Switch the station to music. "Rick Deeze in the morning," a voice says, "tell us what time it is."

Time to go.

ESTEBAN / Diego arrives and parks the car inside the garage. A car big enough for a midget. He looks surprised to see Domingo helping Esteban scoop a fine grayish powder into a mother-of-pearl vial. He opens the door. Climbs out. And from one of the garage cabinets he gets a chamois and starts to dry the rain off the car.

"Grandmother's ashes," Esteban tells his grandson.

Diego grins, and says, "I hear you guys pulled a stunt last night."

Domingo turns to look at Esteban, but he doesn't say anything. Instead he watches as Diego finishes drying the car, goes to the trunk and removes the black-vinyl car cover and puts it over the car.

"It smells funny," Diego says, wrinkling the bridge of his nose.

"She wanted it done this way," Esteban says.

Domingo looks at his watch and reminds Esteban that it is almost eleven. Don Carlos is supposed to come at noon, and they still have to double check that everything they are taking on the trip has been packed. Make sure they don't forget anything.

"Have you packed, Diego?" asks Esteban.

"I have nothing to pack," Diego says. "I'm just taking a pair of jeans, a shirt, and sneakers. That's all."

"We better hurry."

They finish pouring all the ashes in. Esteban holds the vial by the top and stares at it as though he is able to see through it.

"Where did you get the classy container?" Diego asks.

"Your grandmother used to put her miniature roses in it. It was her favorite vase."

Diego leaves the garage and enters the house. Esteban and his friend go in too, Esteban holding the vial with both hands. Lilián and Angel haven't left yet. They don't want to leave until don Carlos comes. They want to say good-bye.

Diego's talking to his mother in the kitchen. "I'm not going on the boat with them," Diego says, "I'm staying behind with the van." He disappears inside the den where Esteban hears him changing.

Angel comes, cleans his pipe by the trashcan, reaches into his back pocket for his bag of tobacco, and fills the pipe. He uses his forefinger to press the tobacco down. Immediately after he lights up, the sweet scent and smoke fill the kitchen. This drives Lilián out. Angel, Esteban knows, doesn't mean to do it on purpose, drive Lilián out, that is. The only place his son-in-law really seems to get any enjoyment out of smoking his pipe is in the kitchen. In the kitchen where the conversations start and end, where they've been known to overheat. Where so many things have been left unsaid, or said too often.

Don Carlos arrives. He knocks on the kitchen door. Domingo lets him in.

The minute Esteban sees don Carlos, he thinks they'll get along. Don Carlos is dressed comfortably in a white-and-blue-striped pullover, white pants, and deck shoes. It looks as if he's just shaved, for his face has an after-shave pallor.

Diego returns to the kitchen. They all shake hands as Diego introduces his boss around. Domingo seems to like him too, holds don Carlos's hand for a while. Don Carlos explains that he has family he wants to go rescue.

"Whenever you gentlemen are ready," don Carlos says and moves back toward the door.

"We're ready," Diego says.

"Don't forget to call," Lilián says to Esteban.

Esteban puts his hand on his daughter's shoulder. Angel shakes don Carlos's hand and excuses himself. Before he walks out of the living room, Esteban shakes his head. Domingo tells him a quick good-bye. So does Diego.

They all follow don Carlos out of the house and to the van, which is parked in the driveway. Esteban can tell it's a family van by how many windows it has. Two on each side and two in the back.

Don Carlos unlocks the back door and pulls it open to reveal a plush interior. A table, reclinable bucket seats (they swivel too), color television, stereo, carpet, everything to make a long trip comfortable.

"The chairs recline," don Carlos says.

They all climb in. Domingo is last. He seems to be dazzled by the van's interior as if he can't believe so many things can fit in.

This is the way they will ride for the first part of the trip: Don Carlos drives, Diego sits next to him with the map, and Esteban and Domingo sit in the back. They should have brought the set of dominoes or chess to play with, Esteban thinks.

"Make sure the suitcases are all the way against the back," don Carlos says and starts the engine.

This is like an airplane, noiseless and smooth.

When don Carlos turns on the radio, the sound comes from all corners of the van. In stereo. Sharp and clear and without any static. The van even has a CB and a radar detector which hangs from the rearview mirror.

"I hope we all have long stories," don Carlos says. "Whoever drives needs to be kept awake."

This seems to tickle Domingo and he laughs like a small child who's just pulled a prank.

Diego's Dodgers' baseball cap sits on the shiny dashboard. He eases the front seat back and reclines it, as though he is ready to take a nap as soon as the van reaches the open road.

Don Carlos tells Esteban all about the boat waiting for them in Key West. Yes, it's got its own crew and everything. It's a pleasure yacht.

In no time they make it to the Long Beach Freeway north, from which they change on to the I-10 and head east. One road connects two coasts, Esteban thinks, like an umbilical cord. The marvel of American ingenuity. Amazing.

Another thing don Carlos asks for is for them to synchronize their watches. Time's important now. "We want to get there in less than seventy-two hours."

"I'll take over the driving as soon as we get to New Mexico," Diego says. "I just don't like the desert."

"What's wrong with the desert?" Domingo wants to know.

"A scorpion bit his ass," Esteban says and laughs.

They all laugh.

"You know what?" don Carlos says.

They all look at him.

"We should fill the cooler back there," he says and points.

"A little booze never hurt anybody," Domingo says.

"Booze in the caboose," Diego says and smiles at his own bad rhyme.

"I prefer beer," Esteban says and leans back against his seat.

"We'll get some of that too," don Carlos says.

So after a brief pause at a Quick Stop and enough supplies bought, they get on the freeway again. "All we got to stop for now is gas," Diego says.

"And the bathroom," Domingo says, "unless you have lead kidneys, in which case you won't need to stop."

"Ever pissed in a bottle?" Esteban asks his friend.

"The hole's too small."

Don Carlos cracks up.

Now Esteban turns and looks out the window as the van starts to climb uphill toward the San Bernardino mountains. In no time they leave the big city behind, its smog and crowdedness. They are in open country. This road leads everywhere and everywhere leads to this road. This mighty four-laned, two-way road.

Imagining what they'll do once they get to Key West, Esteban closes his eyes. With one foot he taps the side of the suitcase to feel the hump of the vial in which Concha's ashes rest.

Domingo has fallen asleep. Salsa plays on the radio. Diego drums the beat of the timbales on his lap while don Carlos sings along. In no time, Concha, Esteban thinks, we'll be home again, so many years gone by. Eyes closed, he succumbs to the steady hum of the wheels and the music and falls asleep.

ANGEL / They sell ice cream all day. Come home exhausted and find a strange aura about the house. After dinner, a deep silence comes from the empty rooms. If he listens hard enough, he can hear the silence. A breathing sound.

Lilián is restless, pacing back and forth from one room to the next. They don't know what to do. To stay in any part of the house for too long, except our bedroom, is to remember. Kitchen: his father-in-law counting and wrapping the change, or smoking. Diego practicing his timbales in the den. The hollow sound of the drums gone now.

Angel decides to turn in early, to kill the boredom. In the bedroom he does everything deliberately, as if in slow motion. After a while Lilián walks in, uses the bathroom, comes out of it dressed in her bathrobe. Towel wrapped around her wet hair. She stands in front of the mirror and dries it by hand.

"How far do you think they've gotten?" she asks, climbing into bed.

"Not too far," he says and doubles the pillow under his head.

She covers herself with the bedsheet. They both lie awake staring at the ceiling. Shapes form and disappear on it. They find it hard to fall asleep. So many things to think about. After a while, though, she closes her eyes. He listens in the dark for her breathing to relax, meaning she has fallen asleep.

From the distance comes the sound of the helicopter spraying malathion, then a jet flies overhead. A long train passes by, its wheels screech against the rails. An ambulance hurries somewhere for someone who's been hurt . . . He is used to the nocturnal noises, of things doing something or going somewhere. Ah, the machineries of the night.

Closing his eyes, he imagines the road. A long shiny road in full shimmer under the sun. How far have they gone? he thinks. In his sleep he sees the van go over and by mountains as red as the crest of a rooster, green valleys with different-colored patches of farmed land, a blue desert with the sun climbing in the horizon, and all the distant cities and towns . . .

There they go.

PART IV

Book of Arrivals

CONCHA / She met him whenever possible inside a toolshed to one side of the garden. The gardener kept the key to it under a flowerpot by the outside water faucet. From there she would take the key, unlock the shed, and wait for Esteban to meet her. This was their most cherished secret. Once he arrived they would kiss and hold each other. It was here she learned that soon he would have to go to the university in Havana to study pharmacy. They also made love there for the first time. Esteban was gentle and careful and whispered in her ear how much he loved her.

HUGO / The sea has turned the color of the sky. Gray in all its meanness. Cold. Most of the debris sank. I imagine the boat at the bottom of the ocean. All around me people are trying to stay afloat, swimming, their heads bobbing in the rough water created by other boats speeding by.

My arms and legs are weak. I'm afraid of getting a cramp, so I move slowly, trying to use the least possible energy to stay afloat. The waves help a little. They sweep upward from under me and push. I see a man swim toward a woman to give her a hand. The woman struggles, her head going under several times. I want to help her but I'm too far away, the boats' line of passage between us.

An American Coast Guard cutter arrives, a small black-and-white boat with bold numbers on its hull. Water gushing out of the scuppers. There is a radar dish turning on top of the cabin. A five-man crew. The men on board inflate rafts and lower them to the water and tie the ropes to the deck railing. People swim toward the boat. A rope ladder is lowered and the people are helped in.

I start to swim toward the boat. Slowly, I tell myself, breathing calmly. My strokes fall short and whatever distance I gain is taken away by the waves. It's a push-and-go situation. I curse the waves. There is only one way of moving, and that's to submerge and move under, away from the crests.

On the surface . . . Below . . . Up again . . . Stroke, stroke . . . Slow . . . Push on, got to make it . . . The raft, I see it . . . It's only a short distance now . . . Almost there . . . Breathe . . . Slow.

I reach the raft and cling to it so I can rest. My breath comes quickly. Tired and weak. My arms tingle. My thighs ache, a burning sensation. An officer on board pulls me in.

"*La balsa,*" he says with a heavy English accent. "*Tome la balsa y yo lo traigo hacia aquí.*"

"Okay," I tell him.

He brings the raft around close to the hull from where the rope ladder hangs. "I got it," I tell him.

"You speak English," he says, surprised. "Were you part of the crew?"

"Crew," I say. "Yes, the crew. I was helping out."

"Pull yourself up," he says, holding the rope ladder steady as I climb.

"What took you so long?" I ask.

"It's crazy out here, man." The officer is young, maybe in his middle twenties, with a bushy blond mustache. Skin turned red under the sun. He's got some kind of cream on the bridge of his nose.

"The boat, it went down hours"—I try to remember the right word "—ago. Hours ago."

On board he hands me a red life vest. "We are out of blankets," he says.

"Forget the blanket," I tell him. I am happy to have made it.

"We've rescued everybody we can carry. Another boat's on its way."

"It's crazy."

"Ah, man, tell me about it."

"Thank you," I say, putting the life vest on. "The rest of the crew is on board?"

"I think so. The captain's filing a report."

"The boat sank fast."

"The weather's a bitch."

A bitch, yes, I think, not certain he means a female dog. I thank the man once again and move away. All I want to do is sit down and rest my arms and legs. Everybody rescued is crowded at the back of the boat. Sitting, kneeling, trying to catch their breath. Several women have blankets over their shoulders.

It starts to rain again, but not as hard. The storm, though, looks far from being over. We start to move. The people on board cheer and thank the captain of the coast guard cutter out loud. On the way we pass boats I think I recognize, the ones that didn't stop.

"We'll be in Key West soon," the captain of the boat says over a loudspeaker.

A woman next to me looks confused, sad. I translate what the captain has just said.

"*Cayo Hueso,*" she says. "*Mi hijo me espera. Sí.*"

She expects her son to be waiting for her. When she says this I start to think about my father. Will he be there? He must look old. But what will he think of me? I have changed since he last saw me, in La Cabaña after I was sentenced.

I also wonder about Lucinda and where she must be right now. I've got to find her in Key West. She knows how to take care of herself, but she doesn't have the advantage I do of speaking the language.

Lord, I'm beat. Something I haven't done in years is pray. I never liked to. I figured that if God was all powerful and almighty, then he could read my thoughts. I didn't have to pray out loud. Maybe Mama Concha's spirit has been looking after me. Out of the storm, she comes to save me. That's it.

I pray now. Pray that I find Lucinda. Thank God that I have a new chance at living. The storm will pass. My father will find me. Lucinda too. It is time to begin again, start from scratch and live the best way possible.

The boat moves on.

ESTEBAN / At Tres Cruces, New Mexico, outside a truck stop where they pulled up to pump gas, Domingo takes over the wheel. Esteban sits next to him while Diego and don Carlos climb in the back. Diego reclines against two pillows and closes his eyes. Don Carlos draws a beer out of the ice chest and opens it. He offers Esteban and Domingo one.

"Not right now, thanks, I don't drink when I drive," Domingo says, checking the position of the rearview and side mirrors.

"Hand me one," Esteban says.

The can of beer is cold, dripping water on Esteban's shirt and pants. He takes a swig, then rests the open can on the wooden cup holder on the dashboard.

Domingo puts the van into gear and moves out slowly. "Never driven something this big before," he says to Esteban.

"Whenever you get tired," Esteban tells him, "let me know. I'll take over."

"You think you can drive with a bum knee, Esteban?" Don Carlos asks.

"I think so."

Back on the highway.

"Esté," Domingo says after a while, "you know what makes this country so great?"

Esteban looks at all the passing cars headed in the opposite direction, thinking about Hugo, so he only catches the tail end of his friend's question. "Great country, I agree," he says.

"I'm talking about the roads. Marvelous. It must have taken years to build them."

"A lot of work."

"Ruth must have called the police."

"Maybe not."

"Knowing her," Domingo says, "she's probably called the White House by now."

"What are you going to do when we get back?" Esteban asks him.

"Maybe I'll stay in Miami for a while."

"What about everything you had?"

"She can keep it all. I don't want anything."

"It's tough to live without . . . "

Domingo reaches for his wallet in his back pocket, opens it, and takes a check out of it. "See," he says and hands it to Esteban. "An old account I closed. This should come in handy for a while. I'm not dumb."

The check is a bank money order for thirty-five thousand dollars. Esteban can't help but smile. "Brilliant," he says. "Fucking smart of you."

"The rest is hers."

"Maybe you can rent a little apartment on the beach, and get some sun. See the girls. They wear very little these days."

"I've got better plans," Domingo says, putting the check in his wallet, the wallet in his pocket. "You know, I think I'll have that beer after all."

CONCHA / She married Esteban when he returned from the university. The ceremony took place in San Basilio's Cathedral. Six hundred people came, friends of the two families. They both wore white, for he insisted on it. Afterward Rosario, her mother, told her that they looked like two angels up on the altar.

Twice the number of people attended the reception at her house. Leon, her father-in-law, thought of a good idea to create more room in the patio of the house. He and her father knocked down the fence separating their yards. Filled with so many people, the patio looked immense.

For a wedding gift her father gave her a new Ford. Her father-in-law helped Esteban with the down payment on the new house. The locale for the pharmacy had been bought two months before the wedding.

That night they spent in the largest suite at the Hotel Versailles, three miles from downtown Santiago, just outside the airport. By far the best hotel in the city: chandeliers, marble columns, Roman bathtubs, and plenty of champagne and caviar for two. From there they flew to Havana for their honeymoon.

Havana was marvelous, except she found it too crowded, and dirty in certain parts of town. She liked El Malecón, the way Morro Castle stood on the edge of a cliff overlooking the harbor. They rode on horse-drawn carriages up and down Prado, which was lined with tall shady laurel trees. They dined in the best restaurants, danced in the grandest nightclubs, and stayed at the Sevilla, which had the largest, most spectacular pool.

The honeymoon lasted two weeks. Upon their return to Santiago, she found her house decorated with furniture imported from Spain. Their house was colonial style, with high ceilings and tiled floors. Rosario commissioned a painting of Concha and Esteban holding hands. The painting hung in the living room. There were enough things to do around the house to keep her busy.

She hired a black woman named Marcelina to help her cook and housekeep. They became good friends, the only person she talked to during the day while Esteban was at the pharmacy.

Every year she planned a vacation, but Esteban had so much work that they kept postponing it. They managed to go to the beach a lot on the weekends. It was something they both enjoyed, she because it reminded her of the summers she spent with her parents at the beach chalet.

During those weekends when they couldn't go to the beach, she would drive downtown and catch a movie, or she would shop. Often, when Esteban decided to open the pharmacy on Saturdays, she took him lunch and spent the rest of the afternoon with him. Several times they found themselves alone, so he closed thirty minutes early and she would lead him inside the stockroom where they made love.

She sat on the rolltop desk with her dress lifted up to her breasts while he kissed her. No doubt, he was a good lover. His searching fingers somehow always found the right places. After she came, she turned around to let him straddle her from behind.

Often they alternated dining at the in-laws. Zoila and Leon, his parents, were good to her. They liked her, especially the old man who kept asking her when she was going to surprise him with a grandchild.

She did. In 1941 she gave birth to a seven-pound-eight-ounce, healthy, black-haired baby whom she named Hugo. The following year Lilián was born. The children brought her the most joy she'd ever experienced in her whole life.

DIEGO / From where the WELCOME TO FLORIDA sign stands to Key West, the road seems to go on forever. Don Carlos drives. Esteban and Domingo are in the back playing cards. Your grandfather's smoking a cigar. The can of beer between your legs has gone warm, untouched. Watching the scenery roll by has made you sleepy, pensive.

Northern Florida is so green, with endless pastures and pine trees. Horses grazing. The unpainted barns, the small brick houses with their air-conditioning units sticking out of the windows. Then the turnpike with the marshes by the side of the road. The egrets and herons, white against the brown and green.

"Alligator land," don Carlos says and points to the expanse of the scenery. "All swamp."

"Must be a great place to fish."

"If you can stand the mosquitoes."

Domingo says something and Esteban laughs. Your grandfather moves up and asks if anybody would like another beer. "Ice is melting," he says, bringing the smoke and the smell of the cigar up front.

"I'll have one," don Carlos says, keeping the wheel steady with one hand.

"How about you, son?" he asks you.

"Naw, thanks, I still have this one."

"What's the matter, Diegito?" Domingo says from the back. "You've been mighty quiet the whole trip."

"Been looking at the sights."

"Beautiful country, huhn?" don Carlos says.

Esteban hands don Carlos the beer, which he places in the can holder. He turns the radio on to country music. Your grandfather returns to the back and he and Domingo resume playing.

"Rummy's their game," says don Carlos. He takes a sip of the beer.

"They play it all the time," you say, watching how the sun seems to move over the marshes as the van speeds on.

The bucket seats are comfortable, but you've been sitting too long. The trip's worn you out, though that was to be expected. Luckily everybody took turns at the wheel. Don Carlos started the trip, you took over in Tucson, then Domingo drove from Tres Cruces to Houston, by far the longest stretch, and your grandfather from there to Baton Rouge, where you took over the wheel to Tallahassee. Don Carlos is driving to Miami, then from there you drive to Key West.

"Don't have the tapes?" you ask don Carlos, for whom you recorded some tapes with the band.

"I'm sorry," he says. "I left them at the office. It's all right though. Once we get to Miami—" He stops talking to look at an accident on the other side of the road. A fender bender it seems—two dent-ridden cars between a tow truck and police car—too many lights flashing.

The voice on the radio predicts a sixty percent chance of thunder showers for tonight and tomorrow.

"I wonder how our friend Nestor's doing at the club?" don Carlos says.

"He can manage."

"Let's hope so. Otherwise you might not have a place to play when we get back." He laughs.

Domingo and your grandfather don't say much; only the cards make any sound against the table, or Domingo tapping on the wood with the rings on his fingers.

Succumb to the softness of the seat and close your eyes. A nap might be a good thing right now, with the steady hum of the engine and the wheels turning on the road.

Where are you going to begin looking? Gustavo, from what Pilar told you, lives in Miami, but where? He might know where his daughter is.

If anybody's going to help you locate V, he will. He has always respected you, even when you and V first separated. "A man needs his own space," he used to tell you. "Go and do what you have to, whether you and my daughter stay together or separate, but find what you are looking for. Get it. Hunt down happiness and . . . " You can almost hear his voice, soft-spoken words, well pronounced. At times you thought Gustavo understood you better than your own father, who spent more time with his ice creams. Even better than Mama Concha used to.

With Gustavo it was easy to relax into friendly conversation. Sports, news, the man could speak about any subject and put it in a way that was thrilling to listen to. Mystery penetrated his voice. Experience, that's what it was; Gustavo had plenty of stories to tell and told them well.

He was the first to approve of you and V getting married. Pilar wasn't too crazy about the idea at first. She thought you were just a punk fresh out of high school, with ideas too big for your own good. "Still wet behind the ears," was the way she used to put it.

You remember the day you went to V's house to be there when she broke the news of the engagement to her parents. Mama Concha had already died, the last semester of high school was almost over, and the band was already assembled and rehearsing every day.

It was a Friday night. You drove over in the Nova your parents owned then. Gustavo and Pilar were having an argument. Vanessa was distraught because her mother, of all nights, chose that one to spoil the surprise. It was a surprise all right. A lot of doors got slammed that night, including the front door when you left.

Pilar called the next day to apologize and said she was very happy for the both of you. Then she invited you over to dinner, and she and Gustavo gave you and V their blessings. They wanted their daughter to be happy.

By August of 1976 you were married and your life, for better or worse, was changed forever.

Shortly after that the arguments and jealousy trips began. V didn't want to go to the club anymore and watch you play. She said she was bored with the same thing all the time. She didn't have you enough. When you weren't playing, you were rehearsing. At the same time, the band was going through severe changes. Danny wanted to do one thing and you another. Then you took command and lost many friendships, Danny's included. He stayed and played but didn't say much to you.

It was he, the morning Mama Concha died, who came to tell you about the news. You were playing basketball and the ball kept hitting the rim and bouncing off. No net on the rim, which was why the ball wouldn't go in. A net made that nice swooshing sound. Working up a sweat, you didn't stop running layups until Danny walked over.

"The coach wants to see you," he said. "Somebody called from the hospital." Then, with a hurt look in his eyes, "I'm sorry, bro."

She was dead. You didn't even bother to go see the coach, instead you headed straight for the locker rooms, undressed, and took the longest shower. The steady spray of cold water fell over your head and shoulders and took you away from everything.

He's with V now to hurt you to get back at you. Wondering how it is possible that Danny and V could end up with each other, you open your eyes and see the rain falling on the windshield. The wipers moving to the slow beat of the country music on the radio.

ANGEL / They are having *arroz con pollo* at El Colmao, a new Cuban restaurant that just opened on Pico. The place is decorated with bull-fighting paraphernalia, posters, banderillas, a red cape with two crossed swords. Above the U-shaped stool counter hangs a glass case with flamenco dancer dolls. Music plays on a jukebox, a song by Camilo Sexto. The mirrored walls make the place seem larger than it actually is.

The waitress brings Lilián the avocado and onion salad she ordered and Angel another beer. They are talking about a dream she had last night, which she now begins to remember.

It is about Hugo and her when they were children. Angel stares at her lips as she talks. Always had nice teeth, he thinks, nice and even. ". . . there was a storm," she is saying, "and the river that ran behind the houses overflowed and flooded the entire backyard. Marcelina had a dog she had tied to a tree."

"Marcelina," Angel says. "I remember her."

"The water rose. Hugo saw the dog drowning. It had no more slack on the rope. Lightning flashed followed by the loudest thunder. He said he was going out to get the dog, and Marcelina told him not to, that she didn't want him to get hurt or catch a cold. But he went ahead anyway. He's always been stubborn."

"Did he save the dog?" he asks and drinks some beer.

"His pants got caught on barbed wire, so he took off his pants and kept going. He reached the dog, untied the rope, and brought the shivering animal back to the house. Entering the kitchen, he put the dog in front of him so Marcelina wouldn't notice he was naked."

He doesn't say anything, so she resumes eating, then after a while she says, "Anxiety probably made me have the dream."

"I hope your father doesn't run into any trouble," Angel says.

"It's not my father I'm worried about, it's him. My brother."

He wonders where his brother-in-law might be right now, how

he managed to escape from La Cabaña, if in fact he got away. Hugo can take care of himself.

"I don't understand why those bastards are letting people out," she says, using her fork to peel the chicken meat away from the bones.

"Neither do I. Maybe they want to get rid of all the people who are against—"

"Are you kidding, then everybody would leave. The whole place would empty." She seems to think about it, then smiles. "Can you imagine that bearded son of a bitch sitting there? Alone. No one around to hear his long speeches."

"Diego said he'd call, right?"

"And my father. Once they get to Key West. Diego's going to look for Vanessa."

"If Pilar didn't tell him, what makes him think Gustavo will?"

"She might be there."

And once he finds her, what then? If she doesn't want him, there isn't a whole lot he can do. Angel believes the reason for his son's attachment to Vanessa is her beauty, but that goes. First the wrinkles, then . . . he looks at Lilián who's kept herself in good shape.

"What do you think he's going to do," he asks, "when he finds her?" Lilián shrugs. "Talk."

Whatever. They should settle things once and for all whether they stay together or separate. Get their lives going again. She was close to him when his grandmother died. Maybe she was the only person he could talk to, open up and let his hurt out.

He is finished with his food. The waitress returns and asks him if he'd like another beer. "No, thank you," he says and reaches for his pipe in his shirt pocket. "Could you bring me a book of matches?"

"No problem," the waitress says, picking up his plate and two empty beer bottles.

Lilián looks at him, then at her and says, "Some coffee for me."

"Don't want dessert? Some flan or—" the waitress says.

They both say no. Angel is thinking that they better hurry back to the house in case the call comes. The cross-country trip, from what he's heard, takes only three to four days, especially if they each took turns driving. Non-stop. In a hurry. He wishes them luck, may they find. . . . the waitress brings the bill.

Lilián figures out how big a tip they should leave, then they pay and leave. On the way home she turns on the radio and they listen for the news, but there's only music. Music to relax them, Angel thinks, and keep them from worrying.

HUGO / As I approach the young coast guard officer who helped me on board, my hands start to tremble. I slip them in my pockets so he won't notice. The clothes are still wet. "Listen," I begin, but stop to let another man pass between us.

He looks at my scalp. "You're bleeding," he says. "Did you hit something?"

"I don't remember," I tell him, and touch the open sores, which, being in the water for so long, have softened. The scabs feel puslike.

He motions for me to follow him around the cabin to the entrance. There, he reaches under a cabinet and takes a red first-aid kit. In it are rolls of bandages, cotton, Band-Aids, iodine, several plastic bags with cotton swabs and wooden applicators, a box labeled SNAKE BITE, and a tube of sunscreen cream.

"Tilt your head down," he says. "Look at the floor."

"Listen," I tell him, "I'm looking for somebody."

"Better have a doctor look at these," he says.

"I must find her . . . this person."

"Was she in the boat with you?" The young man applies the iodine with a cotton swab. It stings, but I don't move.

"No. Not my boat. Another. I believe she's headed this way."

"We have instructions," he says, "to take everybody to Key West."

Without sounding too ignorant, I ask what happens there.

"The immigration department is there. They might be able to help you." He finishes with my scalp. "There," he says. "This should stop the bleeding. Don't forget to see a doctor."

"I used to be a medic," I say, reaching for my scalp.

"Don't touch it," he says.

I thank him.

"I hope you find who you're looking for," he says, putting the kit back.

"One more thing," I say. "If I want to place a call to—to Los Angeles, do you know how much it is?"

The young man explains that I can call collect. All I have to do is dial zero for the operator and tell her that I want to make a collect call, then give her the name and number of the party I want.

"Party?" I ask, not understanding.

"Yeah, person, who you want to speak to."

"Oh, I see."

He looks at me suspiciously. "You lied to me, didn't you? You're not part of the crew."

This is what I tell him: "Look, my father's supposed to pick me up. Then I must find—"

"You want my advice," he says. "When you get to Key West, don't speak any English, okay? Immigration's going to interview you, and if they hear you speaking English, they are going to get suspicious."

"Suspicious? Why?"

"Well, they're gonna want to know how you learned the language. Why you speak it instead of—of Russian or Chinese or something."

"I see, they might think I'm a spy."

"Infiltrator."

The word makes me laugh.

"*You're* not worried about me being one?"

"A spy, no," the young man says and smiles. "That's not my job. My job is rescuing people."

"You do good work," I say and put my hand out for him to shake.

We shake hands, then he tells me to excuse him, that he has other people to attend to. I stay and look at all the navigational instruments inside the cabin. As I return to the back of the boat, I notice everybody eyeing me, looking at my head as if there were something terribly wrong with me.

* * *

DIEGO / Miami. Everything looks flat and washed out. A tall building here and there. Canals with water as dark as ebony. Drawbridges. Had never seen one. San Pedro's the only place where there might be some back home. They are everywhere here.

V might be anywhere in this city. Out there in the heat. At the beach working on her tan. The bitch is still vain after all these years, right. The thought turns over and over . . . tanned legs, back, arms, face. Tan lines where the bathing suit ends and the exposed flesh starts. Exposed flesh.

Remember the day you walked in on her while she was shaving? There she sat on the edge of the tub, legs spread. Shaving cream smeared on her inner thighs . . . her wet skin was dark . . . she worked the Bic razor slowly. The cut hair floated in circles in the water of her bath.

She didn't notice you at first, but she looked up and saw you, and she smiled. "Interesting stuff, huhn?" she said. "Welcome to the private—"

"Shave it," you said. Excitement grew in the lowest part of your stomach and rose to the heart and throat.

"Want to do it for me?"

And you did. You didn't even bother to take your clothes off, just jumped right in the tub with her and started to shave her.

A brief stop to pump gas and get something to eat at a Denny's. Don Carlos says he's hungry. Your grandfather wants to eat at a Cuban restaurant, but Domingo says they have no time.

"This is the best I can do," you say, "on such short notice. Besides, Domingo's right. Let's eat and go."

"Should I call your mother now?" Esteban says, getting out of the van.

"Call her when we get to Key West," you say.

"Things might get hectic down there," Don Carlos says.

"Yes, Esté," Domingo says, "call her from here. Tell her not to spill the beans if Ruth calls . . . forget it. Go. We'll save you a seat inside."

"Call collect," you say.

"Sure," Esteban says. "It'll give me a chance to practice my English with the operator."

The three men walk toward the entrance of the restaurant. You stay behind on purpose. In the wallet you check for some leftover coke, just a trace, a ghost of a trace is all you need. It'll help keep thoughts off the heat. Goddamned humidity too.

Stashed in a crevice of the wallet, the Ziploc bag is empty. Bad luck. There shouldn't be any problems scoring more down here, this is supposed to be the talcum-powder capital of the world.

Esteban is using one of the phones by the entrance. The operator put him through, and he's talking to your mother.

"Give her my love," you say as you walk by and enter the place. Inside Domingo and Big C are sitting in a corner booth. Water and silverware are already on the table. Also the menus. Both men are intent on figuring out what they want to eat.

"Order your grandfather a Super Bird," Domingo says.

"Is that what he wants?" you ask.

"That's what he said," Big C says, looking over his menu. "I'm having the club sandwich."

When the waitress comes to take their order, both Domingo and don Carlos turn on their charm. Too bad your grandfather isn't here; otherwise there'd be more charm at this table than she'd know what to do with.

"Nice breasts," Domingo says when she leaves.

"In English," Big C says, "it's tits."

"Tits," Domingo repeats.

Esteban returns and sits down. He says Lilián says hello. "Nobody's called," he says, opening the menu.

You tell him that the waitress already took the order. Domingo tries to explain what the girl looked like and Big C laughs.

"Okay," Esteban says. "Let's get everything straight before we leave here."

Big C takes over the planning. He suggests that you keep the van until you find V, and that if for some reason you have to leave early, then return to Key West and leave the van parked somewhere, then call Lilián and let her know where it is. The closer to the docks the better.

"That sounds good," you say.

"Yes," Esteban says. "Let your mother know. She's our contact."

"You can still come with us if you change your mind," Big C says.

The food arrives and the waitress whose name is Stephanie serves it with a huge smile on her lips. Working hard for a big tip, she is. Immediately your grandfather jumps in and starts to flirt. He says corny things like, if all the women in Miami are as pretty, then he's going to stay. Sitting there watching him, you realize how much the old man means to you.

ESTEBAN / Diego drops them off at the docks in Key West. He helps them unload, shakes everybody's hand—Domingo gives Diego a hug and says something to him Esteban can't hear—then turns the van around and speeds away, back to Miami.

Concha's ashes are in the glass vial in a gym bag Domingo's carrying. He and his friend walk next to don Carlos, looking for the yacht called the *Arco Iris*. They move in the tumult and commotion of the docks.

"So many people," don Carlos says. "This is a madhouse."

There are all kinds of boats, big and small, new and old, all with people on board. Some are leaving, others are arriving.

"*¡Viva América!*" somebody shouts.

A group of people getting off a boat cheer. They chant, "*¡Carter arriba! ¡Fidel para bajo!*"

Domingo spots the yacht first. It is in dock twenty-seven. Seventy feet of white hull with rainbow-colored stripes running down the sides. The glass windows are tinted. An American flag sways in the breeze over the cabin.

They follow don Carlos around the dock to the on ramp. "It's big," Domingo says.

"Let's hope it gets us there," Esteban says, climbing aboard last.

The skipper greets don Carlos. Don Carlos writes him a check for half of the money. "The other half," he tells Norton, as the skipper is called, "when we return, no?"

"No problem," Norton says. "That's all right with me. Man, I still can't believe all this is happening. Everybody's out here going crazy. Just be glad you found a boat on such short notice."

"What I hope is that my family's there," don Carlos says.

The skipper is American. About as tall as Esteban, but with wider shoulders and stronger arms. He is wearing white bermuda shorts, a pastel-yellow tank top, and a gray bandanna around his neck. His skin looks as tough and wrinkled as that of a turtle.

"How many people are we supposed to pick up?" He wants to know.

Don Carlos, looking around the boat, tells him, counting Esteban's son, plus a brother, a sister, and her family, the number should be six.

"There's enough room," says Norton, "for everybody to be comfortable."

"When can we leave?" don Carlos asks.

"As soon as we refuel and get some supplies and some food."

"Listen," don Carlos says, "would it be all right if we bought some beer and took it along?"

"Sounds better than all right to me," Norton says and flashes an I-thought-you'd never-ask smile.

"Domingo and I will go buy it, don Carlos," Esteban says.

"Here, have some money," don Carlos says, taking a roll of bills out of his pocket. "Get something special." He gives Esteban fifty dollars, then to Norton he says, "Is there a place to keep it cold?"

"Sure," the skipper says. "We have a big cooler."

"Where do they sell beer around here?" Domingo asks.

The skipper says there's a liquor store out past the bait and tackle shop at the corner of the docks.

"How does Michelob sound?" Esteban asks.

"Get a couple of cases, and some sodas," don Carlos says.

"And ice," Domingo adds.

Esteban and his friend get off the boat and follow the instructions to the liquor store. When they get there, there is a line outside, not too long, but a line nevertheless.

While waiting on line, Esteban notices a blond woman approach the door and stand there. He believes he has seen her before, though where he's not sure. She is talking to some men in the front of the line. None of them seems to understand what she is saying.

She is wearing a loose, long-sleeved shirt, faded blue jeans, and white espadrilles. As she speaks, her hands reach up and touch the blond hair. Then the name comes to him: Janna Douglas, the television reporter.

"See that woman?" Esteban says to Domingo. He tries to look over the line. "What do you think?"

Domingo takes a minute to spot her, then, "The one at the door?"

"She's beautiful, isn't she?"

As Domingo moves to the side to have a better view, she looks over. Esteban waves to her to join them.

"Are you crazy?" Domingo says. "What—"

She approaches and stops in front of them, a puzzled look on her face. Esteban introduces himself and tells her, "My friend here just bet me you are on television."

Domingo smiles nervously and doesn't say anything.

"He's right," she says. "I'm a reporter."

Up close, in person, she's really striking. Her eyes are light green, and her complexion is as smooth as her smile. But nothing about her is more revealing than her hands. Her hands are big, strong at the wrists, and her fingers are slender and long, half moons showing under manicured but unpolished nails. Certainly, he thinks, a woman who knows how to take care of herself.

"I'm here to do a special report on Mariel," she says. The confidence in her voice is appealing.

"¿No veo la cámara, Esté?" Domingo says.

"No cámaras, estoy sola," Janna says in a well-pronounced Spanish.

"Alone," Esteban says, figuring that between her Spanish and his English they can have a conversation.

"I'm looking for somebody to take me to Mariel. I want to see it for myself."

"Company won't take you?"

She explains that this is a story she wants to work on on her own, her own time, her own effort.

"I see, I see," Esteban tells her, then translates to his friend.

"Buena idea," Domingo says.

"We go to Mariel as soon as we buy beer," Esteban says. "Maybe we work out a deal, no?"

"Let me hear it," she says and looks at Domingo.

He tells her that if she can use her influence and call the immigration base here to find out if a certain Hugo Carranza has arrived, that they'll take her to Mariel. "I want to make sure he's not here already," he says.

She stands there thinking about it before she says, "A phone call and you'll take me."

"Right. You think you can do it while we buy the beer?"

"Wait here, okay?" she says and walks away.

He watches her go. What a way she moves. What grace! While she's gone he explains everything to Domingo, who doesn't seem to be listening. The line moves and they enter the liquor store where they feel the cool air escaping out of the vents.

"What makes you think she'll call?" Domingo asks.

"There's something about her you can trust," he says.

In the COLD section he finds the beer. A twelve-pack will hold them until the other two cases get cold. A stockboy brings out the two cases of Michelob and a couple of bags of ice. Esteban buys some cigars.

Domingo carries the soft drinks to the counter. Esteban asks the stock boy if he knows of someone who might want to make some quick money carrying the stuff to the boat. The young man takes the job himself. Esteban pays him five dollars and tells Domingo to accompany the young man back to the boat to make sure the beer gets there, while he stays behind to wait for Janna.

Thinking that perhaps Domingo is right about not trusting her, he waits in the shade of the building. He realizes for the first time how hot it really is. Must be in the nineties.

When she arrives, she is carrying a leather bag strapped over her shoulder. "No luck," she says. "Nobody with that name has come." She switches the bag from one shoulder to the other. He offers to carry it for her. "I'm sorry I took so long," she continues, "but all the lines were busy. Then I went to my car to get the bag."

He believes her. The truth is there in her eyes, along with a shimmer of vitality and determination. Determination, he thinks, is on his side. One way or another, if his son is in fact coming, he's going to find him. Expect to hear Diego play live soon, Esteban recalls the line from the telegram.

The yacht is ready to go. He introduces Janna to don Carlos, explains to him the situation, and don Carlos doesn't seem to mind. He says, "We can always find room for a pretty face," and winks at Esteban.

Norton recognizes Janna and welcomes her on board. Domingo and don Carlos walk inside the cabin when the *Arco Iris* moves away from the dock, leaving him and Janna alone.

He watches the choppy water as they pass by other boats coming into the docks. People fill the boats which, under so much weight, struggle over the water.

Janna looks at him and smiles. She thanks him for letting her come along.

"I'm glad I was of some help," he says.

"Who is Hugo Carranza?" she asks, sitting on a stool next to him.

"My son," he says, "whom I haven't seen in eighteen years." He tells her about Hugo.

Domingo brings them a couple of cold beers. He pours Janna's into a chilled glass, and says that it is fascinating to watch the skipper at the wheel. All the controls and instruments look complicated.

Esteban lifts his bottle and proposes a toast, "May everybody get what they want out of this trip," he says.

She translates for Domingo. Domingo extends his bottle. Her hand comes into contact with Esteban's, then she puts the glass to her lips and drinks.

Cheers.

HUGO / Key West, I can't believe it. There isn't room in the water for any more boats. The coastline is hidden behind the vessels. One, a big ninety-footer, tugs a number of smaller crafts. It looks like a mother duck being followed by a line of ducklings.

Tugboats made their way to larger boats that have trouble docking. More cutters arrive. Cutters and patrol boats and utility boats. Horns blow. Clouds of exhaust hang in the air.

I'm surprised to see how flat the land looks. Spotted with scattered pine, palms, and palmettos. Leaden skies behind them. When we come into the docks, people cheer, *"¡Viva la libertad! ¡Viva Carter!"*

Working my way through the anxious crowd—I don't want to be the first to get off—I notice the uniformed authorities ushering the people to one side of the docks.

I look for the young man who helped me, but I don't see him. Anyway, he's already helped me enough. I've gotten this far on my own, and I'm not about to stop. As people start to get off the boat, I sit down and wait.

The struggle's over . . . I'm free . . . now to find Lucinda . . . there's no reason why I shouldn't find her . . . somebody'll help me . . . there are ways . . . she's here, I can feel her presence.

"Hey you!" somebody shouts and points at me. "Off the boat! Come on."

I stand and walk over to where the man in uniform waits. He gives me a hand, pulling me onto the dock. I remember what the young man told me about not speaking any English.

"Follow me!" the man says.

I pretend I don't understand.

"Venga, amigo," the man says with a heavy accent.

Following him, I want to kneel and kiss the wood under my feet, but I realize it isn't ground. The man might think I'm crazy or something and I don't want to get on his bad side.

The man's uniform is dark green with a thin yellow stripe running down the sides of his pants. He's got a cap on with an official seal on it.

Back to the herd, that's where he takes me. Part of the dock has been fenced in and there are people on both sides of the wire. There are families waiting, exchanging greetings through the holes. What a sight.

I follow the man to the end of a line and he gestures for me to wait there. I'm tired, hungry, and in need of a bathroom. Surely, there's got to be a better way. When the uniformed man leaves, I start to make my way down the line, looking everybody straight in the face. These are different faces now, more relaxed, smiles of contentment on everyone.

"Emergencias y ayuda médica," a voice comes from a loud-speaker. *"Formen otra línea hacia la derecha. Por favor."*

When I hear this, I reach for a couple of the scabs on my scalp and scrape them off. The blood starts to flow, I can feel the trickle. Now I'm in need of medical assistance just like the voice said.

Go get in line to be treated. I go. Blood runs behind my ear and slides down the side of my neck. A woman and her child cut in front of me. *"Brazo partido,"* she says, meaning her son's arm is broken.

The kid's face is red and full of hurt, so I forget about the scalp and try to help her. She's having a hard time communicating with the man in charge at the front of the line. Her son's been crying for so long that no tears are coming out, but he's still pouting and moaning.

I interfere though I know it's a stupid move on my part. The man looks at me, sees the blood on my head. "Help him," I tell him and point to the child. "Broke his arm."

The man is taken aback by my speaking English; then he asks if I'm the father. I say no, just someone who wants to help. "You need help too," he says. "You're bleeding a lot."

He pushes the door open and lets us in. The woman thanks me, saying that I'm a miracle. I ask her how it happened. She says that the boy got caught in the middle of a fight that broke out on board the boat they came in. One of the men fighting tripped and fell on her son, whose arm got pinched between the man and the deck. *"Grande y gordo,"* she says, trying to describe the man.

This part of the building is used to provide medical assistance. There are cots, hospital beds, and five stretchers, all occupied. Along the walls there are medicine cabinets marked with a red crosses. Some are locked.

The man we are following leads us to a cubicle and asks us to wait. When he leaves, the child starts to cry. How can I comfort him? I remember what it is like to have a broken arm. A son of a bitch guard broke mine back at La Cabaña, and it hurt like hell.

But soon enough a nurse and a doctor come. They both speak Spanish. The nurse asks the woman what happened. The doctor turns to me and wants to know if I'm the father. I tell him I was helping the woman. He also points out I'm still bleeding.

"Wait outside," he says to me, then to his nurse, "Fix him up, I've got this under control."

The nurse is a young woman in her late twenties, pleasant to look at, but with extremely tired-looking eyes and face. She takes me to another cubicle, where she begins to treat my sores.

She seems to be looking at me with pity. I smile to let her know I'm all right. "The sun did this to me," I say.

"It wasn't because of a fight, was it?" she asks.

"No fight."

After she's done, she walks over to the portable sink and washes her hands. This is when I take advantage of her time and ask her to help me. I tell her about the family in California, about Lucinda being lost, and ask when I can expect to be released.

For the first two she's got answers, but not for the last. Immigration has to check me out first, just as the coast guard officer told me.

"Do you know the telephone number of your father in Los Angeles?"

"No, but I have their address."

"Okay," she says, examining my head again. "What you do is you call the operator and you give her your father's name and address. Now, about your wife, all you have to do is give somebody at immigration her name and I'm sure they'll find her for you."

I feel like kissing her right then and there, but instead I shake her hand and thank her for all her wonderful help.

"One more thing," I say.

She looks at somebody waiting behind the glass door.

"Is there a phone here?"

She tells me there are a couple of them to my right, by the bathrooms. I walk out of the cubicle thinking I can—how does the old saying go?—kill two birds with one shot. No, one stone.

CONCHA / While the children were still small, she had a lot of fun going places with them. Lilián, being the younger, was attached to her brother. Everywhere he went, she wanted to go. At the beach she always helped him build sand castles; but then when little Hugo stepped on the towers and kicked the walls, she cried.

When he told her to stop crying and help him, she would. She took the plastic shovel and threw sand over what had taken them so long to construct.

After they started school, Hugo made a lot of friends. The boys didn't accept Lilián. She was a girl. But, later, she made friends too. Sometimes she brought five or six girls over to the house. It pleased Concha that her daughter had friends of her own. The girls gathered in the kitchen and watched Marcelina cook. Marcelina seemed to enjoy the company; she told Concha that she thought of them as her audience, someone she could teach things to.

Hugo played in the backyard with his friends. Hunting birds with slingshots or playing cowboys and Indians, things boys did. Concha watched her son from the kitchen window. He was the smallest of the group, but the most energetic. It was his ideas the other boys agreed with and followed.

Once they started to go to separate schools, Lilián spent very little time with Hugo, and Concha was aware of this. Not that her daughter didn't enjoy doing things with the family, but she preferred to be alone. Concha went out shopping with Lilián. With Hugo to the doctor or to go see his father at the pharmacy. She and Lilián went to the movies. The girl's favorite movie star was Robert Mitchum. She said she liked the way his eyes drooped, and the way his lips narrowed when he smiled.

Hugo spent a lot more time with his father. Esteban believed the boy showed interest in pharmacy. Most of the time he spent in the stockroom playing with test-tubes and the microscope.

Concha realized that her family was not as united as they once were. But there was very little she could do. Her children were growing up. They did things on their own.

So she thought of ways of getting her family to do things together. Marcelina gave her a lot of ideas. Like having parties Lilián and Hugo could invite their friends to, or having a family dine-out night, or a Saturday they would all help Esteban at the pharmacy. These things worked at first, but then her son and daughter kept making other plans.

She spoke to Esteban about it. He wasn't as concerned. He said it was natural for Hugo and Lilián to want to spend time with their friends. He told her that a lot of Lilián's friends were coming to the pharmacy to talk to Hugo now. His son was growing up, and he had begun to like the company of girls.

Concha saw it differently. Her family was growing farther and farther apart and she felt there was very little she could do about it. But she was happy, as long as everyone else was happy, and everyone seemed to be. Happiness, she thought, was a consolation.

ANGEL / The phone rings. Lilián is in the shower, so he goes to answer it. He was counting the day's change in the dining room. Listening to the news. It's the operator, long distance from Key West, does he accept a call from a certain Hugo.

Hugo's voice fades in and out on the line behind a storm of static and somebody else's conversation. "I'm here, Angel," the distant voice says.

"Where? Where are you, Hugo?" Angel says.

"Oh, it's so nice to hear your voice, you don't know—"

"Your father left to pick you up."

"My father. I'm here in Key West. With immigration. I'm in a temporary medical ward."

"He left four days ago," Angel says, trying to picture the face belonging to the voice. "He should be there by now."

"It's crazy here. Too crowded. Is my sister there?"

Lilián, he almost forgets she's in the house. Shower. "I'm going to put her on, okay," he says, "hold on."

"Hurry, I don't have much time. There are—"

Angel rushes to the bathroom and breaks the news to Lilián as calmly as possible without alarming her. "Your brother's all right," he says. "He's on the phone."

This is when she gets out of the bathroom and runs to the hall phone completely naked, dripping water all over the floor.

As soon as she picks the receiver up and puts her ear to it, she chokes with emotion. Angel can see her tremble. He walks up to her and holds her. The water goes through his shirt, soaks it.

She cries and her words come with difficulty, between sobs. She tries to tell her brother to stay put, not to move from there. To tell her where exactly is he located. Please, let her know everything so she can tell their father.

Angel puts his ear close to the phone to listen, but he can't hear Hugo's voice. He will have to wait for Lilián to tell him.

"Let me write this down," she says and motions for Angel to bring her a pen.

He goes to the dining room and finds a notepad and a black pen and takes them to her.

"Okay, tell me everything," she says. "Start with the number there. It's located on the dial—"

Hugo tells her and she writes it down.

"You say this is part of immigration, right? Try and ask somebody there if they know the address."

There is silence now. Lilian turns and looks at Angel. Her eyes are moist. "They probably missed each other," she says to Angel.

"The important thing is that he's here," he says. "Your father'll find him when he gets—"

"Go ahead," she says. "Yes, I'm here. Tell me."

Another pause.

"What do you mean you have to get off the phone?" she says, her voice getting loud.

She tells him to stay put, that Esteban's going to find him. If she knew where he is, she'd fly down to get him. Immigration takes too many precautions. They are as slow as— "You don't know how happy I am to hear you, brother," she says, then, "Can you tell them to let you talk a while longer. No. Hell."

"What's wrong?" Angel says.

"Don't you worry about a thing," she tells her brother. "We'll find you. Stay put. Remember. I love you." She hangs up.

"Why can't he talk?"

"An immigration officer made him get off the phone, the bastard. I imagine he's in custody now."

"They've got to check him out. It's the way they work."

She stands in the hallway with her arms crossed over her breasts. Tears run down her face. Angel embraces her and wipes the tears away. She slides her arms around him and hugs him hard. They stand there in the silence of the hallway holding one another.

DIEGO / Simple enough. Gustavo Prado's address is in the phone book. 3331 Island Drive in Key Biscayne. You dial the number. After all the purring and clicking on the line comes a busy signal.

Since somebody's there at home, you decide to go straight there. A surprise never hurt anybody, did it? Just in case, if you called first and she's there, she might leave.

Driving in Miami is chaos for a stranger. Confusion waits at every street corner. Whoever mapped out the city should be shot. When you least expect it, the numbered streets change to names, from one direction to the other. It feels as if you are driving in a giant maze. Luckily the tank is full, no trouble there.

Every ten blocks or so you stop to check the map. The tiny lines and curves make the whole thing look like wire mesh. You find yourself somewhere in Coral Gables, not too far from Key Biscayne. A short drive and voilà!

To get inside the place you pass by a toll gate and pay a fifty-cent fee. The black women inside the booth stares at the van with a suspicious look on her face. California plates, that must be it. As soon as the bar goes up, you step on the gas and drive out to the end. You pass Seaquarium where there is a billboard of a giant, three-dimensional Orca.

The street winds and ends facing a canal. You park across the street and notice the dark clouds moving inland. Miami, city of *chubascos*.

The light-blue house stands beyond a nicely landscaped circular driveway. As you walk by you hear the lizards scurry over the rocks and plants to their hiding places. The closer you get to the double wood-and-glass door, the more your nerves tingle. A cold sweat breaks out all over your skin.

For a moment you stand there like a mannequin, rehearsing what to say, observing the patterns on the stained wood of the door. The little light over the doorbell is on. It's now or never, and you are not about to turn back.

Finger touches the button. A nice timbre to the doorbell. No sound at first, then footsteps. Click goes the lock, scrape the chain lock, and bingo!

Gustavo.

"Diegito!" he says.

"Surprise," this first word comes out too softly, so you clear your throat and try again. "It's nice to see you," you say.

"Hell, man," Gustavo says and grabs your hand to shake it, "Something told me I was going to have company today . . . but come right in." He lets go, then, "I was cleaning the pool. The goddamned rain knocks down a lot of leaves. I almost didn't hear the bell ring."

Does this mean he's alone in the house?

Gustavo is dressed in a Miami Dolphins T-shirt and cutoff sweat shorts. His skin in tanned, red around the forehead and cheeks. Barefoot, his feet are white.

"Been catching a lot of sun?" This, you are quite aware, is a stupid question. What else do people do down here?

"I've been spending a lot of time out there," he says and points out past the glass of the living room sliding door and the terrace to the wide canal. "Got a new hobby I want to show you later, but first sit down, relax. Let me make you a drink. What do you drink?"

"Rum and coke will be fine," you say and sit down at the edge of the circular sofa. On top of the four cubes that make up the center table sits a long, wiry sculpture of a statue you think you've seen a picture of somewhere. It's hard to tell if it's of a man or a woman. It's just tall and thin, unrealistic proportions.

Gustavo walks over to the bar to fix the drinks. This gives you the perfect chance to slow yourself down and feel at ease. A couple of breaths gets the heartbeat back to normal. Track lighting illuminates the abstract paintings on the walls. They are all done in reds and blues, warm to the sight.

"Nice place you got here," you say.

"I had always wanted a beach house," he says. "It was a secret dream of mine. After I left Pilar I decided to make it come true."

He's always made good money because he's a fine architect. You remember that V used to show you a lot of the drawings and floor plans he was working on when you first started visiting the house.

"How are your parents?" he asks, bringing the drinks over. His is a gin and tonic, a wedge of lime drowning between ice cubes.

"As always," you say, "busy with their ice creams."

"What do they think of Mariel?" He sits down and puts his drink on top of his knee.

"Oh, my grandfather's here. I mean he's there. My uncle, you see, wrote that he is coming. So I came with my grandfather and a couple of friends."

"I'm glad I don't have any family left over there," he says. "Otherwise I'd be going crazy like everybody else. I've been watching the news. It's suicide the way they are crossing over in those little boats."

"The weather's a bitch."

"I had some vacation time coming, so I said, 'What the hell, take the time off now and keep an eye on what's going on.'"

The drink goes down strong. Too much rum, but after a couple more swallows it starts to flow smoothly. That's the thing about alcohol, too easy to get used to.

The silence spreads thick now. You keep drinking to avoid thinking about how uncomfortable the whole situation is. What if he doesn't know his daughter's whereabouts?

You sit there expecting V to walk in to the living room and surprise you.

"That's good news that your uncle is coming," he says.

"Yes, it is. I've never really met him. I know him through what I've heard about him, from the letters that he wrote to my grandmother."

"You look a little thin," he says, holding up his drink.

What did he expect? you think. "I've lost some weight between Los Angeles and here," you say and smile. "It's a hell of a trip."

"I couldn't take it, driving that long," he says and drinks.

There's nothing left in your glass, except the ice cubes. Gustavo stands and returns to the bar to mix another rum and coke and another gin and tonic. The bar is constructed with black-and-gold formica; there are mirrors behind the shelves, which are crushed with expensive-looking bottles.

"Pilar called me," he says, "and told me what happened."

What can you add to this? You opt to keep silent. When in doubt, let the unspoken speak for itself.

"She's become a very bitter woman since I left her," he says and returns to the sofa and once again sits down.

His legs, you notice, are thin and dark, almost hairless around the thighs and knees.

"She said she knew you were going to come down," he says and smiles. "Her intuition never ceases to amaze me. What a nose for trouble she's got!" He laughs.

The drink trembles in your hand, so you do as he does, hold it steady on your knee.

"I told her you are welcome here any time," he continues. "That just because you and our daughter were having problems didn't mean anything to our friendship."

"I'm afraid they are terminal ones," you say.

"So I've heard."

This is a chance he's throwing your way, don't let it go. "She told you? Was she—"

"She was here, Diegito, and she told me about her decision to leave you."

Was, you repeat, while the disappointment sets in quickly. "She's gone?" you ask.

"From the house," he says. "We got into an argument when she blamed me for what happened between me and her mother. Then she left."

"Did she tell you about Danny? My fucking best friend. Not in a million years would I have guessed."

To this he doesn't say a word. He just sits there and drinks.

"Tell you what I'm going to do," he says. "Then we're going to have another drink and I want to show you what I bought, okay?"

You nod.

"I'm going to give you directions on how to get to the place where you might find her," he says, "but I want you to promise me you won't say a word. I gave her my word I wouldn't tell you, the brat."

Brat isn't the exact word, friend.

"Okay, you got a deal."

While he mixes that third drink—by now you feel indifferent enough so that you can follow him to the bar—he tells you about this discotheque in Hialeah called El Continental, a place like the Toucan Club where Danny is playing with a new band. "Surely," he says, "if Vanessa is with him, that's where you'll find her."

Drinks done, he motions you to follow him out to the terrace, down the stairs to the pool and Jacuzzi, and then around the side of the house to the canal dock. "Here it is," he says, "my new toy."

A brand-new four-engine cigarette boat. The boat is covered with a blue cover, but Gustavo climbs on board and unhooks and removes it.

"One hundred thousand dollars' worth of speed," he says. "This little sucker rides the wave like you wouldn't believe."

The little sucker is called *Lightning*, with letters painted in silver and with the L shaped like a lightning bolt.

"It's beautiful."

"I'm planning to take it out tomorrow," he says. "You can come along if you want. It'll give you a chance to meet my girlfriend."

"I'm sorry, Gustavo," you say, "but I'm running short on time."

"Some other time, no?"

"I've never been on a fast boat before," is all you can offer in order not to hurt the man's feelings. After all, he's still an in-law.

"I hope things work out," he says, covering the boat again.

You give him a hand hooking the cover back in place. "I just want to settle things once and for all," you say.

"Keep your head straight, you know. Don't lose your temper."

"I want to have a talk with her, that's all. Find out what she wants."

"Don't worry about what she wants," he says. "Do what *you* want; don't give in to her wishes."

He's on your side, all right, and when the cover's back on the boat and it's time to go, you shake his hand and thank him for the drinks.

"This is your house," he says, "whenever you feel like visiting . . ."

"I appreciate it," you say and put your hand on his shoulder.

"Remember," he says, "when you find her, don't tell her you've seen me."

You assure him you won't, shake his hand one last time, and leave. By the time it starts to rain, you are out of Key Biscayne and on your way to Hialeah, Cube City, U.S.A.

* * *

233

ESTEBAN / Janna, the American reporter, emerges from the cabin dressed in knee-length shorts and a sleeveless blouse. Her legs are firm and strong, the kind he's seen on women tennis players. Rested, her face and eyes look brilliant. Earlier, when she said she was going down to take a nap, he joined don Carlos and Domingo in the cabin from where the view of the water spotted with so many boats was unbelievable.

Even though the sea is rough and the weather doesn't seem to be improving, the yacht travels smoothly. A good ten to fifteen knots per hour. The skipper believes they'll arrive in Mariel in a couple of hours.

Janna sits with her arms up on the edge of the seat and her legs stretched out. She's wearing new deck shoes. Esteban, drinking the last of his beer, approaches and sits across from her.

"Would you like something to drink?" he asks her.

"Thank you, not right now," she says and smiles. "I'm feeling a little queasy."

"Is queasy like dizzy?" If it weren't for the beer he'd be feeling the same way. But now he feels as safe and steady as if he were on land.

"It's what's left over from a headache," she says. "I'm sure it'll pass."

"I hope so."

From where he sits he can see the cabin. By the time they get there, Domingo's going to know how to navigate the thing, he thinks. Don Carlos's is just worried the boat's headed in the right direction.

"I can't believe it," Janna says, looking at the boat traffic. "None of it makes sense."

"What are you trying to figure out?"

"Why? Why now? Why so many people? Surely there's got to be a catch."

"There's always a catch," he says, "except it isn't evident yet."

"I've been covering the news for a long time," she says and looks at him, "and I've never seen anything quite like this."

"It's called freedom."

"It's been rafts and paddles up to now," she says. "Sneaking out in the middle of the night to avoid the coast guard. I always try to imagine what being on a tire inner tube, floating in the middle of nowhere, must be like. It's the point of view I like to take when I do a story."

"A chance like this comes once."

"I'm interested in the country, its people."

"All I'm interested in is in my son getting out alive," he says, then goes ahead and tells her about Hugo, about the part his son played in the revolution, his incarceration. When he's done telling her, he excuses himself, walks to the cooler, and fetches two beers. He returns and hands her one.

"Drink it," he says. "It'll do you good."

She takes it and holds it for a while before she tilts her head back and drinks.

"I've been keeping track of all the stories. People braving the waters any which way. I want to put together a book of these, maybe some interviews."

He gets curious—has been since the first time he saw her on television. "I'm sure it's going to be very interesting," he says, "just like its author."

Three beers later, she opens up and tells him about herself. She's originally from Texas, a little town outside of Houston. Graduated from Columbia with a degree in political science. From Columbia she went to Berkeley and received a master's in journalism, her true love.

"Are you married?" he asks, not noticing a ring on her finger.

"Once," she says. "I was married to a businessman too interested in business, little in me."

"My wife died several years ago," he says, crossing his feet.

"Sorry to hear that."

"I'm used to not having her around anymore," he says, wondering if he should mention how close she really is.

"The farthest thing on my mind is marriage," she says. "I figure if it didn't work the first time, it—"

"You can't think like that," he says, "a beautiful woman like you."

She blushes. Her eyes try to avert his by staring at the label on the beer bottle.

"Your husband was a fool to let you go."

"I left him," she says. "Anyway, I still have a career to keep me occupied."

Domingo brings more beer and joins them. He looks drunk. His eyes turn red and watery when he's had too much to drink. "Don Carlos is at the helm," he says. "Let's hope the skipper keeps his eye on him." He laughs.

Esteban hasn't seen his friend this happy or this drunk in a long time. Ruth must be out of his head.

"Who are you picking up?" Janna asks Domingo.

"Nobody," he says, "unless I run into a good-looking woman in need of rescue."

"This is the last one for me," she says and lifts her bottle.

"I want to propose—propose a toast," Domingo says and stands. "As the French would put it, bon voyage." He looks toward the cabin and breaks into laughter again.

They all tap bottles and drink. Domingo sits down again. "What are you going to do when you get there?" he asks Janna.

She says she's just going to get a good look. If the authorities let her interview, she's going to do that. She says she brought her handy tape recorder.

"Be careful with it," Esteban says. "That's the kind of equipment they kill for."

"*Mercado negro,*" Domingo says, meaning the black market.

Don Carlos comes over and sits next to Janna. He's got a smile of contentment on his face. "It's easy," he says. "Nothing to it."

Domingo wants to know who needs another beer. Janna declines, but Esteban and don Carlos accept.

Don Carlos discusses his plans of what needs to be done on arrival. First order of business is to ask authorities for information, find the members of Carlos Piñeda's family and Hugo. If for some reason they have trouble finding the people, then Janna can use her influence. But he doesn't see how they can go wrong. Mariel is a small place.

Domingo returns with the beers and apologizes for taking a little time to visit the boys' room.

"It's the girls' room too," Janna says, "and I am going to prove it." She smiles, stands, and walks away.

They all turn to look at her, then don Carlos says to Esteban, "I think if you tell her an interesting story, you might catch her attention, know what I mean?" He winks.

"I think don Carlos is right," Domingo says. "Get her to turn on her machine. I mean her recorder. Sing her a song she might like, that's what I say."

"I don't know any good songs," Esteban says. "At least not clean ones."

They all laugh and drink. Don Carlos puts his hand on the spot Janna was sitting on. All of a sudden he gets serious and says, "Oh my, oh my. Put your hands right here and feel the warmth."

Neither Esteban nor Domingo moves from his spot.

"It's burning," don Carlos continues. "I think we have one hell of a hotblooded gringa on our hands."

"Did she say how old she was?" Domingo wants to know.

"No," Esteban says.

"I'd guess she's in the prime of her time," don Carlos says. "Early forties maybe."

"Good guess," Domingo agrees.

Janna reappears and when she sits down Esteban tries to keep from smiling. He doesn't want to give away that she's been the subject of their conversation.

"You were right," don Carlos says and gets up to return to the cabin. "It's as much the girls' room as it is the boys'."

Domingo leaves too. Once again he finds himself alone with Janna. He looks at her and she catches his stare. It's his turn to blush. "Were your ears geting hot down there?" he asks her.

"They are probably red from all the drinking."

"That's not what I meant," he says. She gets a puzzled look. "We were talking about you."

"You were."

"Don't worry," he says. "It was all good."

"Sure," she says, followed by the killer smile again. "I get the feeling when the three of you are together, you misbehave."

"Maybe you can join the group and we can all misbehave together."

"I might surprise you," she says and puts her legs back up on the seat.

"That calls for more beer," he says. He goes to the cooler and on the way back, the skipper, Domingo, and don Carlos look at him and smile. He flashes them an okay sign with his free hand. There might be a couple of good stories he could tell her after all.

* * *

HUGO / After I hang up with my sister, another man in uniform leads me next door. On the way we pass by the cubicle and I see the woman whose child is getting his arm in a cast. She smiles weakly. I wave back. The man in uniform apologizes for cutting my call off but nobody's allowed to wander.

I don't have to wait on line. The man pushes his way inside. He's got the authority, so I follow him. "What happens in here?" I ask.

"Somebody's going to ask you some questions," he says. "After that I don't know."

Inside there are desks. Desks and more desks lined up in rows. This is where all the interviewing and interrogations are being conducted. There are immigration officers behind each desk. They seem to be intent on what they are doing, leafing through folders, writing, waiting for their questions to be answered.

It is in front of one of these desks that I see her. Her back is turned to me, but I'd recognize that head of hair and body anywhere. The dress too. She is wearing her best dress.

"LUCINDA!" I scream out, and suddenly all is quiet around me. Faces peer.

She turns to face me.

The uniformed man takes hold of my arm. Perhaps he thinks I'm going to attack her. "I know her," I tell him. "Let me go, please. I know her."

He walks over with me, then I pull my arm out of his grip and run to her. She is crying from the excitement. Immediately I work my arms around her and embrace her hard. No words come.

Instead, I begin to cry too. I feel her sobbing against me. She kisses me. Her lips taste salty. They are dry and rough.

Finally these words come: "I thought I'd never find you," I say.

"Oh," she says, "oh, baby." She goes limp against me and I think she's going to faint or something, so I tell the man behind me to pull out the chair for her. She sits down. Won't let go of my hands.

I tell her how I left camp and went to get her, but that she was no longer there.

"They evacuated the place," she says. "I was lucky. I snuck into the group at the last minute and nobody saw me."

"You mean everybody came," I say, meaning all the crazies

were allowed to leave. There were a lot of chronic cases in the ward, disturbed people with violent tendencies.

The man behind the desk is staring; so is the one in uniform behind me. "Can you get her some water? Please." I ask the one in uniform. The man behind the desk nods okay.

I tell Lucinda to stick close to me, to let me do all the talking, that if we don't mention much about our pasts, we'll be able to get processed quickly and out of here.

She squeezes my hand and sits down. Then she hugs me and kisses me and thanks God that I'm alive. "Oh, baby, baby," she says. Her grip tightens around me. She prays out loud.

August, 1958

Dear Mother:

We are coming upon the cane field where Lobo told me to meet him when the sound of two planes arrives with the breeze. From the hills we see what is happening.

The planes circle over the fields. Army trucks brought two or three regiment troops and they have surrounded the area. An ambush.

"They've got no way out," Lucinda says. "Shit."

"Come on," I say. "We've got to do something."

"Wait a minute," she says. "We just can't go down there without planning something."

"There isn't any time to plan. We have to do something now."

"If we create some kind of disturbance," she says, "they'll think they are being outnumbered."

"That's a good idea," I say, "but what do we use?"

"We can fire a couple of rounds."

"No, we might need the ammunition if we get caught."

"A fire then," she says. "We'll set the field behind them on fire."

The closer we draw, the more trucks we see. The whole area is infested with army troops. The planes keep circling overhead. All this time I am thinking that Lobo and his men are going to die.

Sniper fire comes from the tall cane. They are stranded there all right.

"What if we take some of these bastards out from up here," Lucinda says, "at random."

"Might be our only choice."

"Are you a good shot?" she asks.

I stop, hold my rifle steady, and aim. Finger on the trigger, I press. Miss.

She does the same and hits one of the soldiers. I shoot again and score.

They take cover. We can see them scattering, but there's nowhere they can hide except behind the trucks or among the cane itself.

"A couple of grenades," she says, "would blow those fuckers to kingdom come."

Two trucks drive out, turn around, and head in our direction. They stop at the edge of the foothills and troops get out. Lucinda hits two more.

Rapid gunfire comes from Lobo's direction. "He's moving," I say.

"Keep shooting," she says.

"We've got to get back."

The planes drop fire bombs over the field. The army troops trickle out and board the trucks. "Let's get out of here," I tell her.

Lucinda's too busy taking aim and shooting. I pull her away into the green where those bastards know better than to follow.

We run, leaving the sound of machine-guns behind, then stop to catch our breath and think of what to do next. We start to walk around the seam of the valley, in Lobo's general direction. The sound of the planes fades.

> *Your Son, hitting*
> *and running,*
> *Hugo*

DIEGO / A quick stopover at a restaurant to kill some time. The restaurant is located a couple of blocks from your destination, between a row of drab apartment bungalows and a canal that runs parallel to the street.

It's too early to go to the club, so you sit at the counter and eat a steak sandwich. Doubtful the band might even be there.

At the other end of the counter the waitress talks to a fat man who speaks with a slight lisp. The glasses he wears keep sliding down the bridge of his nose and he keeps pushing them up with a greasy middle finger. "I've got him trained not to do that in the house," he says to the waitress, "and God forbid if he does, because . . ." He stops for another mouthful.

The conversation is about dogs. The waitress has a spaniel she just got from a boyfriend. She's training it to go outside to do its necessities.

When she brings over the check, a smile exposes a gold tooth. You give her seven dollars and tell her to keep the change. The sandwich cost $4.95.

Outside can't be any wetter or more humid. The sun has gone down and the streetlights are on. Drizzle falls against the light they shed. Where do the mosquitoes go when it rains?

Feeling the loose change in your pocket, you decide to call home. It takes a while before the call goes through because the operator says the line is busy. "It's an emergency," you say, trying not to get the sticky phone too close to the ear.

"Still busy, sir," the operator says. "Would you like to try later."

What if you really had an emergency? "No problem," you say and hang up. What a stupid thing to do, leave the phone off the hook. They must not have done it on purpose. The coins return and you pocket them.

It's time. The drive to El Continental is a short hop. The building could never compare to the Toucan Club. No way. For one thing, it is not on Sunset but is boxed in the center of two factory warehouses. For another, it doesn't have the glimmer and shimmer of lights and the decor.

The place is already open. Couples have started to arrive for early dinner. You park the van across the street. It has started to rain, so you run across the street and stop under the canvas awning of the entrance. The doorman greets you by saying you should have valet parked.

"I won't be staying long," you say. "Do me a favor and keep an eye on the van for me." You slip him a dollar.

Inside things look better. Classier. With the tables around the dance floor and the mirrors on the wall, it looks more like a restaurant than a cabaret or discotheque. The stage curtains are drawn—no light on underneath.

One thing you've learned from Nestor about bartenders is that if you ever want any information, walk up to the bar, buy the bartender a shot, and ask what you need to know. Except it isn't a matter of asking, but of putting words in a way that will elicit friendly conversation before you move in for the kill.

You follow the first two steps—you approach the bar, tell the bartender you are in a good mood and buy him a drink. After he downs the shot, you buy him another and sharpen the blade. "Listen," you say, pushing one of the stools aside. The more room, the better it is to breathe. "I got a call today from somebody in the band to come and try out tonight."

"Oh, yeah? What instrument do you play?"

"Skins," you say.

"Drums?"

"Close, the timbales."

"You any good?"

Ah, bartenders. "That's what I'm here to find out."

"You mean you don't know."

"I can make those babies sing and weep at the same time," you say. He pours another shot. "So I'm wondering if you can lead me in the right direction."

"The band doesn't start playing until nine o'clock," he says, looking at his wristwatch, a digital plastic job. "Right after dinner. It's barely seven thirty."

"Seven thirty," you say alarmed. One look at your own watch reveals the problem. You are over forty minutes fast. Shit.

You remove the watch and set it right. "It's that west-coast time deal," you say.

"You come from the west coast to try out for the band?" a customer with a crooked bow tie asks.

"Sure did," you say, "but I thought I had synchronized this fucker."

"Maybe you should talk to the manager," the bartender says.

"No, no, I'll be all right once I speak to the band leader, you know." Fake trying to remember the name. "Mr. . . . "

"Shit, I don't know his last name. Around here we call him Flax."

"You mean as in Flaco."

"Yeah, he's a skinny son of a bitch."

That's the man. Another shot for the bartender.

"Three's my limit," he says and puts the cap back on the bottle.

"You know what? Maybe I should go see this guy. He did say that if I didn't find him here I can go see him at home."

By the look on the bartender's face, you figure it's going to take a lot more cunning and the help of Benjamin Franklin. "Listen," you start, "I wrote the address down in a hurry and I seem to have misplaced it." Out of the wallet comes the one-hundred dollar bill. "If you can get it for me . . . "

So they say money talks and bullshit walks and to this bartender money is a parrot with bad manners who doesn't want to stop talking.

"I'll be right back. I think I've seen it on the Rolodex in the office."

"Sure, the Rolodex in the office."

The shots have hit you hard. The old stomach rumbles a couple of complaints. You promise it some Alka-Seltzer soon. Even better, maybe the friendly neighborhood bartender knows who sells good dope around here.

The bartender returns with a three-by-five folded in half. The address is in Hialeah. "Have that third drink," you say and slip the card in your pocket.

"That sounds good," he says and pours.

"One more thing," you tell him. "Know where I can score something for my sinuses? You know, some toot."

"I might be able to introduce you to the right person later on," he says. "Come back."

"If Flax comes in, please tell him I've gone to look for him," you say, shaking his hand.

"Wait," he says. "What's the name?"

"He'll know when you mention the timbales."

Time to go. In the van, the reading lamp on, you check the address on the map and find out which way to go. Pass Forty-Ninth street, on Twelfth Avenue. To the left-hand side, a brand-new condominum.

Parking by the security garage gate, you think that all you've got to do now is wait for Mr. Piano Man to leave so you can have some privacy with the person both of you have in common—share is more like the word, shared in your case. Then you can wait for him to return and the three of you can have a serious adult conversation.

Ah, sarcasm, mother of the tongue-in-cheek!

September, 1959

Mama Concha:

This is a story Lucinda told me:

Once there was an island inhabited by such Indian tribes as the Siboneys, Tainos, and later the Caribs. The Spaniards arrived and (as would become the pattern in all their conquests) thought the semi-naked barbarians' ways evil and uncivilized.

Under the name of Christianity, they ransacked the villages, raped the women (the white men got what they deserved: syphilis and gonorrhea) and killed the men. There are many versions of this legend, but the most striking remains: There, tied to the stake, stood Hatuey, chieftain of the Siboneys. Naked, the straw tickling at his feet. The good Franciscan priest, sweating under his heavy yute frock, offered the chief a last chance at redemption.

Would the noble savage accept God and His heaven?

Noble savage inquired: Do the white men also go there?

Yes, my son, said the priest, We all will if we accept Him.

Hatuey closed his eyes from the glare of the torch which was about to fall on the straw, then spoke these famous last words:

In that case, let the devil be my savior.

A Hug

Hugo

PART V

Book of
New Directions

ESTEBAN / Who would have believed it, Concha? he thinks, as the boat approaches Mariel. Esteban Carranza back here, eh? He's standing in the cabin with Norton. Too bad it is so dark that the light of the other boats is all that can be seen. The whole coast is black. Blackouts, he remembers.

Once in a while a flare is fired. The Cuban coast guard cutters are working like herd dogs, trying to funnel all the boats to the side. They are trying to form a bottleneck around the harbor to screen all the incoming boats. Once in a while they flash their spotlights on the boats. One goes by and from its loudspeaker comes. *"¡Tiren ancla! ¡Tiren ancla! ¡Tienen que esperar hasta mañana!"*

"What did they say?" Norton says.

"We have to anchor and wait until tomorrow."

Don Carlos and Domingo, who are watching from the bow of the boat, return to the cabin. "Son of a bitch," don Carlos says.

"We're in their waters," says the skipper.

"Shit," says don Carlos.

"Where's Janna?" Esteban asks.

"Last I saw her," Domingo says, "she went downstairs."

"I think she's got a weak stomach for the ocean," the skipper says. Then to don Carlos, "I don't think we have a choice."

In order not to listen to don Carlos complaining about having to wait until tomorrow, Esteban decides to go down and get a head start on some rest. He wants to be the first up and around in the morning.

Trying to decide whether he should wait to scatter Concha's remains tonight while it's dark or wait until tomorrow by the light of day, he enters the cabin. The lights are out.

He can hear all the pacing back and forth going on overhead. This is the first time that he's been below.

"Where's the light in this place?" he says out loud to himself.

A lamplight comes on toward the end of the cabin. The gringa's awake. "How are you feeling?" he asks.

"Much better," she says.

She looks fine with the light behind her. Her voice sounds a little sleepy, but other than that she seems to be in top shape. No signs of being seasick.

"I was listening to all the commotion out there," she says.

"I get the feeling it's going to go on all night." He sits on her bunk. "I hope we can all get some rest."

"Rest," she says. "I was making up my mind to go up and have a couple of more beers."

"You're crazy." He starts to remove his shoes.

She sits up and folds her arms over her knees. He can't avoid looking down between her legs where her shorts end and her flesh begins. She looks at him and smiles, but doesn't make the slightest effort to bring her legs down. Maybe she's too tired.

"You know," he says, "maybe I can get us some beers and drink them down here."

"Anything to stop the rocking," she says.

He can think of ways of keeping the rocking going. "This is the first time I sleep in a boat," he says.

"Me too, and I don't like it."

Not bothering to put his shoes back on, he returns to the deck and gets the beer. On the way back he stops in the cabin to ask the skipper a question. "What are the sleeping arrangements downstairs?"

Norton, Domingo, and don Carlos immediately look at him. "Why?" the skipper wants to know.

"Because I think I might not want to be disturbed," he says.

Don Carlos starts to clap and Domingo to laugh. The skipper smiles and says, "There's a sliding door between the sleeping quarters."

"Just make sure you don't make too much noise, huhn," says don Carlos. "You might alarm the coast guard."

They laugh.

He searches for approval in his friend's eyes, but Domingo is already nodding yes.

"I'm not saying that anything's going to happen?" Esteban says.

"I'm sure Concha's not going to mind," Domingo says.

"You've got nothing to lose," don Carlos adds.

Beer ih hand, he goes down. Janna stares at him as he sits down and twists the caps off the bottles. He hands her a bottle.

Now they sit facing each other, drinking, him waiting for the right sign to make his move, all the time thinking he's too old and that he shouldn't even try, not with Concha's remains still on board.

At last he settles for conversation. Words have always come easy to him. He begins to tell her about his youth in Santiago. One thing leads to another and before he realizes it he's telling Janna about the family, mainly Concha and how much she means to him.

CONCHA / As far as she knew, he had never been unfaithful. Not that she was jealous—maybe she was—but early on she learned to trust him. Lilián, in the kitchen with her and Marcelina, asked the question because she said she couldn't stand the jealousy that was eating her up. Her boyfriend Angel worked at La Francia, the department store, and she knew he came in contact with a lot of women buyers, women customers, women representatives, always women.

Concha had never seen Angel before, but that day her daughter showed her a picture. He was handsome all right, carefully groomed mustache, elegantly dressed in a cream-colored suit and a dark-blue tie. Concha turned the snapshot over and read the inscription: *To the one I love, Angel.*

"This sounds serious," Marcelina said.

"He loves you," Concha said, returning the picture to her daughter. "What more do you want?"

"I want him to be with me all the time," Lilián said. "Know what I mean? I want him twenty-four hours of the day with me. Me!"

"You're talking marriage now," Marcelina said and smiled at Concha.

"Yes," Lilián said, "he wants to marry me."

"I'd recommend that both of you wait," Concha said, perfectly aware she was using her motherly voice. "Finish school, no?"

"Ah, mother, you don't understand. I love him; he loves me. I don't see why we have to wait."

"If you talk to your father," Concha told her daughter, "I'm sure he's got a couple of reasons up his sleeve."

Marcelina laughed. She was preparing chicken for dinner and the whole counter was greasy with skin and fat. "I'm sure if he loves you like he says he does, then he won't mind waiting for you to finish school."

"You're always on her side," Lilián said.

"Of course, honey," Marcelina said, "I get paid to be."

This made Lilián so mad she rushed out of the kitchen, leaving the maid and her mother smiling.

"She's just young," Marcelina said, "that's all. Young and in love."

"She thinks I've never been in her shoes."

"I've worn them too. Got hurt," Marcelina said. She was married once, Concha knew, but now lived with another man.

"He is a handsome young man," Concha said.

"They are all handsome. All of them."

DIEGO / The electric garage gate opens. The Mustang appears with who else but Flaco in it. He's using her car, the bastard. Move quickly now, you think. Run and slide underneath the gate just as it comes down.

You go up the stairs to the second floor, find the apartment number, and knock. The door doesn't have a peephole, so the chance of her not opening the door is out of the question. She can ask who it is, but V's careless. She approaches on the other side and opens the door.

The expression on her face is the same as that of someone who has just been told she is dying of cancer.

You stand there without words. Judging from the heat running in your blood, you doubt your expression is any better. But then again what does she expect you to say: I was on my way to Disney World and I thought I'd stop and say hello, isn't it a small world?

"I'm never going to speak to my father," she says, "for as long as I live."

"He had nothing to do with it," you say and push your way inside the apartment. "A friendly bartender at El Continental told me where I could find Flax, that's his name now, huhn?"

"You can't stay," she says and closes the door.

There you stand, in the middle of furniture you seem to recognize, thinking of how a female bird moves stuff from one nest to another, no ill feelings, no regrets.

Welcome back to the new home, her palace of the boxed and canned, the already mixed—just add water.

"Know what?" you say. "You still have the flair for being dramatic. It's the tragic influence in you. You must have inherited it from your mother. Nice lady, your mother."

"I'd appreciate it if—"

"Sit down," you say. "I'm not leaving until—until he comes back. Then we can all have a nice, friendly chat."

"He's not coming back until morning," she says. "The clubs here close later than in L.A."

"Oh," you say, sitting down on the sofa and putting your feet up on its armrest. "I left him a message. I'm sure he'll come back in no time."

"I'm going to call the police," she says.

"Tsk, tsk, tragic, tragic. What are they going to do?"

"You're a royal asshole," she says.

"Look," you say, "sit down. Relax. I just come to give you guys my blessings. Explain to old Mr. Flax the things you like and don't like."

She looks helpless, but beautiful. Had they just finished making love? you wonder. She's got an aura of contentment about her, the same as she used to get back home. Back home is thousands of miles away, back home isn't anymore and will never be.

"Nice place," you say, "though the least you could've done was get new furniture. This secondhand shit doesn't go with the rest of the decor."

"It was mine," she says.

"Very nicely stolen out of the house," you say. "Mrs. Plater told me."

"That's the problem with you," she says, leaning back against the chair. "You've always listened to everything people tell you."

"So far I haven't been misled, have I?"

She stands now. "I couldn't take it anymore," she says, "not a minute more. I felt I couldn't get a word in edgewise. You were always at the club."

"It's called making a living."

"Call it whatever, but—"

"So you left one musician for another."

"Music doesn't mean as much to Danny as it does to you," she says and looks at you fiercely. "Face it, it means more than I meant to you."

"That's not true, and you know it."

"Besides, we were going to keep being unfaithful to each other."

"More excuses out of your bag of excuses."

"Come on, be honest with yourself," she says. "We were bored with each other, except you got bored with me first. Remember?"

"Like I said," you say, "I didn't come here to argue."

"What did you come for then?"

"To wish both of you happiness."

She looks over and smiles.

"Seriously," you say. "I figured since you both had gone out of your way to betray me and be unfaithful—it must be love. True love."

"Fuck you, Diego!"

"So this is it," you say, "a half-assed club in Miami, eh? Sun and Beach City."

"We are happy here," she says. "My mother's going to come live with us."

"You really want to know why I came?"

"Oh, there are more reasons?"

"Because of my grandfather," you say, knowing perfectly well that she isn't going to swallow any of it. "The old man talked me into driving down with him to pick up my uncle. There are other

252

things going on in the world, in case you're not aware of them. Don Carlos came too. He's got family coming."

"Good for everybody," she says.

"Aren't you going to offer me something to drink?" you say. "Let's see if you remember what I drink."

"No alcohol," she says. "Danny doesn't drink."

"Since when?"

"I think you know since when," she says. "That's the problem with you. You get drunk and then you don't remember anything. First it was booze, then coke. How was I supposed to believe anything you said if most of the time you were either drunk or zooming?"

"So it's my fault."

"Look, it's nobody's fault. That's what I'm trying to tell you. I'm not blaming you. But it's over, Diego. I don't love you and you don't love me, okay?"

"Okay. I like it when things are black and white."

"I knew you were going to come," she says.

"Gee, I wonder if Lady Pilar had anything to do with it."

She is telling you to leave her mother out of it, when there's the sound of keys jingling outside the door. Not moving, she braces herself.

"Aren't you going to let him in?" you say, standing and going to the door.

Danny opens the door. He is furious, but Vanessa stands in the way. "Tell him why I came," you say to her.

"Mother fucker," Danny says, "can't you just let things rest."

"Not when my ex-best friend and my wife—last time I checked we were still married—elope."

"She left your ass, see," he says, "because you're a fuckup. A total fuckup."

Skinny and blunt as always, Danny moves to the side and goes to the sofa and sits down. He looks weary, which leads you to believe that he's been banging Vanessa regularly. She does that: want, want, want, until the fine day when she says she doesn't want anymore, and cuts you off completely. Too bad if the cuts bleed.

"Look man," you say, "I came by to make it official. I'm

divorcing her ass. What you do with her is your business."

"How kind of you," he says, "but nothing's official until she gets the papers."

"You've become one hell of a businessman," you say, "but then again you've always had it in you. No room for creativity, just numbers and figures, and if they don't match—"

"Yes, he is," Vanessa says and goes wild, pacing back and forth, from Danny to the door where you are standing. "Oh, yes he is. You want to know how creative he is? Well, let me tell you. I'm pregnant."

The words come out as hard as if she had taken a sledgehammer and hit you on the side of the head. Bang!

Then there is a silence so thick it hangs in the room like fog. Get out now, you tell your legs, but they don't want to move. Vanessa doesn't look pregnant, no noticeable belly under her robe. No wonder Pilar's coming.

"It's Danny's," she says, moving in for the jugular. "You never wanted a kid, remember?"

"Have your lawyer get in touch with mine," you say.

"You still don't understand, do you? I didn't want to hurt you," she says, "not this way. Anyway, I am happy. This is the best thing that has ever happened to me."

Danny's got his face in his hands, not saying anything.

You move to the door, grab for the knob and turn it. "I'm happy for the two of you," you say. "I just wish you wouldn't have been such cowards."

Leaving down the hall, you feel her eyes following you. But you don't dare turn around for a last look. It's over, you tell yourself. Then she closes the door gently.

Now the necessity to hear a friendly voice is great, too overwhelming, so you drive aimlessly looking for a telephone booth. Then you find one at the nearest gas station and you get out and dial the operator, and when she comes on you give her Maruchi's number.

Maruchi's phone rings several times; then the operator asks if you'd wish to call back later. "She's there," you say. "Just let it ring."

Then Maruchi answers.

The operator asks her if she accepts the call, and she does. "Diego, are you all right?"

"Yes," you say and clear your throat. "I just wanted to call and listen to your voice."

"I have bad news," she says. "I called your house and left a message."

"I haven't called."

"Nestor's at the hospital," her voice comes softly. "He's in pretty bad shape."

Brace yourself against the side of the booth and ask what happened.

"He got into some problems with the people he owed money to. They busted his ribs, broke both arms and a leg. Sliced his face up pretty badly."

"Shit! Is he going to make it?"

"The doctor says he's going to be fine. I've been at the hospital since it happened. Susie and I have been taking turns. Just got home a little while ago."

"I'm glad I got a hold of you."

"How are you doing?"

"Seen better days, but I'll make it through."

"Tell me when and I'll pick you up at the airport," she says.

"I've got to take care of some other business first," you say.

There is silence at her end, so you tell her that you have to drop the van off in Key West, then make it back to Miami and catch a plane.

"I'll meet you."

"Thanks," you say.

"Diego."

"What?"

"I miss you," she says.

"I'll be there as soon as I can, babe," you tell her. "Just keep an ear open for my call, okay?"

She tells you she will, then you say good-bye and hang up. No longer, you think, will you be blind to someone as good as Maruchi.

Fucking Nestor, you warned him about doing business with assholes. Damn, busted him up good. He'll make it through, though, he's a strong mother fucker.

The next step is to get out of this fucking place, out of the heat and the rain and the asphyxiating humidity. Out, out. No need to consult the map, the expressway, as the freeway is called here, is up ahead.

Christmas, 1959

Dearest Mom:

I write the letter Lobo sends to Havana. In it he states that communism has a strange way of attaching itself to a cause, and that the revolution was fought for justice, not tyranny. He sends the letter via a courier.

In the meantime we sit and wait.

Lucinda's hair has grown back to the way she had it when she first came. She hasn't had any more attacks. I'm still trying to convince her to go see a doctor. She says she will as soon as we win.

I want to marry her, mother, but she doesn't think it's such a good idea, keeping in mind how much moving around we'll be doing. She wants to work hard and maybe procure a high position in the new government. Social work. She's got more plans than I do. I haven't really changed that much in these past months. I've done my best to survive and that has been enough. I am alive and healthy, maybe a little thin, but you must keep in mind our situation.

When I go visit I would like to have Marcelina make me a big, fat, juicy steak and some fried plantains. My mouth waters . . .

Waiting,
Hugo

ESTEBAN / Conversation comes easily at this late an hour. Esteban is telling Janna about the family's trip from Santiago to Varadero, from where they left on August 31, 1962. "A taxi took us," he says. "I remember what a terrible trip it was. Bad weather caught us midway. The rain fell hard, like bolts falling on tin. Oh, Jesus, and the lightning. Concha kept her eyes closed. Diego slept soundly. Lilián was afraid that we were going to get stuck somewhere along the road.

"Only one of the windshield wipers worked, not the one on the driver's side. Anyway, the man had to stick his arm out to keep his side rainfree, but the rain was falling too fast and too hard. We kept stopping and starting, but no luck, the rain wouldn't go away. So the man cursed and we kept on moving, slower; but as he said, each mile counted. Got us closer to our destination.

"Angel kept quiet. He sat with me up front holding on to the handle on the dashboard. The taxi was an old Chevy, if I remember correctly. Rain leaked through some rusted-out holes in the roof of the cab. At one point a fit of nervous laughter overcame the man, who managed to say that he would get us there one way or another."

Janna's attention is all his, though she looks away once in a while to hide her yawns.

"Well, all our luggage got wet—they were cheap suitcases with cardboard lining on the inside, so you can imagine. Wet clothes and soggy paper. But we made it to Varadero all right. At the airport we paid the driver what we owed him and he helped us with the luggage."

"He charged you," she says, "after what he put you through."

"He did us a favor," Esteban says. "Without him we would have never gotten out of Santiago. Cars—any car—were hard to come by."

It is at this very moment that don Carlos calls Esteban to go up on deck, that Domingo has left the boat.

"Left?" Esteban says. "What do you mean left? Where? Wait a minute. How the hell did he get off the boat?"

"I don't know," don Carlos says. "Me and the skipper fell asleep."

"Over here," the skipper says from the control cabin. "I found something."

Esteban follows don Carlos to where the skipper stands holding a piece of paper. The night, Esteban notices, has dissolved into dawn.

"I think it's a note he's left," the skipper says.

"He's crazy," Esteban says, taking the piece of paper from the skipper.

"Drunk's what he was," don Carlos says. "God knows we all had our share. I just don't understand how he managed to get off."

The instant Esteban opens the piece of paper, it is evident from the careless way the note is written that his friend was drunker than hell. This is what the note says:

Esté:

By the Time you read This I'LL Be on My way to Santiago. Please forgive me for taking Concha's Remains, but think about this: Wouldn't She—she have wanted To be buried closer To home? Her real home. Santiago. Yes. I leave you the check. It should help Hugo Get on his feet. Anyway, Money isn't Going to do me much Good where I'm going. Expect to hear from me.

Cheers!

He can't believe it. How did Domingo get off the boat? The skipper says the emergency raft is missing. "We were so far gone that we didn't hear it inflate," he says.

The money order, which is now signed over to Esteban, is taped to the back of the note. Son of a bitch, Esteban thinks, I hope he makes it. Though he couldn't have guessed it in a million tries, he knows now that that's what his friend wanted. He even thinks maybe Domingo tried to tell him during the road trip, but couldn't bring himself to do so. Jesus, maybe he thought I was going to stop him.

Janna comes up and he tells her everything. She puts her hand over his shoulder and says she's sorry.

"I'm not," Esteban tells her. "I'm sure it's what he wanted."

"I hope he makes it."

"He can't lose either way, can he?" He says and stands close to her as the dawn sheds light on the multitiude of boats. This is the first time in a long time that he's spent a sleepless night, and it feels good. There's a new vitality in his system. A bravura. He can feel it working in his legs. Stronger, he moves about the boat with a sense of assurance. He is anxious to dock and find out what's going on with his son.

January, 1959

Mamacita:

Havana falls shortly after our beloved (here's a little sarcasm) president leaves the country in the middle of the night. How brave a man he is. It is all over the newspapers. He took off in an airplane, destination unknown.

Rebel troops arrive from Havana and help us take over Santiago. What is left of the old guard puts up very little resistance. We do a quick job seizing the city, not one single casualty, no bullets wasted. Whatever government troops are holed up inside Moncada surrender. We take over the radio stations and immediately start broadcasting our success. Pictures of the victory come out in the daily newspaper.

The struggle has ceased, and a feeling of exuberance and joy overwhelms us. Lobo gives a speech over the radio. His voice sounds distant, withdrawn, certainly not the voice of a victorious commander. " . . . the whole idea of Soviet support is unsettling . . . "

After the speech Camilo and two other high-ranking officers come and arrest Lobo, relieve him of command. He is to be held until the commander-in-chief himself arrives to assess the situation.

They take Lobo away and leave us under house arrest

in the old city hall building. Our weapons are taken from us. Nobody's clear on what is going on. The men look restless holed up in this hot governmental latrine of a place. Beaten.

Lucinda approaches me and puts her arms around me. Her breathing's disturbed, as though she has been running. She says she was just downstairs where they have two guards on duty. "I'm afraid they are going to separate us," she says.

"They'll let us go once Lobo sets everything straight."

"Just like a real jail."

When she leaves my side to go back downstairs—it is at this very moment—I feel the urgency to finish this up and get it to you. I might be able to pay somebody to take it to you. Mother, most of this might incriminate me if it is found. Once it reaches you, do with it what you think is best. I'd suggest you destroy it. Burn it. Fire, from what I have witnessed, leaves no clues.

In surrender, Hugo.

DIEGO / Early morning takeoff. Dark sky still. Empty flight. The plane seems to be chasing the westward night. Toward the front the stewardess holds up the safety manual and instructs everybody on how to put on a life preserver, buckle it, and inflate it. From an overhead compartment an oxygen mask is supposed to pop out in case of lack of air at high altitudes.

You left the van in a good spot in Key West. Easy to find. Then called Lilián. After the call, a cab back to Miami: Two hundred and thirty-three dollars in fare.

The aircraft has left the city behind. Miami, only clusters of colorful little lights . . . The captain's voice comes over the loudspeaker, ". . . we'll be leveling off at thirty-eight thousand feet. Our flying time is approximately four hours and thirty minutes. We thank you for flying with us this morning."

Dawn. Its colors blend above a thick bed of clouds. Soothing for some reason. Glad not to have anybody sitting beside you, you lower the window shade and shut your eyes. It'll be better to get some rest; but sleep comes hard, full of visions and emptiness, of things better left far behind.

* * *

ESTEBAN / Offshore, the view of the harbor keeps being interrupted by the passing boats. Boats so full they struggle against the tide. Nothing to see really, just boats and more boats. Coming. Leaving. Never standing still long enough to become one with the background. And through all this, always the coast guard cutters hassling, making sure all the vessels stay together.

Esteban feels strange because he hardly recognizes the place, not that he knew what it looked like before, but there's nothing worth salvaging for the memory. Nothing. Just chaotic commotion. People shouting and waving.

When it is their turn, the skipper docks and immediately don Carlos, Janna, and Esteban jump off only to be met by three armed soldiers, who with ugly gestures move them back on board.

"*¡No se pueden bajar!*" one of the soldiers warns. "*Área restringida.*"

No one gets off. This is a restricted area.

Janna tries to talk to them. She argues that she's an American journalist. They laugh at her, at the way she pronounces the language.

"Gringa go home," the darkest of the three tells her in English.

Don Carlos tries to talk to them too, unsuccessfully. All he wants is to get information about his family. They are aware he's come all this way, but so what. There's nothing they can do.

Esteban begins to wonder if Domingo managed to get through. If caught, he might be in serious trouble. But what can they do to him, jail him?

Behind the soldiers wait a long line of people, poorly dressed, a starved look on their faces. They walk quickly.

"If you want to take somebody home," one of the soldiers says, "take all these degenerates. Otherwise turn around and get the hell out of here."

"Son of a bitch," Janna says, standing next to don Carlos, who mouths those same words but in Spanish.

The skipper wants to know whether he should take all those people.

"If they fit," don Carlos says, "we take them."

"You rented it," Norton tells don Carlos.

Men, women, and children get on board and immediately the boat fills to capacity. Some of the younger men stare at Janna. There's something about her they must recognize as American, Esteban thinks.

"*Viva América,*" a boy says, looking at her.

As soon as the last person climbs on board, the soldiers untie the ropes and push the yacht away from the dock.

"What a fucking waste of time," don Carlos says to Esteban in the cabin.

"We'll find them," Esteban tells him. "From what I can see everybody's leaving this forsaken place."

"I hope that bearded bastard rots alone," don Carlos says. "Maybe he can tape all his speeches and play them back to himself."

The skipper tells don Carlos he's giving the boat full throttle but that, between the weight and the weather, it is going to take a while to get back to Key West.

Esteban finds himself at the stern among strangers. Everybody's face looks haggard, older in appearance then what each person must really be. Suddenly a sad realization comes to him, one that he tries to avoid. If Hugo left, he thinks, this is probably the way he did it, on a boat. Packed in like pickles in a jar.

Janna cuts through the crowds and approaches him. She tells him she is sorry for the way things turned out.

"I'm optimistic," Esteban tells her, a faint smile forming on his lips.

Thunder cracks overhead.

"You'll find Hugo," she says, taking his hand and holding it with both of hers.

"If he made it out, I know I will," he says and puts his arm around her. She feels warm to his touch.

The people in front of them stare. Who knows what they think, he wonders, but they can go to hell if they are thinking that I'm too old to be with this woman. Gorgeous woman, heavenly body.

HUGO / With Lucinda now. We are sitting together, waiting. Waiting for further word from immigration officials. Waiting for the world to stop because we have stopped for the world. I hold her and she holds me. I can feel her hands on my skin, and it is like no other feeling I have felt in a long time. And I am thinking, oh woman, I'm going to destroy you in bed the first chance we get to be alone. I want my tongue to relearn those places on your body . . .

She falls asleep on my lap. Her breathing is slow and easy. It relaxes me just to look at her stomach rise and fall. I feel like kissing her but I hold back. She must be tired. I am tired. We are tired. All around me there are people yearning for sleep.

There's talk of moving us to a so-called tent city in Miami. To some stadium called the orange something or other. We can be processed faster that way. I am sitting next to Lucinda, watching her sleep, and I don't care what happens next. We have made it. We are together and it no longer matters what our fates have decided.

I hold her tight until my hands grow moist with sweat. Next to Mama Concha, I've never loved anybody more than this woman in my arms now. In my arms now, I keep repeating. At last we are together.

CONCHA / The last party to take place at the house was Lilián and Angel's wedding reception. Her daughter married in San Basilio's Cathedral where Concha and Esteban had said their vows years before. The reception got underway early in the afternoon at the house. The whole backyard, converted and arranged into an open-air ballroom, looked beautiful. Flowers were everywhere: roses, begonias, callas, orchids, chrysanthemums, lilies, and gladiolus. Gladiolus she remembered most, because they came in a magnificent burst of colors.

She had never seen so many flowers. Four bouquets on every table, fifty tables.

Oh, and the food. All the catered food to feed five hundred guests. Confections and buffet platters filled with every type of ham and cheese. People seemed impressed by it all. But she imagined what they liked most were the open bars. There were two, at either end of the backyard, serving the best liquors, wines, champagne, and mixed drinks.

The dance floor covered most of the yard. Esteban had complained about it ruining the grass—he wanted to let people dance on grass—but she told him that it would be inappropriate. When people danced they wanted to slip and slide, step to the rhythm of the music. Grass would only slow them down.

There were ribbons and laces and bows and white balloons. Two bands played music continuously. When one took a break, the other played.

Ah, the grandeur of that party, she never forgot it.

Lilián and Angel took more than a hundred pictures: embracing, cutting the cake, kissing, inside, outside, in the car that was to take them on their honeymoon. When they finally left, the party continued until two or three in the morning.

The wedding was announced in the paper as one of the best weddings of the year. In it was the newlyweds' picture. They looked happy, surprised by the camera as they climbed inside the car, Angel holding Lilián's dress so it wouldn't get caught on the door.

People talked about the party for a long time. It made Concha proud to go to the beauty salon and hear her friends compliment her. It filled her with joy and exultation. If Hugo ever got married, she thought, he too would have a party as big and as grand.

ANGEL / Cloudy morning, cool weather. If things continue this way, there will be a sharp decline in sales. Ice cream and bad weather don't mix. He finishes checking the merchandise inside the truck, making up his mind not to go out to sell today. He's been working hard since Lilián's been staying at home.

The extension cord connecting the freezer to the garage electrical outlet seems okay. The last one had to be replaced because the cables overheated for some reason, the plastic wrapper encasing the wires melted, and a short circuit occurred.

He climbs out of the truck and is about to lock the door when a car arrives and pulls into the driveway. It is an ugly brown sedan. A man dressed in a gray tweed suit gets out, reaches into the back for his suitcase, and slams the door shut.

Angel goes up front to greet him.

The man, speaking Spanish, introduces himself as an insurance company adjustor. He is handling the case of the child who was in a hit-and-run accident. "Do you mind if I take a look at the truck?" he asks Angel.

"Go ahead," Angel tells him. "But I am not the guilty party involved."

"Nobody says you are, Mr. Falcón," the young man says. "This is regular procedure. I've been checking everybody's truck, you see."

"Things are getting too tough for the honest," Angel says, "for the people who are out there busting their backs to make a living."

"I know what you mean, and I am sorry to be taking up your valuable time, but—I am going to ask you several questions, Mr. Falcón," the man says, " and I want you to answer them to the best of your knowledge."

"What kinds of questions?" Angel asks, wiping his hands on his work pants.

"Regular procedure," the man says again.

What the hell does regular procedure mean? Angel leads the man to the truck, but he decides to cooperate and not give the man a hard time. The faster he's out of the way the better.

The man inspects the front and back of the truck carefully. "Do you remember where you were the afternoon of March sixteenth?"

"Out selling," answers Angel.

"Selling where, Mr. Falcón, what city? Give me the names of the streets if you remember."

"Well," he says, "in the afternoons I am usually in Bell Gardens. In the vicinity of Garfield Boulevard."

"I see," the mans says, writing it all down.

"I am quite sure of where the accident took place," Angel says, "and I was nowhere near there. I was about five miles away."

"That's far enough, Mr. Falcón. As I've said I am not here to blame anybody."

"I understand."

In profile the young man, dressed so tidily, slightly resembles Diego.

"Have you repaired or painted the truck in the last sixty days?" the young man wants to know.

"No, I haven't. Somebody broke a window and stole some of

my merchandise, but other than that, no."

"How long have you owned the truck?"

"Six years. Yes, I believe it's been that long."

The young man returns his notepad and pen to his briefcase and thanks Angel for his help.

"I hope you find what you're looking for," Angel tells the young man, following him to the car.

The man doesn't say anything further, gets in the car, starts the engine, and drives out. Angel stands by the porch thinking that the son of a bitch who ran the kid over's going to pay one way or another. He hopes they catch whoever did it, so that owners of ice cream trucks can go about their business without any further distraction. God knows with this weather things are tough enough.

HUGO / I am waiting in line to get food when Lucinda runs to me. She is crying. She takes me by the hand and leads me to another part of the building. There's like a recreation room put together in one corner where there are a couple of Ping-Pong tables and a color television set.

She stops in front of the television and points. The people gathered around it look at her as if to say, Get out of the way! I don't have to look twice to recognize who it is she wants me to see.

"It's him, Hugo," she says excitedly. "It's Lobo."

Certainly a resemblance there. If the man on the screen is in fact Lobo Morales, he is much older, thinner, dressed in a suit and tie. The camera draws closer. His name appears at the bottom of the screen.

"Jesus Christ!" I say. "It is! It's him! Look at his eyes. I might forget everything, but not his eyes."

Lucinda leans against me. "He's alive."

"Not only is he alive, but he's been here for two years."

"How do you know?" Lucinda asks.

"That's what was said right now," I tell her. "Now listen, he's going to say something."

Lobo Morales takes his place behind the podium and speaks into the microphone. "I am personally flying to Washington this evening to hold a press conference," he says. His deep voice brings back memories. "Our delegation will hold an audience with

President Carter. Whatever the circumstances, our efforts must not be deterred. I urge both branches of Congress to do whatever must be done, but the freedom flotilla must not be stopped."

The people watching television applaud. Whistle. Cheer.

"We will not abandon a just cause," he continues. "Our fellow men are in need of our help, and we will give it to them at all costs."

When he finishes, he is immediately surrounded by members of the press. Men who appear to be bodyguards try to make way for Lobo out of the conference room.

"He's here," Hugo says. "They freed him and now he's here. I was convinced that he was dead."

After Lobo's arrest and trial, he was taken to La Cabaña. All of Comandante Morales' troops went there. He became stronger in his views. We looked up to him more than ever; then one day they took him out of his cell and he never returned. They told us he had been retired and found guilty of all antirevolutionary charges, shot and killed by a firing squad. And we, being gullible fools, believed it.

"He was going blind," Hugo says. "I remember they kept him locked up in a dark cell."

"He's free now, just like we are," Lucinda says.

"I can't wait to get out of here," I say. "Lobo will help us."

"We've got to find your father first," she says.

I lead her back to the food line where we take our place and wait to be served. Seeing Lobo made me forget how hungry I am, but the minute I smell the coffee and roasted turkey my mouth waters. My stomach growls.

Lucinda looks at me and says softly that maybe after we eat we can go somewhere where it is quiet and dark and be all by ourselves.

ESTEBAN / As soon as they dock in Key West and disembark, the world once again becomes steady, solid underfoot. Esteban realizes it's too late, but he has forgotten to say good-bye to the skipper. It's the nature of his business, he thinks, taking and bringing people to and from places. Nice boat for hire, yes sir. With a captain who drinks beer faster than a distillery can brew it.

A quick step at the nearest pay telephone and he calls Lilián, who tells him the good news. Hugo is here. Esteban tries to listen carefully to his daughter, but all she's got to say is that she misses her brother.

"Where is he?" Esteban asks. "This is a huge busy place, Lili. How am I supposed to find him?"

"He mentioned something about a medical ward," she says. "but he's there. Find him."

As soon as Esteban hangs up, don Carlos leads the way across the docks. He looks angry enough to stop one of these immigration officers and knock him out, but he wants information, not trouble. This is when Janna becomes handy. She gets around a lot faster, with more ease and style. Esteban is delighted to watch her ask her questions.

She leads Esteban and Don Carlos to the immigration detention wharf, a run-down naval station warehouse obviously no longer in use for storage. The security's tight at the door, so she works out a some kind of a deal with the guard, and he lets them through.

"What did you tell him?" Esteban says. He is curious.

"I told him you were Harry Reasoner and don Carlos Ted Koppel," she says.

Esteban knows who Reasoner is, but who is this Ted Koppel?

Inside, the building is filled with malodorous smoke. There are cubicles with people in them, old school desks and chairs. People, people, and more people everywhere. Soon there'll be no more room.

They stop by one of the desks and Janna asks an officer how they go about finding family members.

"This place," don Carlos says to Esteban, "looks as organized as a chicken coop."

"What is the name?" the officer wants to know.

They give the man the names. The man writes them down and walks away toward the rear of the place. He stops at a metal door, opens it, and enters.

While they wait, Esteban looks around. He is searching, but none of the faces are familiar.

* * *

February, 1974

Mama Concha:

Life in prison has no comparison. After so many years I have stopped thinking about the whys and hows and adapted to my cell. Hardly any light, just that which sneaks in through the barred windows. No water, only the buckets brought by the guards in the mornings. Sometimes they bring none. I remember how I kept thinking about the twenty-year sentence—there was never a trial and I often wanted to hear somebody say, "Carranza, we hereby sentence you to twenty years for—" And the more I thought about it the more I resigned myself to endure.

I keep myself strong by exercising. Pushups, situps, I put my hands behind my head and twist from one side to the other. Strong body, strong mind, that's what I think.

The treatment, I get—we get (the other prisoners)—is treatment better suited for dogs, dogs with rabies that is. When it rains the guards force us to march in the mud and some of us catch colds which turn into pneumonia and kill some of the weaker prisoners. When it is hot we pound on bricks and stones with heavy sledgehammers.

Sometimes they feed us, sometimes they don't. Heads-or-tails situations. When they feed us they feed us spoiled food. Some of us die of food poisoning or chronic diarrhea. Fever abounds at La Cabaña. Malaria. You name it, we have it.

But the dead get buried by the living, and the living keep on. Continue to survive. Time has no heart.

I don't know how I survive. A lot of the time, at night, always at night, I feel a presence in the cell. That presence is you, my mother. I know you are here to look after me. My temperament wasn't made to be kept under lock and key, behind bars. I have studied and restudied the situation, milked it for whatever it was worth. I have decided to pretend I am crazy, and sometimes I forget I am only pretending.

Around the guards I keep my mouth shut, but when I

fall in the company of other prisoners I shout and scream like a child rants and raves and I say anything to get a rise out of the guys in the other cells.

Some of them are too weak and worn out to join me.

I don't know why they don't take me out and shoot me. I guess they think that that's what I want. How brilliant they are, skilled in pain and suffering. There are no easy ways out of prison. Suffering feeds on itself, turning the brave into cowards and the strong into the weak.

The years drip-drop. In the morning I get up or am awakened, and I do my exercises. Then rest or take a nap until the afternoon. It is a completely different ball game if they take us out to work. They seldom do, not us politicos. For us they had other plans: to weaken us psychologically with brainwash garbage.

Out of all those years one incident sticks out in my mind. One day I was awakened by loud voices. Voices I wasn't accustomed to hearing. These voices belonged to well-fed men who could speak in fortissimo, resonant voices.

A foreign delegation of some kind. They went from cell to cell, and I could hear their chatter. They spoke in different languages, though most often they settled for English because it was the understood language.

There were five of them. A French-Canadian, a Swiss, too blond for his own good, one Vietnamese, one Chinese, and the last one was from Japan. Two guards ushered them down the corridor past the front of the cells.

They arrived in front of my cell and stopped. I was taking a crap at the very moment. We exchanged glances. They stood there and looked at me as though I were a caged animal, so I decided to act like one.

I stood up, approached the bars, and threw a handful of shit at them. The excrement landed everywhere. On their European-style suits, shoes, and the Swiss got it on his tie.

"I am crazy," I said and wiped my hand on the bars. "Loco!"

They walked away so fast that in a matter of seconds I heard the door at the end of the corridor slam shut. We were all screaming now. "¡Libertad! ¡Libertad!"

What came of their visit?

Apparently, and this is only a guess, they found the facilities so revolting that they filed a petition to have most of us transferred to a mental institution, Mazorra,. and that's where they sent me before the fake pig epidemic broke out all over the island.

Then in Mazorra I found Lucinda and my life, after so many years, started all over again.

           Love and remembrance,
           Hugo

HUGO / "Is there somebody named Carranza here?" an officer calls from the door. "Hugo Carranza."

I grab Lucinda's hand and rush to the door. Somebody's here, I know somebody's come for me. For us.

The officer calls another name out and some more people gather at the doorway.

Lucinda gets worried, but I squeeze her hand to let her know that I'm with her now, that whatever happens is going to happen to both of us.

We are led from one side of the building to the other. In the distance I see my father standing by a desk and my legs grow weak. Lucinda helps me walk across. My father, Jesus Christ, there he stands, unaware of my approach.

The years haven't changed him much, except his hair is thinner and grayer combed back. God, it is him. My father's here for us. I shout, "Papá!"

ESTEBAN / When he hears the voice, he immediately recognizes who it is. Hugo runs to him, teary-eyed, and Esteban barely recognizes him. His son is thin, bald headed—scars on his scalp—and with a sickly pallor to his face.

Before he reacts, Hugo hugs and kisses him. His son weeps hard, and Esteban closes his eyes and says, "Thank God! You—you're alive!"

Hugo is choked with emotion.

"You are free, son," Esteban says and holds Hugo out to have a better look at him. "We're going to get you home."

"I want you to meet somebody special, father," Hugo says. "This is Lucinda, the woman I wrote mother about, remember?"

Lucinda comes forward and Esteban, remembering, embraces her. Big, deep-set eyes grow soft as she smiles faintly, the smell of the sea still caught in her short, spiky hair.

"We are going to get married," Hugo says.

Next to them don Carlos is going through the same thing with his family. Janna's standing to the side, her hands in the pockets of her pants.

"Come meet my son," Esteban says to her.

Janna walks over and shakes Hugo's hand first, then Lucinda's. "I am happy for both of you," she says, putting her hand on his shoulders. His son seems impressed by Janna's good looks.

"I want to get them out of here now," Esteban says to her. "Do you think that's going to be possible?"

"I don't know," she says. "Let me find out." She approaches the officer and the two of them stand there talking.

"Where did you find her?" Hugo says to Esteban.

"She's been a great help, you know," he says. "She went to Mariel with us." He tells Hugo what little he knows about the reporter.

Hugo tells his father about some of the details of how he escaped the camp, the embassy, and how the boat sank. "I called Lilián the first chance I got," he says.

"She can't wait to see you."

"Are they all well?" Hugo asks.

"Anxious for you to come home," Esteban says.

Don Carlos brings his family over and introduces everybody. None of them looks as skinny or as malnourished as Hugo, and this makes Esteban angry, what his son has had to go through. He watches as Hugo puts his arm around Lucinda and kisses her on the lips. She is pretty, Esteban thinks, but looks very tired.

Janna returns and gives everybody the good news that after Esteban and don Carlos fill out and sign some release forms, they can all go home. Immigration will contact them later.

Esteban wonders what's going to happen to her. Is she going to stay here in Key West and finish her story? He wants to know because, in such a short time, he has grown to like her, to care about her.

"What are your plans, Janna?" Esteban asks her, moving closer so he can hear her.

"I'm not sure yet," she says and smiles at Hugo. "I think I'm going to go back home and sort through everything and try to write a story."

"Texas," he says.

"Texas is no longer home," she says and crosses her arms. "I live and work in New York."

Esteban tells her he doesn't know how to thank her for all the help she's given him. "Is there a place I can—you know—I'd like very much to see you again. Take you out for dinner."

"I plan to be in L.A.," she says, blushing. "I'd love to see you again." She takes a piece of paper and borrows a pen from don Carlos and writes her address and telephone number on it. She folds the piece of paper and hands it to Esteban. "Keep in touch," she says.

To Hugo she says, "I wish you and Lucinda lots of luck and happiness."

She says good-bye to everybody and walks away. Standing between Hugo and Lucinda and don Carlos's family, Esteban watches her go, excited at the prospect of seeing her again. Then he takes his wallet and slips the piece of paper inside, next to the money order Domingo left him.

"Okay," don Carlos says. "Let's get those papers filled out and let's get out of here."

Esteban tells Hugo that there isn't enough room in the van—which reminds him he's got to call Lilián again to find out whether Diego's still here, or, if he's gone, where he left the van—so they'll take a plane back to Los Angeles.

"I want to visit Mother's grave," Hugo says.

He better wait before he tells him that Mama Concha's remains are on their way back to Santiago. It might be a while before Hugo can understand. This is yet another beginning, for there's enough time to relive the past and rejoice in the present. In light of this new freedom, his son's future seems certain, and nothing in the world feels better.

"Once we find the van," don Carlos says, "I'll give you guys a ride back to Miami."

"Is there enough room?" Esteban says, figuring he doesn't want to impose.

"It can't be any more crowded than in the boat, right?" don Carlos says and grins.

"Miami," Hugo says as if he were getting the feel for the name.

"When we get there," Esteban tells his son, "we are going to make a stop at a clothing store and I'm going to buy you and Lucinda some clothes and take you to a restaurant."

"A dress," Lucinda says.

Let's hurry, Esteban thinks, and get the paperwork finished; then we can be on our way.

CONCHA / Her grandson was born in the fall of 1958. Hugo was still at the University, making plans to leave for the sierras.

Concha waited at the hospital with Esteban and Angel, whose nervousness had already started to show. The waiting room seemed too small for him. He kept pacing the length of it; then, when he realized how restless he was, he shrugged and kept going. She was glad he didn't smoke; otherwise, he might have filled a couple of ashtrays already.

Esteban ordered sandwiches from the cafeteria across the street. Also coffee, but she told him if Angel drank any, he'd be unbearable.

"He already is," Esteban said.

The baby came at exactly five minutes after two in the morning.

"It's a boy," the nurse told Angel.

Concha's son-in-law's first reaction was to reach out and hug her.

You can see the mother now," the nurse said. "The baby's getting his first bath."

Concha thanked the nurse and Esteban wanted to give her a little gift, one hundred pesos, which in those days was a lot of money for a nurse. But the girl refused.

Angel went in first; and when he came out, he said the baby had been brought and Lilián was feeding it. "Go and see him," Angel told Concha. "He's so tiny. He's so beautiful."

They followed Angel to the room. The baby was wrapped in an embroidered blanket Lilián had brought, only a headful of darkish blond hair showed.

"His uncle looked like this," Lilián said. Her hair was flat, moist with perspiration.

"How are you feeling?" Concha asked her daughter, remembering her own two labors.

"Painful and wonderful," said Lilián. "You can't have one without the other."

The baby's fingers wiggled and when Esteban touched him he grabbed his grandfather's finger.

"Seven pounds, eight ounces," Lilián said. "All male. You should see how big he is, Papa."

"Lilián," Concha said.

"I'm sure I will if I ever get a chance to change his diaper," Esteban said and Angel laughed.

"Oh, you will," Concha said. "Plenty of times."

Esteban got his wish. Lilián brought the baby over to the house plenty of times. Concha's daughter started to gain weight, something the doctor recommended she do.

It was a joy to have the baby over, to hold it, to watch it yawn and stretch and make faces. All that reminded Concha of Hugo were the baby's eyes and thick eyebrows: the rest was Angel. He was born with his father's face, light hair, ears, nose, small mouth, and chin.

When she placed him on her lap, the baby looked up at her in awe, trying to grab her nose, which he did once, and with his pink little nails left a scratch. His big wet eyes looked alert, deep in their bluishness. When he breast-fed, he made loud sucking noises; and if he missed Lilián's nipple, he'd cry.

Concha immediately organized a baptism party to follow the baby's christening. The baby seemed to respond to his name whenever he heard it.

* * *

DIEGO / "Diego! Over here!" Maruchi calls out to you inside the terminal at the airport.

No carry-on luggage, free arms with which to give her a great big hug. How long has it been since you've seen her? Too long and it shows because now that she's trapped in your arms you go about kissing her with a vengeance.

"What do you want to do first?" Maruchi says.

"Let me call my mother," you say. "Then let's go see Nestor."

You call your mother. The fact that she doesn't ask how successful your search for V was is greatly appreciated. She can't wait to tell you Hugo's in America, that she spoke to him on the phone. Good news. You look forward to seeing him. After telling her where you left the van in Key West, you hang up and walk with Maruchi out of the terminal to the parking lot. On the way you tell her about the road trip, all the cities you saw.

Once in the car, Maruchi, too, doesn't make any reference to Miami or ask whether you found Vanessa, but instead chooses to tell what happened to Nestor. "I was working that night," she begins, "and Nestor didn't show up. Don Carlos's wife was upset. I had to keep telling her that he'd show. But he didn't.

"I phoned him at home, at his parents, but nobody knew where he was. Then Susie gets a call from the hospital. She comes to me crying and tells me that the police found Nestor in an alley. As soon as the club closed, me and Susie went to the hospital.

"Jesus, you should have seen him. They had him in intensive care on this orthopedic bed, all boarded up. You could hardly recognize him. His eyes were so bruised and inflamed, it was hard to tell if he'd ever be able to open them again. Several cuts above his eyebrows were stitched and some of the blood—"

"Please, not on an empty stomach," you say, rubbing her knee.

"I'm sorry," she says. "So there was Susie standing next to him, crying her eyes out, and me trying to console her. A nurse walks over to check the respirator and assures us he's going to be fine."

"Jesus, respirator and everything," you say. "They must have really worked on him."

"According to what Nestor told the doctors, all that he

remembers was that they threw him out of the moving car. His right lung collapsed on impact.

"He is doing much better," she says, "though most of his body is in a cast."

Watching the leaden sky—or is it too much smog?—you stick your head out of the window for some fresh air, but all you get is the smell of exhaust. This is home, though. No canals anywhere, no swamp atmosphere and no mosquitoes.

"Remember the night you took me home?" you say, leaning over. "The morning after, hum?" You kiss Maruchi's neck.

"I don't want to think about it," she says. "We're too far from a bed."

"It's over," you tell her. "That's what I went to Miami to find out."

"What do you mean?"

"I'm getting divorced," you say. She puts her hand on your face, drives with the other. "As people say, I'm a free agent again."

"Hey," she says, "my team needs one more player. There's a big bonus if you sign up early."

"What sport?"

"Bed wrestling," she laughs.

Sticking out of her cassette player is a tape that looks familiar. You pull it out and read the label. The Toucan Club Band.

"How did this get here?" you say.

"I took it from don Carlos's office," she says. "I wanted something to—to help me think."

The tape slides in. You turn on the radio and the music blares out of the speaker. Music, you think, great music, something that has always been there to pick you up.

At the VA hospital in Westwood, Maruchi gives you directions to get to Nestor's room; then she says, "You guys need to be alone." She'll be in the cafeteria having some coffee.

The room's located on the third floor of the orthopedic ward.

His is the bed on the far side by the window, out of which downtown Wilshire blends with the azure of the sky. Dick and pussy city. Nestor has his eyes closed, body covered with a cast. A trapeze holds his right leg at a slant. They busted up his face, all right, but you wonder whether it was done before they pushed him

277

out of the car. The bruises have the color of frozen supermarket meat, purple-blue toward the edges.

His eyes open.

"Hey bro," you say, moving closer to bedside. "I got here as fast—"

"Thanks . . . for coming," he says and looks away.

"Maruchi told me you'll be up and running in no time," you tell him. "Maybe we can go shoot hoops, eh?"

"They fucked me up, bro."

"Let me warn you now. I'm not going to stand here and talk about any of that. Forget it all, understand? It's the price you had to pay, and you paid it."

"I know who did it," he says and tries to lift his hand.

"I don't want to know," you say.

"Fist, brass knuckles, guns, you name it, they had it. It was right out of a movie."

"But you're through with them, right?"

Nestor smiles as best as he can without moving the skin around his mouth too much.

"You find her?" he wants to know.

"Found them. Her and Flaco. They're something together, you know. She's pregnant."

"What did they say?"

You tell Nestor what you care to remember, what you've allowed memory to keep, the other has gone to . . . "She doesn't exist," you say.

"Who? Who are you talking about?" Nestor says.

"That's good," you say. "It's the way things work, right?"

"Susie tells me Maruchi's devoted, you know."

"Time," you say, "tests everything. I'm not going to worry about how long the devotion lasts. I'm just taking things blow-by-blow."

"The way I did." He tries to laugh.

Nestor asks about the trip, what you got to see on the way, Key West, and what it was like to be with don Carlos for so long.

"Speaking of whom," you say. "I spoke to him and told him what had happened." Still a good liar. "He told me to let you know your job'll be waiting."

"What a heart, eh?"

"Gold," you say.

"I think I'm going to learn how to play an instrument and join the band," he says. "Shit, remember I tried every instrument back in high school and the only thing I was good at was the piccolo. I liked the sound of it."

"We'll find something for you to play."

"No, I like bartending just fine," he says. "That's where the women are. You dazzle them with music, I do it with my brews."

"Let's go cold turkey on everything," you tell him, "booze, coke, bad love—fuck it all."

"Cut out all the fun, eh," he says. "I'm going to keep bartending. There's nothing like breaking bottle seals."

A pretty nurse enters the room.

"Man," Nestor says, "ah, the care I've been getting around here. Incredible. Go out, get hurt, and ask for the bed next to mine."

All along the nurse smiles. Nestor continues, "Into this room walk nothing but the best. Best doctors, best nurses—correction, gorgeous nurses. Look at this one for example. Isn't she someone who can make you feel a lot better just by looking at her?"

"He can't move, but he can certainly talk," she says, placing a thermometer under Nestor's tongue.

The nurse, you agree, if she were to let loose all her hair, would be quite an impressive sight.

"I better get going, bro," you tell Nestor. "Maruchi's waiting."

"Give her my thanks," he says.

"I'll come see you soon," you say, then tell the nurse a good-bye. Walking out, you hear Nestor flirting with her. Not much has changed, has it? They couldn't knock the charm out of him.

In the cafeteria Maruchi's sitting behind a row of plants. Her shoes are off. The way she sits, the shape of her ass, is appealing and brings to mind a multitude of possibilities.

ANGEL / For Angel to make up his mind about something, a harsh realization has to occur. An explosion of disappointment or discontent that might shatter his goals. The morning after the insurance man leaves, he decides that he and Lilián should own

279

another kind of business. So much of success in the ice cream business depends on good weather that it isn't worth it.

It's not that he hasn't seen worse weather, he has, but it is the routineness of the ice cream trade that, looking out of the bedroom window as the rain falls, appalls him. He's sick and tired of the same shit, day in and day out.

They have enough money saved up to get a small place in a good location and establish a cafeteria like the one they owned in Santiago. La Cubanita. Something simple. With a pleasant atmosphere. He's got enough experience. He can't rely on the ice cream business to be sold. Why wait?

Too, he knows just the right place. He remembers he saw a for-sale sign at the corner of Gage and Lucille, on a fairly new building. It used to be an auto-parts store or something like that. He feels the excitement rising.

It's a good area. Lots of factories. People hungry for lunch every day. They can do takeout too. Cuban sandwiches. They've got money saved up, and more coming if they sell the truck. The freezers they can use.

All day he walks around the house thinking about it, planning, putting a package together to present it to Lilián. Not that she wouldn't agree with his plans, but he likes to consult her. She's got ideas of her own. But she's so preoccupied about her brother's coming that . . . damn, the whole family can help. It'll give Esteban something to do. Hugo too. He can be in charge of inventory and merchandise, help in the kitchen. Lilián can work the register. Angel himself can cook up a storm.

A family thing, yes, that's what he has in mind. He's so revved up that he wants to go out there and see the place, but it's pouring outside and he hates to drive in the rain.

Lilián walks into the bedroom and tells him that they've got to go pick up Esteban and her brother. They'll be arriving soon and she wants to be there. Good, he thinks, the trip'll give him the chance to explain what he's got in mind.

ESTEBAN / During the long flight home, Hugo and Lucinda sleep. His son looks much better fed and with new clothes on. Lucinda needs makeup, but that's no problem. She has fallen asleep wearing the rented headphones. Earlier he bought a round of drinks and now the ice is melting at the bottom of the plastic cups.

Esteban leans his head back against the cushion while disjointed visions of Domingo surface. His friend in Santiago, walking—hands behind his back—through the old streets. Past doors and porticos, paint peeling off walls and brick, cobblestone and trees whose roots have uprooted and cracked the cement of the sidewalks.

He imagines himself there too. Walking, talking, observing how desolate everything seems to be. No flowers up on the windowsills, drawn curtains, birds have flown elsewhere. He can hear Domingo talking, but not himself. When he speaks he hears no sound. Surely, he thinks, his friend must be listening to his words.

Domingo stops at mid-block, points toward the foothills at the end of the street. They go past a useless, dried-up fountain. Moss and mildew have left their scars on it.

They start to climb, Esteban fully aware of what lies on the other side. When they reach the peak, Domingo once again stops and looks around, as if he were admiring the view. The air feels cool on the skin as they come down from the mountains and the sierras.

"This is home," Domingo says, "this grass, this earth, this sky. Ever seen a bluer sky?"

Down, down the other side to the gates of the cemetery. Tombstones and crosses sticking out of the ground. The bas-relief ornaments on the facades of the sarcophaguses appear weather-beaten, the angel faces chipped and worn.

His friend stops one last time. At the front of three graves. The Lara family's remains lie in peace here. Favio and Rosario Lara. Out of the bag Domingo pulls the vial with Concha's ashes.

He holds the vial for a long time; then, slowly, turns it upside down and lets the wind do the rest. The ashes scatter quickly, blend with the ground.

"She might be able to help me," Hugo, who is now awake, is saying.

"Who—who are you referring to?" Esteban says.

"The reporter, your friend," he says. "I'd like to get hold of Lobo."

He understands why his son needs to contact Lobo Morales—

maybe the man can help Hugo put the past behind him once and for all.

"All I want is to let him know we're alive, Lucinda and I." He turns to look at Lucinda.

Home.

The plane lands smoothly, taxis from the runway to the terminal ramp. Lucinda stirs awake with the commotion of other passengers opening the overhead compartments. Hugo unbuckles his seat belt, anxious to get up and off the plane.

They deplane, Hugo carrying the suitcase Esteban took on the trip.

Lilián and Angel wait at the end of the ramp, behind the security metal detectors. Hugo pulls Lucinda as they hurry to the other side. Together now, they all exchange hugs and kisses and more hugs. People walk by and stare. Hugo's still strong enough to lift his sister. Angel embraces his brother-in-law. Hugo introduces Lucinda, who acts as if she's known everybody all her life.

So much to say, but nobody speaks, astounded, awe-struck with surprise and disbelief.

HUGO / Los Angeles, city of glorious freedom. The ride home seems to take forever, but I don't mind. We've got all the time in the world. My sister and Angel are already making plans. They want to buy a cafeteria. I'm welcome to work with them. Lucinda and I have plans of our own. The first thing we are going to do is get married, work, and find a place where we can live and start a family.

Lilián, sitting up front with Angel, asks my father about a certain Domingo. She wants to know if he stayed in Miami.

Esteban doesn't respond, just turns and looks out the window.

"Ruth came by," Angel adds. "She wanted to know if he had gone to Miami."

My father doesn't say anything.

"Papa," Lilián says, "is he all right?"

"Let's just say he's home," Esteban says and smiles at me and Lucinda.

All this time I'm thinking of how huge the city looks. So many

cars and buses. That's another thing, I want to get my driver's
license and maybe later get my own car. It doesn't have to be new
or anything, just inexpensive and in good working condition.

Ah, freedom. Freedom has a definite smell and taste and color
to it, and it's all here.

My sister asks Lucinda what size clothes she wears and Lucinda's eyes light up.

"This skinny," Lucinda says, "a seven."

Lilián tells her she's got a closetful of dresses and shoes that
might fit.

"Will Diego be home?" I ask.

"He'll be there," Angel says, "if he isn't there by now."

DIEGO / Maruchi drives you to the house. The Monte Carlo's
gone and the ice cream truck's parked at the end of the driveway,
so you figure your parents must have gone to the airport. Nobody
home.

"I should go," she says.

"Go? Come on, park the car and come inside for a little while."
It's been raining hard and you don't want her to go.

"I have to work tonight," she says.

"I'm going in too," you say. "I want to be here when my uncle
comes."

She parks in front of the house. The two of you get out of the
car and run to the porch. There, you open the door. No sooner
are you inside than you reach out and embrace her. Smiling, she
responds quickly. Her hands move down to unbutton your jeans.

"I didn't think you were coming back," she says.

"Why wouldn't I?" you ask. "I have everything I want here."

A car pulls up into the driveway. Only when you hear the
doors open do you let go of Maruchi.

ANGEL / The rain has quieted to a light drizzle. His son opens
the front door when they arrive. He's got a girl with him. She steps
out onto the porch behind Diego, who approaches the car and
greets his uncle. Hugo and his nephew hug one another. Then it's
Lucinda's turn. "Your uncle told me a great many things about
you," she says.

"I never imagined you were going to be this tall and strong," Hugo says.

"I want everybody to meet Maruchi," Diego says.

Maruchi steps forth and says hello to everybody. Angel thinks she's just as pretty as Vanessa, but looks don't matter, something he hopes his son has learned by now.

"Let's all go inside," Lilián says, leading the way.

In the house, Esteban searches the kitchen cabinets for a bottle of wine he says he's been saving for a special occasion. Lilián finds the bottle and hands it to her father to open. Esteban pulls the cork out and pours seven glasses full. Angel gets to propose the toast. "Welcome home, Hugo," he says.

They all drink.

Immediately, Lilián takes Lucinda to see the rest of the house. Maruchi goes along. Lucinda says she's very tired.

Esteban, Hugo, Diego, and Angel sit down at the dining room table. This is where all important conversations have always taken place, Angel thinks.

"What happened to Domingo?," Diego wants to know.

Esteban tells them that his friend jumped ship in Mariel. He shows them the note. The old man is probably in Santiago right now. "What did he tell you when he said good-bye to you at Key West?" he asks Diego.

"Not much," Diego says. "I can't remember."

"It says here he left Hugo some money?" Angel, reading, says.

"Thirty-five thousand dollars," Esteban says.

Hugo takes the note and reads it. "Why me?" he says. "He doesn't even know me."

Esteban says Domingo is the best friend a man can have, and his friend knew how much Hugo meant to him.

"What are you going to tell Ruth?" Diego asks.

"The truth," Esteban says. "I'll give her a call and tell her what happened. Anyway, what can she do about it now?"

Diego stands up and pours another round. He carries the glasses to the table. "I read your telegram," he says to Hugo, "and I hope you and Lucinda will come to the club."

"I wouldn't miss it," Hugo says.

"Let them rest first," Angel says and drinks some more wine.

Angel wants to tell Diego all about the cafeteria, but right now drinking this bottle of wine seems to be more important. There will be plenty of time for stories to be shared and plans to be made.

CONCHA / Her memories became everything. Dreams about the good moments. It was as though she were lost in her mind, and her eyes had become shadeless windows through which she saw the past. In the past lived those moments that kept her going, that brought her to this point: to dream, to see, to hear these familiar voices.

This was what the voices said: "Continue, don't give up. Things will turn out all right in the end. You've come this far, you can go further. Joy's all that matters . . . "

And she thought: She must continue . . . she won't give up . . . in the end she knew the Lord would provide an understanding . . . she came this far, she won't lose sight of order . . . yes, joy and happiness were everything.

She moved within her dreams; memories moved her. And the knowledge that when everything was finished—life taken from her—there were still her dreams. Dreams of one day when the family came together. This was her way of paying homage to love and life. Through her the past spoke. The past, that gray-haired man sitting on a wraparound porch, smoking, singing, with eyes closed, snoring loudly at times, loud enough to scare the sparrows nesting overhead in the cornice.

To her mind came the memories of laughter, of songs forever lasting, forever clear.

Brevity—time, she thought, was a great magician, stealing moments. But moments endured. So did memories. Memories prevail the way the earth prevails, like the sky and the water . . .

Epilogue

DIEGO / Live music from the grand ballroom at the Toucan Club in Los Angeles. A gala night. A welcome-home party, a special reason for a celebration. The stage, where the band awaits anxiously to start playing, is dark.

On either side of the dance floor where the tables are, there is a nervousness heard only in the clearing of throats and fingers rapping on champagne bottles. The Carranza-Falcón and Piñeda families have gathered for the party. Upon Esteban's invitation, Janna Douglas has flown in. The men are dressed in tuxedos and the women in glamorous evening dresses. By now Angel, Hugo, and Esteban have drunk their share of champagne and their enjoyment has made Lilián, Lucinda, and Janna vibrant with pleasure. Maruchi, who is off tonight, stands to one side of the stage where she can be closer to you.

They are here to forget about life for a moment, for the exodus continues. The total number of people to arrive from Mariel has gone beyond one hundred thousand, a lot of them are still being held at Eglin Air Force Base, in Ft. Walton Beach, Florida, and at Ft. Chaffee, near the town of Ft. Smith, Arkansas.

The dance floor dims slowly.

"Damas y caballeros," don Carlos says from Tictacs' booth, "I am proud to present a great band, the Toucan Club Band!"

"I'd like to dedicate this song," you say, "to Nestor who is out of the hospital, but could not be here tonight."

One . . . two . . . three . . . The drums begin from the deepest dark of the stage. They go tuc-tuc, tac! Listen to the back beat. Lights on. Tuc-tuc-tuc! Tac! Eyes closed, the heat from the spotlights burns, makes the musicians sweat. Then here come the tumbas and bajas joining the timbales. The sound grows louder, crisper, and it fills the club with a deep, resonant attack which subsides to the tink, tonk! of the timbales, a drumstick hitting a cowbell. Tink! the maracas jump in and the guayo, and the beat picks up. The latin beat has come a long way. Here it is, savor it. Percussion ready, the trumpets and sax and flute go from beeping to weeping. The players' cheeks inflate as they turn from side to side to keep the rhythm steady. After the drums and horns, here comes the electric violin and the bass, for this is the greatest of music. What harmony and pace!

Get ready to salsa, to dance the way dancers should. The players are all dressed in *comparsa* outfits, their ruffled sleeves billowing with the motion. Skintight slacks. Watch them move.

Playing the timbales, you stand behind the microphone and start to sing. Quickly, let the music take over: body, mind, and soul. Let it thrill you—make you forget. Song underway, the dance floor fills and the people dance as though that's all they were born to do.

Good times, bad times, let the beat beat on!

"¡Sabor!"